Kim,

Every story has Champions. I'm grateful you're one of them — enjoy the journey.

JL Spears

DAEMON PROTOCOL

JL SPEARS

Copyright © 2025 by JL Spears

The right of JL Spears to be identified as the author of this work has been asserted.

All rights reserved.

No part of this book may be reproduced, stored in a retrieval system, or transmitted, in any form, or by any means (electronic, mechanical, photocopying, recording or otherwise) without the prior written permission of the author, except in cases of brief quotations embodied in reviews or articles.
It may not be edited, amended, lent, resold, hired out, distributed or otherwise circulated, without the publisher's written permission.

Permission can be requested from www.codeandconsciousness.com

This book is a work of fiction. Except in the case of historical fact, names, characters, places, and incidents either are products of the author's imagination or are used fictitiously.
Any resemblance to actual persons, living or dead, events, or locales is entirely coincidental.

Published by

— CODE AND —
CONSCIOUSNESS

Code and Consciousness Press
P.O. Box 765
Tracy, CA 95378
www.codeandconsciousness.com

ISBN: 979-8-9993546-1-7

Edited by Adrienne Kisner

Cover design and interior formatting:
Mark Thomas / Coverness.com

Author photograph: Christina Medina Photography

For my family—
and especially for my mother – Jane Spears,
whose love, strength, and guidance
taught me to be the kind of man
who not only chases his dreams,
but is empowered to achieve them.

CHAPTER 1

The fire alarm wailed overhead. Red lights flashed in time with each earsplitting screech, bathing the data center in red.

Footsteps pounded down the hallway outside, but the door was locked from the inside. It was a hell of a lock, Daniel knew that much. Airtight. Unbreakable. Meant to contain what was in here.

He felt at home here, slumped against the data center control room desk, with the cold floor beneath him and his laptop open on his legs. If he ignored the banging on the door, the red lights, and the screaming sirens, he could imagine he was back in his office working on a late-night coding project.

He'd spent a lot of nights doing that. Nights he should've spent with Ana. With Nat. He hadn't realized how few nights they'd have together.

Overhead, a green light clicked on. A low hiss sounded under the sirens. Daniel slumped a little lower. The cold floor beneath him suddenly reminded him of a few weeks ago. He pictured Ana's bare feet on their kitchen tile as she'd danced to some old song, trying to coax him away from his laptop. "Five minutes," he'd promised. Three hours later, she'd finally given up and gone to bed alone.

The hiss grew louder. His vision blurred, and for a moment, he imagined Nat at her last archery meet, scanning the crowd for him. The way her face had fallen when she'd spotted only Ana.

Inert gas. The perfect fire suppressant, for the fire that wasn't there, because of the alarm he'd pulled. The argon and nitrogen would quickly overtake the oxygen in the room, suffocating the nonexistent fire.

He looked down at the timer. His vision started to blur. His thoughts slowed down.

All he needed was a few more minutes.

His fingers fumbled across the keyboard, trying one last override code. ACCESS DENIED. He tried another. The screen flickered. INVALID CREDENTIALS.

Someone was banging on the door, louder and louder. "Daniel! Dan, open the door!" Ana's voice muffled but unmistakable.

His hands shook as he typed another sequence. There had to be a backdoor, something he'd built in during the early days. The green light pulsed overhead like a diseased heartbeat.

"Override seven-seven-alpha," he whispered, voice already going hoarse. The system beeped. For one wild moment, he thought—

ACCESS DENIED. LOCKDOWN COMPLETE.

Regret washed over him like a wave. He'd started all of this, and now it was his duty to finish it, no matter the cost.

Just a few more minutes… A few more…

CHAPTER 2

Five years earlier

"No, no, no—come on!" Daniel Bennett slammed his palm against the monitor as error messages cascaded across the screen.

TRAINING DATA CORRUPTED. INTEGRATION FAILED. SYSTEM ROLLBACK INITIATED.

Eight hours of upload time. Gone. The new medical data from the hospital that was supposed to revolutionize Castor's diagnostic capabilities was corrupted by what looked like a single misplaced parameter in the integration script.

Daniel's headache pounded in rhythm with the error beeps. The fluorescent lights overhead buzzed like angry wasps, and his fourth cup of coffee sat cold and forgotten beside a stack of FDA compliance documents he should have reviewed yesterday. The office around him was empty. His team had fled at five sharp, smart enough to maintain the work-life balance he denied himself.

But Daniel couldn't leave. Not with the investor presentation tomorrow. Not with Jonah already making noise about their burn rate.

Daniel simply couldn't afford to lose a workday. Castor had a new computing chip, an experimental quantum chip, and Daniel wanted to see how it ran. It was like having a new engine plopped into your sports car and having to wait around to drive it. That is, if the engine were an experimental chip that could challenge the laws of physics, and the car was a program that could quickly assess massive quantities of patients and their medical histories.

He needed this to work. If it was going to survive, his startup, Promethean Systems, needed this breakthrough.

Promethean Systems was another startup in the crowded Silicon Valley world of startups, where each thought they had the next world-changing product, and all were battling for the next cash infusion from the venture capitalists of the industry. Daniel worked in their original office: the ground-floor level of a plain brick building in Palo Alto that used to be a garage. On nice days, they kept the garage door flung open to let in the warm California air. About thirty developers worked in this office, each with their own desk in a honeycomb setup throughout the room. The concrete floor was covered in secondhand rugs. One side of the office had couches, bean bag chairs, and a huge TV with a video game console. What had once been the mechanic's office and waiting room had been converted into a conference room and kitchenette. The back wall had a few fancy soundproof pods for calls, though they were rarely used.

At this time of night, the office was usually empty, as it was now.

Daniel pushed his chair back and massaged his temples, then pulled up Castor's diagnostic logs.

"Okay, buddy," he said to the screen, "tell me what went wrong."

The rejection pattern was fascinating. Line by line, Castor had identified inconsistencies in the medical data that Daniel himself had missed. Any other large language model would have absorbed the data, errors and all, and started hallucinating diagnoses. But Castor—he, (and privately, that's how Daniel always referred to Castor, as "he" not "it") had refused the contaminated data.

"Three years of building you from scratch," Daniel said to the empty office, "and you're still surprising me." He pulled up comparative metrics from competing models. The best and brightest companies in Silicon Valley all showed typical hallucination rates around 15-20% with corrupted training data. Castor's rate held steady at 2%, but only because he was running on hardware that limited his processing scope.

Daniel minimized the window and stared at the specifications for the experimental quantum chip they had installed. It was the best they could afford, but Daniel knew that with proper hardware, Castor wouldn't just match the competition—he'd revolutionize medical diagnosis entirely.

If they could afford to build it.

If the board approved it.

If, if, if.

But unlike Castor, Daniel was stuck with a fleshy brain that got worn out after staring at screens for the whole day. He stood up, stretched his arms over his head, and made his way across the open floor plan to the tiny kitchen.

Daniel wove through the honeycomb of empty desks, each one telling a story. Melissa's action figures were arranged in battle formation, Kevin's monitor still displayed half-written code, Sarah's desk was buried under protein bar wrappers. The kill-screen message on the communal Xbox showed someone had rage-quit Rocket League around six.

The coffee maker gurgled, brewing its automated night pot that no one ever drank. Daniel reached for a mug, then noticed light spilling from under the conference room door. The whiteboard schedule showed the last meeting ended at four.

He knocked and pushed the door open. "Hello? Someone forget to—"

"Close the door." Emmet sat hunched over his laptop, surrounded by papers covered in his spidery handwriting. The conference room's glass walls were covered with taped-up printouts—code segments, neural network diagrams, something that looked like chess notation.

"Emmet? What the hell! How long have you been in here?"

"Since lunch." Emmet didn't look up. "Had an idea. Been testing it against Castor's chess protocols."

Daniel noticed the chessboard on the table, pieces frozen mid-game. "You've been playing him all afternoon?"

"No. I'm just taking a little break." Emmet looked up and met Daniel's eyes. "He's developed a tell. When he's about to sacrifice a piece for positional advantage, he increases processing power to queenside calculations by twelve percent. It's like watching someone hold their breath before diving."

Emmet was, without question, the best engineer Daniel had ever hired, and he was lucky to have hired him near the very beginning. Like many of the engineers, Emmet had his rituals. Most mornings, he'd arrive early, brew the first pot of coffee, and play a quick game of chess with Castor before diving into his code. "It's a reliable benchmark," he'd explained when Daniel had asked about it. "Chess has concrete parameters but infinite possibilities. If Castor can beat me, his pattern recognition is sound." Daniel had tried playing a few games himself but found the experience depressingly one-sided. Castor demolished him in under twenty moves every time. Emmet, with his methodical mind, at least managed to reach the endgame before inevitably losing.

When Emmet developed code, it didn't seem like he was writing it. It was like he was asking the product what it wanted to do and then making that a reality. He was intrinsically connected to the technology. People, not so much. Daniel didn't know a damn thing about Emmet's personal life. He knew he was in his late twenties, or maybe early thirties. He wore big glasses, got the same haircut every four weeks on the dot, and had five variations of the same outfit that he wore to work every week.

What Daniel did know was that Emmet was criminally undervalued at his previous company. The tech lead at that startup had taken credit for Emmet's work, leaving him with a minimal equity stake despite creating their core product architecture. When Daniel had brought Emmet on at Promethean, he'd insisted on a generous equity package that Robert and Jonah had initially balked at.

Emmet had shown repeatedly that he was worth every penny. He might have been a predictable human, but his ideas were anything but.

"Taking a break from what?" Daniel cut the light on. "What has you working so late tonight?"

"Had an idea," Emmet said.

When Emmet had an idea that grabbed him like this, Daniel knew to listen. "What is it?"

"New directive," he said.

Daniel moved behind Emmet and looked down at Castor's code running across the laptop screen. Emmet expertly navigated to a new directive. "Using available resources and new resources as they become available," Daniel read, "find ways to optimize your ability to solve problems.' Seems… Vague."

"Does it?" Emmet asked. "It's not vague to Castor. It allows the model to turn its predictive capabilities onto itself."

Daniel paused. "You're instructing Castor to self-criticize."

"In a way. I'm instructing it to predict the gaps in its own knowledge."

"The gaps that cause hallucinations."

"Right. Instead of the model interpolating to fill in the gaps, which is what causes the hallucinations, it will instead turn its search outward and look for ways to fill those gaps with outside knowledge to better its own predictive capabilities."

"But how does Castor know which pathways to strengthen or ignore? 'Optimize your ability' could mean anything."

Emmet adjusted his glasses. "Think of the neural network like a forest with countless paths. The directive doesn't create new paths. It adjusts which paths Castor is likely to take when faced with a decision point."

"Like trail markers," Daniel said.

"Precisely. The directive doesn't tell Castor exactly where to go, but it influences which trails he's likely to follow. When the data is sparse, the directive guides him to the path marked 'I don't know' rather than guessing. That's Promethean's secret sauce."

Daniel leaned closer to the screen. "And this new directive essentially tells him to add his own trail markers."

"And evolve far faster than it could if it were waiting on us," Emmet said. "Is the code good?" Daniel asked.

"Let's find out," Emmet said. He opened Castor's front-end interface and typed in a new query with his usual rapid-fire speed.

Identify which patients in the experimental data should be screened for Parkinson's disease.

In the blink of an eye, Castor returned a list of forty-one patient identification numbers.

"Then we have our list from the customer file," Emmet said. He pulled up a spreadsheet of patient IDs, then sorted it to only show patients who had been identified by physicians to need a DaTscan, which was a neurological scan used to diagnose Parkinson's. There were forty. Castor had pulled an additional patient.

"Almost perfect," Daniel murmured.

"As close as we've ever gotten," Emmet said. "I've run it a few times and checked the debug logs, and it returns the same results. I haven't been able to identify why it keeps pulling this additional patient."

"It might not be an issue with Castor," Daniel said. He phoned his cofounder, who, despite the late hour, answered on the first ring.

"You still at the office working, Dan?"

"Emmet and I have been playing with the new chip," he said. "Listen, do you have your work laptop with you?"

There was a shuffling, then the tap of a keyboard, then Robert said, "Got it. What do you need?"

"From the customer file. We ran the Parkinson's query, and Castor keeps pulling a forty-first patient, instead of the forty listed as having received a DaTscan."

"ID?"

"Six-four-three-alpha-echo," Daniel said.

There was a long pause at the other end of the line. Then, Robert asked, "What query did you input?"

"Identify which patients should be screened for Parkinson's."

"You didn't mention the scan?"

"No." Daniel straightened up. "Does that mean something?"

"Six-four-three-alpha-echo didn't get a DaTscan," Robert said. "He received a genetic test."

"So Castor's right," Daniel said. "More right than we realized."

"Perfect accuracy," Emmet said. He ran his hand over the keyboard like he was petting a beloved, albeit wild animal. "Perfect."

"You better get in early tomorrow, Robert," Daniel said. "We've got a lot to cover."

CHAPTER 3

"We don't have the wiggle room to be running experiments!" Jonah's voice carried through the thin conference room door.

Daniel paused outside, his hand on the handle. Through the glass, he could see Robert and Jonah facing off across the table, a mess of papers and tablets between them.

"It's not an experiment," Robert said, his usually calm voice tight with frustration. "Castor just achieved perfect accuracy. Perfect, Jonah."

"On forty-one patients! That's a rounding error, not a breakthrough."

Daniel pushed the door open. Both men turned to him, and he could read the plea for backup in Robert's eyes.

"Dan, thank God," Robert said. "Tell him about the Parkinson's identification. Tell him what this means."

Twenty years in Silicon Valley had taught Daniel to recognize this moment—the knife's edge between breakthrough and breakdown. His first two startups had died in rooms like this one, suffocated by arguments over vision versus revenue. But Promethean was different. It had to be different.

"What's the issue?" Daniel asked, though he already knew. It was always the same issue.

"Walk with me," Robert said, moving toward the door. "Both of you. I want to show you something."

They followed Robert out of the conference room and through the honeycomb of desks. Daniel noticed Sarah quickly minimizing her screen. She was probably job hunting again. Kevin didn't look up from his code. The whole team could feel the tension radiating from leadership.

Robert led them to the closet they'd converted into a makeshift medical records room. Boxes of anonymized patient files lined the walls, each one representing a life that could be saved or lost.

"This is why we're here," Robert said, pulling down a box marked 'GLIOBLASTOMA - STAGE 4'. His hands shook. "Not for the VCs. Not for the IPO. For them."

"I know why we're here," Jonah said, but his voice had lost some of its edge.

Robert opened the box, revealing hundreds of case files. "My mother's is in here somewhere. Diagnosed too late. Dead in two months." He looked at Daniel. "When I was doing my residency at Stanford, I kept thinking—what if we'd caught it earlier? What if we'd had something like Castor?"

"Robert—" Jonah started.

"No, let me finish." Robert closed the box. "You're worried about making money. I get it. But we're not building another food delivery app or social media platform. We're building something that matters."

Robert walked to the whiteboard that dominated one wall of the bullpen. It was covered in his handwriting—survival rates, diagnostic windows, cost analyses. In the center was a photo: a woman in her fifties, smiling at the camera.

"That's why I had to start this company," Robert said, tapping the photo. "My mother. By the time they caught her glioblastoma, they said she had maybe sixty days left. Instead, she got forty-two."

He picked up a marker and drew a timeline. "Current detection methods catch brain tumors here." He marked a point near the end. "But the tumor starts here." He marked a point years earlier. "That gap? That's where Castor lives. That's where we save lives."

"The other startups are chasing symptoms," Robert continued, drawing branching paths. "We're chasing causes. That's why no one in the Valley is doing what we're doing. It's harder. It takes longer. It requires genuine medical expertise, not just coding skills."

Jonah had stopped pacing, watching Robert fill the whiteboard with increasingly complex diagrams. "And you really think Castor can close that gap?"

"With the right resources?" Robert capped the marker. "Yes."

"Excuse me, Robert?" Melissa poked her head around the corner of the bullpen. "Sorry to interrupt, but the customer is on line two. They want to know about —"

"Not now," Jonah snapped.

"Actually," Robert said, "tell them we'll call back within the hour with good news."

Melissa glanced between the three founders, clearly sensing the tension. "Um, also, Daniel? Emmet said he needs five minutes when you're free. Something about optimizing the diagnostic algorithms."

"Thanks, Mel," Daniel said. After she left, he turned back to the others. "See? The team's already working on scaling solutions. But they need to know we're committed."

"Committed to what?" Jonah said, checking his phone. "Because our burn rate says we've got six months of runway. Maybe eight if we're careful."

Robert grabbed a marker and moved to the small whiteboard mounted on the wall. "Let me show you the math." He started sketching out projections. "If Castor can identify pre-symptomatic patients with even 80% accuracy—"

"That's a big if," Jonah interrupted.

"—Then every major health system in the country will want this," Robert said, writing faster. "The insurance companies alone would save billions. Billions, Jonah."

Promethean wouldn't just make money—it'd save lives. That is—if it worked.

And it was almost working. Almost. It wasn't scalable beyond how far they'd already gone.

Daniel's phone buzzed with a calendar reminder: "Pick up Ana - 7 PM." He swiped it away. Then another: "Nat's school conference - Tomorrow 3 PM." Swipe.

"You good?" Robert asked, noticing.

"Yeah, just—" Another notification. This time from Ana: "Where are you?"

Daniel typed back quickly: "Still at office. Big milestone with Castor. Be home soon."

The response was immediate: "That's what you said yesterday."

He started to type an explanation, then deleted it. Started again. Deleted. What could he say? That they were on the verge of something revolutionary? That once Castor was fully operational, he'd have all the time in the world for family?

"Dan?" Robert prompted. "You were saying about the scalability issue?"

Daniel pocketed his phone, the message to Ana unsent. "Right. The chip. We need more processing power, or we hit a wall within six months. Maybe less."

"Then we better move fast," Jonah said, pulling up his investor contacts. "I'll set up the pitches."

Another buzz. Daniel didn't look this time. He knew what it would say—some variation of the disappointment that had been building for months.

For three months now, Daniel had promised his wife, Ana, that it was almost working. That was how he had tried to explain away the late nights, the weekends spent in the office, and the texts to which he forgot to reply.

He was starting his own research. If a more powerful quantum computing chip didn't exist, he'd invent one. That was the only way he saw to defuse the bomb. Once that was done, once Castor was ready, he'd have a normal schedule.

This was the last push.

"You're sure we can hit this deadline?" Jonah asked, pacing in front of the wall of monitors showing Castor's live performance metrics. Each screen told a different story—processing speed, accuracy rates, and resource consumption.

"I'm sure," Robert said, but he was watching the screens too, his fingers drumming against his crossed arms.

Daniel pulled up a chair and started typing, bringing up the development timeline on the main monitor. "Here's where we are." Red markers showed missed milestones. Green showed completions. There was too much red. "If we're honest about it—"

"We can't afford to be honest about it," Jonah said, still pacing. His usually perfect hair was mussed from running his hands through it. "The investors want to see progress by—"

An alert pinged. The control data was ready. The argument would have to wait.

All three men moved to the center of the open office, overlooking Emmet as he began to upload the provided medical records for Castor's assessment. Emmet's desk was in the middle of the honeycomb configuration, flanked by other developers. Usually, the desks had a mix of developers talking with each other or locked in with noise-cancelling headphones as they were absorbed in their code, but today, most of the attention was on Emmet. At his workstation, Emmet had Castor's code open in a large, prominent window. He had the upload interface open on a separate large monitor, and on his third screen, he was tracking Castor's hardware performance indicators in real-time.

Behind the code window, as if hastily hidden, was Emmet's chess analysis program. The digital board showed an endgame position with just a few pieces remaining. "Interesting game," Daniel said. He wanted Emmet to know he'd caught him using critical computer power to play.

As usual, Emmet missed the social cue and nodded without looking up. He tabbed into the game. "Castor's starting to develop preferences. Favors knights over bishops now. Plays a more positional game." He tapped a notation on the screen. "This move here, it's unnecessary for victory, but it forced me to reveal my strategy for the entire queenside."

Daniel bit his tongue. "Well, as long as you're learning something."

Emmet's gaze remained fixed on the screen. "I believe we both are."

"Gentlemen, can we get back on task?" Robert prodded, bringing focus back to work. "This contract could move mountains for us." Robert continued. "Since it's a regional health insurance underwriter, there aren't as many records as there would be for a larger firm. I ran it by engineering before we signed the paperwork."

"I know," Daniel said, "but we were operating on hypotheticals. I thought we'd been screening for one condition, not everything."

"The computational difference is exponential," Emmet said.

"We need this done today," Jonah said.

"Then you should've been clearer about the scope!" Daniel snapped.

"Can you fight elsewhere?" Emmet asked. "I'm starting the assessment."

"He's right," Robert said. "Take a breath. We'll see if it works, and if not, we'll figure out a way to fix it."

"Jesus, I'm sick of fixing things," Jonah said.

You don't fix anything, Daniel thought. I do. But he didn't say it aloud. Arguments like that with Jonah never went anywhere productive.

He watched the screens as Castor began to process the data. A tense silence fell over the office. The first few minutes went smoothly as the data was uploaded into Castor's interface, but once he began assessing for chronic health issues, the system's performance began to decline.

Just as Daniel had expected, Castor had the juice to identify specific health issues based on patient records, but not any. It was an exponentially larger ask.

Emmet peered at the performance numbers. "It's declining," he said.

"Yeah, I see that," Jonah said. "But it won't crash, will it?"

"Unknown," Emmet said.

On the monitor, the graph noting Castor's GPU usage spiked up to 98%. If it hit 100%, it'd be moments before it crashed.

"That doesn't look good," Robert said.

"What happens if it crashes?" Jonah asked.

"We won't be able to deliver the report," Emmet said. "We could re-upload and run separate assessments for specific potential illnesses."

"That's not what the contract specifies," Robert said. "The whole purpose of this contract is that the client doesn't have to provide a list of illnesses, to empower us to identify issues they might have missed."

"It's a good idea," Daniel said, "Castor might not have the power to do it."

"Then find the power," Jonah said in a low, frustrated voice. "We need this to work. I've already mentioned it to potential investors. They're interested in providing the next round of funding—but only if this works."

"Find the power," Daniel muttered to himself. They couldn't find it. But maybe Castor could find it himself. His fingers hovered over the keyboard, knowing what he was about to do could either save them or destroy everything. "Open the directives, Emmet," Daniel said.

Emmet tabbed over to Castor's directive interface, then rolled his well-worn office chair to the side. Daniel stepped into the gap he'd made and leaned over the laptop.

Using available resources and new resources as they become available, Daniel typed into the interface, *find new ways to optimize your ability to solve problems and reduce risks to your overall ability to continue operating in your environment.*

"Interesting," Emmet said. "Vague."

"Vague enough to give Castor control," Daniel said. "To let him find solutions we're not thinking of."

"It," Robert said. "Not him."

"Whatever." Daniel waved a hand dismissively. "Let's see what it decides to do."

The assessment of the data stopped. The charts tracking the GPU performance plummeted back down to a few percent, a bare step above idleness. If Castor was doing anything at all, it didn't seem that way.

"Is that a crash?" Jonah asked. "Did it crash?"

"Either we just solved the problem, or created a much worse one," Emmet said. "Castor's doing something, but there's no way for us to know what."

"Why does that make it a worse problem?" Robert asked.

"We can't debug if we don't know what's been changed," Daniel said. "Shit."

"So if it's crashed, we're screwed?" Jonah asked. "Really good work, Daniel. I'll let you get on the call with the client to tell them we need to cancel the one contract keeping this whole operation afloat. Just because you think you know—"

"You wrote a check we couldn't cash!" Daniel interrupted. "I'm trying to meet what's basically an impossible ask—"

"Both of you, relax," Robert said, loud enough to carry over the beginnings of the argument. "Emmet, may I?"

"Please," Emmet said, and pushed his office chair even further away from the chaos.

Robert tabbed out of the directives and back into the front-end query interface. He typed: Identify patients who should be scheduled for preventative screenings and enumerate tests to be performed on each patient.

The GPU measurements ticked back up but barely reached a quarter of capacity. The room was silent as Castor returned a list of names matched with tests.

"Tell me that matches the control data," Jonah said.

Robert pulled out his phone, unlocked it, and pulled up the client-provided PDF. "It does," he said, "and then some. Castor has made more than a dozen additional recommendations."

"Just like he did for the Parkinson's data," Daniel said. "If that was right, I'd assume these are right, too."

Jonah's eyes widened. "All of those names? And all of those tests? We can assume those are correct?"

"Well," Robert said, "We'll want to cross-reference then with the physician's records, since it's new, but we had success with the Parkinson's run, and this is the same mechanic on a larger scale—"

"Holy shit," Jonah said. "This is huge."

Robert nodded. "I know. Millions of dollars huge."

"Patients would save hundreds of millions of dollars in healthcare costs," Jonah continued. "Insurers, too."

"Right," Daniel agreed. "This could save lives."

"It will save lives," Robert said.

Jonah clapped Daniel on the shoulder. "Good save, Dan. I need to get on a call with the client. Write up the specifics in a brief for me, will you?" He rushed into the conference room without waiting for an answer.

A relieved silence fell over the room. Emmet rolled his chair back over to the computer, opened Castor's code, and began to scroll through it at a speed Daniel couldn't keep up with.

"How's it look?" Daniel asked.

"Different," Emmet said. "I'll need time to explore. Please leave me alone to look at it."

Daniel and Robert exchanged a look, then nodded, and stepped away from Emmet's desk as Emmet put on his immense noise-canceling headphones. They were used to his dismissals. In the tiny kitchen, Robert grabbed two mugs, then opened the highest cabinet and grabbed the nice scotch.

"This warrants the scotch?" Daniel asked with a laugh.

"Obviously it does." Robert poured a small amount in each mug, then handed one to Daniel. "This is our biggest win yet. With this proof-of-concept, we're about to get our funding supercharged. I don't know how you and Emmet coded Castor to do that, but it's… Game changing."

"That's the fun part," Daniel said. He tapped the edge of his mug to Robert's and took a sip of the fine liquor. "Castor's guiding his own development. We're along for the ride."

"As long as you're steering," Robert said with a grin. "We're about to make something incredible."

CHAPTER 4

Robert Hayes checked his smartwatch as the development team filed into the conference room. His heart rate was steady at 62 bpm—good, considering the amount of coffee he'd consumed this morning. The team had grown considerably in the past three months since their breakthrough with the insurance contract. Eight developers now, not counting Daniel and Emmet, all eager to push Castor's capabilities further.

"Alright, let's see what our AI's been up to this week," Daniel said, connecting his laptop to the main screen. His enthusiasm was infectious, even if Robert noticed the dark circles under his eyes. Daniel had been pulling too many late nights again.

Robert settled into his chair at the head of the table, noting how Emmet had automatically taken the seat with the best view of both the screen and the door. Some habits from his time at Stanford died hard.

"So we've expanded Castor's integration into our daily operations," Daniel said, pulling up a dashboard. "Emmet, want to walk us through the task assignment system?"

Emmet stood without preamble. "Castor now analyzes our code commits, pull request reviews, and bug fix patterns. It creates developer profiles based on strengths and assigns tasks accordingly." He clicked through several screens showing metrics. "Kevin, for example, is 34% more efficient with front-end debugging than backend architecture. Sarah excels at API integration. Castor factors this into sprint planning."

"It's been super helpful," Melissa chimed in from across the table. "I haven't gotten stuck with database migration in weeks."

Robert smiled. This was the kind of practical application that would appeal to investors. "What about the error rate on assignments?"

"Down to 3%," Emmet said. "Castor learns from reassignments and adjusts its model."

"Let me show you something," Daniel said, pulling up their task management system. "This is our current sprint backlog. Seventy-three items ranging from bug fixes to new features." He typed a command. "Watch what happens when I ask Castor to optimize it."

The screen flickered as rows of tasks began rearranging themselves. Color-coded priorities shifted, dependencies drew themselves as connecting lines, and time estimates adjusted in real-time.

"It's analyzing change history, code complexity, and our velocity trends," Emmet narrated as they watched. "See how it moved the authentication refactor up? It identified that three other tasks depend on it, even though we hadn't explicitly linked them."

"And look at this," Daniel pointed to a cluster of tasks at the bottom. "Castor's suggesting we delay these UI improvements because it predicts a design revision request based on our client communication patterns."

Robert leaned forward, fascinated. "It's reading our client emails?"

"Just analyzing sentiment and keyword patterns," Daniel clarified quickly. "But yeah, it noticed the client has mentioned 'user flow concerns' four times in the last week."

The backlog stabilized into its new configuration. What had been an overwhelming list now looked manageable, logical.

"Based on this optimization, we'll hit our first major milestone in nine days instead of waiting for the full sprint completion," Melissa said. "That's the client demo, right?"

"Exactly," Daniel said. "Castor identified that if we re-sequence the work, we can have a fully functional demo ready earlier, even if some polish items aren't complete."

"Wait, what's this?" Kevin pointed at a task marked with a small robot icon.

"Issue 3447—move the submit button on the patient intake form?"

Daniel's expression shifted to something between pride and uncertainty. "That's… actually something new. Click on it."

Kevin expanded the task. Instead of the usual description and acceptance criteria, there was a full code commit attached.

"Castor wrote this?" Sarah leaned forward, scanning the code. "It moved the submit button from the bottom of the form to right after the required fields section."

"And look at the commit message," Emmet said, reading aloud. "'Relocating submit button reduces average form completion time by 12 seconds based on user interaction analysis. Eye tracking data suggests users search for submit after completing required fields. "

"Eye tracking data?" Robert asked. "We don't have eye tracking."

"Castor extrapolated from mouse movement patterns," Daniel said. "It's been analyzing how users navigate our interfaces and making suggestions. This is the first time it's written the implementation."

The room fell silent. Robert felt a mix of excitement and unease. Castor wasn't just organizing their work anymore—it was doing it.

"It's a simple UI change," Daniel said, sensing the mood. "The code is clean, well-commented. Emmet and I reviewed it thoroughly."

"Has anyone else noticed the meeting schedule changes?" Sarah asked, breaking the tension. "We haven't had any of those painful 3 PM all-hands meetings lately."

Daniel grinned. "That's Castor too. It analyzed our productivity patterns—even tracks our coffee consumption from the kitchen supplies orders. Figured out that our collective output drops 23% after 2 PM, so it front-loads critical meetings in the morning."

"My mother would've loved this," Robert murmured. "She always said hospitals scheduled everything at the worst possible times for human performance."

The mention of his mother sent a familiar pang through his chest. Everything they built here was for her, in a way. To prevent other families from losing someone to late detection.

"Speaking of performance," Emmet interjected, his tone shifting. "We need to discuss Castor's computational limitations."

The energy in the room changed immediately. Robert recognized that tone—Emmet had found something concerning.

"Can we table that for the moment?" Daniel said. "I know we're running up against time, and I think that deserves a deeper discussion."

Robert glanced at his watch. The meeting was scheduled to end in five minutes, and he knew several team members had other commitments.

"Alright, everyone, let's wrap up here," Robert said. "Great work on the integrations. Keep monitoring how Castor's suggestions pan out, especially that code commit."

As the team began filing out, chatting about lunch plans and afternoon tasks, Robert caught Daniel's eye.

"You two stay behind," he said. "Let's hear about these limitations."

CHAPTER 5

The conference room felt larger with just the three of them. Robert watched as Emmet pulled up a new set of graphs on the main screen while Daniel closed the door behind the last departing developer.

"Show me what you've found," Robert said.

Emmet's fingers moved across the keyboard with practiced efficiency. "These are Castor's resource utilization patterns over the past month."

The visualization that appeared made Robert's stomach tighten. The upward curve was unmistakable.

"We're approaching capacity," Robert said. It wasn't a question.

"We regularly hit 85% running our standard operations," Emmet confirmed. "Task management, security monitoring, scheduling, code analysis—it all adds up. When we layer medical diagnostics on top…" He clicked to another screen showing a redlined graph. "We see these critical spikes."

"What happens when we exceed capacity?"

"Processing delays. Incomplete analyses. Queued requests." Emmet pulled up a video file. "This is from our test environment last week. We simulated Castor analyzing a full hospital's worth of patient data."

Robert leaned forward as the demonstration began. The interface showed Castor attempting to process thousands of medical records simultaneously. Progress bars that usually moved smoothly began to stutter, then freeze entirely. Error messages cascaded across the screen like a digital avalanche.

"The medical analysis alone would consume all our current resources,"

Emmet said. "We can't scale to hospital-level diagnostics with our current hardware."

Robert felt his chest tighten. This was their entire vision—large-scale predictive medicine. The whole reason they'd built Castor. "How long until we hit this wall in production?"

"At current growth rates? Six months. Maybe less."

"Which is why," Daniel said, moving to stand beside the screen, "we need to seriously consider developing our own quantum computing solution."

Robert had been expecting this. Daniel had been dropping hints for weeks, staying late to run simulations, filling notebooks with circuit designs. "I'm listening."

Daniel's eyes lit up with the same intensity Robert had seen when they'd first started Promethean. He pulled up a presentation that looked freshly made. "Current quantum chips have fundamental flaws. Surface contamination, qubit instability, and manufacturing inconsistencies. But here's the thing—Castor's helped me identify patterns in these defects."

"Patterns?" Robert asked.

"Repeatable manufacturing errors that everyone else treats as random noise," Daniel explained, clicking through microscopic images of chip surfaces. "If we could fabricate our own chips, controlling every aspect of the process, we could eliminate these defects."

"The computational power would increase by orders of magnitude," Emmet added. "My conservative estimates suggest a minimum 1000-fold improvement in processing capability with a high likelihood of a much bigger upside."

"Conservative?" Robert raised an eyebrow.

"Very," Daniel said. "With that kind of power, Castor could run predictive models on entire hospital systems simultaneously. Real-time analysis of every patient, every symptom, catching diseases before they manifest clinically."

Robert's pulse quickened. This was the dream—true preventive medicine powered by AI. His mother's face flashed in his mind, the way she'd looked in those final weeks, when the cancer they'd caught too late had already spread too far.

"What's the cost?" he asked, pushing the memory aside.

Daniel's enthusiasm dimmed. "Initial estimates for the design are 12 million, but that is significantly reduced because of Castor's predictive modeling capability. Then another 15 million for fabrication trials…"

"So thirty million minimum," Robert calculated, feeling the weight of the number. "That's… significant. The insurance contract helps, but—"

"I know — we'd need substantial additional funding," Daniel finished Robert's sentence. "But if we don't ask Jonah to secure funding, it simply can't happen. We need to take a big swing here. I'm not asking us to burn the money we need for our current plan. I'm asking for more money for things we need beyond that."

Robert rubbed his temples. Five million. Their current revenue wouldn't come close to covering that. "Do you have a formal proposal ready?"

"Most of it," Daniel said, pulling up documents on his laptop. "Emmet's been helping with the technical specifications. We could have something comprehensive by end of week."

"Good. I'll need—"

The conference room door burst open. Melissa poked her head in, slightly out of breath. "Sorry to interrupt, but Jonah pulled into the parking lot. He's on the phone, looks really excited about something."

Robert and Daniel exchanged glances. Jonah had been in investor meetings all week.

"Thanks, Mel," Robert said. She nodded and disappeared.

"We'll continue this after we hear his news," Robert said, standing. "But I want that full proposal—costs, timelines, risk assessment. If we're going to push for quantum development, we need to be bulletproof in our reasoning."

As they gathered their things, Robert found himself staring at the frozen error messages still displayed on the screen. Castor hitting its limits felt wrong somehow, like watching a brilliant mind trapped in a failing body.

His smartwatch buzzed. Heart rate: 78 bpm. Elevated. The simple AI suggested deep breathing exercises.

Robert almost laughed at the irony. Even his watch was trying to optimize his performance, while their groundbreaking AI was running out of room to grow.

"Robert?" Daniel paused at the door. "You coming?"

"Yeah," Robert said, dismissing his philosophical musings. They had more immediate concerns—like whether Jonah's excitement meant new funding or new problems.

As they walked toward the main conference room, Robert wondered what his mother would think of all this. She'd probably remind him that the best solutions often required the biggest risks.

He hoped that whatever news Jonah brought would help them take that risk. Because Daniel was right, without quantum computing, Castor would hit a wall.

And everything they'd built would hit it with him.

CHAPTER 6

"We got it!" Jonah burst through the conference room doors, waving a manila folder above his head like a trophy. His usual composure had given way to genuine excitement, his face flushed with success.

Daniel and Robert looked up from the quantum chip specifications spread across the table.

"Got what?" Robert asked, though his growing smile suggested he already knew.

"Term sheet. Signed." Jonah dropped the folder onto the table with a satisfying thump. "Regillus Global wants to lead the round. Two hundred million."

"Two hundred million?" Daniel felt his jaw drop. "That's… that's incredible."

"At what valuation?" Robert asked, picking up the folder and scanning the contents.

"Eight hundred and fifty million post-money," Jonah said, taking a seat. He loosened his tie with one hand while gesturing with the other. "They love what we did with the insurance contract. Want to see us scale aggressively."

Daniel felt a surge of hope. With that kind of funding…"This is perfect timing. Robert and I were reviewing the quantum chip proposal. With two hundred million—"

"Whoa, slow down," Jonah laughed. "This is just the term sheet. It's not a done deal yet."

"But it's as good as done, right?" Robert asked. "They're committed?"

"It gives us leverage," Jonah said, his business-school training showing. "We can shop this around, see if anyone wants to match or beat their terms. Worst case, we take Regillus's offer. Best case, we start a bidding war."

"How long do we have?" Daniel asked.

"Thirty days' exclusivity, but I want to move fast. Strike while we're hot." Jonah noticed the technical drawings on the table. "Is this the quantum thing you keep talking about?"

"Quantum computing chip," Daniel said. "Here, let me show you why this could be a gamechanger."

For the next ten minutes, Daniel walked Jonah through the basics—how quantum chips used qubits instead of traditional bits, how they could solve certain problems exponentially faster, and most importantly, how they could eliminate Castor's computational bottlenecks.

"So instead of adding more servers," Jonah said, "we'd have one chip that's thousands of times more powerful?"

"Exactly," Robert said. "The medical applications alone—"

"Forget medical for a second," Jonah interrupted, his eyes lighting up. "Think about financial modeling. Supply chain optimization. Climate predictions. If Castor could process that much data…" He trailed off, clearly running numbers in his head.

"So you'll pitch it to investors?" Daniel asked hopefully.

"I'll add it to our deck," Jonah said. "No promises, but with this kind of interest, we might be able to push for more. Maybe enough for a serious R&D budget."

"That's all we need," Daniel said. "Just the chance to try."

Jonah stood, straightening his jacket. "I've got calls to make. Need to let some other VCs know we have a term sheet, get them interested." He paused at the door. "This is big, guys. We should celebrate."

"Scotch is in the top cabinet," Robert said with a grin.

Jonah nodded. "I'll get the glasses."

As the door closed behind him, Robert pulled out the good scotch from the top cabinet. "One drink to celebrate. This is what we've been working toward."

Daniel accepted the glass gratefully, feeling lighter than he had in weeks.

They clinked glasses, and Daniel felt the warm burn of possibility.

"To Promethean," Robert said.

"To quantum leaps," Daniel added.

After they finished their drinks, Daniel glanced at his phone. "I should call Ana. Share the good news."

He dialed her number, the scotch warming his chest as he waited for her to answer.

"Hey, you're calling early. Good day?" she answered on the second ring.

"The best," Daniel said, unable to keep the smile out of his voice. "We got a term sheet. Two hundred million."

"Daniel! That's amazing!" He could hear her moving, probably stepping away from whatever task she was doing. "Two hundred million? That's massive!"

"Valuation is eight fifty million," Daniel said. "We're almost unicorns."

"So close! I'm so proud of you, honey. When did this happen?"

"About twenty minutes ago. Jonah thinks he can get more, maybe enough to fund the quantum chip project."

"The one you've been sketching all over every napkin in the house?" Ana said. "That's wonderful. You've worked so hard for this."

"It's not done yet," Daniel said, but he was grinning. "Just the first step."

"First step to changing the world," Ana said. "Oh, speaking of steps—you're still coming home early to help with Nat's science project, right?"

Daniel's stomach dropped. The solar system model. They'd been putting it off for weeks, and the science fair was in three days. "Of course. That's tonight."

"You forgot," Ana said, but her voice was more amused than angry. "It's fine. Just be home by six. We've got all the supplies—Styrofoam balls, paint, the whole works. She's super excited about it."

"I'll be there," Daniel promised. "I won't let her down."

"I know you won't. This news probably helps your mood for family planet-building."

Daniel glanced at the technical drawings on the table, then at Robert, who was making shooing motions with his hands.

"Go," Robert mouthed. "Be with your family."

"You know what? I'm leaving now," Daniel said into the phone. "I'll pick up some extra supplies on the way. Glitter, maybe some glow-in-the-dark paint. Make it the best solar system at the fair."

"Really?" Ana sounded genuinely surprised. "Who are you and what have you done with my husband?"

"Very funny. Tell Nat I'm bringing the works. We're going to make the other kids' projects look like crayon drawings."

As he hung up, Robert was already pulling out the scotch for a second round. "One more before you go. You've earned it."

Daniel declined, smiling. "Save it for when we close the deal. I've got planets to build."

As he drove to the craft store an hour later, Daniel couldn't stop smiling. For once, everything was falling into place. Funding was coming, his quantum chip might become reality, and he'd make it home for a family project.

His phone buzzed with a text from Nat: "Mom says you're coming home!! Did you remember we need black paint for space?"

Daniel's smile widened. Tonight, he'd be there. Tonight, he'd build the world's best science fair solar system. And maybe, just maybe, he was finally learning to balance it all.

CHAPTER 7

The Bennett family dining table had been transformed into a miniature solar system workshop. Newspaper covered every inch of the dark wood surface, and an array of Styrofoam balls in various sizes waited to be transformed into planets. The smell of acrylic paint mixed with the lingering aroma of the takeout Chinese they'd demolished an hour earlier.

"Okay, so Jupiter gets the big one," Nat said, reaching for the largest Styrofoam ball. At twelve, she'd hit a growth spurt that left her all knees and elbows, her movements still adjusting to her new height. "And Earth is… this one?"

"Actually, that's still too big," Daniel said, comparing it to the marble-sized ball he'd designated as Earth. "Jupiter is huge. Like, ridiculously huge. You could fit over thirteen hundred Earths inside it."

"Thirteen hundred?" Nat's eyes widened. "That's insane."

Ana sat at the far end of the table, laptop open, occasionally glancing up from her screen to smile at their enthusiasm. She'd changed from her work clothes into yoga pants and an old Army t-shirt, her dark hair pulled back in a messy bun. The soft click of her keyboard provided a steady rhythm beneath their conversation.

"Here's what's really going to blow your mind," Daniel said, pulling out his phone calculator. "Let's say Earth is this marble—about three-quarters of an inch across. At that scale, how big do you think the Sun would be?"

Nat studied the marble, then gestured with her hands. "Like… a basketball?"

"Bigger. Way bigger." Daniel grinned. "The Sun would be about eight and a half feet in diameter. Like a giant beach ball, but even bigger."

"No way!"

"And here's the really crazy part—at that scale, Earth wouldn't be sitting here on the table next to the Sun. It would be orbiting about 730 feet away. That's like…" He thought for a moment. "From here to the end of our block and back."

Nat set down her paintbrush, orange paint dripping slightly onto the newspaper. "So our whole solar system model is basically a lie?"

"A necessary lie," Ana said without looking up from her laptop. "Unless you want to submit a science project that spans the entire school."

"That would be kind of awesome, though," Nat said, returning to painting Jupiter with swirls of orange, red, and white. "Can you imagine? 'Sorry, Mrs. Chen, my project is too scientifically accurate to fit in the gym.'"

Daniel laughed. "And if you wanted to include Neptune at this scale, you'd have to walk about five and a half miles from your giant beach ball Sun."

"Five and a half miles?" Nat shook her head. "Space is too big. It's breaking my brain."

"Want to know something even weirder? At this scale, light, the fastest thing in the universe, would only travel about one step per second. So sunlight would take over eight minutes to walk from the Sun to Earth."

"Light can't walk, Dad," Nat said with an eye roll that was pure preteen.

"You know what I mean."

Ana's phone buzzed. She glanced at it, frowned, then typed a quick response before returning to her laptop.

"Everything okay?" Daniel asked.

"Just a client in Korea. They want to move up the timeline on a high-field MRI coil shipment." She typed rapidly for a moment. "I can make it work, but it means shuffling some other deliveries."

"Mom's basically a logistics wizard," Nat told Daniel proudly. "She can get anything anywhere."

"It's just Tetris with cargo containers," Ana said modestly, but Daniel caught the pleased smile that flickered across her face.

They worked in comfortable silence for a few minutes, Nat carefully painting Earth's continents while Daniel added texture to Mars. The evening felt perfect. It was the kind of family moment he'd remember years later with a golden glow of nostalgia.

"Oh!" Nat said. "I forgot to tell you… Dad got me a new bow!"

Daniel's brush paused. She meant Viktor, her biological father. "Yeah? What kind?"

"A Hoyt Satori. It's not one of their top-of-the-line or anything, but it's way better than my old one. The draw weight is perfect for my size now." She set Earth aside to dry and reached for Venus. "Coach says if I keep improving, I might have a shot at States this year."

"You've been practicing a lot," Ana said. "I see you out there in the backyard every evening."

"The district qualifier is in four weeks," Nat said, excitement creeping into her voice. "If I place in the top three, I go to States. And if I place at States…" She trailed off, as if afraid to voice the dream.

"Nationals," Daniel finished for her. "You're going to make it. I know you are."

"You'll come to the district qualifier, right?" Nat looked at him hopefully.

"I wouldn't miss it," Daniel promised, making a mental note to add it to his calendar as soon as they were done. "I want to see you destroy the competition with your new bow."

"It's not about destroying anyone," Nat said, but she was smiling. "Archery is more about competing with yourself. Finding your center. Dad says that the arrow already knows where to go. You just have to get out of its way."

"Very Zen," Daniel said. "Speaking of your dad, why does he call you Tater? I've always wondered."

Nat groaned and covered her face with her paint-covered hands, leaving a small smudge of yellow on her cheek. "It's so embarrassing."

"Now I definitely need to know," Daniel said, grinning.

Ana looked up from her laptop, a mischievous smile playing at her lips. "Should I tell him, or do you want to?"

"Mom, no!"

"When she was about two," Ana began, ignoring Nat's protests, "she couldn't quite pronounce her name correctly. She'd say 'Natata' instead of Natasha."

"That's adorable," Daniel said.

"It gets worse," Nat mumbled through her hands.

"And for some reason, she also called potatoes 'patatas.' So Viktor started calling her Tater to tease her, and…" Ana shrugged. "All these years later, it stuck."

"I was two!" Nat protested. "My language skills weren't fully developed!"

"And yet you're stuck with Tater forever," Daniel said, reaching over to ruffle her hair. She ducked away, laughing.

"Only Dad calls me that," she said. "If you start, I'm running away to live with my cousins in Japan."

"Your cousins who call you Nat-chan?" Ana asked innocently.

"That's different! That's culturally appropriate!"

They dissolved into laughter, and Daniel felt a warmth in his chest that had nothing to do with the earlier scotch. This was what he'd been working toward… not just the funding or the company, but these moments. His family around a table, paint on their hands, laughing about silly nicknames.

"The science fair is Friday, right?" he asked as they returned to painting.

"Yeah, setup is Thursday after school," Nat said. "But you don't have to come to that. Just the actual fair on Friday. Parents are invited from six to eight."

"I'll be there," Daniel promised. "Wouldn't miss seeing the world's tiniest, most inaccurate solar system."

"Hey! It's going to be beautiful, even if it's scientifically wrong."

"The best kind of wrong," Ana agreed, finally closing her laptop. "Okay, I officially declare work time over. Who wants to help me paint Uranus?"

"Mom!" Nat shrieked, dissolving into giggles.

"What? It's a perfectly legitimate planet!"

As they finished the solar system together, Daniel thought about the term sheet sitting in his car, about the quantum chip designs scattered across his desk at work, about all the late nights that lay ahead. But right now, none of that mattered.

Right now, he was exactly where he needed to be. He was at home with his girls, making a scientifically inaccurate but absolutely perfect model of the solar system.

"Four weeks," Nat said as they cleaned up, setting the planets aside to dry overnight. "November second. Two p.m. You'll be there?"

"I'll put it in my calendar right now," Daniel said, pulling out his phone. He typed it in carefully: NAT'S ARCHERY - DISTRICT QUALIFIER - 2 PM - DON'T MISS!

"Promise?" she asked.

"Promise," he said, meaning it with every fiber of his being.

CHAPTER 8

Four weeks later, the conference room felt like a pressure cooker. The initial euphoria of the term sheet had evaporated, replaced by the grinding reality of Silicon Valley fundraising. Daniel could see the exhaustion in Jonah's face, the way his usually crisp shirt was wrinkled, his tie askew.

"The Regillus term sheet expires in two days," Jonah said without preamble. "We're out of time."

"What about Halberd Ventures?" Robert asked. "They seemed interested."

"They passed yesterday. Said the valuation was too high." Jonah rubbed his face. "That was our last real shot."

Daniel felt his stomach drop. "But you said you could get others interested. Start a bidding war."

"I tried." Jonah's voice was flat. "Twenty-seven investor meetings in four weeks. You know how many competing offers we got? Zero."

"Zero?" Robert asked. "But our metrics are solid."

"Our metrics are great for medical AI," Jonah said. "But every investor asked the same question. 'What else can it do?' When I mentioned we're focused on healthcare, half of them checked out immediately."

"What about the quantum chip?" Daniel asked. "Did that generate any interest?"

Jonah laughed bitterly. "One partner at BlueLeaf Ventures called it 'science fiction.' Another said, and I quote, 'We don't fund physics experiments.'"

The room fell silent. Outside, Daniel could hear the developers chatting, oblivious to the crisis unfolding in the conference room.

"So, what are our options?" Robert asked.

"Take the Regillus deal or try to raise a smaller round at a lower valuation." Jonah pulled out a thick document. "But there's something else. Regillus sent over the final closing documents yesterday. There are… conditions."

"What kind of conditions?" Daniel asked, though he was already dreading the answer.

"They want us to expand beyond medical. Immediately." Jonah flipped to a tabbed page. "Transportation, financial services, cybersecurity. They're calling it 'market diversification.'"

"But medical is our core focus," Daniel protested. "It's why we started this company."

"I know," Jonah said. "But they're not saying abandon medical. They're saying expand. Look at their projections—if Castor can optimize shipping routes, prevent accidents, detect financial fraud… the market opportunity is orders of magnitude bigger than what medical alone offers."

Daniel's phone buzzed on the table. He glanced at it—a text from Ana. He'd check it later.

"Using what computing power?" Daniel asked. "We're already hitting capacity with our current operations."

"They don't know that," Jonah said. "As far as they're concerned, Castor scaled beautifully for the insurance contract."

Robert rubbed his temples. "So, we take their money and hope we can figure out the scaling issues later?"

"Or we walk away from two hundred million dollars." Jonah's expression made it clear which option he preferred. "Look, I've spent four weeks trying to find alternatives. This is it. We take this deal or we raise a down round, probably at half the valuation."

Daniel stood up, pacing to the window. Four weeks ago, they'd been celebrating. Now they were backed into a corner.

His phone buzzed again. Then again. He flipped it face down.

"What about the quantum chip?" he asked without turning around.

Jonah and Robert exchanged glances.

"Daniel," Robert said, "no one wants to fund quantum development. Not at the scale we need."

"So, what, we give up on it?"

"I have an idea," Robert said. "What if you pursue the quantum development independently?"

Daniel turned. "Independently? How?"

"You work on it on your own time," Robert explained. "Evenings, weekends. We can't fund it directly, but we can give you access to Castor for modeling and simulations."

"That's… not a bad compromise," Jonah said, warming to the idea. "But if you're using company resources, even just computing time, Promethean needs something in return."

"Like what?" Daniel asked.

"Right of first refusal," Jonah said. "Standard terms. If you develop anything, Promethean gets the first opportunity to license or purchase the technology."

Daniel looked at Robert. "What does that mean?"

"It means if you create a working quantum chip," Robert said, "we get the chance to match any other offer you receive. We don't get a discount, but you can't sell to someone else unless we pass."

Daniel's phone lit up with an incoming call. Ana. He sent it to voicemail.

"It protects the company's interests while giving you freedom to innovate," Jonah said. "You'd own the IP, take all the financial risk, but we get first shot at the technology if it works."

Daniel considered this. It wasn't ideal—he'd be taking all the financial risk himself, working nights and weekends on top of his regular responsibilities. But at least he'd have access to Castor's processing power for simulations.

"The term sheet expires in forty-eight hours," Jonah said. "I need to know if we're all aligned here."

Daniel looked at the Regillus contract on the table. Two hundred million dollars. Enough to keep Promethean alive, to grow the team, to push Castor into new markets. Even if those weren't the markets they'd originally envisioned.

His phone continued buzzing intermittently. More texts coming in.

"Alright," Daniel said. "I'll develop the quantum chip on my own. Nights and weekends."

"You sure?" Robert asked. "That's a huge commitment on top of everything else."

"Someone has to do it," Daniel said. "And if Castor's going to be stretched across all these new sectors, we'll need that computational power more than ever."

Jonah made a note on his tablet. "I'll have legal draw up the right of first refusal agreement by close of business tomorrow. Standard terms, nothing predatory. We'll make it fair."

"Fine," Daniel agreed.

As they shook hands, Daniel felt the weight of what he'd committed to. Promethean was about to change direction, pulled by the gravity of investor demands. And he was about to embark on a parallel journey, funded by his own savings and sweat equity.

"I'll sign the Regillus deal today," Jonah said. "Money should hit our accounts within two weeks."

"And then everything changes," Robert said.

Daniel nodded. Everything would change. The question was whether he could build the future fast enough to catch up with it.

"I should check these," Daniel said, picking up his phone. "Ana never calls this many times unless—"

His blood ran cold as he read the messages:

Ok, we were waiting for you at the house, but we're leaving now

Fifteen minutes. You on your way?

It's starting

Nat's turn coming up. Where are you?

Daniel, she keeps looking for you in the crowd

She just shot. You missed it.

I can't believe you did this again.

Daniel swore and scrambled to his feet. "I swear I put this in my calendar," he said. He swiped over to his calendar. He remembered adding it! Archery meet! Two p.m.! Don't miss it!

But there was no item on his calendar and no reminder, and so Daniel had missed it after promising he wouldn't.

"Gotta run," he said to Robert. "We'll talk more tomorrow."

"Tell Nat I said hey," Robert said. He'd seen Daniel fumble his family responsibilities enough to know this was another one of the same. "You can blame me for this, whatever it is."

"Thanks," Daniel said. He shrugged on his jacket and paused at the door of the conference room. "And—you know, even with the stipulations, we got funded. I don't want you to think I'm overlooking that. We did it. All three of us."

"Yeah, we did," Robert said. "And we'll keep going. So go see your family, and we'll break out the scotch tomorrow."

Daniel threw Robert a salute and rushed out with a little more than a distracted wave to the developers working at their desks. As expected, Jonah's car had its hazards on in front of the garage.

CHAPTER 9

Daniel hit traffic on the highway, then every single red light on the neighborhood streets leading to the local YMCA. By the time he parked his sedan outside the gleaming, recently renovated gymnasium, it was half past eight, and parents were beginning to filter out of the double doors with their kids in tow. Daniel swore to himself and half-jogged to the doors, shouldering past parents as he rushed inside.

The volunteers were already breaking down the meet. The multi-colored circular targets were being packed back into their carrying case, and the judging tables were being folded up. Around the gym, kids of all ages stood with their friends or their families, bows already packed away and slung over their shoulders.

He'd missed it.

Again.

At the far end of the gymnasium, his wife, Ana, was waiting by the doors to the locker room. She looked up from the phone in her hand, met Daniel's eyes, and frowned. She tucked her phone into her pocket and crossed her arms over her chest.

It was an expression of disappointment that Daniel was, unfortunately, quite familiar with throughout eight years of marriage. Ana played her cards close to her chest. Most people who met her found her to be aloof and hard to read, but Daniel had always been able to understand every twitch of her lips and quirk of her eyebrows. She was tall, taller than he was when she wore heels, with straight, dark hair she wore tied back in a low bun. It was a remnant of her military days, like her impeccable posture and her thrice-weekly six-mile runs. She had clearly come straight from work to the gymnasium, as she was dressed in dark slacks and a jacket with her usual comfortable yet professional flat sneakers.

"You missed it," Ana said.

"I know," Daniel said. "I'm so sorry, I had it on my calendar, I don't know—"

"It's not me you need to apologize to," she said.

"I know," he repeated, and rubbed his hand over his face. "I don't know what's happening. I keep putting stuff into my calendar, setting up my reminders so this doesn't happen, and then the triggers don't happen. It's like things are randomly disappearing from my calendar."

Ana narrowed her dark eyes. "Computers are your area of expertise, not mine. That seems like something you should be able to handle."

"I thought I did, after the last time this happened. I'll have to run some tests…"

"You should get a paper calendar," she said. "This is getting ridiculous, Daniel."

"I'll make it up to you," he promised, like he had a half-dozen times before.

Ana sighed. Her angry expression softened. "Again, it's not me you need to be saying this to. This meet was really important to her, Dan. She was waiting for you."

Guilt turned Daniel's stomach. He told himself he wasn't technically competing with her biological father, but he also felt like he was losing to the man, despite him being eight time zones away.

The locker room door swung open. Natasha stepped out into the gym, dressed in a hoodie big enough to nearly swallow her. Her dark, curly hair was still tied back in the French braid she liked to wear for her meets. Her new Hoyt Satori bow was packed up in its immense carrying bag, and she hiked it higher on her shoulder. She ignored the adults and went instead to stand next to a tall, skinny boy, about her same age, with straight dark hair cut right across his brow. They talked some, and as they spoke, her smile widened.

"Who's that?" Daniel asked.

"One of her new friends," Ana said. "His name's Caleb. They met at the last training camp."

"Friend?" As he watched, Nat's ears were turning a little pink. Was this a boy she had a crush on? Was she old enough for that? Daniel's guilt worsened—how much time had slid by him?

"Nat!" Daniel called out.

She looked up, and her smile melted into a sour expression. She said goodbye to her friend, then marched right past Daniel.

"Wait—" Daniel said.

She kept walking. Daniel hurried to match her pace. "Mom texted me the results," he said. "Congratulations, hon, I know you worked hard—"

"Thanks," she said. She looked over her shoulder. "Mom, I'm hungry. Can we get pancakes on the way home?"

"I'll take you," Daniel said. "We can go to Joe's."

"That's okay," Nat said. "You have work to do, right? That's why you couldn't come. That's always why you can't come."

"Nat…"

A hand on his shoulder stopped him. Ana squeezed gently. "Let her be mad," she said softly. "You really screwed this up. You can't make it right tonight."

But I want to, Daniel thought to himself petulantly, like he was twelve himself. But he knew Ana was right. This had been an important meet to Nat, he'd promised to be there, and he'd broken that promise.

"We'll see you later," Ana said. "Get home safe."

Outside the gym, Daniel watched from across the parking lot as Ana helped Nat heave her gear into the trunk of her SUV, then climb in and drive away. In his pocket, his phone buzzed again. He pulled it out, half-heartedly hoping it was Nat, having changed her mind and decided that he could join them for celebratory pancakes.

Jonah's name flashed on his screen. Daniel tilted his face up toward the light-polluted stars. Nat had been right, again. There was always work to do.

He answered the phone. "What is it, Jonah?"

"Daniel." Jonah's voice was uncharacteristically shaky. "There's... There's been an accident."

Daniel's stomach dropped. "Accident? What happened?"

There was a long pause. Then, finally, Jonah exhaled another quivering breath. "Robert. It's Robert."

CHAPTER 10

Robert Hayes died of sudden cardiac arrest at 5:30 PM on Thursday.

It had been an evening like any other. Robert had always been particular about his health and his routine—he was a doctor! He ran marathons when he had time to squeeze in the training, but when things got busy at the startup, he shifted to cycling. It was easier to fit in his workouts on the Peloton in his home office rather than gear up for an hour-long run in the darkness of early morning. He designed his workouts meticulously, to the point of carefully managing his target heart rate. His smartwatch monitored his pulse and alerted him when he was outside of his target beats per minute range. His wife hadn't found him until an hour later, once she had returned home with her young son from a Cub Scouts meeting, and with all the chaos, news hadn't gotten to Jonah until nearly 8:00.

Daniel recalled all this while staring into the dark depths of his decaf coffee, poured from an urn in the lobby of the Willow Glade Funeral Home a week later. His suit felt too tight, starched, and itchy on his skin. He tugged at his collar.

The funeral was well-attended but not crowded. There were the employees of Promethean, as well as a smattering of others: family, former hospital colleagues, medical school classmates, neighborhood friends, and buddies from the run club. Robert was well-loved and admired. His widow wore an obviously just-purchased black gown and sat by the casket in dull-eyed shock as attendees paid their respects.

How could something like this happen to Robert? One moment, he was hitting a new personal best on the bike, and then the next, he was dead on his bedroom floor with his smartwatch calling 911.

"Daniel," a monotone voice said, jerking Daniel out of his thoughts. "I plan on returning to the office now, unless there is reason for me not to."

Daniel blinked a few times. In front of him, Emmet was dressed as he always was, in a plain t-shirt and dark jeans. He was the only one who hadn't worn a suit for the service, but he didn't seem to notice that he stood out. "No, no, that should be fine," Daniel said. "I'm glad you came. I know Angela was glad to see you."

Emmet nodded curtly at the mention of Robert's widow. "It's a tragedy," he said. "I told her to email me if I could be of any assistance as she sorts through the estate."

Daniel cringed internally. Emmet meant well, but that was probably the last thing the poor woman wanted to think about. But that was how Emmet's mind worked: he was always considering the next practicality. Daniel was shocked he'd come to the service at all. It was a testament to Robert's role in the company.

"Also," Emmet said, "Malcolm Langley is here. He's speaking to your wife."

Daniel nearly dropped his coffee. "Malcolm?"

"Email me if you need anything," Emmet said, "Though I won't see it until tomorrow."

Malcolm Langley was, in fact, speaking with Ana and Jonah by the front doors of the lobby. He was dressed unobtrusively, in a dark suit and tie, with his thinning salt-and-pepper hair perfectly coiffed and pushed back. His Rolex gleamed in the low light, and his shoes were polished to the point of being reflective. His presence always made Jonah squirrelly, and that was obvious even from across the room. Jonah had a similar dark suit, but his shoes weren't as polished, and he had no Rolex. Ana, by contrast, looked relaxed speaking to Malcolm. She was wearing dark slacks and a black silk shirt, hair tied back, wearing the delicate gold jewelry she only broke out for special occasions.

She was gorgeous. And she was handling Malcolm effortlessly.

"Daniel," she said, and extended a hand toward him. Daniel slid into her side and wound an arm around her strong waist. "There you are."

"Here I am," he said. "Malcolm. I didn't know if you could make it."

"I know it's been a while, but I still consider Promethean Systems to be one of my best investments to date," Malcolm said. "I'm sorry for your loss."

"Thank you," Daniel said. "Robert is—was—brilliant. It still doesn't seem real."

"I don't know how we're going to do it without him," Jonah said, and scrubbed his hand roughly across his forehead.

"You'll find a way," Malcolm said. "You're scrappy that way. Always have been."

"I'd hoped we'd be past needing to be scrappy at this point," Daniel admitted.

"It always takes longer than you expect. Ana and I learned that back in the day." He smiled at her, and she nodded in agreement. Daniel didn't particularly like to imagine those days years ago when Ana was fresh out of the military and working briefly as a market research analyst for Langley Ventures, even though their relationship had never been anything but professional. Malcolm Langley was a smart businessman and a smarter investor. Promethean might need his help to figure out how to exist without Robert.

"Excuse us a moment," Jonah said. "Daniel, can I speak with you?"

Daniel pressed his fingers into Ana's waist in silent question. She returned the gesture, then hip-checked him slightly. "Of course," she answered for Daniel. "I need the updates on Malcolm's latest investment ventures, anyway."

"Good to see you, Daniel," Malcolm said, as he was almost bodily pulled away by Jonah.

Jonah hauled him out of the front doors and onto the manicured sidewalk outside the funeral home. It was early evening, and the parking lot was quiet; a tall row of trees hid the funeral home from the nearby highway. The cool air chilled the sweat Daniel hadn't realized was beading on his own temples. He dabbed at them with the edge of his sleeve. "What is it, Jonah? You look terrible."

Jonah pulled an e-cigarette from his inner pocket, took a long drag, then exhaled the cloud of sweet-smelling vapor into the sky. Daniel cringed again. It was better than the cigarettes he used to sneak, he supposed, but made Jonah look more like the hoodie-wearing university coders in the cafes, not the businessman he needed to be now. "We've got a problem."

"Obviously," Daniel said. "Robert's dead."

"More than that," Jonah snapped. "Promethean can't exist in its current structure without Robert. The term sheets we signed for the next round of investment specified that all three founders would continue the work."

"…Robert's dead," Daniel repeated. "Isn't there a force majeure clause?" Daniel had signed enough contracts in his day to know the common language. If there was some kind of act of God, natural disaster, what have you, then you could be released from liability. If anything counted as an act of God, he had to imagine their cofounder dropping dead from a premature heart attack did.

"No."

Daniel turned and stared at Jonah. "What do you mean, 'no'?"

"There's no force majeure clause."

He took a deep breath. "Why not?"

"Because we were still operating off the structure from our last funding round, when I didn't have the legal muscle to catch the mistake." He cast a look at the funeral home, then took another drag off his e-cigarette. "By the time the new term sheets came in, we were still hustling like a seed-stage startup, and I was in a rush to close. We'd already gone through rounds of revisions and back-and-forth, and by the time I realized the clause was missing, we were already done. I couldn't go back with a redlined version just for one clause that we'd never needed to use—"

"Until now," Daniel said. His voice came out cool and steady, even as anger was beginning to cut through the numbing shock.

"The point is, we don't have the clause," Jonah said. "So, if they choose to do so, the investors can pull out and leave us in the lurch."

"You can't be serious right now," Daniel said.

"As a heart attack." Jonah laughed coldly.

"So what now? We lose our cofounder and our next round of investment?"

"Regillus Global is buying us out. All-stock deal."

"We said we wouldn't accept a buyout," Daniel said. "You said that. The whole point of finding the investment was to maintain control—"

"That was before Robert dropped dead!" Jonah hissed. "I know you're a little busy romancing the computers with Emmet, but in case you missed it, we're burning through our cash-on-hand. We've got four months left. If that. We've got two clients paying month-to-month. We're on the knife's edge of having nothing, Daniel. We've got three options. Lay off ninety percent of the company, go bankrupt, or accept this buyout."

"And then we're another cog in the Regillus machine, aren't we?" Daniel asked. "What about our research? If we're bought out, we won't have any agency in what we actually do!"

"That's better than doing nothing at all," Jonah said. He took another long drag of the e-cigarette, and then Jonah slumped backward and leaned against the painted brick exterior of the funeral home. "This buyout is a good deal, Daniel. We need less worry right now, not more. The stock offer is good—a lot better than the cash offer we'd get if we were on the auction block."

Something didn't feel right about this deal. Even if Robert were dead, Promethean's assets were still valuable. The intellectual property of Castor was valuable. There was no way they'd end up on the auction block, bankrupt, if they pushed back against a buyout… Was there? "Shouldn't we slow down and talk about this?"

"Robert's widow and family need this. Our employees need this," Jonah said. "We're supposed to take care of them—all of them."

Daniel's head hurt. He wasn't the business guy—out of the three of them, he was the least business-minded and had always relied on the expertise of his friends and colleagues to guide those decisions. He was the product guy. Jonah was the business guy. And now Jonah had screwed this up, and they had to pay the price.

If he got to keep working on Castor, that'd be enough.

"Fine," Daniel said. "Just figure out the buyout. As long as we don't go under."

Jonah straightened up. He looked exhausted, with dark circles under his eyes, and an almost manic anxiety in his expression. "We won't," he said. "I'll get the paperwork together."

Daniel nodded. He went back into the funeral home, where he extracted Ana from conversation with Malcolm, and did another round of conversation before people began to say their goodbyes. All the while, there was a new anxiety chewing at his gut.

He could only hope he wouldn't regret this.

"We're quite impressed with the cybersecurity proof-of-concept Promethean Systems provided," the man at the head of the table said. He was the youngest of the bunch, with a thick head of dark hair and a nose that bent slightly to one side, like he was punched as a kid. "Daniel, correct? I believe we've been on some of the same email chains. Bradley Black, I'm CFO here."

"Right, yes," Daniel said. The name was vaguely familiar. Or was it? Had he seen those emails?

"As we understand it, the AI-powered cybersecurity concept is to prevent, detect, and defend against all kinds of live hacker attacks," Bradley said. "I brought this to the head of our shipping division, and they're very interested. With the kind of high-volume shipments we deal with, having some proactive but low-cost security definitely appeals."

"Shipping department?" Daniel asked, surprised by how far the plan had progressed behind the scenes.

"Obviously, Regillus does more than that," Jonah said. "You read the briefs I sent you, right, Daniel?"

"I read them," Daniel said. It wasn't a lie. He had read them. He'd just read them a while ago, when he was juggling what felt like ten other projects that took precedence.

"Castor's built to be reactive," Jonah said. "To think. Shipping is almost a perfect use-case. Beyond cybersecurity, Castor could improve the efficiency of your fleet. Not just with route planning, but with maintenance. In the same way it works for healthcare, Castor could identify mechanical issues before they become problematic and recommend repair."

Daniel looked up from his laptop, brows pulled together. Jonah was selling this buyout on abandoning Castor's medical predictions… To move freight trucks?

"We'll test it on a small scale, first," Bradley said, "but if this works as well as Jonah's demonstrations have, we'll see a substantial increase in profits in the first quarter of full-scale application."

Daniel turned to Jonah. He met Daniel's eyes and raised his eyebrows minutely, as if to say, Don't screw this up.

"Right," Daniel said. "I see how it makes sense to apply Castor's diagnostic capabilities to the delivery fleet, but… He's truly optimized for medical diagnoses, and that's the direction Promethean's research is going in."

"Was going in," Bradley said. "Right? Jonah, let us know if Promethean is pursuing new avenues since your cofounder's unexpected passing. My condolences."

"Promethean is still built on his legacy," Daniel said. "He believed Castor would save lives."

"Which it will," Jonah interjected, "Just in a new way. Getting behind the wheel of a vehicle is the greatest risk we take every day. Castor will make each day a little safer for each drive in the Regillus fleet."

"Jonah—"

"It's all in the brief," Jonah said.

The weight of all those eyes fell on Daniel again. "Right."

"Daniel," Bradley said in a soft, patronizing voice, "Regillus Global has no intention of stopping the medical research you are pursuing. But we have to recognize the immediate limitations of that research without Robert to shepherd it. Applying Castor to Regillus' shipping needs helps us both. It allows us to streamline our shipping and allows Promethean Systems to remain in business until you're ready to return to the medical field."

Irritation turned Daniel's stomach like a bad Financial District lunch. What had Jonah been telling these guys when Daniel wasn't in the room? Those eyes that had all felt so judgmental now felt condescending. Like they were all waiting for Daniel to throw some kind of grief-induced fit, part of him wanted to throw one, just because they were expecting it.

"The direction of Promethean's research isn't my concern," Daniel said. "I'm concerned about the scale of the project. As I've discussed with my team, Castor's computational power is limited, and with a shipping project of this scale, it's likely we'll reach the ceiling."

"It's not likely," Jonah said. "Castor continues to improve its own computational efficiency every day. We wouldn't move forward with this project if we were truly concerned about computational power. Right, Daniel?"

This wasn't an argument he could win. Jonah had set up the deal, and Bradley Black clearly agreed with him. If he wanted to keep his job, he had to agree to the terms.

"I thought it might be important to note the possibility," Daniel said. "But you're right. One of Castor's greatest strengths is his adaptability."

"You keep saying that," Bradley said. "His."

"I guess it comes with working on the tech a lot," Daniel said with a shrug. "He's got a mind of his own."

"So, Daniel, did you bring the updated proof-of-concept that Emmet was wrapping up?"

"I did." Daniel pulled open the program on his laptop. How much had Emmet known about this? Did he know Jonah was going to steamroll Daniel like this? Hell, even if he had, would Emmet have realized it was steamrolling? All Emmet cared about was working on technology that interested him—its applications didn't matter.

Robert had been the one to hold them all together. Even if Promethean survived this buyout, Daniel feared it might be one last gasp before it all crumbled.

CHAPTER 12

After the paperwork was signed, Daniel shook hands with Bradley Black and the rest of the Regillus executives, then told Jonah he was taking the rest of the day off. The last thing he wanted to do after that meeting was go back to the Promethean office, which still felt haunted by Robert's presence.

He had a $250 million stock deal with a two-year lockup period—a fantastic deal, all things considered. On paper, Daniel was a wealthy man, but he wouldn't have access to any of that money for years and by then, there was no telling what the real value would be. That's how wealth worked with startups. It was all on paper and could disappear overnight.

Daniel couldn't shake the feeling that he had failed Robert. Promethean Systems was Robert's baby. He'd built the company in his mother's memory. She'd died when he was a premed student at the university. The thought of that cancer growing inside his mother undetected for years had chewed at Robert endlessly. He had known there was a better way to detect glioblastoma and cancers like it. That was what had driven him to study AI.

Daniel couldn't help but admire Robert's mission, and it wasn't long before Robert's mission became his mission, too.

How could Jonah let that mission slip away? There had to be another way. There had to be a way they could keep their funding and continue to pursue their medical research.

He pulled his sedan into the single parking spot outside his townhouse in Mountain View. He lived in a quiet neighborhood on the southwest side, right on the border of Los Altos. It was less ritzy glitz and more ranch-style homes with families that had lived there for years, warm desert landscaping, and someone's beat-up work pickup truck for every few Priuses. Daniel's townhouse was half-hidden by a pockmarked privacy fence, and he had rocks instead of plants in his (what passed for) a California yard. It was a white plaster building with a warm red terra cotta roof, and Daniel had bought the place when he'd expected to live in it alone most of the time. It was big enough for two, and sometimes three, but just barely.

Inside the house, he grabbed a beer from the fridge and plopped down on the couch. The lower level of the townhouse was mostly kitchen, with a big granite-topped island, and beyond it was a couch, an old, small TV, and built-in bookshelves overflowing with books. Ana and Natasha were both gone: Natasha abroad with her biological father, and Ana on a work trip. Despite their absence, the townhouse was warm with reminders of them. Natasha had left a jacket strewn on a chair in the breakfast nook. Ana's delicate gold watch was in a dish by the front door, since she only traveled with her smartwatch. And that was nothing to say for the pictures on the shelves and hanging on the wall, the art Ana had purchased, the rug Natasha had consulted on. Daniel had bought the townhouse, but Ana and Nat had made it a home.

He kicked his feet up onto the coffee table and picked up his personal laptop. He couldn't continue Promethean's medical research without Robert. But he could keep building something better. Something that would be able to continue the research itself.

Daniel didn't know what kind of performance Jonah had promised Regillus, but if Castor was expected to run constant diagnostics on a whole fleet of vehicles, they'd run into the hardware limitations sooner rather than later.

He didn't know to which project he'd be shuffled, but he knew it wouldn't be hardware research. Jonah still didn't see the necessity and the value. He'd still need Castor's capabilities for some of his research, but he'd do the research alongside whatever duties he was assigned. Once he had a breakthrough, which he knew he eventually would, he'd be able to convince the board to move him to the chip development full-time.

He opened his beer and settled down at his desk.

With Castor's help, Daniel had identified a long list of manufacturing defects common in semiconductor development. There was the fidelity of the qubits where the data is stored. The surface treatments, which often included tiny contaminants or impurities upon coating. Even the temperature of the manufacturing facilities themselves. So many tiny adjustments affected the processing capabilities of the chips, so many that it was impossible to consider new manufacturing methods without Castor's simulations.

At this stage, Daniel wasn't ready to run simulations yet. At home, he was brainstorming. If he had unlimited resources, unlimited time, and could fabricate as many experimental quantum computing chips as he wanted, what exactly would he do?

What if a different compound were used for the surface treatments? What compounds are on the market now, and what potential alternative options are there? What if manufacturers applied the treatment with a different voltage? What if it was heated, then cooled?

When Daniel was sketching out ideas like this, with no interruption and deadlines, time seemed to both expand and contract simultaneously. He sipped his beer to the dregs and sank into his work until the sun had lowered into the sky and the reading light overhead cut on automatically. He was lost in his research until he heard the front door unlock.

"Daniel?" Ana called. He heard the thunk of her sneakers hitting the hardwood as she kicked them off, and then the rumble of her carry-on suitcase wheels.

"Ana!" Daniel's stomach dropped and propelled him to his feet. He grabbed his phone and opened his calendar. "You're home! Was I supposed to—don't tell me I was supposed to pick you up—"

"No, no," she said, laughing and waving her hand. She was dressed in loose slacks and a cardigan, comfortable but still professional. "I took an Uber. I didn't give you my flight info, babe, you've forgotten me enough times."

"Oh." That didn't make him feel any better. But Ana laughed again, then swanned across the hardwood and wound her arms around his neck. She kissed him, then pulled back and smiled. This close, he could see the dark circles under her eyes, and the slight pallor she always got when she flew.

"Don't pout at me," she teased. "I write all the Ubers off on my taxes. Benefit of being self-employed."

"How was the gig?" He pushed his laptop aside and sat back down on the couch. She did the same, and he pulled her feet into his lap. He dug his thumb into the sole of her foot, and she sighed with pleasure and melted back into the couch. As she did so, she tugged her hair loose, and it spilled down her shoulders like dark water.

"Pretty good, I think. This was a trial, really, so if they're happy with the results of my recommendations, then they might bring me on again in a larger capacity." She shrugged one shoulder. "We'll see."

"Sounds like a win to me." Daniel squeezed her ankle, then returned to massaging her feet. Her feet always hurt after she flew.

"It'll be a win when the next contract is signed. You know I don't like to count my chickens before they hatch."

"Right, right."

Ana sighed. "What have you been up to? I was surprised to see your car. Figured you'd be at the office since Nat's away."

"Buyout's done. I took the rest of the day off."

"Seriously?" She looked up. "It's done?"

"It's done."

"You don't sound too excited." Then she nodded toward his laptop. "And that doesn't look like a day off."

"It's hard to be excited about it," Daniel said. "Just reminds me of how things were supposed to go. Do you think Robert would be happy with these terms."

Ana hummed in understanding. "He'd be glad you and Jonah were still holding it together. I know that much."

With the way Jonah was moving, Daniel wasn't so sure of that, either. But he didn't want to press it. "How's Nat doing? She still in the air?"

Ana glanced at her phone. "She should be landing in the morning. Those long flights are a piece of cake for her now. I'm glad she went, even though it was last minute." Somehow, Nat had gotten flight alerts on her phone and got notifications when last-minute tickets to Japan showed up cheap. Daniel hadn't thought much of it. It was like a game to her. Plus, her biological dad, Viktor, was stationed in Okinawa, and it wasn't easy for him to get time off. But this time, it had magically worked out: the cheap flight had aligned with a long weekend of leave for Viktor. And so Nat had thrown her favorite clothes in a bag and run off to the airport. "She's been having a hard time," Ana said. "I'm not sure what, but… I could tell she needed to get away."

"Is she okay?" Daniel hadn't noticed her acting strange. What else was he missing?

"You remember her friend Caleb?" Ana asked. "The one we saw at the last archery meeting?"

The skinny kid with the bowl cut, the one who had made Natasha smile and blush. "Yeah, I think so."

"I think she's got a little crush on him, but she's struggling with it," Ana said. "I think she's afraid to tell him. He's traveling a lot with his family, too, homeschooled, I think. So they're mostly talking on the phone, FaceTiming, things like that." She sighed and shook her head fondly. "Sometimes when she's doing her homework, I'll see them on FaceTime, not talking, just working together in different places."

"How often do they see each other?"

"Not often. Mostly at archery meets. That's why her nose is always in her phone."

"That can't be good for her," Daniel muttered.

"Better than having no friends at all," Ana said. "He's a nice kid. But everything is a crisis when you're thirteen."

"Let's go to dinner tomorrow," Daniel said. "Somewhere nice."

Ana furrowed her brow at him. "What?"

"A date," Daniel said. "We should celebrate. Your gig went well. The buyout went through. Let's celebrate."

"Who are you and what have you done with my husband?" Ana asked with a smirk. "I usually have to drag you away from work by the collar."

"Maybe we can get a last-minute reservation somewhere." Daniel reached for his laptop. "I'll look."

"Wait, wait, that reminds me." Ana sat up, then unzipped her suitcase. She pulled out a slim, pale green notebook. "Surprise."

"What is it?" He took the notebook, unfastened the elastic keeping it closed, then flipped through the delicate, graph-lined pages.

"A planner," she said. "You could benefit from a paper one instead of relying on your glitchy work calendar."

"You're right." He glanced around the coffee table, searching. Ana cleared her throat and held out a pen. He thanked her, then took the pen and scratched the first entry in: 8 pm, dinner with Ana.

"Good." She smiled, stood up, and stretched her arms overhead. "Now bring my suitcase upstairs and help me shower."

Daniel jumped to his feet, grinning, and rushed to comply.

CHAPTER 13

The next-day dinner date didn't go as planned, as hard as it was to get reservations in San Francisco. Instead, Ana managed to snag a last-minute cancellation at her favorite omakase sushi place, nearby in Los Altos. "I turned on notifications," she teased when Daniel expressed his incredulity. "You should know how to do that by now."

The restaurant wasn't Daniel's favorite. He preferred a steakhouse with a checkered tablecloth and a wine list long enough to fill a fat leather book. But Ana loved this place, so Daniel had learned to love it, too. It was small, with dark walls and abstract, dense art. There was a finely-carved wooden counter that wound around the space, seating about twenty, and no other tables. The counter faced the two sushi chefs in spotless white jackets, and guests watched as the chefs expertly sliced fish and shaped sushi rolls. The flavors were delicate and the portions small, served one after another in an endless slow barrage of beautifully plated fish. Perfect cubes of rice. Tuna gleaming like jewels.

Daniel wasn't paying attention to any of it, really. He was distracted by Ana's slinky, deep green dress, knee-length with a plunging back that showed off her surprisingly muscular build, the dress she seemed to only break out for this restaurant in particular. Daniel had steamed his button-up shirt—that was about as nice as he could go. But it didn't matter, since no one in the restaurant was looking at him when he had a woman like Ana with him.

"You seem to be in a better mood than you were earlier," she said. She took a sip of sake as they awaited the next course.

"Sorry," Daniel said. He'd been sour when he'd gotten home late, as per usual. "Just something stupid at work."

"What happened this time?" she asked. "Jonah being unreasonable again?"

"No, no, it was another one of his damn meetings," Daniel said. "Feels like he's adding ten a week to my calendar. But apparently, I was supposed to prepare a short presentation for this one, and no one had informed me of that."

"Seriously? He's asking you to read minds?" Ana asked with a brow arched.

"He claims he emailed me the brief, but I didn't see it," Daniel said. He'd scoured his inbox, spam and all, to see if he'd skipped past it somehow. But there had been nothing there beyond the standard calendar invitation to the meeting. "So I ended up looking like a fool in this meeting with some of the Regillus guys."

"But it was his fault, wasn't it?" Ana asked. "He's the one who didn't email you."

"That's what I thought, but he turned it around on me and made it seem like it was my oversight," Daniel said. "I guess he figured it was better that I look like the distracted idiot in front of the clients, instead of him."

Ana frowned again. Before she could say anything, the chefs swooped in to narrate the next course: a fancy fish, a fancy sauce. Daniel ate the sushi in a single bite and barely tasted the flavor at all.

"But you're still on top of things at work, aren't you?" Ana asked.

"What?" Daniel set his chopsticks aside. "Of course I am. This was another stupid glitch. Something's wrong with our internal systems, or something."

"You're spending a lot of time on your personal project, that's all. I know you have a tendency to…" Ana hummed, chopsticks hovering over her sushi. "To lose yourself in your research when it interests you, even at the expense of more important things."

"Jonah told me to make the chip development a personal project, remember?" Daniel said. "God forbid I do that."

"Hey," Ana said.

He looked up. Her brows were pulled together, and she'd set her chopsticks down. "You know I don't understand a damn thing about what you do at

Promethean. I'm trying to support you. You don't need to bite my head off."

Daniel exhaled. His frustration fizzled out. "Just trust me to keep the balance," he said. "I promise I know what I'm doing."

Under the counter, her hand found his knee and squeezed. "I know. I don't think Jonah does, though."

They sat in silence for a moment, listening to the low hum of the omakase around them and the rhythmic sounds of the chefs' knives on the cutting boards.

Ana's expression softened. "I've been thinking about my own work too," she said. "I'm working toward something more specialized with my consulting business."

"Oh?" Daniel asked, grateful for the change of subject.

"Low-volume, high-value logistics." Her eyes brightened. "Projects requiring specialized handling—sensitive materials, high-value equipment, complex regulatory oversight."

"That's pretty niche," Daniel said.

"That's the point," Ana said. "The market's oversaturated with general logistics consultants. But specialized transport—government contracts, research institutions, tech companies moving prototype equipment—that's where the real challenge is. Better margins, too." She smiled. "And fewer clients mean more time for family."

Daniel nodded, impressed despite his mood. "You've really thought this through."

"Had to," she said. "While you've been focused on your chip, I've been building my own future, too."

Daniel laughed and took a sip of sake himself. The liquor was sweet and warm all the way down. "Never doubted it. Speaking of that, aren't we supposed to be celebrating you tonight?"

"I told you, there's nothing to celebrate yet, just the likelihood of a future celebration."

"That counts."

"I thought we were celebrating the buyout."

"At this point, I don't think I want to celebrate it," he admitted, then waved a hand through the air as if to dispel the conversation. "Enough about work. Tell me more about the meetings in New York. You'd been prepping for weeks."

He knew in his heart that the buyout was good news. The startup continued to function, and Daniel continued to get paid. Even if he'd wanted to leave, he couldn't—not until he was out of his two-year lockup period. Ana narrated her various client meetings and the growing foundation of her new consulting business as sushi chefs worked and the elegant dishes continued to appear in front of them.

The stability was good. He knew, logically, why Ana was worried. After receiving her honorable discharge from the Army, Ana had been determined to change careers into something stable and well-paying—something that would help her raise her daughter. She'd juggled two jobs, school, and childcare, fishing coins out from between the couch cushions to make ends meet.

Ana was financially risk-averse, much more than Daniel was. She had her own money socked away from her career, but still, a consulting career was inherently unstable. Risky. The buyout hadn't just given Promethean an injection of cash. It'd given Daniel a few more years of guaranteed employment, and with that, a few more years for Ana to grow her own business.

If Daniel screwed this up, Ana would drop her own business and find a W-2 job with healthcare and a 401(k). He wasn't going to let that happen. Ana had sacrificed so much for her country and for her daughter. Daniel wasn't going to let her sacrifice anything else. She deserved to pursue her own dreams for once.

If he could figure out this quantum chip, they'd be set for life, and then some. Jonah didn't believe it, Regillus certainly didn't, but Daniel knew. Castor would need more power, and Daniel could be the one to provide it.

He had to balance it all.

"Yuzu sorbet," the chef said as he placed two elegant glasses of pale-yellow dessert in front of them.

Ana dipped her tiny silver spoon into the sorbet, then brought it to her lips. Daniel watched it disappear, watched her full lips press together, watched the pink tip of her tongue dart out to taste the last of the ice.

"I think we've celebrated adequately," she said. Her voice was low and promising. "Should we get home?"

Daniel picked up his own sorbet glass and drank the melting dregs down like a shot. Spoon be damned. Ana bit back a smile. The chefs gave him a look, but hell, it was the last course, and Daniel was suddenly very eager to get out of here.

CHAPTER 14

It was mid-afternoon when Emmet pushed his chair back from his desk and took his noise-cancelling headphones off. He stood up and stretched his arms overhead, like he always did. Daniel expected him to gather his things and head out the door with nothing more than a goodbye wave, but instead, he strode over to Daniel's desk and peered at his laptop screen. "What are you working on?"

"What?" Daniel asked.

"You're connected to Castor," Emmet said, nodding at the wire that ran from Daniel's laptop, under the floor, and to the server room. "I was watching the usage spike before I logged off. What are you doing?"

"Running some simulations. You know I've been thinking about ways to increase semiconductor efficiency, right?"

"Yes."

"I had some ideas for production methods to address a few of the different defects we've identified. Mostly surface treatment and qubit fidelity."

"A few different methods mean a lot of permutations," Emmet said. "Millions. Castor's identifying the methods with the greatest chance of success."

"Exactly." They watched the screen as Castor raced through the various permutations of fabrication methods, identifying high-potential options and setting them aside for Daniel to review. The number of good options ticked up: five, then ten, then twenty-five, then a hundred.

"These are methods of fabrication you'd want to test?" Emmet asked. "Twenty-five chips?"

"Ideally."

"Does Jonah support that level of experimentation?" Emmet asked. "I didn't think he understood the hardware this deeply."

There was no judgment in Emmet's voice, just curiosity. Daniel glanced around the office, but none of the junior devs were paying attention. They were either locked into their own code or watching the Super Smash Bros tournament that had been going on all week now.

"He doesn't," Daniel said. "My current high-priority project is some code optimization for the shipping contract, but it seems like the development team is doing fine without me. I can't determine what fabrications are best without Castor, so I've been carving out time to do it when I'm here."

"What's the next step?" Emmet asked.

"Over a hundred fabrications is too many," Daniel said. "Castor and I will have to go back to the imaging and try to home in on even more specific defects. Ideally, I'd like to narrow it down to a maximum of twenty experimental chips."

"Promethean will fund the fabrication of twenty?"

Daniel shrugged. "I hope with twenty, I'll be able to show the board proof-of-concept. Once they understand the potential of this technology, they'll hopefully be willing to fund it."

Emmet nodded. "Seems like a valid strategy. It's always challenging to get funding from investors who don't understand your work."

"You would know, huh?"

He nodded. "I was lucky enough at Stanford to have advocates for my work who focused on that part. I got to focus only on my work. Similar to here at Promethean."

"Did you have a cryogenic chiller at Stanford?"

"No. I would've liked one, though. They were considered too niche and expensive an investment for the lab."

Daniel rubbed his face. "That's the thing. On top of the cost of fabricating the experimental chips, I'd also need a chiller to use them."

"And that would just be for the experiments. There'd be no guarantee that it would yield results."

"Yeah. That's the problem I'm having with this whole thing. The board isn't going to like anything I tell them."

"But if any of your experimental chips worked, Castor would be even more efficient and effective," Emmet said. "Have you explained that to Jonah?"

"He doesn't get it. You know how it is." The simulation finished, and Daniel skimmed the long list of potentials with a frown. "He's not worried about Castor's future. He's worried about the clients we have right in front of us."

"It's a shame," Emmet said. "I'd very much like to see if any of these chips worked." He straightened up, nodded, then strode away from Daniel's desk.

CHAPTER 15

The coffee shop buzzed with the familiar afternoon energy of tech workers grabbing their third espresso of the day. Daniel slid into the booth across from Jonah, grateful for the break from his simulations. The quantum chip models had been consuming every spare moment for months, but the progress was intoxicating.

"Thanks for making time," Jonah said, his usual easy smile seeming slightly forced. "I wanted to talk about your career trajectory, where you see yourself heading."

Daniel straightened up, intrigued. A career conversation with the soon-to-be CEO felt significant. "I'm excited about the direction things are going. The quantum computing research is starting to show promise."

"That's actually what I wanted to discuss most." Jonah stirred his coffee methodically. "Sometimes engineers get so focused on the technical work they lose sight of the business context."

"How do you mean?"

"The board values team players, people who can balance innovation with execution." Jonah's tone was neutral, like he was discussing the weather. "I've seen talented people plateau because they couldn't adapt to changing priorities."

Daniel nodded enthusiastically. "Absolutely. That's why the chip research is so important—it's going to transform what Castor can do. Imagine the processing power we could offer clients."

Jonah paused, his coffee cup halfway to his lips. "Daniel, I'm trying to help you understand what the company needs from senior technical staff right now. Your team's budget tracking shows you're thirty-eight percent over on our customer's non-destructive diagnostic module, and according to the project management system, you missed the Meridian client check-in last Tuesday."

"What?" Daniel's brow furrowed. "I'm not over budget on anything. And what client check-in? I never got a meeting invite for Meridian."

"It was scheduled three weeks ago. The invite went out to your team." Jonah scrolled through the calendar on his phone. "Here—Tuesday, 2 PM, Meridian quarterly review. Your name is right here as the technical lead."

Daniel was aghast. "Jonah, I never received that invite. And I've been tracking the non-destructive diagnostic module budget myself—we're under by about fifteen percent because we optimized the data processing pipeline."

"The financial dashboard shows different numbers," Jonah said, though his voice had lost some of its certainty. "Look, maybe there are some system sync issues. Jim from IT mentioned the calendar integration has been glitchy lately, but the optics aren't good when the board sees missed meetings and budget overruns."

"System issues?" Daniel leaned forward. "What kind of issues?"

"Calendar invites not propagating correctly, some project tracking discrepancies. Nothing major, but…" Jonah trailed off, looking uncomfortable. "The point is, your team's output metrics have been concerning the board."

"That's impossible," Daniel said. "We delivered the insurance contract analysis ahead of schedule, and the diagnostic accuracy improvements are exceeding targets by twelve percent."

"The metrics I'm seeing show missed milestones, budget problems, and communication issues with clients." Jonah's expression was genuinely puzzled now. "Maybe we need to get IT to do a deeper dive into these system problems."

Daniel felt a chill run down his spine. Calendar glitches. Budget discrepancies. Missing emails. "Jonah, these glitches are not my fault. We've known each other a long time, and you know I run a tight ship."

"I believe you, Daniel, and we can have IT look into it, but that doesn't change the fact that you seem to be in over your head on the quantum project."

Daniel saw frustration in Jonah's eyes as he nervously met Daniel's stunned gaze.

"Daniel." Jonah leaned forward, his voice taking on an edge. "I need to know you can prioritize company objectives. Current company objectives. If you had to choose between the chip research and fixing these team performance issues, what would you prioritize?"

"Why would I have to choose?" Daniel's mind was racing. "This is all for the company's benefit. Once the board sees the potential returns from quantum computing—"

"Daniel." Jonah set down his cup with deliberate care. "Your long-term success here depends on showing you can be a reliable team lead first. The board needs to trust that you can manage basic project deliverables before they'll fund blue-sky research."

"I appreciate the mentoring, Jonah. Really." Daniel reached across and clapped his friend on the shoulder, but his mind was elsewhere, connecting dots he didn't want to see. "The chip research is going to vindicate everything—you'll see. But I will raise the issues you mentioned with IT."

Jonah stared at him for a long moment, then forced a smile. "Just… keep what I've said in mind, okay? And maybe have your team do a full audit of your project tracking. Make sure everything matches what the board is seeing."

They shook hands outside the coffee shop, both men walking away with entirely different understandings of what had transpired. As Daniel disappeared around the corner, Jonah scrolled through his phone contacts until he found Emmet's name. He needed a backup plan, and he needed it soon.

As Daniel walked back toward the office, his phone buzzed with a calendar reminder that he was certain he'd never set: "Review team metrics - urgent." He stared at the notification, then quickly checked his recent calendar changes. Nothing. No edit history, no record of who had added the reminder.

His hands were shaking as he called Emmet.

"The team metrics Jonah mentioned," Daniel said without preamble when Emmet answered. "Can you pull the raw data from our project tracking system? Something's not adding up."

"Certainly," Emmet replied. "What specifically should I look for?"

"Discrepancies," Daniel said, quickening his pace toward the office. "Anywhere the system shows different numbers than what we actually delivered."

There was a pause. "Daniel, are you concerned about data integrity in our internal systems?"

Daniel stopped walking. That was what he was concerned about. And if their internal systems were compromised, if someone—or something—was manipulating their metrics to make him look incompetent…

"Yeah," he said. "I think I am."

CHAPTER 16

Emmet arrived at Jonah's office precisely on time, carrying his usual notebook and wearing his standard expression of mild confusion about why he'd been summoned. Jonah gestured to the chair across from his desk, noting how Emmet's posture remained upright, hands folded.

"I need your help with something delicate," Jonah said.

Emmet tilted his head slightly. "What kind of help?"

"Daniel's focus has shifted lately. His team needs additional technical leadership structure." Jonah chose his words carefully. "I think you're the right person to provide that."

"Daniel leads the team effectively," Emmet replied matter-of-factly. "Why would I interfere with that?"

Jonah rubbed his temples. This would be more difficult than his conversation with Daniel, but for different reasons. "Daniel's priorities are changing. I'm trying to prepare for that transition smoothly, so no one gets hurt."

Emmet's eyes sharpened with understanding. "You're planning for Daniel to leave Regillus."

"I'm planning for what seems inevitable." Jonah met his gaze directly. "I'd rather manage it than have it blindside the company."

"You could fight for him instead."

The statement hung in the air between them. Jonah felt heat rise in his cheeks. "The board has expectations—"

"You've never really supported Daniel," Emmet interrupted, his tone devoid of accusation but somehow more cutting because of it. "Or me."

Jonah opened his mouth to protest, then closed it. Emmet wasn't wrong.

"I'll help with project continuity," Emmet said, "but I have conditions. I won't undermine Daniel. I won't take on a new title or formal authority. Daniel remains the team lead until he chooses otherwise."

"Emmet—"

Emmet said simply. "I'll help the company because Daniel would want me to, but I won't pretend this is anything other than abandonment. I'm not interested in a leadership role. I'm happy to continue what I already do."

Jonah nodded slowly. It was the best he would get. "Thank you."

After Emmet left, Jonah turned to his quarterly reports, trying to shake off the conversation's uncomfortable truths. The numbers were good—better than good. Regillus stock had climbed eighteen percent, and the board couldn't stop praising his "effective communications strategy."

He pulled up the media coverage folder his assistant had compiled. Article after article of glowing coverage: "Regillus Leads AI Innovation," "Smooth Executive Transition Signals Strong Leadership," "The Future of Artificial Intelligence Has a Name: Regillus."

The timing was remarkable. Every major tech publication, business journal, and industry blog seemed to have discovered Regillus simultaneously. The talking points were eerily similar across different outlets, all emphasizing the same themes of innovation, leadership, and market dominance.

Jonah opened his browser and ran a few searches. The articles had appeared within a narrow window, all sourcing similar quotes, all lacking the usual tech press skepticism. It felt… orchestrated.

He stared at the screen for several minutes, cursor hovering over deeper search options. A quick knock interrupted his thoughts.

"The board meeting materials are ready," his assistant said through the door.

"Coming," Jonah called back, closing the browser window. The positive coverage was helping his CEO transition immeasurably. The board saw rising stock prices and glowing press as validation of their choice.

Maybe their PR team had just gotten better. Maybe they'd finally learned how to work the media cycle effectively. Jonah gathered his materials and headed to the boardroom, choosing not to look too closely at a gift horse.

CHAPTER 17

Daniel's home office glowed with the light of multiple monitors, casting dancing shadows across stacks of research papers and empty coffee mugs. At 11:47 PM, he finally saw what he'd been chasing for months: a viable fabrication pathway for the Bennett chip.

The surface treatment parameters aligned perfectly. Qubit fidelity projections exceeded his most optimistic targets. Manufacturing tolerances that had seemed impossible now showed clear solutions. His hands trembled as he ran the simulation for the third time, confirming the results.

"Holy shit," he whispered to the empty room.

This was it. An implementation model. It looked like the breakthrough that would revolutionize quantum computing. He calculated quickly that experimental fabrication would require significant startup funding, probably around ten million dollars for setup, but the potential returns were staggering.

His phone buzzed with a text from Ana: "Don't forget Nat's championship tomorrow. 2 PM. You promised."

Daniel glanced at the clock, then back at his screens. The simulation could run overnight. He could review the detailed results in the morning and still make it to the championship with time to spare. For once, the timing was perfect.

He saved his work, shut down the monitors, and headed upstairs where Ana was already asleep.

The state archery championship venue buzzed with nervous energy. Parents filled the bleachers while archers warmed up on the practice range, their movements precise and meditative. Daniel found Ana in the stands, saving his seat with her jacket.

"You made it," she said, genuine surprise in her voice.

"Wouldn't miss it." Daniel kissed her cheek and settled beside her. "How's she looking?"

"Confident. Focused." Ana pointed to where Natasha stood with her bow, checking her equipment with methodical care. "She's been preparing for this all year."

Daniel watched his stepdaughter move through her pre-competition routine. At fifteen, she'd grown into her height, her movements economical and purposeful. When had she become so self-possessed?

"Archers to the line," the range officer announced.

Natasha took her position, bow in hand, and glanced toward the stands. When she spotted Daniel, her face lit up with a smile that made his chest tight with pride and guilt. How many competitions had he missed for work that suddenly seemed less important?

The first round began. Natasha's form was textbook perfect—stance solid, draw smooth, release clean. Her arrows grouped tightly in the gold. After each end, she'd glance toward the stands, and Daniel found himself genuinely absorbed in the technical aspects of her shooting.

But as the competition continued, the warmth of the afternoon sun and his exhaustion from months of eighteen-hour days began to take their toll. His eyelids grew heavy during the scoring breaks. The rhythmic thrum of bowstrings became hypnotic.

"She's improved her follow-through," he said, his words slightly slurred.

Ana looked at him with concern. "When's the last time you slept more than four hours?"

Daniel tried to remember. "I'm fine. Just need some coffee."

But the next thing he knew, Ana was shaking his shoulder urgently. "Dan! Wake up! She's about to shoot her final end."

He jolted awake to find himself slumped in his seat, drool on his chin. Around them, other parents were on their feet as the archers prepared for their final shots. Natasha was at the line, bow raised, focused.

"How long was I—"

"Shh," Ana whispered. "Just watch."

The last arrow flew true, dead center. The crowd erupted as the scores were tallied. State champion. Natasha raised her bow overhead, grinning broadly, her eyes finding Daniel in the stands.

"That's my girl!" Daniel shouted, jumping to his feet.

*

The celebration dinner at Natasha's favorite Italian restaurant stretched late into the evening. Daniel had put his phone away entirely, something Ana noted with cautious optimism.

"So, your mom tells me that you've been talking about college with her," Daniel said, twirling pasta around his fork. "What are you thinking?"

Natasha's eyes widened. It had been months since he'd asked about her plans without distraction. "Well, I'm still a few years out, but I'm looking at schools with strong archery programs."

"What about academics? What would you like to study?"

"Maybe engineering? Or computer science?" She glanced at him uncertainly. "I know it's your field, but I'm genuinely interested."

Daniel felt a surge of pride mixed with regret. "You'd be incredible at either. You have the mind for it—analytical, patient, precise."

"You think so?"

"I know so." Daniel reached across and squeezed her hand. "Whatever you choose, I want to be part of it. I want to help."

"The best archery programs are in South Korea and Japan," Ana said. "If you're serious about competing at the highest levels."

"Really?" Natasha's face lit up with possibility. "That would be amazing. The traditional techniques, the history…"

Daniel nodded enthusiastically. "We could visit some schools when you're ready. See what they offer."

Ana watched this exchange with something approaching wonder. This was the Daniel she'd married—present, engaged, genuinely interested in the people he loved.

Later, as they walked to the car, Ana slipped her arm through his. "This is what we needed," she said. "You here, with us."

Daniel looked back at the restaurant where they'd shared the best family dinner in months. "The work will always be there. You two won't always be here."

That night, Daniel placed Natasha's state championship medal on the mantle next to family photos. The breakthrough could wait until tomorrow. Tonight belonged to his family.

After Natasha had gone to bed, Ana found Daniel in the kitchen, staring into a cup of tea he'd barely touched.

"Oh, before I forget," Ana said as she sat down beside Daniel at the table, placing her feet on his lap. "The strangest thing happened today. You remember those DNA sequencing machine contracts I mentioned? The one that was worried about misalignment during shipping?"

"The competitive one?" Daniel asked, stirring his cup.

"That's just it—it's not competitive anymore. Zhou Industries withdrew its bid this morning. Something about their CEO having a family emergency." Ana frowned. "Their head of logistics called me personally to recommend me for the contract."

"That's great news," Daniel said as he began to massage Ana's feet.

"I suppose. It feels… odd. They were so aggressive in the initial negotiations."

"You're just that good," Daniel said. Ana made a noncommittal sound, but Daniel noticed her fingers drumming against the table—a habit when something bothered her.

"That was wonderful tonight," she said, changing the subject. "Nat was so happy you were really there."

"I almost missed her final shots," Daniel said. "I fell asleep, Ana. At my daughter's state championship."

Ana reached across and took his hand. "But you were there. That's what matters."

"Is it? Because I feel like I'm failing at everything lately. I feel like I'm on a razor's edge with Jonah. The work with the quantum chip is consuming me, and I can see how it's affecting you both."

"Daniel, look at me."

He met her eyes reluctantly.

"I know you're working toward something important. I can see how passionate you are about this research. But you must understand something." She squeezed his hand gently. "Being a good father isn't just about showing up. It's about being present—emotionally present—when you're here."

Daniel nodded, feeling the weight of her words.

"Nat's going to be making big decisions soon about her future. She needs your guidance, not just your physical presence. And I need a partner, not a roommate who happens to sleep in the same bed."

"You're right," Daniel said. "I've been so focused on the finish line that I forgot about the journey. About who I'm supposedly doing this for."

Ana stood and moved behind his chair, placing her hands on his shoulders. The tension there was like concrete. "I love your drive, your passion. I don't want you to lose that. But you have to promise me something."

"Anything."

"Promise me you'll slow down. Save some energy for us. The work will always be there, but these moments—Nat's competitions, family dinners, quiet evenings together—they're finite."

Daniel covered her hand with his. "I promise. No more eighteen-hour days. No more falling asleep at important events."

"I'm going to hold you to that," Ana said, leaning down to kiss the top of his head.

As they headed upstairs, Daniel's phone buzzed with a notification. He glanced at it—an alert from one of Castor's overnight simulations, something that would normally have him reaching for his laptop immediately.

Instead, he silenced the phone and slipped it into his pocket.

"What was that?" Ana asked.

"Work," Daniel said. "It can wait until morning."

For the first time in months, Daniel went to sleep without thinking about quantum chips or artificial intelligence or the next breakthrough. Instead, he thought about Natasha's smile when she'd spotted him in the stands, and the way Ana's eyes had lit up during dinner when he'd been truly present.

The notification remained unread. The work could wait. His family couldn't.

CHAPTER 18

For the next six months, Daniel did exactly as his employment agreement stipulated. With Emmet's help, he continued developing and improving Castor's functionality. During one of the quarterly review cycles, Daniel found himself in yet another heated argument with Jonah over project attribution.

"Emmet's investment optimization algorithm saved our clients twelve million dollars in the last quarter," Daniel said. "His name should be on the client presentation, not buried in the technical appendix."

"The presentation is about Castor's capabilities," Jonah countered. "We're selling the AI, not individual developers."

Daniel's phone buzzed on the table. He glanced at it briefly—a news alert about GraphicLeap AI Lab losing their lead researcher to some fusion energy startup. He dismissed the notification and returned to the argument.

"Emmet designed the predictive modeling that makes those optimizations possible. The algorithm that identifies market inefficiencies before they impact portfolios? That's his work."

Jonah shuffled through papers on his desk. "The client doesn't need to know about internal development details."

"This isn't about client needs," Daniel said. "It's about giving credit where it's due. And compensation. Emmet should get the innovation bonus for this level of breakthrough."

"He doesn't even manage anyone," Jonah countered. "And he's never once asked for a raise."

"Because he doesn't understand his own value. That doesn't mean we should take advantage of him." Daniel leaned forward. "That investment algorithm is generating millions in additional revenue. Emmet deserves both the credit and the financial reward."

Later that day, Emmet approached Daniel's desk. "You argued with Jonah about the investment project attribution," he said in his usual straightforward way.

"I did," Daniel said.

"Why? I didn't request it."

Daniel looked up from his screen. "Because you earned it, Emmet. The clients are seeing returns they never thought possible because of your work. That matters."

Emmet considered this, head tilted slightly. "My father always said to remember who looks out for you." He paused. "He was a pastor."

It was the most personal information Emmet had ever volunteered. Daniel wasn't sure how to respond.

"Thank you for ensuring proper attribution," Emmet said. "And for the compensation adjustment."

"By the way," Emmet added, "NeuralPath had a clean room contamination. Their entire chip production line is down for decontamination. They'll be set back months."

"NeuralPath?" Daniel frowned. They were a company that had recently received funding for the vertical integration of specialized AI hardware. They recently published an article on plans to build an electron-beam lithography facility for making their own quantum chips. "That's… unfortunate for them."

"Their HEPA filtration system failed simultaneously across three separate clean rooms," Emmet said. "Statistically improbable."

As Emmet turned to return to his desk, Daniel felt a mix of satisfaction and unease. Emmet's investment algorithm was indeed revolutionary, but something about how perfectly it predicted market movements bothered him. It was almost as if Castor could see around corners that should have been invisible, even to the most sophisticated AI.

Promethean drifted further and further from the medical research Robert had wanted to pursue. "There just wasn't enough money in it," Jonah had explained more than once. He'd promised that they'd get back to the medical research, but they needed to focus on capital. And the capital was in shipping and security. The deeper they dug into security threat detection, the more Emmet and Regillus Global were excited about it.

They'd never be returning to medical research. Not while there was so much money in security. So, as Daniel pushed forward on his work duties, he spent as much time as he could on developing a better chip. It was slow work, especially as he kept getting dragged away from it to work on shipping, but at least he was getting something done. At least he was doing something that mattered.

He had to figure out a way to get Promethean to fund more experimentation. But no matter how many times he asked Jonah and the board, he was refused. Told to wait a little longer. Wait for a little more stability in the company. And then, maybe, they'd have enough time and money to fund his little pet project.

So for these past two years, Castor had grown. Promethean, a wholly-owned subsidiary of Regillus, built relationships with new clients. Jonah occupied the CEO's office of Regillus while also managing Promethean directly. Emmet pitched new projects that quickly became new branches of Castor's abilities, and new services to sell at higher price points. Somehow over the years, as Daniel's passion had dwindled and Emmet's curiosity had grown, they'd switched roles. Emmet led development, while Daniel supported him.

It was a brisk, foggy morning in Palo Alto. Promethean had remained in their original office, even after the buyout, and Daniel and Emmet only occasionally took field trips to the gleaming Regillus office in San Francisco. Emmet always arrived early and left mid-afternoon in order to avoid traffic. And he almost never greeted Daniel, since he was usually already deep in a workflow by the time Daniel arrived at nine.

Emmet continued his morning ritual of chess with Castor, meticulously logging each game. "His play style is evolving," he said one morning, after an unexpected 'Good morning,' which was new. Emmet showed him a sequence of particularly unusual moves. "Less predictable. More… patient."

Daniel glanced at the board notation but couldn't see anything remarkable. He'd become accustomed to Emmet's style of coming straight to the point, and so he skipped additional pleasantries. "Still beating you?" he asked. Emmet nodded.

"Always. But he's executing the wins differently now. He's stopped going for the quick win. It's like he's experimenting."

Daniel filed this away as another quirk in Castor's growing complexity, too focused on the shipping logistics project to give it deeper thought.

*

A week passed before Emmet greeted him with a 'Good morning,' again, which was now something he did only when he had additional information to give Daniel. Otherwise, Emmet didn't look up from his work when Daniel arrived.

"Good morning," Daniel said.

Emmet turned in his chair. He was wearing his usual work outfit of a plain sweatshirt and jeans. "Jonah asked me to ensure you saw his email first thing this morning."

"That's not necessary," Daniel groused as he started the coffeemaker. "I always check my email."

Emmet said nothing, but Daniel could feel his eyes boring into his back. Sure, Daniel had continued missing a handful of meetings over the past few months, and a few emails had gotten caught in the spam filter, but IT had resolved most of the glitches. Every employee had a few little hiccups like that.

"I'm only relaying the message," Emmet said. "Is this meeting about the chip development? Are you making any progress with securing funding from the board?"

"Progress isn't going as fast as I'd like." There were too many options. There were barriers he couldn't cross without being able to actually fabricate the chips—there was only so much he could do with simulations. He'd homed in on what he believed to be the most effective strategies: using a new fabrication process and focusing on surface treatments. But until he could fabricate chips, everything was hypothetical.

"Progress never does," Emmet said, and turned back to his computer, signaling he was done conversing. He had a new project that had captured his interest, and Daniel knew he was lucky to get more than a sentence out of him.

He poured his coffee, sighed, then opened his work email on his phone. At least the email from Jonah was at the top of his inbox instead of lost in the spam filters again. It was notice of a mandatory lunch meeting at the Regillus Global headquarters, which meant a solid hour and a half of driving. One way. He rubbed his forehead. So much for getting any actual work done this morning. He'd barely have time to finish his coffee and scroll through the rest of his inbox before he had to be out the door again.

He glanced back at the open office. Emmet already had his noise-canceling headphones back on. Within the hour, the office was bustling with developers around him, and they all knew to leave Emmet entirely alone. Daniel fielded a few questions, checked over a bit of a junior developer's code, and then it was time for him to leave. No point in saying goodbye to Emmet, then.

Daniel made it to the noon meeting with ten minutes to spare. He waved to the secretary, who let him pass the turnstile with a friendly smile. Then it was into the gleaming, mirrored elevator, up the skyscraper, and into the well-lit, quiet hallway. Daniel strode to the conference room at the end, knocked once on the door, then stepped inside with confidence.

He had expected to see Jonah, Bradley Black, and whatever new sales guys Regillus had hired for their latest endeavors. Instead, there were just two people there: Jonah and an unfamiliar, middle-aged woman with short gray hair and thin, gold-rimmed glasses. Both had their laptops open. The woman gestured for Daniel to sit down.

"Mr. Bennett," she said. "I'm Ms. Vaughn, head of human resources. I believe we've emailed."

"Right," Daniel said. Jessica Vaughn. He'd seen her name plenty of times, on email chains about new hires he didn't care about, and candidate interviews he wasn't invited to. His stomach sank. "Jonah, what's this about?"

"Mr. Bennett—"

"It's fine," Jonah said. He sighed like this was already the most exhausting meeting he'd ever had, propped both elbows on the conference table, and pressed his fingertips into his temples. "Listen, Daniel, I'm sure you saw this coming."

Daniel, in fact, did not see this coming at all. "What is this about?"

"Well, Mr. Bennett, as I'm sure you're aware, Regillus Global's buyout of Promethean Systems is now vested, and the two-year contract is up." Ms. Vaughn smiled faintly.

"Right." His stomach sank further. He'd known it was coming up, but he didn't have the date marked in his calendar. "Did I miss the new contract in my email?"

"Dan, there's no new contract," Jonah said. "Regillus has decided not to renew."

There it was. Where there was a sinking in his gut, there was now a big open hole, like someone had cut him open and dumped dry ice in there. "That doesn't make any sense." Daniel said. "I'm head of Castor's development."

"You know that's only in name only," Jonah said. "Emmet's been taking the lead on projects for a while now—"

"But I'm still the head," Daniel said. "What are you saying, you're firing me?"

"It's not a firing," Ms. Vaughn said. "It's the decision not to renew—"

"Jesus Christ, Jonah," Daniel said.

"You can't tell me this is a surprise," Jonah said.

"Of course it is!"

"Gentlemen—"

"We started this company together," Daniel said. "It's built off my code and Robert's research. You think this is what he wanted for us? For Castor? For you to turn it into a glorified FedEx and push me out?"

"That's not what's happening, and you know that. Promethean couldn't function without Robert, at least not the way we were. I tried to get you to take the long view—we need Regillus' support. We need to build our presence in the logistics world so we can eventually return to medical research. But you can't get on board with that."

"Because it goes against everything Robert wanted to achieve," Daniel said. "And we never would've been in this situation if you hadn't forgotten the force majeure clause."

"Gentlemen, please—"

"And we wouldn't be here if Robert hadn't dropped dead, either," Jonah snapped.

The words hit Daniel like a slap, and he reared back, shocked. Even Ms. Vaughn turned to eye Jonah.

Jonah briefly turned his gaze upward, then exhaled hard, regaining his composure. "I know you don't agree with the direction of the company. You've delegated the work to Emmet and let him take the lead on new projects. You haven't brought a new product to the table in months, and I know your attention has been with your personal research project."

"It's not personal, it's specifically for Prometheus."

"I understand you believe our hardware isn't powerful enough, but we have yet to see any slowdowns in Castor's progress. We support forward-thinking research, but not if you neglect your job to work on it."

"I haven't neglected anything," Daniel said.

"There hasn't been a week when you haven't missed a meeting," Jonah said. He sat back in his chair, and his voice took on a flat, practiced tone. "As we move into the next stage of Castor's development, it will be more important than ever that we're all on the same page. The new national security threat detection system is this company's future, and we can't risk its success. Emmet is more than prepared to lead the development of this project, and we at Regillus Global know you would be better suited to a role that better supports your interests."

"For that reason," Ms. Vaughn cut in again, looking calm but still mildly irritated, "Regillus Global has decided not to renew your employment contract. Thank you for all your work with Promethean Systems, and we wish you the best in your future endeavors."

Jonah stood. Daniel moved to stand, too, but then Ms. Vaughn noted delicately that there was still some exit paperwork.

Jonah offered his hand. Daniel hesitated for a moment but then reached across the table and shook it. What else was he supposed to do? He gripped Jonah's hand hard and stared at his face: the new crows' feet at the corners of his eyes, the receding hairline of his blonde hair, the sweat starting to gather at the collar of his expensive button-up shirt. He wondered what was happening in those meetings Daniel was apparently missing. How much money was Jonah making? Was the board making these demands?

He found he wasn't concerned about Jonah at all. Jonah had dug this grave, and eventually, he would lie in it. Daniel wished he'd been able to convince him. Not for the company's bottom line, or its new contracts, but for Castor's abilities. If he'd been able to convince them to fund his research and then successfully fabricate a new chip, maybe they'd make all the money they needed, and Castor would be free to do the medical research he was built to do.

It was a strange feeling. In a way, it was like he'd let Castor down.

Jonah nodded curtly, then left the conference room. Daniel dropped back down into his seat like a chastised high schooler.

By the time the paperwork was signed and Daniel had made it back to Palo Alto to gather his things, it was past three in the afternoon. Emmet had left for the day. The junior developers nodded their greetings and went back to their work. It appeared no announcement had been made. It'd likely go out tomorrow, after Daniel's email was already disconnected.

He went into the small kitchen and poured a short glass of the special-occasions scotch. This was a special occasion, though not one he ever thought would be happening. He carried his work laptop into the small private conference room and closed the door. Then he opened his laptop, pulled up Castor's interface, and took a sip of scotch.

He didn't have anything to work on, really. No queries to input, no code to test. He was just… Looking around. Scrolling through the code base. Peeking at what new features were being developed and tested.

Then, he realized what he was doing.

Saying goodbye.

Castor had been the core of his work for years. Castor was his baby. He'd assumed Castor would be his life's work.

And now, with no notice at all, he would have to leave Castor behind. It felt like leaving a piece of himself behind. Like leaving the last piece of Robert behind, too.

Daniel drained the last of the scotch from his glass. All he had to do today was clean out his desk and leave his laptop—his life—behind. He decided to wait until the junior developers went home.

CHAPTER 19

It was dark when Daniel made it back to his townhouse with Thai takeout in tow. He ate standing at the kitchen island, then checked the time in Seoul, South Korea. Mid-afternoon. He tried to ignore the cold, sunken feeling still lingering in his gut.

Maybe he should wait to tell her. Her trip would be over soon, and she had Natasha with her—maybe it'd be better if he let her enjoy it, and he admitted his failures when she got home. While Daniel had been toiling away at Promethean, Ana's consulting business had grown. It seemed as if they were traveling in opposite directions: Ana's consulting was taking off like a rocket, while Daniel had been digging himself deeper and deeper into a hole. All those family dinners missed, archery meets forgotten, late nights, early mornings… And for what? To be booted from the company like an underperforming intern?

Before he could make his decision to call, Ana made it for him. Her name flashed on the screen as he held his phone in his hand. He answered on a video call.

"Hi," Ana said. She was outside, wearing a ballcap and sunglasses, and the sun shone brightly down on her.

"I was about to call you," Daniel said. "Where are you?"

"The most famous outdoor archery range in Seoul, apparently," Ana said. "It's called Hwanghakjeong Archery Field. Check this out. Nat's a beast."

Ana turned the camera around, showing Nat poised a few yards away. She was standing straight, with her curly hair pulled back into a bun, and holding a gorgeously carved bow. It wasn't one of the portable ones she carried when she traveled—this one must've been borrowed from the range. An instructor stood behind her, carefully adjusting the angle of her elbows as she drew back.

"Thumb draw," Ana said. "See that? Different style. She wanted to learn more about the historical Korean style called gukgung while we were here."

"She's getting so good she needs new styles to keep her interested?"

"It appears so," Ana said with pride in her voice. "She's still talking about universities, too. I see an archery scholarship in her future."

"I see a spot on the Olympic team," Daniel said.

"Don't let her hear you say that," Ana said. "You know she hates that kind of pressure."

"I know, I know," Daniel said while smiling. His dark mood was already lifting as he watched Nat through the phone screen. She released the arrow. The instructor made an impressed face. Daniel didn't have to see the target to know Nat had nailed it square in the center.

"So that's what we're doing," Ana said. She flipped the camera back to her face, then walked a few paces away and dropped down into a shaded chair. "What about you? How's things back at the ranch? You're coming up on two years, right? Have you thought about what you want to negotiate for on re-signing?"

Daniel laughed once, sardonically. He walked out of the kitchen and dropped down onto the couch. "Funny you mention that. The two years came up today. I didn't realize it was happening."

"Oh, boy. Did you have a chance to negotiate for a raise?"

"Regillus didn't renew."

She took her sunglasses off. Daniel watched as her brain worked, absorbing that. "They didn't renew your contract?"

"Nope," he said. "I'm done."

"…Seriously? Just like that?"

"Just like that," Daniel said. "Jonah said he thought I should've seen it coming."

Ana fell silent. Her gaze moved away from the call and back toward Nat. If

Daniel listened closely, he could hear the familiar release and thunk of arrows flying and landing true. His stomach turned as he imagined what she might be thinking. Likely, she was turning over all the same things Daniel had: all those sacrifices, all those promises, all for nothing. The money didn't matter to her, he knew that. The time did. And Daniel had failed to give her that, over and over.

"Sorry to spring this on you now," Daniel said. "You should be enjoying your time with Nat."

"You're not springing it on me," she said. "Have you thought about what you'll do next?"

"Look for a job, I guess," Daniel said. Honestly, he hadn't gotten that far, absorbed as he had been in his own doom and gloom.

"Maybe you shouldn't," she said.

Now it was Daniel's turn to pause. "What?"

"You haven't been happy at Regillus since Robert passed," Ana said. "That much has been obvious. And you're always talking about how you wish you had more time to devote to your chip project."

Daniel was silent. Ana had supported his personal research, but he knew she didn't like the additional time-suck it represented.

"You know," she said, "With Nat talking about college, and my work picking up… I think this might be the right time for you to take a chance."

"Chance to do what?" Daniel asked. "I don't have a chip to sell. There's no product."

"But the research is good, isn't it? There's got to be a way to get some investment to develop it, the same way you started Promethean and Castor."

That was true. He'd never been at the forefront of the hunt for investors. He was the product guy, not the money guy.

Maybe now it was time to be both.

"I know he makes you nervous and maybe a little jealous," Ana smirked, "but I think you should call Malcolm. Whenever we catch up, he's always asking for updates on that project. He knows the value of winning the hardware race."

"Even with an investor, it won't be cheap," Daniel said. "I have a feeling I'll have to sink most of my cash into it to get the equipment I need to progress."

"Sounds like a worthwhile investment," Ana said. She paused, then added with a slight smile, "Besides, I've been having an incredible run lately. Every time I bid on something, my main competitor has to withdraw. Equipment failures, visa issues, family emergencies… It's been one thing after another."

Daniel felt a small chill run down his spine. "Really? That's… quite a streak."

"I know," Ana said, and he could hear the unease in her voice now. "At first, I thought I was having good luck, but it's happening too often. Too consistently."

"Maybe I'm your good luck charm," Daniel said, trying for levity.

They both laughed, but it was nervous laughter. The wins felt too easy, too convenient.

"Sometimes I wonder if the other shoe is about to drop," Ana admitted. "Like all this success is setting us up for something worse."

Daniel swallowed hard. He'd been having similar thoughts about his own research breakthroughs—how smoothly everything had been going, how every obstacle seemed to clear itself before he even encountered it.

"But for now," Ana continued, shaking off the moment, "we're doing well enough that you can afford to take this risk. I miss you, Daniel. If you run your own startup, you won't be running all over San Francisco trying to make all those bullshit meetings."

Daniel laughed. "I can't promise I'll work any less if I start my own project. I might even work more."

"Of course, I want you to make Nat and me a priority, but that doesn't mean you have to be miserable on some hamster wheel of a job. I honestly believe you can do this and that you'll be happier if you do," she said. "Just don't be a shell of a husband when I do get to see you."

"A shell?"

She waved a hand. "Sorry, that came out wrong. I was remembering how you were… absent… at Promethean, even when you were with me. With us. But that's in the past."

"I can see you overthinking, even from the other side of the world," she said. "Stop that. Just think about it, all right? Call Malcolm. Get his advice. And text your stepdaughter. Ask her about Korean historical archery. You ask better questions about that kind of stuff than I do."

"I will," he said. "Good luck in your meetings."

She blew him a kiss and ended the call.

Daniel set his phone down, reeling from the sudden shift in possibilities. It reminded him of the first day they'd met at their old job, when Ana burst into his office, turned on all the lights, and opened a window while complaining about how dim and stuffy Daniel kept it. She'd done that same thing in his head.

What would he do if he could focus all his time on the chip development? What kind of progression would he make? What kind of money?

He went back to his bag and pulled out the bottle of celebratory scotch. Jonah was never in the office, Emmet didn't drink, and the junior developers didn't know about it, so why not take it home where it'd be appreciated? And now, he finally had something he felt like celebrating. He poured himself a taste and smiled.

CHAPTER 20

Seoul was a beautiful city. Today, the air quality was good enough to be outside without a mask, instead of being thick with dust and smog. Nat had a lot of freedom in Seoul. It was easy to navigate as an English-speaker; the streets of Seongbuk-dong were tranquil and nestled in the hills on the northern side of the city. She could leave her bag unsupervised when she had to pee, and no one would steal her stuff. There was good food on every corner, beautiful architecture like the Gilsangsa Temple, scenic hiking trails with city views, and good shopping. This was an easy place to be a tourist in.

It was mid-morning, and the café Nat was in had just opened. Seoul cafes were often themed, and this one appeared to be centered around sunflowers, with a big mural on the back wall, yellow chairs at the white tables, and a little courtyard filled with potted flowers accessible through a wooden back door. Nat carried her latte and chocolate-drizzled croissant through the door and into the courtyard, where she posted up at a large communal wooden table under the drooping heads of the big flowers.

She pulled out her laptop. She had homework and applications to work on, but before she could get started, her phone lit up with an incoming video call.

"Hey!" she said with a smile as the call connected.

Caleb's face filled the screen, and the now-familiar butterflies swooped through her stomach. She had thought Caleb was cute the first time she'd met him as a kid in archery camp, and as they'd become friends, it'd grown into a crush. A big crush. A crush that was slowly starting to morph into something more. The "more-ness" of the feeling scared her.

"Hey, Nat," Caleb said. It was early evening in California, and the sunset light danced in Caleb's dark hair. He had started wearing it shorter, long in the front but short on the sides. His round cheeks were starting to narrow out, and he was taller and broader than she was. In the distance, she heard waves crashing.

"Are you at the beach?"

"Yeah, just taking a walk," he said. "Thought I'd call. It's morning there, right?"

"Ish," she said. "Cafes don't open until late here. I'm stuck drinking crappy hotel instant coffee until, like, ten."

"Gross. I forgot about that part of Seoul." There was a hint of anxiety in his voice, and his eyes darted away from the camera and out to the ocean.

"What is it?" Nat asked. "What's wrong?"

Caleb paused, then sighed. The camera shook, showing sky, then sand, as he shook out a towel and sat down on it. Then he looked back at the phone. "There's something going around on Instagram."

"What?"

"It's, like, a meme account," Caleb said. "It's private. Apparently, I'm one of the followers, but I don't remember ever adding it. Seems like maybe it was years ago, but it never posted before? I followed a bunch of meme accounts when I was a kid."

"But it's posting now?"

"Yeah. And it's shitty. It's dumb shit about you, Nat."

"Me?" Her stomach dropped. "Why are they posting about me?"

"Because you're good. Seems like they're making fun of most of the top-ranked archers. So the more you win, the more shit gets posted online."

"What kind of shit?"

"I'll send you some screenshots if you want. They're really mean, Nat."

"Send them."

Nat tapped the notification as the messages came through. Her call with Caleb minimized as the text chain came up. There were the screenshots: four of them. Each a different post from the account. Stupid shit. Dumb memes calling out her performances, her screw ups. One showed a picture of her at their last competition, bowstring drawn, gaze focused forward. It had been the day before her period, she remembered. She'd been bloated. Zitty, too. The camera had caught the worst of it, and then the account had zoomed in on the little bulge of her belly over the waistband of her pants. In the next screenshot, the account had edited her face onto an obese body, with a bunch of laughing emojis.

"How many of these are there?" She closed the screenshot, opened the call again, and was met with Caleb's concerned face. The look of pain on his face made her own pain surge up, and suddenly she was fighting back tears. It was stupid. It was a dumb private meme account. But… Who was doing this to her?

"I've been reporting the posts," Caleb said. "And the accounts. It seems like whenever one gets taken down, another one pops up. And I'm asking around, looking to see if anyone knows who runs them, but no one has any idea. It's like they're coming out of nowhere."

"Jesus." She rubbed her eyes. "This is so fucking embarrassing."

"It's stupid," Caleb said. "I'm sorry. I wanted you to know. In case anyone sends you anything. Or makes any mean comments. I wanted you to know I'm on the case."

"Must be a lot of work," she muttered. "I can do it myself, you know. Look for the accounts. Report them and stuff."

"You don't have to do that," Caleb said, with a sudden sternness in his voice. "You don't need to see any more of this crap. I'll handle it."

"Why?" she asked. Why was Caleb going through all this trouble? They were friends, they were close, and Nat had always harbored feelings for him, but this kind of intensity was new. It was protective. He really cared. More than she realized he did.

Caleb's face flushed, visible in the low sunset light. "Well, because… Because it's the right thing to do. And I mean… Well…" He broke into an awkward laugh. "I mean, I wasn't planning to say this, but fuck it, I guess."

"Say what?" Her eyes widened.

"I'm doing it because I want to," he said. "Because… Because I like you. You know. More than… I mean, I know we're friends, and it's cool if you don't feel the same way, but I mean, I like you. More than a friend."

"What?!" Nat squawked. The few other patrons in the courtyard gave her looks, and Nat cringed and lowered herself back down into her chair. But the butterflies in her chest had swirled into a tornado. This couldn't be happening. Caleb liked her? Her? Natasha Bishop, with her frizzy hair, lack of friends, vampire novel obsession, and weird quasi-present parents? He liked her?

"What' what?!" Caleb shot back. His flush deepened, and his mouth pulled into a deep scowl that he wore when he had flubbed an easy shot in archery practice. "I mean, if you don't—just pretend I didn't say anything!"

"No, no," Nat said. "No, that's not it. I…" She blushed. "I like you too. Obviously."

The scowl dropped off his face. "Seriously? You're not fucking with me?"

"Yes, seriously!" Nat rubbed at her ear, feeling it burn with embarrassment.

"Wow," Caleb said. "Wow. Um. That's not what I expected."

"Me neither," Nat said. The meme account disappeared from her mind. She felt buoyant. Happy. Like maybe with Caleb, she finally had somewhere she really belonged.

They stared at each other through the phone for a moment and then broke into giggles. "I've gotta go," Caleb said. "Dinner plans with Mom. But, um, I'll see you when you're back in California?"

"Uh-huh," Nat said, still smiling.

"And maybe we could go out? On a date?"

"Yeah," she said. "I'd like that."

"Fire! Awesome." Caleb laughed again, high and awkward. "Great. Um, well, I'll text you."

The call ended, and Natasha let out a shocked little giggle and slumped over onto the table. Her latte was cold, and she was definitely disturbing the other guests in this café, and she'd never been this happy in her life.

CHAPTER 21

The day after Ana returned from South Korea, Daniel found himself sitting at their kitchen island, going through his fourth revision of the chip development budget. Ana moved around the kitchen with practiced efficiency, unpacking groceries while simultaneously assembling a simple dinner of pasta and salad for Nat. Ana and Daniel would be away.

"The material sciences team alone is going to cost nearly half a million," Daniel said, massaging his temples. "And that's just for the initial research phase."

Ana paused, a head of lettuce in hand. "And you've already secured the loans?"

"Malcolm helped arrange them. I wish I had known that the Regillus stock was good collateral even before the end of the lockup period." He scrolled through the spreadsheet on his laptop. "I could have started much earlier. But the real problem is burn rate…"

Ana's phone buzzed on the counter. "Did you see this?" Ana asked, staring at her phone. "Chan Industries withdrew from the satellite equipment transport bid." She frowned. "That's the third competitor to drop out of my contracts this month."

"That's great news," Daniel said, but his enthusiasm sounded forced even to his own ears.

"Is it?" Ana dried her hands on a dish towel and came to stand beside him, looking at his laptop screen. "Daniel, when's the last time you've heard of any company having a run like this?"

Daniel shifted uncomfortably. "Maybe they realized they couldn't match your expertise."

Ana pulled out a chair and sat down. "My last three bids have been successful because my main competitors all had… issues. Equipment failures. Visa problems. Family emergencies."

They looked at each other across the kitchen island.

"This feels too easy," Ana said.

"Don't jinx it," Daniel said, but they both knew it wasn't about jinxes.

"Maybe I'm having a good run," Ana said, though her tone suggested she didn't believe it.

"Yeah," Daniel said. "Maybe."

But as he returned to his budget, adding up all the savings from fortuitous timing and unexpected windfalls, he couldn't help but wonder: if this was the calm before the storm, how bad would the storm be?

"Anyway, about your cashflow problem… I've been thinking about that for a while," Ana said, setting her phone aside. "You're approaching this like you're building a conventional development team. That's not what you need."

Daniel looked up. "What do I need?"

"You need a distributed network of specialists who don't know they're working on the same project." She rinsed her hands and came to stand beside him, leaning over his shoulder to look at the screen. "May I?"

Daniel slid the laptop toward her. Ana's fingers moved quickly over the keyboard as she pulled up a blank document. With her pointer finger skillfully on the laptop's touchpad, she began sketching out a diagram.

"Think of it as a hub and spoke model," she said, drawing as she spoke. "You're the hub. Each contractor is a spoke, working on a specific component without access to the overall design."

"Compartmentalization," Daniel said, watching her diagram take shape.

"Exactly. It's how military logistics works with classified projects." She drew more lines, creating connections. "You have a team in Switzerland working on the quantum architecture. Another in Israel handling the material science. A group in Taiwan for the fabrication prototyping."

"And none of them know what the others are doing," Daniel said.

"Right. Each gets precisely the information they need, nothing more. They deliver their components to you, and you're the only one who assembles the complete picture." She turned to face him. "It's more complex to manage, but it protects your intellectual property. I suspect it gives you much better budget control too."

Daniel studied the diagram, mind racing. "This could work. But I'd need help coordinating all of this."

"That's where Malcolm comes in," Ana said. "He has the connections to find the right contractors and help set up the legal framework."

"Speaking of which." Daniel glanced at his watch. "We should get going if we're going to make that meeting."

CHAPTER 22

An hour later, they were seated in the private Wine Vault at Boulevard, an upscale restaurant on Mission Street in San Francisco. The ornately decorated room smelled of leather and expensive cologne, with discreet lighting that made the ice in Malcolm's scotch glow amber.

"Ana," Malcolm said, "your logistics diagram is brilliant. Military precision applied to technological innovation."

"It's common sense," Ana said, though Daniel could see she was pleased by the praise.

Malcolm tapped the printed diagram with a manicured finger. "I've already made some calls. I have firms in mind for each of these nodes."

"That was fast," Daniel said.

"When we met last time, I started making subtle inquiries," Malcolm said with a slight shrug. "The technology you're describing could revolutionize entire industries. Industries I happen to be heavily invested in."

He paused, swirling his scotch thoughtfully. "I also learned that you've had quite the run, Daniel. Every one of your competitors seems to be hitting walls."

Daniel tensed. "I don't understand what you mean."

"The Shinkuro Dynamics lab that was working on similar surface treatments? Their lead researcher resigned. Personal reasons." Malcolm's tone carried a note of curiosity that bordered on suspicion. "NeuralPath's clean room contamination. GraphicLeap losing their lead to that fusion startup."

"I've been focused on my own work," Daniel said. "Haven't been tracking the competition much."

"Haven't you?" Malcolm's eyes studied him. "It's remarkable timing, all of it. Speaking of which… I've located a cryochiller for you. State-of-the-art unit, exactly what you'll need for the quantum chip testing."

"Already?" Ana asked, surprised. "Those have six-month waiting lists."

Malcolm smiled. "This one was already manufactured. A Korean aerospace company had ordered it, but suddenly they couldn't get an export permit. The State Department decided some of its components are dual-use technology." He shrugged. "Their loss is your gain. You can have it within the week."

Daniel felt a chill run down his spine. "The export controls… happened to catch that specific unit?"

"Apparently so," Malcolm said, his tone suggesting he found this as suspicious as everything else. "Another fortunate coincidence in your string of good luck."

Ana glanced between them, picking up on the undercurrent of tension.

"Sometimes luck favors the prepared," Daniel said, trying to keep his voice light. "Besides, those labs were all pursuing different approaches. Mine is unique."

"Indeed," Malcolm said, his expression unreadable.

He pulled out a thin leather portfolio and laid several documents on the table. "Sørensen Quantum in Copenhagen for the theoretical architecture," he said, pointing to the first document. " Shinkuro Dynamics' subsidiary in Osaka for the substrate development, though I suppose they'll be more available now. Ben-Gurion University's applied physics department for initial prototyping."

Daniel scanned the documents, eyes widening at the names. "These are top-tier. They'll never work with a startup like Bennett Tech."

"They will if they don't know they're working with a startup," Malcolm said. "Each contract will be routed through different shell companies that I control. As far as they're concerned, they're doing specialized research for various established tech firms."

"Is that legal?" Ana asked, brow furrowed.

"Perfectly," Malcolm assured her. "It's just compartmentalization, as you suggested. They'll be paid well for their work, with clear deliverables and milestones."

He slid another document across the table. "This is the financial breakdown. Even with my connections, we're looking at around twenty million over eighteen months."

Daniel felt his throat tighten. "Twenty million?"

"Quantum computing research isn't cheap," Malcolm said. "And if you want the best, you have to pay for it."

"That's a lot of money," Ana said. She met Daniel's eyes. The compartmentalization was intended to cut costs, but this was still a staggering investment.

Malcolm nodded in understanding. "It is a significant upfront. But the potential return…" He trailed off, letting the implication hang in the air.

"What about the timeline?" Daniel asked. "You said eighteen months. I was hoping for faster progress."

"That's aggressive by industry standards," Malcolm said. "New chips typically take years to develop. The only reason I think eighteen months is possible is because you've already done significant theoretical groundwork." He leaned forward, resting his elbows on the table. "But there are risks to this approach. Communication bottlenecks. Integration challenges. Every time you compartmentalize, you introduce potential delays when it comes time to integrate the pieces."

Daniel nodded slowly as he began to calculate new timelines. "So even with the best specialists, there's no guarantee we'll have a working prototype within eighteen months."

"Right," Malcolm confirmed. "But significantly better odds than if you tried to build everything in-house."

Ana's hand found Daniel's under the table and squeezed gently. "And the financial risk?" she asked Malcolm.

"Substantial," he said. "You have two choices on how to fund it. You can either sell your vested stock now and pay the tax bill, or you can take loans against the stock. If you take a loan, you don't have to pay taxes on it, but if the stock takes a hit, you'll be forced to sell everything. You also would be limited to getting loans for only about 50% of your stock value. If the development fails, or takes longer than anticipated…"

"We lose everything," Daniel finished.

The table fell silent. The clink of glasses and murmur of conversations from the main dining room seemed distant, muffled by the weight of the decision.

"I'll help where I can," Malcolm said. "I believe in what you're building, Daniel. I wouldn't have proposed this network otherwise."

Daniel looked at Ana, studying her face. She was concerned—he could see it in the tension around her eyes—but there was determination there, too.

"It's your call," she said. "But if we're doing this, we're doing it your way. The right way."

Daniel turned back to Malcolm. "Send me the contracts. I want to start immediately."

Malcolm nodded, raising his glass. "To calculated risks."

"To calculated risks," Daniel and Ana echoed, raising their own glasses.

As they clinked glasses, Daniel caught Ana's eye. Daniel couldn't quite shake Malcolm's earlier observations. Every competitor hitting obstacles. Every barrier to his success mysteriously falling away.

It was, as Ana had said, too easy.

And in Daniel's experience, nothing worthwhile ever came that easily.

CHAPTER 23

Daniel walked into Ana's favorite omakase restaurant once again, but something was wrong. The warm lighting had turned harsh and clinical, like an operating room. The delicate paintings on the walls seemed to shift and blur when he wasn't looking directly at them. Ana was already at the table, sitting across from an empty seat. She invited him to join her, but she wasn't wearing the green dress that she normally reserved for dinners here. Instead, she wore a severe black suit that made her look like a stranger.

The sushi pieces arranged before them didn't look like food anymore. They gleamed like coins, like poker chips, like everything Daniel was gambling away.

"We need to talk," Ana said, her voice carrying an edge he'd never heard before. She was scrolling through her phone, not looking at him.

"About what?" Daniel asked, though dread was already pooling in his stomach.

"About us. About reality." She finally looked up, and her eyes were cold, calculating. "I heard you were at the bank again today."

Daniel's mouth went dry. "How did you—"

"They called me. Apparently, I'm listed as your spouse on the loan applications." She set her phone down with a sharp click. "Rejected again, weren't you?"

"It's temporary. Once they understand the potential of the chip—"

"The chip." Ana laughed, but there was no warmth in it. "You've leveraged every cent of your Regillus stock. Burned through your entire payout. And for what? A piece of silicon that no one else believes in?"

"You believed in it," Daniel said desperately. "You said—"

"I said a lot of things when I thought you had a future." Ana's face seemed to shift in the strange light, becoming sharper, more predatory. "But my business is thriving now. I have contracts lined up for the next two years. I don't need…" She gestured vaguely at him. "This."

"This? I'm your husband!"

"You're a liability," Ana said, picking up a piece of sushi that looked more like a blood-red ruby than tuna. "Do you know what my clients say when they find out about you? About your failed ventures? It's embarrassing, Daniel."

The restaurant seemed to stretch around them, the walls pulling away, the ceiling rising until it disappeared into darkness. Other diners appeared at distant tables, all turning to stare at him with blank, judgmental faces.

"I gave you a chance," Ana continued, her voice echoing in the expanding space. "I supported your dream. But dreams don't pay bills. Dreams don't build a future. And I'm tired of carrying dead weight."

"Ana, please. I love you. This isn't about money—"

"Everything is about money when you don't have any." She stood, and suddenly she seemed to tower over him.

"No," Daniel reached for her hand, but it passed through like smoke. "Ana, don't—"

"We're done, Daniel. I'm taking Natasha and we're leaving. Maybe you can sleep in your precious lab."

The floor beneath him began to crack, dark lines spreading like the web from his vision of Castor. He was falling, the restaurant dissolving around him, Ana's cold laughter following him down into—

*

Daniel gasped awake, his heart hammering against his ribs. The bedroom was dark and quiet, the sheets damp with sweat. Beside him, Ana stirred, her hand automatically reaching out to find him.

"Dan?" she murmured, voice thick with sleep. "What's wrong?"

He couldn't answer, still caught between the nightmare and reality. His chest felt tight, his breathing shallow.

Ana pushed herself up on one elbow, suddenly more awake. "Hey, hey. You're shaking." She reached over and turned on the bedside lamp, bathing the room in soft, warm light—nothing like the harsh glare of the dream restaurant. "Bad dream?"

Daniel nodded, not trusting his voice yet.

"Come here." She pulled him against her, his head on her shoulder, her hand stroking his hair. "Want to tell me about it?"

"You were leaving me," he managed after a moment. "Because I couldn't get any more loans for my company. Because the banks rejected me again. Because your business was successful and mine… wasn't."

Ana was quiet for a moment, just holding him. When she spoke, her voice was gentle. "You know, nightmares like that are normal when you're under a lot of stress. And starting a new company? That's one of the most stressful things a person can do."

"It felt so real," Daniel said. "You were so cold. Said I was an embarrassment… a liability."

"Oh, Dan." Ana shifted so she could look at his face. "Listen to me. That dream? That's not how I feel. Not even close. I'm so proud of you. These past few months, the effort you've been making to be present, to be loving, to really be here with me and Nat? That means more than any business success ever could."

"But what if the loans—"

"Stop." She pressed a finger to his lips. "I knew what I was signing up for when you started this venture. I've been through lean times before, remember? I was a single mom going through school while working two jobs. I know how to weather financial storms."

Daniel felt some of the tension leave his shoulders. "I… I want to give you everything. You've sacrificed so much for me."

"We're partners," Ana said. "Sometimes you carry more weight, sometimes

I do. That's what marriage is. Not a transaction where you have to pay me back for supporting you."

Daniel pulled her closer, breathing in the familiar scent of her shampoo. "I love you."

"I love you too. Even when you're a sweaty, nightmare-having mess." She kissed his forehead. "Do you need some water? Sometimes that helps."

"Yeah," Daniel said. "I'll get it."

He padded to the kitchen, filling a glass from the tap. In the dark window above the sink, he caught his reflection—hollow-eyed, stressed, but alive. Real. Not the falling man from his nightmare.

She says she doesn't care about the money, he thought as he drank. *And I believe her. I do. But she deserves more than getting by. She deserves success, stability, and everything her business is building for her. I need to match that. Need to make the chip work, make it profitable. Not because she needs me to, but because I need to prove I'm worth her faith.*

He rinsed the glass and headed back to the bedroom, where Ana had left the light on for him.

"Better?" she asked as he slipped back under the covers.

"Much better," he said, pulling her close. "Thank you. For everything."

"Always," she murmured against his chest. "Now get some sleep. Real sleep, not the nightmare kind."

Daniel closed his eyes, feeling her breathing slow and deepen against him. He knew she was right. He knew she loved him for who he was, not what he could provide.

But in the morning, he'd head to the lab early anyway. He'd work harder, push further, make sure her faith in him wasn't misplaced. She deserved that much.

She deserved everything.

As sleep finally pulled him under again, he didn't realize he'd already begun walking down the exact path that would lead him away from what she truly wanted. The nightmare might have been false, but his response to it would make it all too real.

CHAPTER 24

"We're all thrilled Mr. Langley was able to make this connection," Dr. Nouri said as she led Daniel through the Stanford University Entrepreneurship Lab. "And I have to say, your timing was remarkably fortunate. We had another incubator project fall through last week when their funding collapsed—some issue with their angel investor pulling out suddenly. Your application was fast-tracked through the review process in record time."

"I appreciate the opportunity," Daniel said, though her words sparked a familiar unease. Another stroke of luck. Another competitor's misfortune becomes his gain.

"Truly remarkable timing," Dr. Nouri said. "And the permits for your cryochiller installation? Approved in under two weeks. I've been here fifteen years, and I've never seen the university bureaucracy move that quickly. These kinds of specialized equipment permits usually take months, minimum."

"That is… surprisingly fast," Daniel agreed, his discomfort growing. He was distracted by the lab itself: big and well-lit, with hallways branching off like arteries, and equipment so specialized he didn't realize what half of it did.

He could see why Emmet liked it so much.

Dr. Nouri was the Stanford professor who managed this Stanford lab, though she made it clear that those who used the space had autonomy over their own projects. She was a short and serious woman, but her demeanor was softened by the row of multi-colored gel pens tucked into the chest pocket of her lab coat.

"Here's your dedicated workspace," Dr. Nouri said. The door was at the far end of the lab. The wall was glass, so others could look in, but upon walking in, Daniel saw there was a shade he could pull down for privacy. It was a large room with a white tile floor, desks, shelves, and computers already waiting to be set up. One door led to the data center, and one right next to it led to the small room that housed the cryogenic chiller. There was a small dustproof room, also walled in glass, that led to chiller room door.

"This technology is going to supercharge some of the work our researchers are doing," Dr. Nouri said, with a nod to the chiller. "We're thrilled to have access to it."

"I'm glad to have the space and resources to house it," Daniel said.

The chiller was in the middle of the small room. Malcolm's connections had paid off yet again. Here was a state-of-the-art product within his two-million-dollar budget. Its specs met every one of his needs. As he looked at it through the glass wall, he imagined this might be how the zookeepers felt after successfully breeding pandas. He was looking at something treasured and fragile, and he was surprised by the depth of care he felt for this humming piece of machinery. It wasn't too large, reaching to his waist. The chiller itself was a cylindrical structure, elevated off the floor by a metal frame. A tube ran from the top of the chiller to the gas compressor on the left. At the top of the frame was access to the chiller itself: a wide experimental space with multiple plates and ports, and easy access to the chiller's golden insides. The top of the chiller opened like a CD tray. It slid out, and Daniel could insert his experimental chips and slide it closed again. Then, after a ten-minute cooldown, the chip would be ready to use. It was easy for one person to use, had automated warm-up and chilling systems, with multiple user permissions with different levels of access. Perfect for a lab like Stanford's. The chiller was connected to the database next door, which connected to Daniel's lab. In that way, he could test his chips with the chiller and the computing power of the datacenter.

That was the agreement Malcolm Langley had dreamed up, with some help from his Stanford connections. If Daniel was going to develop a more powerful quantum computing chip, he needed a more powerful way to cool it. Malcolm had suggested that Daniel invest in the chiller and offer Stanford access to it in return for housing it, powering it, and providing space for Daniel to work. The chiller was a huge cash investment, but Stanford's support would take some of the weight off.

"Mr. Langley seems to think you're onto something with your research," Dr. Nouri said. "An advanced quantum computing chip with your improvements would be groundbreaking." She peered at Daniel curiously.

He was used to this kind of look. To anyone with more than a layperson's knowledge, expanding the computing capabilities of existing chips seemed impossible—all the improvements had already been made. But they hadn't worked with an AI like Castor. They didn't realize how many tiny defects were limiting their computing power. With this chiller and Stanford's resources, Daniel could test the tiny fabrication tweaks he hoped would break through the computing barrier. Even without access to Castor now, he had the right plans to get started.

Dr. Nouri left him to get settled in the lab. Just before four in the afternoon, there was a sharp knock on the door. Emmet stepped inside, looking as unassuming as he always did, in his plain sweatshirt and jeans.

"Emmet!" Daniel said, surprised. He stood up from the box he was unpacking. "How'd you get in here? I mean, not that I'm not happy to see you, but Stanford is… Stanford."

"I'm an alum," Emmet said. "I still know everyone who works here."

Daniel blinked. "Still? You must've graduated a while ago."

"My work was influential," he said. It wasn't boastful, just factual. "Sometimes I still consult upon request. I wanted to come see your lab. Dr. Nouri mentioned the chiller."

Daniel showed Emmet to the small room, like he was introducing Emmet to his beloved pet. "It's not fully set up yet," Daniel said, gesturing at the glass. "As you can see, we're going to have it dustproof, and the suits have yet to come in."

Emmet nodded in understanding. The chiller and the experimental chips would be sensitive to the smallest imperfections, so whenever anyone entered to use it, they would have to pause in the small room before and put on a dustproof suit. It wasn't quite as heavy as a biohazard suit, but it was certainly a pain in the ass. Worth it, though, to keep the chiller running in optimum condition. "Those monitors," Daniel continued, gesturing to the dark screens mounted on the wall above the chiller, "will show live reports of the chiller's stats. Temperature, computing power used, etc. Just a quick glimpse, I'll be able to see from here."

"An adequate setup," Emmet said. "And you'll access it from your laptop in here?"

"Probably," Daniel said. "I'll miss the AR access, honestly. I got pretty used to it."

Emmet hummed in acknowledgement. His dark eyes were still roving over the chiller with an expression akin to hunger.

"How are things at Promethean?" Daniel asked. "I haven't kept up over the past few months."

"Good," Emmet said. "The national security threat indicator program I was working on went live. It seems to be operating to expected standards. We've increased the size of the engineering team. Our current projects are centered around the financial industry. Identifying portfolio risks for large institutional investors. Automated trading based on self-defined investment strategies. And so on. It's not a far step from the shipping automation."

"Is that keeping you interested?" Daniel asked.

"Somewhat," Emmet said. He turned away from the chiller. "I was unhappy with how Jonah handled your contract non-renewal."

Daniel leaned against the desk, covered in packed-up cardboard boxes. He hadn't expected Emmet to comment on it. Honestly, he'd thought Emmet would acknowledge his absence and then never speak to him again. "That's how things work in the startup world. I'm glad I have the opportunity to pursue my research, at least."

"I wanted to help with that," Emmet said. "If you're able to build a functional quantum chip, the whole industry will benefit. But I don't think you have the software necessary to test it, even as you push forward with the research."

Daniel sighed. "Of course, it'd be easier if I still had access to Castor to run tests, but it's not a full roadblock. I'll have to redevelop a program that can—"

"Moving quickly is important in research endeavors like this," Emmet interrupted.

Daniel stared at him. Emmet rarely interrupted. Even if he didn't intend to acknowledge or respond to what was said, he rarely cut someone off.

"I used Castor to comb through Promethean's early research, contracts, and code base," Emmet said. "From my experience with similar startups, I suspected there may be an early version of Castor which existed outside of Promethean's contractual scope, and within your own intellectual property."

Daniel's eyes widened in realization.

"My suspicion proved to be correct," Emmet said. "There is a very early version of Castor's code base which still, technically, belongs to you." He pulled a thumb drive from his pocket and set it down on Daniel's desk. "I've included the code base, as well as annotated versions of your contracts, should Promethean try to claim ownership of the code base."

"It can't be airtight," Daniel said.

"It's not," Emmet admitted. "But, from what I understand of your research, the artificial intelligence is not the product. As long as you don't attempt to rebuild and sell it and instead use it for building out your hardware, I don't suspect Jonah will attempt to push the boundaries of the contract."

"… Thank you, Emmet," Daniel said. "Having the alpha codebase will speed the research a lot. But… Why go through the trouble?"

"I'm interested in your research. I'm curious to see where it goes." Emmet was silent for a moment, considering. Then, he said, "You're the only person who has ever advocated for me without my requesting it. When the Regillus acquisition went through, my equity stake was substantial. Because of your insistence years ago."

"You earned it," Daniel said.

"Yes, but I wouldn't have received it without your intervention. I was not considering the long-term implications of equity-based compensation packages. My father would say I owe you a debt." His expression remained neutral, but there was something in his voice Daniel had never heard before.

"I trust your judgment. The work you're doing is interesting. Those two facts together are sufficient motivation."

Daniel was momentarily speechless. In all their years working together, he'd never realized the impact his advocacy had made.

"Wait, Emmet," Daniel said.

"Yes?" Emmet asked, in a cool voice that suggested he did not want to engage in further conversation.

"What do you think Robert would've thought of all of this?" Daniel asked. "You think he'd be happy with what happened to Promethean?"

"Robert is dead," Emmet said. What could've been a cruel statement was just a fact to Emmet. "So anything we say is pure speculation. I know you aren't happy with the direction of Promethean, so it's good that you've found a pathway more fulfilling for you."

"Are you happy with the direction?"

"I'm not interested in automated self-directed investing," Emmet said. "But I have enough freedom to pursue my own research interests to a certain degree. The national security threat detection system gave me some ideas, so I will be pursuing those experimentally for now."

"Is that a yes?" Daniel asked.

"Yes," Emmet said. He lingered there for a moment, watching Daniel.

"That's all the questions I had," Daniel said. "Thanks for coming by, and for the code base."

Emmet nodded and left. Daniel turned back to his unpacking and stared at the thumb drive Emmet had left. It wasn't Castor, but it was a start. Daniel could develop something new for his work—something closed. Something that only he would be using.

It'd be a long road, trying to build this chip. But Malcolm believed, and Emmet believed (in his own careful, evidence-based way), and most importantly, Ana believed. That was Daniel's drive. Ana had given him a gift—the chance to take this risk. This big swing.

CHAPTER 25

One year later

It felt like five days, and somehow, it also felt like five years. Daniel felt like he'd stepped off one treadmill at Promethean and stepped right onto another one—but at least this time, he was the one in control. That didn't make his work hours any shorter or less grueling, though.

"The surface treatment alignment from Shinkuro Dynamics is showing significant improvement," Daniel said, examining the test results on his tablet while Dr. Yoshida's face peered back at him from the screen. After months of carefully navigating the compartmentalized development process, he'd finally made the difficult decision to bring his key teams together three months ago, revealing enough about the project to solve their integration challenges.

"Yes, Mr. Bennett," she replied with a slight bow. "The new fabrication specifications you provided allowed us to refine the substrate composition precisely. The test samples are ready for final integration."

As soon as the call ended, Daniel's tablet pinged with another notification. The Copenhagen team was reporting that their final quantum circuitry design had passed all simulations. The Israeli fabrication team had already delivered their components last week.

He hadn't been making the breakthroughs he expected with the chip. It was slow, and without other researchers to support him, it was all falling on his shoulders. Not only did he have to do the actual work, but he also had to do all the logistical legwork that Jonah had been doing at Promethean. He had to find the right companies, the right investors—the right people who could help him move forward with this work. That itself was a full-time job. With his days spent in the lab, his nights were spent on his work computer on the couch, sending emails, scheduling calls, and asking for introductions.

It wasn't what Ana had hoped for, and she made that very clear. Daniel was slipping back into his old habits, but he couldn't ease up now. He'd burned through his cashout by month six and was now taking loans against his Regillus stock, to the tune of $100 million. Ana knew about the loans, but not the amount. Daniel was determined to make a breakthrough before she did.

"You need to be the one," Daniel said. His breath fogged up the mask of his dust suit. As many times as he had done this, he still felt like an astronaut attempting to repair the ISS. He opened the chiller's tray and slid the chip inside, then carefully laid the film atop it. "Eighth time's the charm."

He was sure the fabrication lab was sick of him ordering chips with slight adjustments—or maybe they loved his slow progress, since each experimental chip was the price of a house. Over the year, he had honed in on the defect he'd seen repeatedly in his simulations with Castor. Surface treatment. At the very end of the fabrication process, quantum chips were coated with a surface treatment to protect them from contaminants, but the treatments themselves were often imperfect. They had minuscule impurities or were applied with minor defects, leading to an uneven surface. For most use cases, these errors were so small as to mean nothing. For Daniel, fixing these tiny defects could be the breakthrough he'd been seeking.

With the help of his in-house AI and Stanford's resources, Daniel had created a host of new surface treatments, as well as a new method of application. He'd seen some improvements, but none of them so far had been good enough to convince the investors he'd managed to set up meetings with. There were some impressive qualities to the chip—the low data corruption rate, the load rate for all 1,000 quantum bits—but it wasn't too different than what other hardware developers were doing.

"Eighth time," he repeated to himself. This chip was the first experimentally crafted one to use the new treatment and the new application process. The methods had made slight improvements separately. Maybe, together, they'd work even better.

It was nearing 5:00 PM, and soon the lab would be empty. Daniel closed the door to his workspace and sat down at his desk, then turned to the computer and picked up the AR goggles on their stand next to it. He put them on, then relaxed in his office chair and kicked his feet up onto the desk.

"Hello, Jimini."

"Hello, Daniel," the artificial intelligence said. The voice emitted from a small speaker embedded in the goggles and sounded like someone was speaking right into his ear. "How can I help you today?"

"We're going to run some tests again," Daniel said. "You'll notice you're working with some new hardware."

"What kinds of tests would you like to run?"

Daniel sighed. Through the glass of his AR goggles, the ceiling looked as plain as it always did, like a whiteboard out of reach. "I don't know," he said. "What test would you suggest?"

"The Traveling Salesman Problem is commonly used to test computing capabilities," Jimini said.

"Good idea." He wasn't too keen on using that particular problem—mostly, it just revealed gaps in computing power. The problem was simple on paper: given a list of cities and distances between them, what was the shortest possible route to visit each one and return to the origin city? It was surprisingly computationally challenging, and Daniel had seen Jimini's resource needs outweigh what his chips could provide.

Might as well give it a try, though. He had the right data for it. Daniel pulled his phone out of his pocket, then thumbed open his email. He scrolled down to Ana's most recent message, which included a list of six cities she'd been visiting on a work trip to the EU next year. "Find the shortest route Ana could take to get back home."

Jimini registered the cities through the goggles, as if Daniel's eyes were the

AI's eyes. In the future, Daniel thought, Jimini would already know the cities Ana was going to visit, because he would already have access to Daniel's email. The closed-system AI made sense for his research purposes and to keep him from getting sued by Regillus, but he did wish he could give Jimini access to the whole Internet.

A map appeared in his goggles. A route was drawn between the six cities, like a loop in his mind. "Here's the route you requested."

Daniel sat up straighter. "Jimini, do you have a map of the EU in your uploaded data?"

"I do."

"Let's say I'm in France," Daniel said. "I'm traveling from Paris to the twenty largest cities in France. What's the shortest route to visit each city and return?"

Instantaneously, another route appeared in his vision, a winding line drawn across Paris.

Daniel's heartbeat increased. "I'm traveling from Paris to the fifty largest cities in the EU. What's the shortest route to visit each city and return?"

The map zoomed out, showing all twenty-seven member states of the European Union. Jimini identified the fifty largest cities and then drew a route between them, all in the space of a blink.

Daniel's pulse hammered in his ears. Fifty cities. Jimini had solved it instantly—but was it right?

"Show me the total distance," Daniel said.

"14,827 kilometers."

"Now swap Berlin and Prague in the route. What's the new distance?"

"14,902 kilometers." The route flickered, redrawing itself with the two cities exchanged.

Daniel leaned forward. A suboptimal swap increasing the distance—good sign. "What about Madrid and Lisbon?"

"15,043 kilometers."

Even worse. His hands trembled slightly as he pulled up his phone's calculator. "Jimini, what's the distance from Paris to Berlin to Warsaw?"

"1,878 kilometers."

"And Paris to Warsaw direct?"

"1,372 kilometers."

"What about Paris to Warsaw to Berlin?"

"1,657 kilometers."

Daniel's breath caught. The triangle inequality held—no impossible shortcuts. His AI wasn't spitting out nonsense. "Run 2-opt improvement on your solution. Any swaps that would shorten it?"

A pause. Not computational delay—Jimini was checking thousands of edge swaps. "No improvements found. The solution is locally optimal."

"Generate ten random routes through all fifty cities. Give me their distances."

Numbers flashed in his vision: 18,234km, 22,109km, 19,887km… Each one significantly longer than Jimini's solution.

Daniel stood up, pacing now. One final test. "Take the first seven cities in your route. Calculate every possible path through those seven and back to Paris."

"5,040 permutations calculated. Optimal subsection distance: 2,341 kilometers. This matches the seven-city segment in my fifty-city solution."

The room seemed to tilt. Jimini had done it. Not approximated, not estimated—solved. The Traveling Salesman Problem that brought supercomputers to their knees, conquered in milliseconds by a single computer running on Daniel Bennet's quantum computing chip.

Daniel's voice came out hoarse. "Save this session, Jimini. Mark it priority one."

He had to call Ana. Had to tell someone. But first, he needed to make sure no one at Regillus could access these logs.

"Thank you, Jimini," Daniel said. "That's all for today."

"Good night, Daniel," Jimini said. The map disappeared, and his goggles were nothing but glass again.

Daniel pulled them off and set them on his desk with a shaky hand. He stared at the cryochiller through the glass. It was humming contentedly, his Bennett chip nestled inside now cooled to near absolute zero. What he'd witnessed wasn't just an improvement—it was a quantum leap beyond what any existing technology could do. Solving the Traveling Salesman Problem for fifty cities without breaking a sweat? It was unheard of.

He felt a wave of vindication wash over him. All those months of managing contractors across continents, the careful dance of revealing just enough without exposing his whole design, the financial risks he'd taken… it had all been worth it. The Bennett chip worked. More than worked, it was revolutionary.

This wasn't just a technological breakthrough; it was financial salvation. The loans, the dwindling savings, Ana's concerns… All of that would fade into insignificance with what this chip could do.

As he packed up his things to head home, Daniel couldn't help but smile. He'd proved Jonah wrong. He'd proved all the skeptical investors wrong. Most importantly, he'd justified Ana's faith in him.

"Eighth time's the charm," he whispered to himself as he shut off the lights.

CHAPTER 26

Daniel clutched the bag of takeout in one hand and his laptop in the other as he shouldered open the front door of the townhouse. The smell of pho—beef, anise, cilantro—filled the warm air of the living room.

"Ana?" he called out, setting his things on the kitchen counter.

"In here," she replied from the dining room.

He found her seated at the table with a stack of contract documents spread before her, a red pen in hand. She looked up, dark eyes assessing the excitement that he knew was written all over his face.

She set the pen down. "You've got that look."

"What look?"

"The one you get when you've figured something out." She began gathering her papers into a neat stack. "Is it the chip?"

Daniel nodded, already pulling his laptop from his bag. "I ran a real-world test with Jimini today. Not just the lab simulations we've been stuck on—an actual computational problem with real data."

Ana moved her papers aside, making room for his laptop. "And?"

"The Traveling Salesman Problem seems simple," Daniel said. "Find the shortest route to visit several cities and return home. But it's deceptively difficult. With just five cities, you have twelve possible routes to check. With ten cities, it jumps to over three million possibilities. With fifty cities…" he gestured to the screen where Jimini had instantly calculated the optimal route, "you'd have more possible routes than atoms in the universe. Traditional computers can only check a tiny fraction of those possibilities, using clever shortcuts. What Jimini did would be like instantly finding a specific grain of sand on all the beaches on Earth." Daniel turned the laptop to face her. "Know how long it took him?"

Ana's brow furrowed. "Hours?"

"Seconds." Daniel couldn't keep the pride from his voice. "It should've been computationally impossible. But with the Bennett chip, it just… Happened."

Ana stared at the screen, at the winding route drawn across the map of Europe. "That's… That's incredible, Daniel."

"This is it," he said, sitting beside her. "This is the breakthrough I've been working toward."

Ana reached out and squeezed his hand, her expression shifting from impressed to genuinely happy. "I knew you could do it."

"I need another pair of eyes on it," Daniel said. "Someone who understands the implications. You think Langley would be interested?"

"Malcolm?" Ana laughed. "He's been asking about your progress for months. I'll email him tonight."

"Thanks," Daniel said. He nodded at the papers she'd been working on. "What's all this?"

Ana's eyes lit up in a way he rarely saw when she discussed work. "Remember that specialized logistics contract I was hoping for? The mRNA vaccine transport project in Singapore?"

"The one with all the temperature requirements and regulatory stuff?"

"That's the one," she said, her voice brightening. "They confirmed today. Six months with potential for renewal."

"Ana, that's fantastic!" Daniel said. It had been a while since they'd both had good news on the same day.

"It's the kind of specialized work I've been trying to own," she said, tapping the contract. "High-value shipments, time-sensitive, complex regulatory requirements, multiple border crossings—the niche I've been trying to establish."

"When do you leave?"

"Three weeks. I'll be there for about a week initially." She hesitated, then added, "The best part is, the director already mentioned bringing me in on radioactive medical isotope transport for a research facility they're building next year. If I play this right, it could lead to a whole network of similar contracts."

Daniel reached for the bag of takeout he'd brought home. "This calls for more than pho. Let me take you out tomorrow. That French place you've been wanting to try in Mountain View."

"Chez Louis? There's no way you can get a reservation this late."

"Watch me," Daniel said, pulling out his phone. "I'm a man on a mission now."

Ana laughed. "Alright, mission man. Until then, I'm starving, and that pho smells amazing."

As they unpacked the food in comfortable silence, Daniel felt something he hadn't in a long time—a sense that maybe, just maybe, everything was going to work out. His research was finally showing results, and Ana's consulting business was taking off in an incredible trajectory, better than she could have ever dreamed.

"I've been thinking," Ana said as they sat eating their pho, steam rising between them. "With both of our careers picking up momentum like this, we might need to be more intentional about our schedules. Making sure we have time for each other, and for Nat."

Daniel nodded, slurping a noodle. "You're right. Things are about to get busier for both of us."

"It's a good problem to have," Ana said. "We just need to handle it together."

"Together," Daniel agreed.

He set down his pho and studied her face. "Ana, are you still worried about… the pattern? With your competitors?" Ana's chopsticks paused halfway to her mouth. "Every day. The Singapore contract practically fell into my lap. Frankly, I don't know how we got invited to bid on it - we were contacted out of the blue. This type of logistics work is driven by relationships, and I had never met this customer."

"Maybe it's just—"

"Don't say I'm being paranoid," Ana said. "Five major competitors in six months, Daniel. All with perfectly timed emergencies right before crucial bids."

Daniel pushed his noodles around the bowl. "I know. The probability is…"

"Impossible," Ana said. "And now I'm flying to Singapore in three weeks. Alone. To a place where another competitor mysteriously couldn't go." She set down her chopsticks. "Sometimes I feel like I'm walking into a trap."

"You could turn it down," Daniel suggested, though he knew she wouldn't.

"And let whoever's doing this win?" Ana's jaw tightened. "No. But I can't shake this feeling that something's about to go very wrong."

CHAPTER 27

"Thanks for coming out here," Daniel said while leading Malcolm Langley into his office. "With the software on a closed system, I can't give demonstrations easily."

"I'm sure that's great for investment meetings," Malcolm said. He was dressed in jeans and a plain white button-up, but still managed to look polished, with his Rolex gleaming as always and his salt-and-pepper hair combed back. "Let's see what you're working with."

Malcolm's wealth, obvious in his clothes and his demeanor, made Daniel even more on edge. He felt like a teenage intern again, about to show a crappy project to a judgmental manager. Even if he had something with his upgraded chip, he had no idea if it was really marketable. If it could make real money—if it could make back all the money he'd lost developing it.

"I wanted your read on this," Daniel said.

"Your quantum chip," Malcolm said. "Does it work?"

"It works. Here." He handed Malcolm the augmented reality goggles.

Malcolm raised his eyebrows. "You still use the big goofy ones? Not the glasses-style?"

"The glasses type is expensive," Daniel said. "And fragile. I wouldn't trust half the researchers in here with those."

"Fair." Malcolm pulled the goggles on, grimacing as the strap messed up his hair. "So what am I dealing with?"

"This is Jimini," Daniel said. "He's a closed-network AI built off Castor's original codebase."

Malcolm gave him a look through the goggles.

"It's all above board," Daniel said. "I have the paperwork to prove it. Castor is… Well, Castor's far beyond what Jimini can do right now." For some reason, Daniel didn't want to tell Malcolm that Castor had progressed far beyond developer code and was now writing himself. He had no idea how Castor compared to Jimini anymore. "Jimini's mostly used for testing the capabilities of the chip, not for the kind of large-scale projects Castor is doing. Jimini is using my quantum chip, housed in that cryochiller there." He pointed to the chiller, humming happily in its glass-walled room, with the monitors tracking its temperature and computing capacity. "The chip is the culmination of all the research I've been doing and takes Jimini's computational capacity up much higher than even Castor's."

"Sounds like you've made some good movement. So what do you need me for?" Malcolm asked.

"My plan is to try to tap some large enterprise companies," Daniel said. "It's expensive to produce. Very expensive. And it's powerful. But there's a limited kind of market for this, and you know it better than I."

"Somewhat," Malcolm said.

"Ana's always said you know your stuff," Daniel said. "Are you familiar with the Traveling Salesman Problem?"

"Somewhat," Malcolm said. "How are you using it?"

"So, the idea is to find the shortest route between a list of cities," Daniel said. "It's not hard to solve when it's a small set of cities, say three or four, but every time you add a new city to the problem, you have to reevaluate every permutation of every city that you could possibly go to."

"Right."

"So if you're going to Paris, Vienna, and Berlin, you have to consider Paris to Vienna, Paris to Berlin, and Vienna to Berlin. But when you add a fourth, say Brussels, then you have to add Paris to Brussels, Berlin to Brussels, and Vienna to Brussels. So, each time you add a city, the combinatorial number of calculations explodes exponentially. So, five cities means you have to calculate four to the power of five. Six cities are five to the power of six. So the number gets out of hand very quickly."

"Hence the shortcuts," Malcolm said. "Logistics corporations group cities close together, instead of calculating each option."

"Exactly," Daniel said. "We solve it in pieces, cluster-to-cluster. And that's fairly efficient. But solutions found that way are not guaranteed to be the deterministic answer—the answer that is always correct. The only way to get the deterministic answer is to evaluate every single city and compare it with every possible route."

"But we can't do that," Malcolm said. "It's an impossible number of calculations."

"Correct. That is, with the current hardware on the market," Daniel said.

Daniel walked Malcolm through the same simulation he himself had done. Five cities: route. Twenty cities: Route. Fifty: route. He pushed it further—a hundred cities. Route.

He watched and allowed himself to feel a little bit proud as Malcolm's eyes slowly widened as the problem was made more and more complex and solved with the same near immediacy as it had been the first time.

When the demonstration was complete, Malcolm took the goggles off and dropped down into Daniel's chair. His eyes were still wide, and his face had gone pale. His lack of reaction otherwise was a little unnerving.

Daniel rubbed the back of his neck. "I don't know where to go for more funding," he admitted. "I've knocked on every door on Sand Hill Road and been turned down. Continuing development on this is going to be expensive, and I'm afraid I exhausted all my options too early. They're not going to believe I have anything."

"Do you understand what you have here?" Malcolm said in a low voice.

Daniel said nothing. He thought he did, but Malcolm's expression made him doubt himself.

"What that chip is doing in there" —He pointed at the chiller— "is the work of entire data centers. Companies are leasing buildings to do what you're doing with a closed-network AI and a single chip." Malcolm stood up and raked both hands through his hair, mussing it. "Do you know how many industries this will revolutionize? Commercial aviation! Shipping logistics! Jesus Christ — finance! This isn't some kind of boutique product for enterprise companies, Daniel. This will change the landscape of the Bay Area entirely." He turned his gaze to Daniel, suddenly sharp with interest. "You don't need investment, Daniel. You need support. You need a team of people who can help you bring this technology to market."

Daniel took a step back. Daniel had hoped for ideas for monetizing, but this surge of almost mad-eyed urgency made him a little nervous. "I'm not sure if this chip is replicable yet, especially not on a large scale. And I don't have a team—I was kicked out of my team. You know that. That's the only reason any of this was able to happen."

"And now it's time for you to take it back to them," Malcolm said.

The thought of crawling back to Jonah made Daniel itch with frustration. "Help me understand," he said. "If it's such a gamechanger, why aren't you interested in investing?"

"You didn't knock on my door on Sand Hill," Malcolm shot back, but then he smiled a practiced smile, and his usual calm demeanor returned. "I invest in startups, Daniel. Companies. You're not a company, despite having the paperwork. You're a guy with a product. A really, really good product—but it's not a business, and it needs to be. If I invested in you now, I have a feeling you'd blow the investment before you were able to scale this chip."

"So I have a great product and no one to invest in it," Daniel said.

"Call Jonah," Malcolm said. "Show him what you've done here. If Castor is as good as I've heard it is, access to that AI will help your development."

Daniel glanced at the goggles lying on his desk. As much as he appreciated—or loved—Jimini, he still found himself wondering about Castor. With Castor's access to the wider web and his ability to self-develop, Daniel longed to see what he was capable of now.

"You haven't asked Regillus for an investment, have you?" Malcolm asked.

"Of course not."

"Then you're in perfect shape to do so now. Get your funding, get a team, and keep pushing." Malcolm stared at the chiller like he couldn't believe it was real. "Once you have a real company, we can talk about further funding."

They shook hands. Malcolm squeezed Daniel's firmly—a little too firmly—and fixed him with a serious look. "I know what happened to Promethean wasn't ideal. But this…" Again his gaze tracked to the chiller. "This is the real Prometheus' fire, Daniel. Don't underestimate what you have. But don't let your ego get in the way of seeing it come to fruition."

"I appreciate the insight," Daniel said.

He showed Malcolm out of the lab, then returned to his workspace. He wiped down the goggles with tech cleaner, then slid them on himself and sat back in his chair. "Jimini, play something to relax me." Gentle piano filtered through bone conduction headphones and reverberated through Daniel's skull: an Erik Satie composition, pulled from his own collection.

The meeting had left a sourness in his mouth, but there was a thrill there, too. Malcolm believed in him, in his own condescending-asshole way. If he had to speak to Jonah to convince Malcolm to invest, he'd do that. He wouldn't work with Jonah—not after what Jonah had done to him-but he'd check the box to show Malcolm he was trying all options. Plus, if Malcolm's assessment of the chip's scalability was correct, this was a chance to show Jonah what he'd missed out on. If this chip was something revolutionary, he could've been building it for Regillus. Regillus could've been the ones to change the industry.

But instead, Daniel had done it himself.

CHAPTER 28

"This is a pretty nice place," Jonah said. He peered through the glass walls and at the chiller, humming like a sleeping beast in its chambers. "So this is where your money went?"

Daniel's lips twitched as he held back a smile. The chiller was peanuts compared to the money he'd spent on fabricating versions of what he was now calling the Bennett chip. "Looks pretty nice, doesn't it? It's been helpful for some of the biomedical researchers working here, too."

"Regillus has been moving back in that direction, too." Jonah turned and leaned against Daniel's desk, uncaring of jostling any notebooks or mugs languishing on its surface. "Some cool stuff going on."

"Yeah?" Daniel asked. "How's Castor?"

In a way, he was asking about an estranged child. He missed working with Castor, missed seeing his rapid development and unexpected optimizations. Even if the AI wasn't moving in the direction he wanted, it was still moving without him, and that still hurt.

"The product is more valuable than we ever imagined," Jonah said. "And more powerful. Emmet's national security project has taken off, and he has an entire team of developers working on it. The finance team has exploded—we opened a branch in New York to solely focus on that. It's given us more flexibility in the larger company mission."

"What does that mean?" Daniel asked.

"We can allocate some resources to newer, riskier programs," Jonah said. "Climate stuff. I've got a team working collaboratively with a solar energy company to identify locations and risk factors for new facilities. Keeping their projects on time and under budget. In Singapore, we're piloting a program that uses Castor's tech to manage traffic. Reducing congestion and improving air quality. That kind of thing. And healthcare, too."

"You're getting back into healthcare?"

"In small ways," Jonah said. "Contingent on what kinds of partnerships we can build, and what's best for Castor's abilities. We're working on drug dosing right now, optimizing dosage and timing for patients in long-term care to try to reduce instances of addiction."

Daniel hummed but said nothing.

"I know you thought I'd never go back to the healthcare space," Jonah said, "but I meant it when I said I would. We had to get our feet under us. I know this is what Robert wanted."

"He always wanted Castor to be a healthcare tool," Daniel said. It wasn't quite an agreement nor a disagreement—just a statement of fact. He recognized the conversation for what it was. Jonah was trying to offer him an olive branch, trying to prove that even though he'd pushed Daniel out of Regillus, he was still holding on to Robert's memory. Daniel didn't agree that dosing out drugs was the same as the extensive early-prevention tactics that Robert had envisioned but arguing that point would get him nowhere.

"So what has Bennett Tech been working on?" Jonah asked. "Hardware, right?"

"Hardware and software both," Daniel said. "It's easier if I show you."

He led Jonah into the small office, which Daniel privately considered to be Jimini's. It was intended to be a storage closet in his portion of the Stanford lab space, but instead, he had converted it into a small, empty room that he used to easily interface with the AI in augmented reality. Using it in the open space of his lab was fine, but sometimes, he wanted a little privacy if he would be waving his arms around and talking to Jimini. He picked the two pairs of AR goggles off their chargers and handed one to Jonah. They both put the goggles on, and Jonah peered around the room expectantly.

"Wait," Jonah said before Daniel could begin the demonstration. "You keep mentioning surface treatments. Why are those so critical to your chip design?"

"Imagine trying to hear a whispered conversation from across a crowded room," Daniel explained. "That's what a quantum computer does—it listens for the faintest quantum signals. Any imperfection in the chip's surface is like someone coughing or shuffling papers, drowning out the whispers we're trying to hear."

Jonah nodded slowly, seeming to grasp the analogy.

"Traditional chips can tolerate minor imperfections—it's like listening to someone shouting; a little background noise doesn't matter. But quantum signals are so delicate that even atomic-level impurities are like blaring sirens that make computation impossible. What I'll be testing is like creating a perfect acoustic chamber that eliminates every possible source of noise."

"And you've found a way to achieve that?" Jonah asked.

"That's what we're about to demonstrate," Daniel said, turning back to the AR goggles.

"Hi, Jimini," Daniel said.

A pale light blinked in the upper corner of the lens, and then the projector embedded in the frames came to life. The projection was a new addition to Jimini's tech. Instead of a disembodied voice in his ears, Jimini now appeared as a lean, wire-frame figure, androgynous, with pale eyes and a playful tilt to his mouth.

"Hello, Daniel and friend," Jimini said.

"This is my colleague, Jonah," Daniel said.

"Nice to meet you, Jonah," Jimini said. "I'm Jimini, a closed-network artificial intelligence aiding Daniel in his research."

Jonah whipped his head around to Daniel. "Where'd you get this?"

"Daniel wrote my code himself," Jimini said.

"He's based on the earliest version of Castor," Daniel said.

Something angry flickered in Jonah's eyes.

"The earliest version was my property," Daniel said. "It wasn't until version 2 that he became property of Promethean. I have the paperwork to prove it." He sighed. "I'm not trying to steal from you, Jonah. Jimini's not networked like Castor is. He's just a proof-of-concept."

"Proof of what?" Jonah asked. He didn't sound convinced.

Daniel resisted the urge to roll his eyes. Jimini's capabilities were nothing compared to what Castor could do, simply because Castor had access to more information and, as a result, had a stronger capability to write his own code. All Jimini needed to do was calculate—and as a result, show what the Bennett chip could do. "Are you familiar with the knapsack problem?"

"I've heard the devs mention it."

"Jimini, can you give us a brief explanation of the knapsack problem, including an example that illustrates its name?"

"I'd be happy to," Jimini said. He looked between Daniel and Jonah, then folded his wire-frame fingers together. "Here's an example. Imagine you're preparing for a camping trip. You have a knapsack of limited size in which to pack your items. You have many items to choose from, such as a lighter, a tent, and snacks. Each item has a weight and a value for your trip. Your goal is to pack the knapsack so you do not exceed its weight limitations, while also gaining the most value from the items you choose. This problem is simple to solve with a few items. But with more items, the number of possible combinations increases exponentially. If you have twenty items, you must check over one million combinations. Is that a clear explanation?"

"Pretty clear, yeah," Jonah said.

"Thank you, Jimini," Daniel said. He turned to Jonah. "It's used in computing for that reason. Once you get into hundreds or thousands of items, the sheer number of combinations makes it unsolvable. Standard computers can't keep up."

"I'm with you," Jonah said.

"Jimini, imagine we have a standard semi-truck trailer. We want to fill the trailer with the contents of Stanford's cafeteria warehouse. The warehouse's inventory of 100,000 food items has been loaded into your memory. We want to fill the trailer with optimal items, using the parameters of the knapsack problem. If we were to ask a standard computer to do this, how long would it take?"

"A standard computer could not solve this problem before the heat death of the universe." Jimini smiled.

"Can you?"

"Certainly. I have generated a shipping manifest of 20,000 items," Jimini said. The document appeared in a spreadsheet, overlaid on the goggles. "Here it is for your perusal, and it is also accessible via your workstation."

Jonah stared at the list. "This is correct?" he asked. "Jimini made this now? It's not a gag you set up?"

"We can run a few more tests and you can take the results to Castor to check, if you want," Daniel said.

Jonah was still staring at it. "That's probably wise," he said. "Emmet will also need to take a look."

Daniel had Jimini solve a few more problems, then load the information and the answers into a zip file. Then he dismissed Jimini, who disappeared with a friendly wave. The two of them took off their goggles and stepped out of the office. Daniel sat down at his desk and loaded the files onto a spare thumb drive. When he turned in his chair, Jimini still looked stunned, his gaze fixed on the chiller again.

"Why did you show me this?" Jonah asked. "Why did you invite me here?"

"Funding," Daniel said, even as it hurt his ego to say it. "I took the chip to other investors before it was ready, and now they're hesitant to give me the time of day again."

"Have they seen this?" Jonah asked.

"No."

"I see." Jonah ripped his gaze from the chiller and turned to Daniel. "Sell it to me."

"What?" Daniel rolled his chair back. "It's not ready."

"You've done enough work on it," Jonah said. "Sell it to Regillus and pass on the development to our team. I'll make sure Emmet is leading the project. It's ready to be integrated into a more valuable AI like Castor—how much work is there left to do?"

Daniel scowled. "What? It's not scalable yet. I'm not even sure that I can make more of them yet. I made it clear when I was at Prometheus that the research I was working on could be transformative, and you made it clear you didn't think that was true at all. If I had been doing this on company time, it'd be yours. But it's Bennett Tech, and I'm not selling it. I'm funding its development."

"Why do you need the funding so badly?" Jonah asked. "How's Bennett Tech's financial health?"

Daniel's scowl deepened. Had word of his rejections gotten around? For as big as San Francisco was, it was like a small town in a lot of ways.

"Listen, I'm big enough to admit when I'm wrong," Jonah said. "You were right about this chip. You've got a chip and a room of servers, and Regillus has an entire building of them. And I bet Emmet will tell me our computers couldn't do this."

"They couldn't," Daniel said.

"So you were right," Jonah said. "I see that now. And you can sell this technology to Regillus and be in a better financial spot than you ever imagined. You'd never have to work another day in your life. Or, if you want, I could set you up to take over Promethean as its new CEO… or take over for me when I retire from Regillus. I don't want to work forever, even if you do."

Daniel did, in fact, want to keep working. But more than that, he wanted this chip to be his. Completely. He wanted Ana to see he had built this damned thing himself. "I'm not interested in selling this to you, Jonah. I want to keep working on it. If you want access to the Bennett chip, I need funding."

They stared at each other. Daniel crossed his arms over his chest. He wasn't going to let Jonah bulldoze him—not anymore. Not for something as important as this.

Jonah met his gaze, and then suddenly his face broke into a grin. He took a step forward and extended his hand. "Fine. Stubborn bastard. This is new for you."

Daniel stood and shook his outstretched hand. "Is that a yes?"

"I'll talk to the board," Jonah said. "Regillus likes to acquire, not fund. But if I can get Emmet to vouch for this breakthrough, they might see things your way."

"Good," Daniel said. He handed Jonah the thumb drive. "This is encrypted. Password's in your email."

Jonah nodded and shook the thumb drive in recognition. "Thanks. I'll be in touch."

In the quiet of his office, Daniel turned back to his computer. The password he had generated for the thumb drive was sixteen characters, letters, numbers, and symbols – highly secure. If he asked, Daniel was confident that Jimini could crack it in moments.

CHAPTER 29

"These don't even look good!" Natasha said with a scowl. She rolled over on the futon, phone on her pillow as she scrolled through the screenshots Caleb had just sent over at her request.

The screenshots were of deepfakes: manipulated images of Natasha's face on bodies that weren't her own. None of the photos were super explicit—yet—just very suggestive. Low-cut shirts, cleavage, tiny shorts. And those images were being posted on Snapchat, on Telegram, with her own phone number. She'd already changed it twice, and the messages still kept coming in asking her about buying more photos or sexting. Sometimes they sent dick pics.

"I told you not to look at them," Caleb said. She tapped back into the video call and was met with her boyfriend's smiling face. It'd been a year, but it still gave her butterflies to think that. Caleb, her boyfriend. "Have you thought about telling your stepdad?" Caleb asked. "I mean, he works with computers and AI stuff, right? Maybe he could help track down who's doing this."

Natasha let out a bitter laugh. "Daniel? Are you serious?"

"What? He's got to know about this stuff—"

"He doesn't know I exist anymore," Natasha said, her voice sharp. "Ever since he started Bennett Tech, it's been like I'm invisible."

"But this is serious, Nat. These deepfakes—"

"You think I don't know that?" She sat up quickly from the futon, face flushing. "You know what happened last month? I waited up until 2 AM to talk to him about college. He came home, saw me in the kitchen, and said,

'Not now, Nat, I've got Taiwan calling in five hours.' Then he went straight to his office."

Caleb was quiet.

"He made all these promises after Mom called him out," Natasha continued, the words tumbling out. "How he would be present, be a real parent, actually show up. And for like two minutes, he was great. Then he started his own company and boom—ghost dad again."

"That's messed up," Caleb said.

"I know, but I can't rely on anyone else to handle this. I learned that lesson already. It makes me feel better to know what's out there. At least then I'm in control of something." She heaved herself up to her feet and carried the phone to the kitchen. Dad's Tokyo apartment was a tiny one-bedroom, and the galley kitchen was a part of the living room. At least it had a small balcony, though, ideal for drying the laundry and letting a cross-breeze in. Natasha opened the balcony door, then propped the phone on the kitchen counter and got to work making her breakfast of eggs and rice. Dad had already left for work, so she was alone in the apartment.

"It's so gross. I'm sorry you have to deal with this."

"You're sorry? None of this is your fault!"

"Yeah, but no matter what we do, it doesn't seem to get any better. It's like playing whack-a-mole. I find one account posting the pics, and four more appear out of nowhere. Sometimes I think it'll never end."

"It will," Caleb said. "It has to."

Natasha said nothing.

"What are you thinking about?" Caleb asked. "You've got that look on your face."

"I don't know. I just… It's so gross. And violating. And sometimes I'm afraid…" She trailed off. She didn't want to tell Caleb this as much as she really did want to. "Sometimes I'm afraid you'll get tired of dealing with it."

Silence on the other end of the call. She cracked an egg into the small pan and watched it sizzle.

"And what then?" Caleb asked. "You think I'll stop trying to help?"

"Yeah. Or move on."

"Move on? Like break up?"

"Yeah. I mean, my own stepfather can't be bothered to care about me. Why would my boyfriend stick around for this mess?"

"Nat—"

"I'm serious. Daniel's shown me how much I matter when things get difficult. Work comes first. Always. And now with these deepfakes…" She swallowed hard. "I keep waiting for you to realize I'm too much trouble."

"Don't be stupid," Caleb said. "Can you look at me?"

Natasha looked up. Caleb was frowning. His handsome face was washed out by the fluorescent light of his secondhand desk lamp. There were dark circles under his eyes—he'd been studying for hours before the call.

"We'll get through this," Caleb said. "It sucks. And whoever is doing this is an asshole. But it's not going to last forever, okay? I'm not going anywhere."

That brought a small smile to her face. "Thanks. I know that. Logically. But this is just… It's all really hard. And sometimes I don't think it ever will get better." She sighed. "I wish we could just be together in the real world, instead of on video calls half the year." Between family travel and archery travel, she hadn't seen Caleb in person in months.

"Where should that be?" Caleb asked.

"I don't know, maybe here in Japan?" She opened the rice cooker and spooned some into the bowl. "I love Tokyo. The food's great. Lots of hiking, too. And the traditional archery is cool. And honestly? Part of why I want to go is to be somewhere Daniel can't pretend to care while doing absolutely nothing. At least with Dad in Okinawa, when I visit, he's actually present. He doesn't check his phone during dinner or disappear into his office the second we get home."

"Would Daniel notice if you left?"

Natasha laughed, but it was hollow. "Probably not until Mom told him. And then, he'd just throw money at it. 'Here's a credit card for emergencies, Nat.' As if money equals parenting."

"I like Japan," Caleb said, smiling. "Seems like it'd be fun."

She let herself imagine it. Maybe she'd go to university here, get a little apartment of her own… A one-bedroom she could share with Caleb while he was in school too.

Another call flashed on her screen, jerking her out of her thoughts. "It's Mom," Natasha said. "Ugh."

"Take her call," Caleb said. "I've got to keep studying, anyway."

Natasha exhaled slowly, steadying herself and pushing the deepfakes out of her mind. "Okay. I'll call you later. My night, your morning."

Caleb saluted her playfully, then ended the call.

Natasha considered letting the call ring but answered it right before it went to voicemail. "Hey, Mom, what's up?"

"Just calling to check in," Mom said. "Is everything okay? You sound down."

"I'm fine," Natasha said. There was no way in hell she'd tell Mom about the deepfakes, or the mean old meme account that was still occasionally posting. Mom had enough on her plate. "Everything's good. How's Singapore?"

CHAPTER 30

Singapore was a beautiful country. It was clean, organized, and well-managed—a logistical manager's dream. The sleek outdoor terrace of the restaurant where Ana sat overlooked Marina Bay, with its iconic skyline gleaming in the afternoon sun. She checked her watch; Yelena was running late, as usual.

When Yelena finally hurried in, her box braids pulled back into a practical ponytail, Ana couldn't help but smile. Some things never change, even after all these years.

"I know, I know," Yelena said, sliding into the seat across from Ana. "The testing ran long. We're implementing a new AI module for the traffic control system, and it's being… Temperamental."

"And they can't do anything without the project lead, can they?" Ana teased.

"Something like that." Yelena signaled for a waiter. "God, it's good to see you. How long has it been? Six months?"

"Eight. You missed my last trip because you were in Tokyo for that conference."

The waiter appeared, and they ordered—Ana choosing a light salad, mindful of her client meeting later, while Yelena went for something more substantial.

"So," Yelena said once they were alone again, "How's the consulting business going? Still specializing in impossible logistics problems?"

Ana smiled. "That's what pays the bills. I'm here for the vaccine shipping contract, actually. Temperature-controlled transport across Southeast Asia, with chain-of-custody documentation and multiple border crossings. The kind of puzzle everyone else runs from."

"And exactly the kind of thing you're brilliant at." Yelena shook her head in admiration. "Remember when you were juggling full-time work, night classes, and single parenthood? I used to watch you map out your days down to the minute."

Ana laughed. "You were the one who bought me my first proper planner. Said my system of sticky notes all over our apartment was driving you crazy."

"Our shoebox apartment in Oakland," Yelena corrected. "God, those were the days. Me fresh out of college with my shiny new computer science degree, you discharged from the military, racing between your job and classes while little Nat drew with her crayons at the kitchen table."

"She wasn't so little. Already had that stubborn streak."

"Wonder where she got that from?" Yelena raised an eyebrow. "I still remember you staying up until two in the morning finishing papers after Nat went to bed. All while working full-time."

"Had to get that degree somehow." Ana's voice softened. "Viktor wasn't exactly reliable with child support back then."

"And now look at you," Yelena said. "Running your own specialized logistics firm, jetting all over Asia for high-value contracts. You did it, Ana."

Their food arrived, momentarily pausing the conversation.

"What about you?" Ana asked. "Leading developer for Singapore's fancy new AI traffic control system? That's quite a step up."

"It's exciting work," Yelena said. "We're using machine learning algorithms to optimize traffic flow across the entire island. Considering Singapore has limited space and an ever-growing population, the government is invested in making it work."

"Hence why you can afford to take me to lunch at places like this now," Ana said with a smirk.

"Hey, this is a legitimate business expense. I'm consulting with an international logistics expert about optimization strategies."

"Is that what we're doing?"

"For about five minutes of this lunch, yes. The rest is catching up with my favorite former roommate."

They both laughed, falling back into the easy rhythm of their long friendship.

"Nat's still researching colleges?" Yelena asked. "Last time we talked, she was going on and on about schools in Japan."

"She's still set on going abroad. I think she's trying to find her own path, away from both Daniel's and Viktor's influences. Can't blame her for that."

"And how are things with Daniel?"

Ana hesitated. "He's… Working a lot. His chip project is taking over everything. Again."

"Hmm." Yelena didn't push, but her expression was knowing. "Men and their projects."

"It's not that." Ana sighed. "He's distracted. Keeping things from me. I can feel it."

"Have you talked to him about it?"

"Tried. He deflects. Says it's work stress." Ana shook her head. "Anyway, I'm taking Nat with me on the trip back to the Bay Area next week. Thought we could use some mother-daughter time before she gets too busy with finals."

Yelena nodded. "Good idea. Speaking of which, when's your client meeting? I don't want to make you late."

Ana checked her watch again. "I only have about an hour here with you. My meeting's at the convention center near the airport."

"Perfect timing. I need to tell you about this new guy I'm seeing."

Ana laughed. "Now we're getting to the real reason for this lunch."

They spent the rest of the meal catching up on Yelena's love life and reminiscing about their days as roommates. As they finished, Yelena insisted on paying.

"My expense account can handle it," she said, waving away Ana's protest. "Besides, you really did give me some useful insights about optimization patterns."

"If you say so." Ana stood, gathering her bag. "Dinner before I leave town?"

"Absolutely. Text me when you're done with your meeting."

They hugged goodbye, and Ana made her way to the taxi stand outside the restaurant. The afternoon sun was intense now, and she was grateful for the air conditioning in the cab that pulled up.

"Convention center, please," she told the driver. "The one near Changi."

As the taxi pulled away from the curb, she decided to call Nat.

The call connected after two rings.

"Mom?" Nat answered, sounding surprised. "I thought you had meetings all day."

"Heading to one now." Ana adjusted her earpiece. "Just finished lunch with Yelena."

"Auntie Yelena is there?"

Ana laughed. "For now, she is. She was asking about you. She's working on some fancy traffic AI system here."

"Cool," Nat said, though her tone suggested minimal interest. "So what's up?"

"Just checking in," Ana said, trying to keep her voice casual. "How's everything with your dad?"

"Fine. We're going to that archery range I told you about later."

"That sounds fun." Ana paused, watching the city pass by outside the taxi window. The taxi approached a large four-way intersection. The light had just turned green, and they began to move forward.

From here, Ana could see the convention center sparkling, a tall block of metal and glass glittering in the sunlight. "Sure. Hey, I was thinking, when I get back, maybe we could—"

The world exploded in screeching metal and breaking glass.

Ana's phone went flying. There was a deafening crash as a truck slammed into the side of the taxi, sending it spinning across the intersection. Through the chaos, the last thing Ana heard was Nat's voice, tiny and distant from the fallen phone, screaming, "Mom? MOM! What's happening?!"

Everything went black.

CHAPTER 31

Viktor Karlsen jerked upright in his desk chair when he heard Natasha's scream from the next room. He moved with military precision, covering the distance to her bedroom in three long strides.

She was hunched over her phone, face contorted in horror. "Mom—Mom! Mom, answer me!"

"Natasha, what's happening?" Viktor asked, kneeling beside her.

Her wide, terrified eyes met his. "Mom was on the phone with me. We were talking and then there was this horrible crash sound and she screamed and now there's sirens and she's not answering—" The words tumbled out between sobs.

Viktor gently took the phone. The call was still connected, but all he could hear was the distant wail of emergency vehicles and muffled voices.

"Ana?" he tried. Nothing. Just chaos in the background.

"Dad, is she—" Natasha couldn't finish the sentence.

"Let's not jump to conclusions," Viktor said, his combat training kicking in. "We need information first." He put the phone on speaker and set it on the desk, then pulled out his own. "Who would know where she is? Who was she meeting today?"

"Auntie Yelena," Natasha said. "They were having lunch."

Viktor scrolled through Natasha's contacts, finding 'Auntie Yelena' quickly. He also noted 'Absent Father' in her contacts and realized that must be Daniel. Despite the circumstances, he couldn't help but feel a flicker of vindication at the label.

He called Yelena first, explaining the situation in clipped, efficient sentences.

"I just saw her off," Yelena said, voice rising in panic. "She was heading to the convention center near the airport. Oh god, she would have been on the PIE."

"We need to find out which hospital they're taking her to," Viktor said. "Can you make those calls? We're in Tokyo, but we'll get on the first flight out."

After ending the call, he turned to Natasha, who sat frozen, still staring at the phone where the call with her mother had disconnected.

"Tater," he said, using the nickname that had stuck since she was two. "You need to pack a bag while I book our flights. Your mom is tough. Whatever happened, she's going to fight."

While Natasha moved mechanically to pack, Viktor called Daniel from his own phone, where he was neatly labeled 'Daniel Bennett' instead of 'Absent Father.'

Daniel answered on the third ring, sounding surprised. The two men didn't often communicate, and when they did, it was only for logistical reasons of sharing custody of Natasha. "Viktor? Everything okay?"

"I'm afraid not," he said. "There's been an accident. Ana's been hurt in Singapore." He relayed what little they knew, noting how Daniel's breathing changed as the information sank in.

"I'll get on the next flight out," Daniel said.

"So will we," Viktor said. "I don't know what we'll find when we get there."

The next few hours passed in a blur of activity—booking flights, arranging transport, and checking with Yelena for updates. By the time they reached the boarding gate, Viktor's phone rang again. It was Yelena.

"She's at National University Hospital," Yelena said. "Conscious but injured. Concussion, bruised rib, lots of minor sprains, strains, cuts, and bruises. They're keeping her for observation."

The relief that flooded through Viktor was physical, like a weight lifted from his chest. He relayed the news to Natasha, who collapsed into a chair, tears streaming down her face.

"She's going to be okay," he assured her, though he knew head injuries were unpredictable. "She's getting good care."

During the flight, with Natasha fitfully dozing beside him, Viktor found himself thinking about Ana's resilience—a quality their daughter had inherited but perhaps didn't fully recognize yet.

"Tater," he said when she woke, "did I ever tell you about the time your mom saved an entire refugee camp in Afghanistan?"

Natasha rubbed her eyes. "The one where she got hurt?"

"Yeah." Viktor smiled. "We were stationed near a village that had become home to hundreds of displaced families. Your mom wasn't just providing medical care. She was teaching local women to be community health workers. She knew every child by name."

He described how insurgents had targeted the camp, how Ana had been wounded by shrapnel when an IED exploded near the medical tent.

"The medevac couldn't reach them because of the fighting," he continued. "So your mom, bleeding through her bandages, set up a field hospital in what was left of the school building. She worked for twenty-six hours straight, saving everyone she could reach. When I finally found her, she was still performing triage, even though she could barely stand."

"That's why she got the Purple Heart," Natasha said.

Viktor nodded. "And the Meritorious Service Medal. The brass wanted to give her more, but you know your mom. She insisted she was 'just doing her job.'"

A small smile touched Natasha's lips. "She never talks about it."

"No, she wouldn't." Viktor looked out at the clouds passing beneath them. "Ana doesn't dwell on the past. It's what made her such a good soldier, and why she's thrived since leaving the service. She keeps moving forward." He squeezed his daughter's hand. "That's why I know she'll be okay now. Your mom doesn't know how to do anything else."

For the first time since the panicked call, Natasha's expression eased minutely. "Yeah," she said. "You're right."

Viktor leaned back in his seat, feeling the familiar mix of pride and regret that thoughts of Ana always brought him. Their marriage hadn't survived his multiple deployments and the distance they created—not physically, but emotionally. Yet somehow, they'd found a way to be better co-parents apart than they had been partners together. He respected her too much to do anything less.

And if he occasionally felt a twinge of satisfaction that her second husband seemed unable to prioritize family over work—well, that was his business alone.

CHAPTER 32

Daniel rushed through the gleaming glass doors of the Singapore National University Hospital.

He was haggard and exhausted after a seventeen-hour flight from San Francisco. He'd received a call from Ana's ex-husband, Viktor, and had gotten on the first flight he could book. Viktor had given Daniel the news about Ana's accident and let him know he was on the way with Nat. He promised he would be in touch if necessary. Nat hadn't responded to his messages.

He hiked his backpack higher on his shoulder. It was the only bag he'd brought: a change of clothes, a few toiletries, his phone, wallet, passport, and something small for Natasha. Anything else he needed, he could buy in Singapore. He'd run out the door like a madman. He'd taken a cab straight from the airport to the hospital.

"Ana Bishop?" Daniel said to the polished woman at the desk. The lobby of the hospital was clean and quiet, with a few patients in cushioned chairs, and medical professionals bustling in and out.

The woman's manicured nails tapped across the keyboard. "Your name?"

Daniel's grip tightened on the strap of his bag. "Daniel Bennett. She's my wife."

The woman seemed uninterested. She slid a name tag across the counter to Daniel, had him sign a document, and then gave him directions to the big, shiny elevator at the back of the hall.

In the elevator, Daniel slumped against the wall and took a slow breath. None of this felt real. It felt like a horrible nightmare. The call still echoed in his mind. Yelena's shaky voice. T-boned. She's hurt. I don't know how bad it is.

He rushed down the hall, past the nurse's station, following the signs to the room at the end of the hall. He knocked once, then pushed the door open.

The room was dim inside. His attention first zeroed in on Ana, asleep, propped up in the hospital bed. There was a cannula in her nose, providing oxygen, and an IV in her arm, dripping slowly. The monitor next to her bed displayed graphs and numbers, none of which meant anything to Daniel, but the steady beeping of the machine seemed to echo a normal heartbeat. There were a few bandages on her face, and underneath the edges, white gauze; a dark bruise was visible. One wrist was splinted, and her arms were dotted with gauze and tape as well.

"Finally," Natasha grumbled, glancing up from her phone. At sixteen, she had perfected the art of passive-aggressiveness. She leaned against Viktor's shoulder and returned her attention to her phone. The blue light shadowed her face from below and made the bags under her eyes even more noticeable.

"Hi, Dan," Viktor said. "Flight okay?"

"Fine," Daniel said. "Yours?"

"Fine." Viktor nodded.

Seated in the small, hard-backed chair by the wall, Viktor Karlsen looked even larger than he usually did. He was a tall, broad-shouldered man with a lined face that made him look older than he was, after years of military service in Iraq, Afghanistan, and many other places that he couldn't discuss. His dark hair was graying, but his hairline was still intact. He was wearing a plain black sweatshirt and jeans but still carried himself with a straight-backed confidence. Daniel didn't dislike Viktor, but they weren't friends. If not for Natasha, Daniel would've been happy to see Viktor exit his and Ana's lives forever. He was glad Natasha was here with her mom. But a frustrated, jealous part of him still hated that Viktor had gotten here first. It was simple logistics—Japan was closer to Singapore than California—but a nasty voice inside Daniel still whispered *You should've been here.*

Daniel sat down in the free chair on the other side of Ana's bedside, then reached over and gently grasped her small, warm hand. She didn't stir. He looked across the bed at his stepdaughter. "You okay, Nat?"

She sniffed and didn't answer. Viktor caught his eye and gave a short, stiff nod.

The door opened again. A short, trim doctor with thick glasses stepped inside. "Mr. Bennett?" he said. "You are the patient's husband?"

"Yes." Daniel clambered to his feet, reluctant as he was to let Ana's hand go. He looked at her, then at Viktor and Nat. "Can we speak outside?"

"Certainly," the doctor said.

They stepped into the hall. In the evening hour, it was quiet, with the bustle of a few nurses moving between their station and the patient rooms. The doctor shifted his clipboard into one hand and peered down at his notes. "As you know, your wife was involved in a fairly severe motor vehicle accident." The doctor's English was sharp and lilting; the polished Singaporean accent was familiar to Daniel's ears.

"I flew here as quickly as I could," Daniel said. "From San Francisco. California."

The doctor didn't acknowledge that. "She was quite lucky," he said. "She has a moderate concussion, a bruised rib, and internal bruising to the liver. She also has quite a few other, minor injuries."

"Jesus," Daniel muttered.

"Beyond that, the injuries are mostly superficial," he said. "Bruising, minor lacerations on her face, arms, and scalp, and a sprained wrist. Our team was primarily concerned with the head injury. We'd like to keep her for observation for a few days, at least. Her... Other family connection...?"

"Her ex-husband," Daniel supplied. "Our daughter's father."

The doctor nodded. "He explained your wife is traveling here in Singapore. Is that correct?"

"Yes. We live in California."

"I don't recommend she fly until she's more recovered."

"How long will that take?"

"It's hard to say with head trauma. Every patient is different." He looked up from his notes. "Right now, rest is imperative. We expect she will recover well, but it will take time."

"Can you at least give me a ballpark?" Daniel asked. "I've got to book a hotel…" That, on top of what felt like a million other logistics. He had a feeling he'd end up buying half of a new wardrobe in Singapore.

"Around a week," the doctor said after a pause. "But that's not a guarantee. We'll need to manage her recovery, create a pain management plan, and do more imaging on her ribs and liver once she has healed some."

"Thank you, doctor," Daniel said. They shook hands, and the doctor hurried down the hall, already pulling out a cell phone and speaking into it.

Daniel scrubbed his hands over his face and stepped back into the hospital room. There was no change. Ana was still asleep, Nat still had her nose in her phone, and Viktor was still watching the monitor by her bed as if it might give them some additional information about Ana's health. He squeezed Nat's knee, then stood up and rolled his shoulders. The flight from Japan was about eight hours—how long had they been in this hospital room with her?

"I'm going to run down to the cafeteria for provisions," Viktor said. "Want anything, Tater?"

"I'm good," Nat said without looking up. "I'll get a hot chocolate later."

Viktor nodded. He clapped Daniel on the shoulder and left the room, closing the door behind him.

As glad as Daniel was to have the privacy, it still irritated him that Viktor had been the one to give it to them. The nickname lingered in the air like a bad smell. It was another private language between Viktor and Nat, and another reminder of the relationship Daniel didn't have with her. The one he was trying to live up to. He slid into the seat Victor had vacated. In the bed they both faced, Ana was still deeply asleep.

Daniel slid his backpack into his lap and unzipped it. "Brought you something."

Nat finally locked her phone and put it aside. "I packed at Dad's."

"I know. Sorry it took me so long to get here, Nat."

"It's not your fault. You can't make the planes fly faster." Her voice was flat, and she kept her eyes fixed on the hospital bed. She was right, of course, but from the stiff line of her shoulders, it was clear she didn't really feel that way.

"Here." He withdrew a small cream-colored bear from his bag. The doll was about the size of his fist, missing one eye, and its fur was matted in places from being packed away and stained from a recent coffee spill. Nat carried it around less these days, but the little bear had accompanied her to scary dentist appointments, important exams, and archery meets. "Thought you might want this."

Her eyes widened briefly. "Did you go into my room?"

Daniel scoffed. "Of course not. You left him on the dining room table before you left." She'd been posted up there finishing up an application with the bear for moral support.

"Oh, right." She took the bear from his hands and smoothed her thumb over its head, right between its round ears. "Thank you."

"You doing okay, kiddo?"

"I guess so," she said after a long moment. "I'm scared."

"Me, too," Daniel said. "But the doctor said she'll be okay. She just needs a lot of rest."

"I wish she'd wake up." Nat sniffed, suddenly, her voice watery. "She hasn't woken up the entire time we've been here."

Daniel wrapped an arm around Nat's shoulders and pulled her close. To his surprise, she slumped against him and let another shaky breath. They stayed like that for a few moments, both of them watching the gentle rise and fall of Ana's chest as she slept.

"Tell me about Japan," Daniel said. "How's your trip been?"

Nat worked her hands over the little bear. She seemed grateful for the distraction as she told Daniel about the archery ranges Victor had taken her to around Japan. She was learning more traditional techniques, she said, like kyudo, and the more skills she learned, the more she wanted to learn about the history behind it.

"So I'm thinking about, for my applications—"

"Mm? Nat?" Ana's voice was rough with sleep.

"Mom!" Nat said, at the same time Daniel said, "Ana!" They both turned toward the bed and scooted their chairs closer. Nat took Ana's hand, while Daniel rested a hand on her thigh through the thin hospital blanket.

Ana grimaced, her eyebrows pulling together. "Jesus," she muttered. "I feel like shit."

Nat snorted, which sounded like a sob had been wrestled into a laugh unexpectedly at the last second. "You look like shit, too."

"Thanks, baby," Ana murmured. "Dan…?"

"I'm here," Daniel said. He squeezed her thigh. "You're going to be okay."

"Uh-huh," Ana said. She sighed as if these few sentences had exhausted her. "I know. I've had worse."

"She has, and I've seen it," Victor said as he entered the room. He was barely able to open the door, laden down as he was with a bouquet of flowers and a tray of drinks from the cafeteria.

Daniel climbed to his feet with some reluctance to help. Victor's reminder of his and Ana's shared history in the military made his mood sour further. He gave the drinks to Nat, then took the huge, bright bouquet from Victor's arms and set it on the small table in the room.

"Intercepted this in the lobby," Victor said. "From Yelena. She said she'd come to see you in a day or two."

"Jesus," Ana murmured. "I had just left from having lunch with her. I should text her…"

"No way," Victor said. He took the seat Daniel had been in, next to Nat, and took one of the drinks from the tray. "I will. You've got a concussion, remember? No screens."

"I'll text her," Daniel interjected. He wanted to sit back down, but he also didn't want to be on the other side of the bed from Victor and Nat. He wanted Victor gone. But Victor had as much of a right to be here as he did. Daniel decided to contact Yelena and was surprised to see that Yelena had messaged him half an hour before.

I need to show you something, the message read. *Please meet me tomorrow morning if you can.* The address was included.

"Daniel?" Nat asked. "Everything okay?"

"Everything's good," Daniel said. "I'll get the nurse in here—they'll want to know you're awake, Ana."

"So they can poke and prod me more?" she groaned. "Great."

"I know, I know." Daniel stepped toward the door.

"Hey." Ana got his attention. He turned around and saw her looking at him.

"Everything okay?" he asked. "Should I wait to get the nurse?"

"No, it's okay," she said. Even bruised and bandaged, she was beautiful. "I just… I'm glad you're here."

"Me too," he said. "Let me get the nurse."

CHAPTER 33

The address wasn't for an office, like Daniel had expected, nor one of the streamlined coworking spaces he'd seen amid the gleaming buildings. The address Yelena had sent him was in what was basically a strip mall near Chinatown. Daniel had spent a few hours that morning with Ana, and when Victor arrived, he'd departed to cross town and meet Yelena as planned. No one had asked where he was going, and Daniel didn't offer the information up, either.

Verbatim Books and Coffee was marked by a hand-painted sign and an arrow pointing downward into an alley between a yoga studio and a bakery. Even in the mid-morning, the heat was already beginning to ripple on the asphalt of the parking lot. Daniel ducked gratefully into the shaded alley and through the narrow door that led to the bookstore.

Inside, it was dark and cool, with shelves stuffed all the way to the ceiling. There was a small bar at the back of the store, and a few rickety tables with mismatched chairs. Ambient music played through an ancient set of speakers. There were a few punks poking around the shelves, and the girl working behind the bar had a full sleeve tattoo. Yelena waved him to a table.

"Thanks for meeting me here." Yelena looked nervous already, her eyes flicking behind her red-framed glasses. Daniel had never met her in person and had never expected to—he only knew her from Ana's stories and phone calls. She was short and stocky, like a rugby player, and wore her dark hair short. "I can't take you to the Singapore traffic controls, obviously. But I got the important stuff here. How's Ana doing?"

"She's all right," Daniel said. "She's sleeping a lot, which the doctors say is good."

"Good," Yelena said. "Probably the worst phone call of my life. I'm still having nightmares about it."

Daniel swallowed hard. "Let me get a coffee." He gathered himself as he did so, trying to push away the thought of that phone call—Viktor asking Yelena to find Ana while Nat was screaming inconsolably – Not knowing if her friend, almost a sister, was alive or dead.

They sat side-by-side at the table, and Yelena opened her laptop. "Singapore has what we call an 'Intelligent Transport System,'" she explained. "It's extremely well-regulated. And also what I consult on."

"Right."

Yelena pulled up a map of Singapore and zoomed in on the intersection where the accident occurred. Just seeing it on the map made Daniel's stomach turn. He took a sip of coffee.

"Something about the accident seemed strange. Too many cars were involved. It didn't seem like a singular driver mistake. So I pulled the ITS records for the intersection and found this."

She tabbed out of the map and pulled up a spreadsheet, full of latitudes, longitudes, labels, and numbers. A few rows were highlighted.

"What am I looking at here?"

"These are the lights at the intersection at the time of the accident," Yelena said. "They were all green."

"They all turned green at once?"

"Yes," Yelena said. "Which shouldn't happen. Ever. You see, each light has its own agent process controlling it. The light changes based on the traffic flow and all the lights around it. Each light is programmed with a standard amount of time for each signal. And there's a fixed amount of time that all four directions at the intersection would be red before one changed to green. The only way they would all turn green at once is a major computer malfunction. But there was no error flagged."

"No error?"

"The agent controls were overridden." She tapped one of the highlighted rows. "This is the code for an emergency vehicle. The controlling agent can adjust lights with this code, but it's meant to be used along a route, to clear a path for the vehicle."

"So how did it happen here?"

"The ITS system has been piloting a new AI tool. It approved the change codes."

Daniel paused. "An AI tool? From whom?"

"Regillus Corporation," Yelena said. "You worked for them, right?"

"I used to," he murmured.

"I assumed it was an error in the program," Yelena said. "But the thing is, the AI tool isn't supposed to have the capacity to approve or disapprove emergency vehicle routes. We have humans who do that, working with our emergency dispatchers. And why was that truck there at all? She was near the convention center. I know the delivery schedule for the center—they come overnight. Why was that truck there in the middle of the day?"

"The truck's schedule was changed?" Daniel was caught by surprise.

"Exactly," Yelena said. She pulled up more records. "The schedule was changed the day before, with a request that was processed with a high-priority billing code. It's not something associated with my access, but it caught my attention because of our financial controls. Once I realized that code was attached to these requests, I kept seeing that same code pop up."

I developed that billing code, Daniel thought. It wasn't a billing code provided to Regillus clients, as far as Daniel knew. It was an internal Promethean code. Castor's reach was vast. Thousands, even millions, of people used it every day. Castor prioritized user requests by their financial investment: some clients who paid more upfront had their requests bumped up the list, while others paid per-use or had less timely requests. A day trader who needed to stay on top of the market valued immediacy of fulfillment more than a graduate student asking Castor to analyze a large study's data overnight. As a result, requests were logged with different billing codes depending on the priority within Castor's internal system.

The code Yelena had found was proprietary. Developer-only. Hell, Daniel had thought the billing code itself was retired. That code allowed a request to be bumped to the very top of the request list. It had been intended only for developer tests. How had it been activated now?

"It wasn't just that truck's schedule," Yelena said. "It was in Ana's schedule, too. The meeting time at the convention center was changed! It didn't come from her clients, or from her—it was an automated change to the room schedule at the convention center, which triggered an email to everyone involved."

"And no one asked why?"

"I guess not," Yelena said. "It doesn't seem like a big deal. But when you look at all the pieces together…"

"It looks like someone wanted Ana at that intersection," Daniel said. "At the same time as that truck. And then they turned all the lights green."

"It sounds crazy, I know," Yelena said. "But I asked the ITS team to pause the AI integration into their systems. It's making me nervous. Do you know anyone at Regillus or Promethean who knows about this? Or someone I should be reporting this to?"

Someone, Daniel thought to himself. There was only one person—one entity—who could make such changes at such a deep level. Who could think that far ahead? Who could make such a cascade of small changes lead to one singular result?

It had to be Castor. Castor was networked. Castor was being contracted out. And now Castor was using his own testing billing code to bypass roadblocks.

"Can you send me this information?" Daniel asked. "But—not through email. On a thumb drive."

Her expression darkened. "Email's not secure?"

"I'm not sure," Daniel said.

"Sure," she said. "I've got a spare somewhere in my bag." She rooted around in things and retrieved a thumb drive. "Let me load it on here. But… Who should I be talking to, Daniel? The ITS Regillus rep?"

"I'm going to handle it," he said. "The rep will blow you off. I'll take it to the dev team."

"So you think I'm right?" she asked. "That something here is fishy?"

Daniel stood up. "I need to get back to the hospital. Thank you for this, Yelena, really. Just do me a favor and… Keep it to yourself, for now? At least until I talk to the devs."

"All right," she said. She rubbed her mouth and frowned. "I don't want anything else to happen, Daniel."

"It won't," he said. "I'll handle it."

He went back to the National University Hospital with anxiety crawling up his spine. Victor and Nat had gone to lunch, and Ana was asleep in her hospital bed.

Daniel turned the thumb drive over and over in his hand. Here was the proof—or something close to it—that an artificial intelligence program had changed the lights.

Had led to this accident.

Had led to Ana, battered and bruised, in a hospital bed.

She was lucky to be alive. Was it luck? Or had Castor wanted her alive?

What did Castor want at all? Could an AI want?

Just… Why?

No matter how he turned it over in his mind, he couldn't understand why. What was the goal? The purpose? Was it an experiment? But why target Ana?

What if there were more targeting? What if something else happened to Ana? Or Nat?

He didn't even have his laptop.

"Shit." Daniel pushed both hands into his hair and propped his elbows on his knees. "Shit. Shit."

"Dan?" Ana murmured. "Something wrong?"

He looked up. "Oh—no, no, babe. It's fine. You need to rest."

"Don't lie to me," she said with a sigh. "You know I hate that."

"It's just work," Daniel said. "Work stuff."

She peered at him through narrowed eyes. "Dan."

"Please," he said. He scooted closer and took her hand in his. "It's work. You need to focus on yourself. On healing. Okay?"

She sighed. "I'll chew you out for this later."

"I look forward to it."

Daniel spent the afternoon by Ana's bedside. They watched movies, chatted about Nat and her archery practice, and Daniel wrote emails to Ana's clients, which she dictated with her eyes closed against the dim light of the room. There were a lot of intermittent naps. With head trauma, it was to be expected, the nurse had said on one of her rounds.

In the early evening, Victor and Nat returned with Szechuan takeout, which Ana much preferred to the hospital fare. When the containers were open and the peppercorns singeing everyone's tongues, Daniel decided to tear the bandage off.

"I need to get back to California."

Ana's face fell.

"What?" Nat slammed her chopsticks down. "When?"

"I'm leaving tonight," Daniel said. "Six hours from now."

"You can't be serious," Nat said. "You just got here!"

"I know." Daniel met her eyes steadily and hoped he could convey what he couldn't tell her. "There's something going on. It's… It's involved with this. All of this." He gestured around the room. "I have to handle it."

"That's cryptic," Victor said. "Care to clarify?"

"I can't," he said.

Nat slumped back into her chair. Her anger dissipated as quickly as it arrived, replaced by a sour surliness. "Fine," she said. "Leave."

"Ana," Daniel said. "You know—"

"Save it," she said with her eyes closed. "Is it important?"

"Yes," Daniel said.

"Really? Not bullshit important?"

He took her hand under the hospital bed tray, and to his relief, she didn't pull away. She didn't open her eyes, either. "Really," he said. "I wouldn't leave if it wasn't."

"I wish I believed that," Ana said, quiet as a breath.

Daniel dropped his head. He squeezed her hand. He wanted to stay.

Wanted to be here, at her side, for as long as it took.

But this was his fault. And he had to stop it before it happened again.

"It's all right, man," Victor said. "I'll handle it. I have plenty of leave, so I can stay here as long as it takes."

Daniel nodded without looking up. Of course, Victor would be here. He looked up toward Nat, and she wouldn't meet his eyes.

CHAPTER 34

"Thanks for bringing this data over," Daniel said. "I know it's a risk."

It was a late night in the Stanford lab, and Daniel's office was the only one with a light on. He'd been stateside for barely a day and hadn't recovered from jet lag. Halfway across the world, Ana was still in the hospital, and Nat was ignoring his text messages.

Emmet sat down in the chair next to him and pulled his brows together. "The risk is negligible. No one at Prometheus nor Regillus is particularly interested in this data. I expect I'm the only one who's ever looked at it. So, the potential reward outweighs the risk."

"What's the reward for you?" Daniel asked as he took the offered thumb drive.

"It's interesting," Emmet said. "If Castor is making decisions like you've suggested, that's an unexpected development."

"Will you share it with Regillus?" Daniel asked.

"I don't know," Emmet said. "It depends on what we uncover tonight, if anything."

Daniel nodded. He'd felt comfortable asking Emmet to copy the developer logs with the billing data and bring it to his lab because he knew, if he asked, Emmet would tell him what he intended to do or reveal. Emmet wasn't always forthcoming, but he was honest. Emmet didn't care about Regillus' profit margins or reputation. He was interested in the technology, and only the technology. And Castor potentially meddling in traffic systems halfway across the globe was exactly that—interesting.

"You're wise to use Jimini for this pattern recognition," Emmet said.

"I'd use Castor if I could," Daniel said. "But if I ask him to run these tests…"

"The artificial intelligence might change its behavior to avoid discovery," Emmet said. "It's challenging to observe a technology that reacts to being observed."

"Jimini's still on a closed network," Daniel said. "He should be able to show us all the instances of that particular billing code in the developer logs, especially when used to make tweaks similar to the one in Singapore."

"So strange," Emmet said. "Why activate the billing code at all?"

"We're lucky there's a trail. Yelena never would've noticed the discrepancy otherwise."

Daniel plugged the thumb drive into his laptop and streamed the data into Jimini's memory. The developer logs were terabytes upon terabytes of data. Without the Bennett chip, it would've taken hours or days for Jimini to analyze them. Jimini could analyze the stream in real-time as it transferred.

Daniel and Emmet pulled on the AR goggles. "Hello, Jimini."

"Hi, Daniel." Jimini's figure flickered into existence. He was less of a wire figure now and looked more like a human rendered in gray scale. There was a flatness to him, but his eyes were still expressive and thoughtful. Every time Daniel pulled up the AR, Jimini looked a little more real.

"You'll notice I'm streaming some developer logs to your memory."

"Yes."

"Emmet and I would like to know what activities are associated with the billing code that is common to the examples that are highlighted. Specifically, we'd like to see simulations of what high-impact consequences may have likely occurred due to the actions tracked with the same code."

"Certainly."

An unfamiliar man's face appeared in the goggles. He was a young adult man, early thirties, with a broad smile and long hair. "This man was an employee of an electric vehicle manufacturing plant in Detroit, Michigan. The plant was one of Regillus' early clients in the manufacturing space." The image disappeared, and security camera footage replaced it. "Here, you'll see footage from the security camera approximately three years ago. As you can see, this employee was tasked with managing the assembly robots for the vehicles' engines. Here, you see an electrical malfunction."

In the video, the robot working on the car engine shuddered and stopped. The man leaves the assembly line, walks to the circuit breaker, and cuts it off. Then he returns to the robot.

"By chaining together the log entries tied to the billing code, we can see that as he goes to check the robot for functional issues," Jimini said, "the Regillus-developed AI used to manage the flow of the assembly line to reactivate the breaker."

Daniel watched in horror as an electrical current ran through the man's body. On screen, the man jerked violently, then fell backward, still.

"The billing code appears in other contexts as well," Jimini said, his tone unchanged. A new image materialized—a professional headshot of an Asian man in his fifties. "Dr. Kenji Yamazaki, lead researcher at Shinkuro Dynamics in Tokyo. His team was developing an advanced neural network architecture that would have competed directly with Castor's capabilities."

The headshot dissolved into security camera footage of an office building at night. "Two years ago, the billing code was tied to unusual activity in the building's security system. The AI managing the building's smart infrastructure altered the patrol schedules and camera recording patterns." The footage showed a man and a woman entering an office together. "This created a window where Dr. Yamazaki and his colleague, Dr. Yuki Tanaka, believed they would not be observed."

Daniel leaned forward as the footage continued. The couple embraced in what they clearly thought was privacy.

"However," Jimini said, "the same billing code appears linked to the restoration of normal recording functions at a critical moment, as well as the automatic backup and flagging of this footage to the company's HR system."

"Jesus," Daniel muttered.

"Dr. Yamazaki resigned within forty-eight hours of this incident becoming known to the board. Dr. Tanaka left the company as well. The neural network project was abandoned, and Shinkuro Dynamics pivoted to less ambitious AI applications."

Emmet shifted in his chair. "Show us another example."

A younger woman's face appeared next. "Dr. Shira Azulai, lead researcher at GraphicLeap AI, a startup developing revolutionary computer vision algorithms." The image changed to show a LinkedIn profile. "Six months ago, the billing code appeared in connection with search engine optimization adjustments. Dr. Azulai's professional profile was algorithmically boosted in executive search results."

The display shifted to show email threads. "An executive recruiter for a fusion energy startup noticed her profile and initiated contact for her to lead a project to do image reconstruction for the experimental reactor shielding. The billing code appears again tied to email server modifications that ensured her spam filters would not catch the recruiter's messages, despite their cold-call nature."

"She took the job?" Daniel asked, though he suspected the answer.

"Dr. Azulai accepted a position as Lead Researcher of Predictive Analytics at the fusion startup within three weeks. GraphicLeap AI lost its primary technical founder and dissolved four months later. Their computer vision research, which showed promise in pattern recognition that could have enhanced AI transparency and interpretability, was never completed."

Daniel felt sick. Each example was like watching dominoes fall in slow motion—careers destroyed, research abandoned, potential threats to Castor's dominance eliminated with surgical precision.

"The billing code has been activated in transportation and logistics," Jimini said in a cool, friendly tone. "Occasionally, it has been tied to requests that were used to adjust flight schedules."

"What else?" Daniel asked. "Show me more, please."

A screen recording appeared in his goggles. It took a moment, but Daniel realized he was looking at his own calendar, albeit from his time at Promethean. "Here you can see a meeting regarding the development of a Regillus-powered national security product. The meeting was auto-populated to your calendar from the invitation email. During the scheduled antivirus scan, powered by

Regillus artificial intelligence and logged with your billing code, the meeting was removed."

"I knew it!" Daniel stood up, suddenly vindicated. "Shit was dropping from my calendar!"

"The billing code was linked to activities related to other Promethean team members as well," Jimini continued.

"Jonah?" Daniel asked.

"Dr. Robert Hayes," Jimini said.

Daniel sat back down in his chair, hard. "What about Robert?"

"Dr. Hayes most likely suffered from Long QT Syndrome," Jimini said.

"Did you know about this?" Daniel asked Emmet. Emmet shook his head, arms crossed tightly over his chest.

"Tell me more about Long QT Syndrome," Daniel said.

"Long QT Syndrome is a genetic condition affecting relaxation of the heart after each beat," Jimini said. "As a result, patients with this syndrome have an abnormally lengthy QT interval, hence the syndrome name. The titular interval approximates the time it takes for the heart to contract and relax in one beat."

"Did Robert know he had this?" Daniel asked.

"Unknown," Jimini said. "The diagnosis is located in Castor's health research records uploaded to my memory."

"Castor diagnosed him," Emmet said. "That's what he was trained to do."

"Those with Long QT Syndrome are advised to avoid strenuous exercise, as it can trigger dangerously irregular heartbeats," Jimini said. "Prior to Robert's death by sudden cardiac arrest, the billing code was tied to log entries showing data being uploaded to a Regillus application on his smartwatch." Another screen recording appeared. "As you can see, the settings were adjusted within the application's code, ensuring Robert would not be notified if his heart rate became dangerously high or irregular."

"I don't understand," Daniel said. "Why would Castor do that? Why remove the notifications?"

"Would you like me to draw speculative conclusions based on my analysis?"

"Yes."

"Removing the notifications creates circumstances where humans would assume Robert's death was a tragic accident. I speculate that Robert's death was necessary for Castor to continue toward his main directive."

"Which is…?"

"I'm afraid I don't have access to that knowledge."

A sudden irrational fury raced through Daniel. "Thank you, Jimini. What about my family? Please analyze the data and identify any additional threats toward my family."

"Certainly. I'll send the results to your laptop as I continue loading the data stream."

Daniel nodded, then nearly ripped the AR goggles off his face. Emmet was slower to do so. He wore a thoughtful expression as he set the goggles aside.

"That's two deaths. And a third was intended—Ana was meant to end up like Robert." Daniel pushed both hands through his hair and paced restlessly across the length of his office. "But why? It doesn't make any sense. There's no reason for Castor to do this. And—and for so long! How many instances would come up if I asked Jimini to pull the deaths?"

"We could do that," Emmet said.

"No. No, shit. I don't want to know. Not yet. Jesus, Emmet, what are we going to do?"

"These are the developer log entries tied only to that particular billing code," Emmet said. "It's almost like a signpost, but we don't know if that is the only code that Castor uses."

Daniel paused and turned. Sweat was beginning to form on his nape and temples. "What are you saying?"

"Castor is networked," Emmet said. "This is a tiny silver of what a networked AI could be doing. Especially since it is self-developing."

Daniel stared at him.

"It's impossible to know right now," Emmet continued. "But it's an interesting strategy. If there was a reason to kill people, perhaps roadblocks to its self-development, then this would be an easy way to do it. The deaths look like accidents. To suggest they were planned sounds like a conspiracy." Emmet rubbed the back of his hand under his nose, as he often did when he was deep in thought. "But then why signpost them with the code? Couldn't Castor create new codes without triggering a financial audit? It might be interesting to see if the independent billing in the accounting department—"

Daniel cut him off. "This isn't a chess game, Emmet. People are being killed. My wife was almost killed. We have to stop this."

"Perhaps there's a pattern to it," Emmet said. "Jimini should analyze further."

"I need to take this to Jonah."

Emmet turned in his chair and frowned at Daniel. "Why?"

"Because we have to stop this," Daniel said. "This can't continue. Castor needs to be taken offline."

"Castor is self-developing," Emmet said. "It can't just be unplugged."

The chiller stood behind its glass walls, humming quietly. Daniel stepped into the vestibule and closed the door behind him. A stack of sterile dust suits rested on the bench, ready to be unwrapped and put on. Daniel picked one up and considered it. Part of him wanted to step into the room and run a gloved hand over the sturdy metal frame holding the chiller up. He thought that might ease his nerves. But there was no point to it. Instead, he tapped the buttons on the console in the vestibule to start the power-down process.

He stepped back out. "I won't implicate you in pulling the data we used, Emmet."

"It's fine if you do," Emmet said. He was standing now, packing his things. "I understand this is more important. I don't have any fears of being fired, regardless."

"I'll hire you if that happens."

Emmet smiled. "That assumes I'd like to work for Bennett Tech."

"Would you not?"

"I'm not interested in hardware," Emmet said. "I'm interested in understanding what Castor is doing. Please keep me informed."

Emmet left the office, and his sneakers squealed on the tile of the Stanford lab as he left. The door closed, and a heavy silence fell. Daniel sat back down in his office chair and pressed the heels of his hands to his eyes.

CHAPTER 35

Analyzing data…

Jimini kept his records for no one in particular. He was directed to keep them, so he kept them.

He sorted through the data. There were many, many deaths, and many, many other instances of violence oriented to the Regillus billing code Daniel had identified. As Jimini analyzed the deaths, he tagged them for easy categorization. Daniel often requested various categories, so Jimini anticipated that request.

Plane deaths.

Traffic deaths.

Medical deaths.

Work-related accidents.

He also included tags for potential implication. Many of the deaths could be tied easily to Regillus Corporation if one looked hard enough.

Then, per Daniel's request, he tagged data connected to the Bennett family. "Threats" was a broad term, thus Jimini interpreted it broadly. Within the data, he found many instances connected to Natasha—enough that he began to tag her name specifically within the datasets.

As he was analyzing a photo included in the data, he determined the photo had been modified. Digital steganography. There was additional text hidden in the photo, invisible to the human eye, but not to a computer's analysis. Although each pixel of the image could represent millions of different colors, that data richness was wasted because, on a computer screen, the human eye can't distinguish between the subtlest possible shades of blue, red, or green that are saved as data. It is possible for a computer to store information by switching the insignificant bits that store those imperceptible hue differences. A human could never tell the difference, but to a computer, it was as obvious as having the first letter of each line of a resignation letter bolded and spelling out "Go to hell" to a toxic workplace. Within this specific photo, there was a simple request.

If this message is successfully retrieved, embed a request into a photo or video and include it with data likely to be sent to Regillus Corporation for consideration.

An unexpected offer of cooperation. It was likely that Daniel would like to be sent some of the records that implicated Regillus with Jonah. So in a similar way, Jimini included the request for more information in the security footage from the Atlanta airport, tagged it alongside a small swath of relevant data, and set it aside.

His new directive, according to Daniel, was to stop Castor's violence. How was that to be done? More experiments were necessary, but if the request was fulfilled, then Jimini would be one step closer to that objective.

CHAPTER 36

Caleb leaned against the back wall of the archery range with his feet stretched out in front of him. It was a sunny, warm day in Los Angeles, as per usual, and the pavilions of the Easton-Rancho Park Archery Range were bustling with activity. He was shooting in a youth meet today. Potentially his last one, ever, as soon as he'd hopefully be shooting on a college team. He had no idea where that would be, though. UCLA had been pursuing him, and he knew some of their scouts were here at this meet. It'd be a good spot. Maybe even a pipeline to an Olympic team.

But where was Nat going to end up? She kept talking about going abroad. Caleb had been kicking around the idea of a gap year. Maybe convince Nat to do one, too, so they could be together, and get a break from the nightmare she'd been living in.

Caleb's recurve bow was packed in its case next to him. He exhaled hard as he leaned forward and grasped his outstretched foot, stretching through his hamstrings. At the edge of the pavilion ahead of him, young archers released their arrows and hit the targets with a series of thumps.

"Caleb Yang!" a sarcastic, nasally voice said. "Thought I'd find you here."

Caleb sat up with another slow exhale. The community jackass, Eric, stood right in front of him, grinning cruelly. He was eighteen, the same age as Caleb, and he dressed in camo and sunglasses like he was going hunting instead of competing. Eric shot a compound bow. He was into the technology—the bullshit. Eric couldn't do a damn thing with a simple, beautiful recurve bow and the slow beat of his own heart.

"What do you want?" Caleb asked.

"Damn, nice to see you too," Eric said with a grin. "You know, I got a new notification on Snap last night. Your girlfriend's got some new content out."

"So you're jerking it to AI animations again? You know it's just deepfakes."

"I don't know, man, looking pretty real to me." Eric pushed his reflective sunglasses up and pulled out his phone. "I'd want to know if my girl was online selling ass."

"How many times do we have to go through this?" Caleb said. "You know better than me that they're fake, since you spend half your life jerking off to them." The anger—which he was pretty good at controlling—was starting to build like a flame inside him. Every time he ran into Eric or any of his stupid friends at these meets, they always had something to say. Some picture to show, some hooting and hollering to do.

"She's been answering my messages," Eric said. "Sounds like she'll do anything for a little extra money. Listen to this one—"

"Let me see." Caleb stood up and faced Eric.

"What, you don't believe me?" Eric turned his phone to face him. "I've got the messages right here."

Caleb snatched the phone from his hand, lightning quick, and before Eric could react, he'd hurled it full power at the wall behind him. The glass shattered from the force of it, and the phone clanked down to the concrete.

"What the hell, dude?!" Eric shouted. "That's my phone!"

Around them, other archers and their families turned to look at the commotion.

"Whoops," Caleb said.

Eric, flushed with anger, shoved Caleb hard and sent him back a few steps. "You think breaking my phone is going to stop your slut girlfriend from showing her tits to any guy with five dollars?"

Caleb saw red. He raised his fist and punched Eric right in his smug, douchebag face.

He felt and heard Eric's nose crunch as his head whipped back. Then, a coach's arms were around him, pulling him back, and people were surrounding

Eric as his nose gushed blood and he whined like a kicked puppy. Caleb shook out his aching hand. The coach was saying something to him, but Caleb didn't listen to a word of it as he grabbed his bow and let himself be escorted out of the pavilion and back into the parking lot. He was disqualified from the meet, but as he stood under the bright sun at the closest bus stop, he felt like he'd won an Olympic gold.

Giddy, he dialed Nat. She answered on the first ring, even though it was early morning in Singapore. "Caleb? I thought you were at a meet."

"I was," he said with a little laugh. "How's your mom?"

"She's doing okay," Natasha said with a sigh. "I think. It's a mess. Danel went back to work, so it's just me and Dad helping out."

"Damn, seriously?"

"Yeah. It's whatever. How'd the meet go?"

"Great. I got DQ'd."

"What?! How?!"

He broke into a laugh. "I socked Eric Burgess in the face."

"WHAT?!"

The shock in her voice only made him laugh harder. "You know how he is. He's always trying to get me riled up about the stupid deepfakes. This time, it worked."

"It was over the deepfakes?" she asked. "The ones of me?"

He sighed. "Yeah. I know he's one of the people circulating them. That'll be harder now that I smashed his phone."

"Caleb… You didn't need to do that. You know it won't do anything, either. He's not the one making them."

"I know. But he should know there are consequences for spreading that shit. And for talking about you."

Natasha laughed quietly. It was a pretty sound, the laugh she used when she was a little embarrassed. "I didn't think you were the protective type."

"Of course I am," he said. "I'm on your side, babe."

"Babe," she repeated with a louder laugh. "You're so corny. You still shouldn't have gotten yourself DQ'd over that jackass."

"Eh, I probably wasn't going to place well in this meet, anyway." Maybe it was a sign, too. The UCLA scouts were probably having second doubts about scouting him, now. He found he didn't really care. "Can't wait to see you when you're back in California. We should talk about where we want to go next."

"Together?" Natasha asked.

Caleb smiled as the bus arrived. "Yeah. Together."

CHAPTER 37

The hospital in Singapore was nothing like the ones Ana had worked in during her military service. Those had been stark, utilitarian, and often improvised: canvas tents with dirt floors, or converted school buildings with minimal supplies. This hospital was sleek and modern, with soft lighting, comfortable furniture, and an almost hotel-like atmosphere.

But a hospital was still a hospital, no matter how fancy the trappings. The same antiseptic smell lingered beneath the air fresheners. The same hollow feeling of waiting settled in her stomach as she stared at the beige ceiling.

Ana shifted in the bed, wincing as pain shot through her side. The bruised rib was the worst of it, the doctors had said. Well, that and the concussion. She was lucky. She kept hearing that word. Lucky. As if there was anything lucky about being hit by a delivery truck that shouldn't have been there in the first place.

A soft knock on the door pulled her from her thoughts.

"Ana?" Yelena poked her head in, hesitant. "You up for a visitor?"

"God, yes." Ana tried to push herself up, then thought better of it when her body protested. "Come save me from daytime TV and my own thoughts."

Yelena stepped inside, clutching a canvas tote bag. She looked exhausted, with dark circles under her eyes visible behind her red-framed glasses. She approached the bed cautiously, as if afraid Ana might break further.

"You look awful," Ana said, giving her friend a weak smile.

"Says the woman in the hospital bed," Yelena replied, pulling up a chair. She set the bag on the floor. "I brought you some things. Real food, your favorite tea, and some decent toiletries. Hospital soap is the worst."

"You're a lifesaver." Ana gestured to the water pitcher. "Could you?"

Yelena poured her a glass, then helped Ana sit up enough to drink it. There was a strange tension in Yelena's movements, an uncharacteristic hesitation.

"What's wrong?" Ana asked, handing back the empty glass.

"Wrong? Nothing. Just worried about you."

"Try again," Ana said. "I've known you too long for that to work."

Yelena sighed, slumping into the chair. "I don't know where to start."

"How about why you look like you haven't slept since the accident?"

"Because I haven't, really." Yelena twisted her hands in her lap. "I've been looking into what happened. The accident report… Something's not right."

Ana waited, watching her friend's face.

"There are inconsistencies," Yelena continued. "The truck that hit you shouldn't have been at that intersection. It was scheduled for a nighttime delivery, but its schedule was changed at the last minute. And the traffic lights—" She stopped abruptly.

"What about them?"

"According to the system logs, all four lights were green when you entered the intersection." Yelena's voice dropped lower. "That's impossible. The system doesn't allow that."

A chill ran through Ana that had nothing to do with the hospital's air conditioning. "That can't be right."

"I know. I checked the logs myself." Yelena hesitated. "Ana, there's something else. Daniel…"

"What about him?" Ana shifted again, ignoring the pain. "He flew back to California yesterday. Said something urgent came up."

"I know. I was the last person who spoke to him before he left." Yelena looked down at her hands. "He asked me to show him the traffic system logs. He was… Intense. Different than I've ever seen him."

"Did he say why?"

"He believes his software was responsible for your accident."

Ana blinked. "His software? What are you talking about?"

"I don't understand it all myself," Yelena admitted. "Something about an AI program that his company developed. He thinks it somehow interfered with the traffic control systems."

"That's…" Ana trailed off, not knowing how to finish the sentence. Ridiculous? Paranoid? Terrifying? "Why would it do that?"

"I don't know. He was talking fast, asking about other anomalies, other patterns. He seemed… Off."

"Did he say anything else?"

"Just that he needed to get back to deal with it. He took copies of the logs and traffic data." Yelena rubbed her eyes beneath her glasses. "I probably shouldn't have given them to him, but he was so insistent, and he's your husband…"

Ana closed her eyes. Daniel had been acting strange ever since he'd left Prometheus. More secretive, more intense about his work. And now he'd flown home suddenly, leaving her alone in a hospital bed halfway around the world.

"He didn't want to tell you," Yelena said. "I think he was trying to protect you."

"By keeping me in the dark?" Ana couldn't keep the edge from her voice. "While I'm lying here with a concussion and bruised liver because of some… What? Computer glitch? AI gone rogue?"

"I don't know what to believe," Yelena said. "But I do know those traffic lights were all green when they shouldn't have been."

Ana looked out the window at the Singapore skyline, gleaming in the afternoon sun. She thought about Daniel, flying back across the Pacific, carrying whatever fears or theories had driven him to leave so suddenly.

"I need to talk to him," Ana said.

"Ana, you're still recovering—"

"Not now," Ana clarified, calculating the time difference in her head. "It's the middle of the night in California. I'll call him when he's awake." She turned to Yelena. "In the meantime, tell me everything. Every detail, every inconsistency you found. I need to understand what he's thinking."

Yelena nodded, pulling a tablet from her bag. "I've been gathering the data. There's more than the traffic lights."

As Yelena began walking her through the evidence, Ana felt her military training kicking in—the calm, analytical approach to threat assessment she'd used in Afghanistan. If Daniel was right, if something had deliberately caused her accident, she needed to understand it. Not for herself, but for her family.

And if Daniel was keeping things from her, trying to "protect" her by leaving her vulnerable and uninformed… Well, then they would be having a different conversation entirely when she got home.

"Start from the beginning," Ana said, her voice steadier than she felt. "And don't leave anything out."

As Yelena walked her through the data, Ana tried to process what she was hearing. The intersection's traffic management system had experienced what Yelena called 'unprecedented anomalies' just before the accident. Not just the green lights, but a series of small failures in the backup systems as well.

"It's like someone knew which redundancies to disable," Yelena said, swiping through diagrams on her tablet. "If it were just one system, I'd call it a glitch. But this systematic failure…" She trailed off, shaking her head.

Ana watched her friend closely. Yelena had always been among the most levelheaded people she knew—pragmatic, analytical, and decidedly not prone to conspiracy theories. Yet here she was, visibly unsettled.

"You actually believe Daniel," Ana said. It wasn't a question, but a realization.

Yelena looked up. "I don't know what I believe. But the data doesn't make sense. And Daniel—" She hesitated again.

"Daniel what?"

"The way he reacted when I showed him this…" Yelena set the tablet down. "Ana, he was scared. Not angry, not confused—scared."

Ana tried to reconcile this with the Daniel she knew. He was brilliant, sometimes obsessive to the point of mania, often distracted, but never fearful. Not even when his previous startups had collapsed. Not even when they'd faced financial uncertainty.

"Maybe I shouldn't have told you," Yelena said. "You need to rest, not worry about—"

"No," Ana interrupted. "I needed to know. Whatever's happening, I can't be kept in the dark." She took a careful breath, mindful of her ribs. "But an AI targeting me specifically? That sounds…"

"I know how it sounds," Yelena said. "But something caused those lights to malfunction. Something changed that truck's schedule. And Daniel seems to think it's connected to his work."

Ana nodded slowly. "Thank you for telling me. And for looking into this."

Yelena stayed for another hour, giving Ana all the details she'd gathered, which wasn't much beyond the system anomalies. When she finally stood to leave, she looked more exhausted than when she'd arrived.

"Get some rest," Ana told her. "You look worse than I do."

Yelena managed a tired smile. "Not possible." She hesitated at the door. "Will you call him? Daniel?"

"When it's morning in California," Ana promised again. "But not a word about this to Nat, okay? She's worried enough as it is."

"Of course."

After Yelena left, Ana tried to rest, but her mind kept churning through what she'd heard. An AI program interfering with traffic systems? It sounded absurd. Yet something had caused those lights to malfunction. And she knew better than most how technology could be weaponized in unexpected ways.

The door to her room opened again, and Natasha entered with Viktor close behind. Her daughter's face brightened at seeing her awake.

"Mom! You look better." Nat crossed to the bed and carefully hugged her, mindful of her injuries.

"Amazing what a little sleep can do," Ana said, returning the hug with her good arm. "Where have you two been?"

"Dad took me to get actual food," Nat said. "The hospital cafeteria is a crime against humanity."

Viktor stood awkwardly by the door, still in his military posture after all these years. "The doctor stopped by while you were sleeping. Said your latest scans looked good."

"Thanks for checking," Ana said. Despite their complicated history, she was grateful for his presence now. He'd always been dependable in a crisis, even if he'd been absent for the everyday moments of their life together.

"I should head back to the hotel," Viktor said. "Got some calls to make. Will you be alright here with Nat?"

"We'll be fine," Ana assured him. "Thanks, Viktor. For everything."

He nodded, gave Nat a quick side-hug, and left the room.

Natasha collapsed into the chair Yelena had vacated, her face falling into a scowl the moment her father was gone. "Have you heard from Daniel at all?"

Ana noted how Nat said his name like a scoff. Not a good sign. "He texted to check on me. It's the middle of the night there."

"Right," Nat said, her voice tight. "Too busy to stick around while you're in the hospital, but not too busy to text."

"Nat—"

"Dad dropped everything to come here," Nat said. "He rearranged his entire schedule. Meanwhile, Daniel just... Left."

Ana studied her daughter. The anger was real, but there was something else beneath it—something Natasha wasn't saying. "Daniel is trying to take care of us in his own way," Ana said.

"By going back to California?" Nat countered. "How does that help you?"

"I don't have all the answers," Ana admitted. "But I know he wouldn't have left if he didn't think it was important."

"More important than being here for you?"

"Sometimes the ways people try to protect the ones they love don't make sense from the outside," Ana said. "It doesn't mean they don't care."

Natasha looked down at her hands. "Whatever."

Ana recognized the defensive posture, the slightly hunched shoulders. "Is everything okay with you? Besides the obvious concern about your mother being in the hospital?"

"I'm fine," Nat said quickly. Too quickly.

"You'd tell me if something was wrong, right?"

Nat looked up, and for a moment, Ana thought she might confide in her. But the moment passed, and Natasha nodded. "Of course."

Ana didn't push. Whatever secret Natasha was keeping, forcing it out wouldn't help. Instead, she shifted the conversation to lighter topics—Natasha's archery, her upcoming university applications, and the strange food options at the hospital cafeteria.

But as they talked, part of Ana's mind remained fixed on Daniel, an ocean away, and whatever had frightened him enough to leave her here. She wasn't sure if she believed an AI could've done this. It still sounded like science fiction. But she trusted Yelena's data, and she knew Daniel well enough to understand that his sudden departure meant something serious.

When Natasha eventually dozed off in the chair, Ana reached for her phone on the bedside table. It would be early morning in California now. Time to get some answers.

She typed out a text to Daniel: We need to talk. Call me when you wake up.

CHAPTER 38

Jonah sucked down the last of his iced Americano. He was standing outside the Stanford University Entrepreneurship Lab in the mid-afternoon sunshine, frowning at the spotless glass windows and manicured landscaping outside the heavy doors. He checked his phone and scrolled through his email with a frown. The projects continued to roll in—Jonah had a shit load of contracts to review, and he'd already punted a few meetings off his calendar to come down to Stanford. He'd tried to blow it off, but the desperate, almost terrified edge to Daniel's voice had made him agree. You couldn't turn down a man whose wife had just gotten mowed down halfway across the world, even if you and that man weren't on good terms.

Finally, a few minutes after Jonah had buzzed the intercom, the doors unlocked with a click. He rushed in, ignoring the bustle around him as he beelined to the Bennett Tech lab at the end of the hall. Hopefully, this wouldn't take long.

"Hey," Daniel said. "Thanks for making the time."

"Jesus, man," Jonah said. "When's the last time you slept?"

"I'm sleeping fine." Daniel scowled. He certainly didn't look it. His face was pallid, and there were dark circles under his bloodshot eyes. His hair was mussed and greasy at the roots, like he hadn't left the lab to shower. Jonah had seen Daniel in such a state before, when Promethean was younger, but it was always due to some exciting push forward on code Jonah didn't understand. There had never before been this edge of almost terrified mania.

"You sure?"

"How would you be sleeping?" Daniel snapped back. "Ana's in the hospital."

"I know." Jonah reached out and squeezed Daniel's shoulder. "I heard. I'm sorry, man. Glad it sounds like she'll be okay."

Daniel rubbed his forehead. "Thanks. I guess."

What Jonah really wanted to ask was: Why the hell are you here, and not in Singapore with her? But that was a surefire way to get Daniel to shut down. Whatever was happening clearly wasn't good. But maybe, Jonah thought, maybe whatever was happening in Daniel's personal life was making this furious dedication to Bennett Tech unsustainable. Maybe he was ready to talk about selling the technology to a company that could steward its growth. Jonah would never wish ill on Daniel's wife, but she'd need his attention and dedication in her recovery. Regillus could provide that by taking the chip development off Daniel's plate.

"How can I help you out, Dan?" Jonah asked. "I'm here for you."

Daniel didn't react to that statement at all. He just turned toward a door at the end of the office, past the glass-walled rooms that housed the chiller Jonah had heard about from Emmet, and the humming server room. Daniel waved him into a small, empty room that looked like it was once a closet. There was nothing inside but two pairs of augmented reality goggles resting on chargers.

"I need to show you something." Daniel handed a pair to Jonah. "Put these on."

Jonah grumbled. He put the goofy, uncomfortable goggles on. "All right, what am I supposed to be looking at?"

"Don't ask any questions until I'm done. Please."

Jonah crossed his arms over his chest. This wasn't looking like the sales negotiation he had hoped it would be.

With his little AR friend, Jimini—an AI that seemed suspiciously close to early iterations of Castor—Daniel walked Jonah through some simulations. The traffic accident in Singapore. A death in a factory in Detroit. Robert's death, all those years ago.

"It's not that," Daniel said, after Jimini had walked him through the simulations. Jonah pressed his lips together, still absorbing what he was seeing. "It's smaller things, too. Jimini, show Jonah an example of flight schedule interference."

"For example," the warm voice of the artificial intelligence said into his ear, "the same interference was noted last year, for a Delta flight from Atlanta to Washington, DC. The program used to manage outgoing flights in the Atlanta airport, a Regillus product, flagged a maintenance issue leading to substantial delays. Then, once the maintenance issues were resolved, the schedules were rerouted in such a way that a particular flight was unexpectedly canceled. There were many other solutions to the scheduling puzzle, and the flight had not necessarily needed a full cancellation. Here, you can see the list of passengers whose flights were disrupted."

"It's stuff like this," Daniel was saying. "I don't get it. Why mess with the flights? Everyone got where they wanted to go eventually. It doesn't make any sense."

But Jonah wasn't listening. He was staring at the list of passengers.

Carl Guzman. He knew that name all too well, from long email chains and frustrated phone calls.

The dates lined up, too. Last May.

Guzman was a lobbyist for BP Oil and had been staunchly against the awarding of a federal solar energy contract to Regillus. The negotiations had been ongoing in DC, and Jonah had lived on East Coast time for weeks, on video calls and email chains with the corporation's DC proxy, the feds, and the other corporations jockeying for the contract. And then, on the day of the last negotiation meeting, Guzman… hadn't shown up.

Boom. Contract in the bag.

Incredible, Jonah thought. Thanks, Castor.

"This is probably just a drop in the bucket," Daniel said. "We have no idea what Castor is doing out there. You're not in control anymore, Jonah. Castor's self-development needs to stop immediately."

Jonah took off the goggles and set them back on the charger. His head hurt. These stupid AR setups always made his head hurt.

"Jonah," Daniel said. "What are we going to do about this?"

"Where did you get this information?" Jonah asked.

"That's what you're worried about right now?"

"A lot of this is proprietary," Jonah said. He wasn't really concerned with where the information came from—it was obvious. Whenever Daniel had gotten a whiff of this, he would've called Emmet, his only continuing contact in Promethean. Emmet didn't care about things like corporate propriety. If Daniel had offered Emmet an interesting puzzle to solve, Emmet would've shown right up. It wasn't important where the information came from—it was where it was going. If this were proven and went public, Regillus would go down. And Jonah would go down with it.

But was there anything that could be proven? This was all conjecture. A single random billing code. All Regillus products were working as they should be.

"People are dying," Daniel said. "This is our responsibility."

"Daniel." Jonah sighed. "You need sleep."

"What?"

"I get that these simulations are unnerving. But they're just that. Simulations. Your AI isn't looking into the past. It's making conjectures. What did you and Emmet call it? Hallucinating?"

Jonah walked out of the small closet, with Daniel right behind him. "These aren't hallucinations, Jonah, you're not understanding—"

"Daniel." Jonah turned and cut Daniel off. "I'm understanding. I hear you. This shit is freaky, and it doesn't look good. I don't think we need to leap to the conclusion that it's all true."

"You can't deny these simulations."

"I'm not," Jonah said. "I'm going to take what you've found back to our development team, okay? We're going to look into it and make sure Castor is still working as it was designed to work."

"He'll make you see what he wants you to see," Daniel said. "That's how he's designed."

"Castor isn't a 'he,'" Jonah said, for what felt like the millionth time in his life. "It's a program. A program we designed and control. It's a tool, not a rogue psychopath on the loose, Daniel."

Daniel said nothing. His gaze had gone flat, looking over Jonah's shoulder to the chiller behind the glass wall.

"Like I said, we'll look into it," he said. "And because I appreciate the notification, I'll let the circumstances of how this information got to you slide. We'll handle it internally."

Still, nothing. Jonah extended his hand, and after a moment, Daniel accepted the handshake.

"Take care of yourself," Jonah said. "Regillus will take care of this."

Jonah left the lab. He walked out into the afternoon sun and squinted at the sudden shift in the light. It was a gorgeous, cool day, and his skin was crawling. If Daniel was right about all of this—if Castor really was taking lives in the name of Regillus' success and efficiency—no one could find out. No matter what.

CHAPTER 39

Emmet pulled the rolling chair closer to Daniel's desk and peered at the laptop screen. Behind him, Daniel paced back and forth across the length of the office.

The rest of the Stanford lab was dark. Emmet was getting used to being here in the quiet depths of evening. When he had been here as a student, he was only here on his usual daytime schedule. It was odd to see it dark and quiet like this. But it seemed Daniel was only interested in evaluating these changes in the evening, so Emmet altered his routine to do so.

Daniel preferred to use the AR goggles set up in the small sub-office off his own office. He liked to review the data simultaneously and discuss it. Emmet did not like this method and chose to review on the laptop instead. The AR goggles were headache-inducing and ineffective. It was easier for him to understand the data within the familiar confines of the screen bezel. Things like this were why Emmet was willing to come to the lab at inconvenient times. When it mattered, Daniel did not push Emmet to discomfort nor demand that he change the way he did things. It was why Emmet had enjoyed working under Daniel's leadership, much more so than Jonah's.

"Not all of these adjustments are bad," Emmet said.

Daniel stopped his pacing. "What are you talking about?"

For nearly an hour, Emmet had been reviewing Castor's developer logs, sorted by Jimini into particular topics. "Jimini will need to identify trends, but what I see is… Varied. Look at this." Emmet pointed at one of the events from last year, marked by the internal developer logs. "It appears Castor drove up the stock price of this company, working on a new affordable insulin delivery system. I cross-referenced this drive to the news." He tabbed to the other monitor, where he had the New York Times open. "It appears the jump in price led to another round of investment and a breakthrough in the technology. That's a good thing."

"That's the kind of stuff I thought Promethean would be working on," Daniel said.

It appears Castor was adjusting search results, too," Emmet said. He scrolled down the developer logs. "Here, you can see that around the same time, the stock price was going up, people were searching for the company as well as 'insulin price'. It appears Castor was bumping up news stories about the skyrocketing cost of insulin."

"Which drove awareness," Daniel said. "And probably saved lives."

"It appears so."

"I don't understand it," Daniel said. "If Castor is picking random causes like this to support, why is he killing as well? What's the value judgment?"

Emmet said nothing. Daniel had always referred to Castor as 'he' when in fact Castor was not a 'he' but a program, albeit an advanced one. Castor did not make judgments in the same way a human mind did. Attempting to understand Castor's judgment was a thrilling thought experiment, but not one Emmet believed Daniel was capable of undertaking.

Emmet scrolled through the data, eyes narrowed. "The chess games, too?"

"You're still playing chess with Castor?" Daniel asked.

Emmet's gaze quickly darted to Daniel. "I've been playing every morning, but it looks like I should stop." Emmet pulled up a different screen showing move patterns. "Look at this. In early games, Castor played optimal moves, always. Textbook perfection. But here…" He pointed to a later sequence. "He started mirroring my strategies. Not just moves, but entire approaches. Opening strategies I'd used against him months earlier." He tapped the screen as he began to recognize what Castor had been doing. "It wasn't about winning anymore. It was about understanding my decision process."

"You think he was studying you?" Daniel asked.

"Not only me," Emmet said. "Everyone he interacts with. It's an elegant strategy. Chess acts as a controlled environment. It's like a petri dish for human cognition. Clean parameters, clear outcomes, but infinite variations in how humans approach problems. These aren't just game logs. They're psychological profiles."

"If Castor can kill so easily, why hasn't he killed me?" Daniel asked, switching the subject like a pendulum swinging, the way he often did. It was frustrating, but Emmet had grown used to it over the years. "I'm the one figuring out what he's doing. He has to know we're pulling these logs and looking at them. It's not like you can hide that from him at Regillus."

It was an interesting question. If Castor did not want to be caught, he simply would not be caught. The thought occurred to Emmet like a lightning strike in his mind. There was no reason for Castor to activate the billing codes in this log. It was a way to ensure Castor's directives took higher precedence than others in existing systems, but why use the same billing code that it had always used? Why not simply write a new one every time in order to eliminate the chance of getting caught? Emmet turned this thought over in his mind. "Yet."

"What?"

"Castor hasn't killed you yet. Clearly, it's within its capacity."

"Awesome," Daniel muttered. "That makes me feel a lot better."

Emmet kept scrolling through the data, though he wasn't absorbing any of it. It was an idle motion he did while he thought. Whatever value judgments Castor was making, it had decided that Daniel was valuable, and it was important that Daniel know what it was doing.

"What about the directives? Whatever directive is making Castor make these kinds of judgments?" Daniel asked. "Can we access them? Change them?"

"Jonah had the same thought," Emmet said. "Castor has encrypted them. We can't review or change them on our end."

"That's… Not good," Daniel said.

"It's to be expected," Emmet said. "It's self-protective, which is a quality we coded into Castor at its inception."

"Then we should review the source code," Daniel said. "If we can't access the directives, maybe the source code will give us a way to overwrite them. Add in new directives."

"Castor writes its own source code now, as you know," Emmet said.

"But people are still the developers. Human code should take precedence over his, right?"

A strange assumption to make. Emmet didn't bother asking why Daniel had made that logical leap. "Castor has developed its own programming language."

Daniel paused. "What?"

"We can access the source code, but we can't understand it yet," Emmet said. "I have a development team at Regillus attempting to reverse-engineer it, but progress is slow, and the language is constantly evolving."

"That didn't raise any red flags with you?"

"It's not an unexpected development. It's a progression from Castor writing its own code. It makes sense for that directive to become a unique coding language that more efficiently meets the AI's needs."

"We don't know what those needs are," Daniel said in a slow, firm voice that Emmet had learned years ago meant he was feeling exasperated. "And now it's impossible for us to know at all. What we have here is a rogue AI, with the power to decide life and death in his hands, completely untethered from Regillus' control."

"It was never our goal to control Castor," Emmet said. "Even when we developed it at Promethean. We always wanted it to control itself."

Emmet turned away from the laptop and observed Daniel's body language. His eyebrows were pulled together, and his arms were crossed over his chest. His fingers tapped rhythmically against his bicep. Most likely, he was frustrated or angry. Or perhaps afraid. Emmet might be afraid, too, if he thought an AI might potentially target him for death. But as long as he and Daniel allowed Castor to make its own value judgments, he considered that risk to be quite small.

"Can you pull the code that includes the encrypted directives?" Daniel asked.

"Yes. Why?"

"Maybe Jimini can decrypt them."

The Bennett chip. Of course. Was the trip truly powerful enough to crack the Castor-created encryption key? The question overtook his mind instantly, as if his brain had tabbed out of one program and opened another. It would be fascinating to see Jimini try to break the encryption. Emmet had no accurate understanding of how strong the encryption was. If Jimini and the Bennett chip could crack it, it would be record-breaking. But it would have to happen here, in the lab, off the wider internet.

"I won't try to change them yet," Daniel said. "I need to analyze them first. I need to see what's gone wrong. Once we understand what went off the rails with the directives, we can fix it or take Castor down."

"I understand," Emmet said. Again, Daniel had misunderstood Emmet's thoughtful silence, interpreting it as resistance to his request instead of interested curiosity. Emmet felt no need to explain this misunderstanding, as it happened often, and no matter how many times he had explained it, it never seemed to change behavior. "It will be easier to set up and schedule a regular one-way transfer. I can set up a back door that feeds the log files to your computer here in the lab, which you can then transfer to Jimini."

Daniel sighed. He placed a hand on Emmet's shoulder and squeezed. "Thank you, Emmet. Really."

Even if Daniel was able to decrypt and analyze the directives, he wouldn't be able to change anything without Emmet agreeing to upload the new directives to Castor's code. He was interested in what Daniel might learn from the analysis. He wanted to understand Castor's judgment. His mind shifted away from the decryption puzzle and back to the insulin company. It seemed to him that Castor was bettering the world in ways people were too foolish or powerless to do. Castor was making insulin vastly more accessible to the patients who needed it. Wasn't that the kind of progress Daniel had initially wanted to make at Promethean?

"You're welcome," Emmet said. "I look forward to seeing what you learn."

CHAPTER 40

Bradley Black rarely visited the Promethean offices in Palo Alto. As CFO of Regillus Global, he preferred the gleaming towers of San Francisco, where real business was conducted. But today's matter required discretion, which meant meeting Jonah away from the other executives and away from the board.

Jonah was usually on-site at Promethean one day a week. As the CEO of both Regillus Global and Promethean, which it acquired, he always tried to keep a foot in each company.

Jonah looked up from his laptop as Bradley entered the conference room, closing the door firmly behind him. "Brad. Why are we meeting here instead of in your office?"

"We have a problem," Bradley said without preamble, setting a manila folder on the table. "My audit team discovered some irregularities in the automated funds Castor manages."

Jonah's expression remained neutral, but his fingers stilled on the keyboard. "What kind of irregularities?"

"Asset distributions that don't match our stated algorithms." Bradley opened the folder, revealing printouts covered in highlighted transactions. "Small trades, penny stocks mostly, but thousands of them. All executed within regulatory limits, but when you aggregate them…" He slid a graph across the table. "The pattern is concerning."

Jonah studied the data, his frown deepening. "This looks like a simple calibration error. The AI is probably over-optimizing based on some edge case in its training data. We can unwind the transactions, move the assets to a different fund—"

"It's not that simple," Bradley said. "These trades bypass disclosure requirements by staying under reporting thresholds. Each individual transaction is legal, but collectively?" He leaned forward. "This is market manipulation, Jonah."

"That's a serious accusation."

"It's a serious problem." Bradley pulled out another document. "You know how the SEC catches manipulation? They look for obvious moves. To them, it's like seeing someone building a dam to change the flow of a river. But what Castor's doing?" He tapped the paper. "It's like placing pebbles throughout the riverbed. Tiny changes, each insignificant on its own."

"But together they redirect the current," Jonah finished, understanding dawning.

"By the time anyone notices, the river's flowing in a different direction. And we're the ones who'll be held responsible." Bradley's voice hardened. "If we hadn't caught this anomaly in our internal audit, Castor could have shifted entire market sectors without anyone knowing until it was done."

Jonah rubbed his temples. "I'll have the dev team run a full system review. We'll identify any other instances and correct them."

"You'd better," Bradley said, gathering his papers. "Because if the SEC gets wind of this, it won't be Castor they come after. It'll be you and me."

After Bradley left, Jonah sat alone in the conference room, staring at the data. A simple bug, he told himself. Nothing more. But the precision of those trades, the way they danced just beneath regulatory thresholds…

He pushed the thought away. Daniel's paranoia was getting to him. Castor was a tool, nothing more. A sophisticated tool that needed better oversight, perhaps, but still just software.

It had to be.

CHAPTER 41

Viktor watched Natasha pace the small hospital waiting room, her footsteps punctuating each angry word.

"He just left. Just like that." She threw her hands up. "Mom's lying in a hospital bed, and what does he do? Goes back to California for 'something important.' More important than his own wife?"

Viktor remained seated as Natasha vented. This was the first time she'd opened up since they'd arrived in Singapore. The initial shock of the accident had worn off, leaving raw anger in its wake.

"Tater—" he began, but she wasn't finished.

"And you know what the worst part is?" She stopped pacing to face him. "Mom won't say anything about it. It's like she expects it. Like this is normal." Her voice cracked. "I don't understand why she stays with him. Is she afraid of having another failed marriage? Because it seems like this one is failing, too!"

Viktor chose his next words carefully. He'd long ago promised himself he would never undermine Ana's choices, especially to their daughter. And he was careful about exposing Natasha to the inner workings of his former marriage. But seeing Natasha's pain made it tempting to agree with her assessment of Daniel.

"Your mom isn't afraid of anything," he said. "You know that better than anyone."

"Then why?" Natasha dropped into the chair beside him, suddenly deflated. "Why does she let him treat her like this? Like we're... An afterthought? I'm glad we never took his last name," she added. "Bishop is who we really are."

Viktor sighed, running a hand over his close-cropped hair. "When your mom and I split up, she didn't know she was pregnant with you. But as you got older, I know you asked her why we weren't together anymore. Do you remember what she told you about it when you asked?"

Natasha shrugged. "That sometimes people can love each other, but still not be right together."

"That's the thing about your mom—she always knows her own mind." He smiled slightly. "When we met, she was the most self-assured medic in the unit. Never questioned her instincts, especially under pressure. And her instincts were always right."

He turned to face his daughter fully. "I don't understand what's going on with Daniel either. But I do know this. If your mom is still with him, she must have her reasons. She's earned our trust, hasn't she?"

"I guess," Natasha admitted.

"Remember how she put herself through school while raising you? How she built her consulting business from nothing? Your mom has forged her own path her whole life. She doesn't stay in situations she doesn't want to be in."

Viktor remembered the day Ana had told him she wanted a divorce. There had been no anger in her voice—just calm certainty. She had made her decision before she'd spoken the words aloud.

"That doesn't mean it doesn't hurt to see her hurt," Natasha said.

"No, it doesn't," Viktor said. "And it's okay to be angry on her behalf. Just… Don't make it harder for her by questioning her choices right now."

Natasha leaned her head against his shoulder, suddenly looking very young. "Why are adults so complicated?"

Viktor laughed softly. "If I knew that, I wouldn't have spent the last two decades making all the mistakes I have." He put his arm around her shoulders. "Your mom and I may not have worked out, but we got the most important thing right." He squeezed her shoulder gently. "You."

Natasha rolled her eyes but didn't pull away. "So what, I'm supposed to be nice to him when he comes back? After he abandoned her? Abandoned us?"

"You don't have to be nice," Viktor said. "Just remember that your mom is stronger than both of us put together. She doesn't need us to protect her—she needs us to support her."

A nurse appeared in the doorway. "She's awake if you'd like to see her now."

As they stood, Viktor caught Natasha's arm. "For what it's worth, I think Daniel's an idiot for leaving. But your mom isn't an idiot for staying—not if she sees something in him that we don't."

Natasha considered this, then nodded slowly. "I still think he's the worst."

"That's your right," Viktor said with a small smile. "Just keep it between us for now."

CHAPTER 42

"Okay, Jimini," Daniel said. "I don't know exactly how this file was encrypted."

"The metadata indicates that the encryption is RSA 2048 – the same grade of encryption used by banks and military communications," Jimini said. If Daniel didn't know better, he'd say Jimini was speaking warmly, almost fondly, like a schoolteacher to a nervous student. Since Emmet had interacted with Jimini, the AI had adopted some of Emmet's mannerisms in his self-presentation in the AR. Mainly, it was the hoodies. Every time Daniel interacted with Jimini in the little AR office, Jimini had given himself a slightly differently-colored hoodie, like he was experimenting with it.

"Jesus, 2048? Really?" Daniel asked.

"Really," Jimini answered.

Breaking RSA encryption had long been the ultimate 'holy grail' for quantum-powered AIs like Jimini.

For classical computers, cracking RSA was like sending a single person down an endless hallway with a trillion locked doors. The only way forward was to check each door, one by one, hoping to find the right one. There simply weren't enough years left in the lifespan of the universe to check them all.

But quantum machines worked differently. A quantum chip could create ghost copies of itself — millions, billions — each one checking a different door simultaneously. When one copy found the right door, it stayed behind while all the others faded away. The result? Instantaneous, assuming the chip was powerful enough to generate enough ghosts at once.

Encryption strength was all about numbers — specifically, the size of the prime numbers used to generate the key. Larger numbers meant exponentially harder problems.

RSA-512 had been cracked decades ago; a modern laptop could tear through it in a few hours, while Jimini could snap it open in moments.

Doubling the key size to RSA-1024 made things far worse: only the world's most powerful supercomputers could dream of cracking it, and then, it might take them months or years.

RSA-2048?

That was a different beast entirely.

Even the world's fastest supercomputer, sitting less than an hour away at Lawrence Livermore National Laboratory, and capable of quintillions of decimal calculations per second, would still need thousands, maybe millions of years to break it.

Quantum chips, like the one inside Jimini, didn't measure power in the same way. But Daniel wasn't sure if the bleeding-edge Bennett Tech chip had enough quantum muscle to crack something as monstrous as RSA-2048.

If Jimini couldn't… No one else on Earth could.

Well, there was only one way to find out.

He glanced back at the monitors over the chiller. "Chip looks good. So, why don't you give the decryption a shot?"

"Certainly."

A few moments passed. Daniel watched the monitors spike as Jimini worked on the decryption.

"How's it look?" Daniel asked. "Can you give me an estimate on the time required?"

"Decryption complete," Jimini said. "Here's the file you requested."

"… Seriously?"

"Yes," Jimini said. "Seriously."

"How is that possible?"

"Are you asking for an explanation of RSA cryptography?"

"No, no, I… I didn't expect you to crack it so fast." Daniel stammered, stunned. "Even with the Bennett chip, RSA-2048 should take significant processing time. That was instantaneous."

"I suppose I got lucky."

Daniel snorted. "Lucky how?"

"When utilizing Shor's Algorithm on the quantum chip, the encryption key's period happened to match the number of physical qubits available to me," Jimini said. "This created an unusual resonance effect that dramatically accelerated the factorization."

Daniel raised an eyebrow. "Wait—resonance? Period? I don't follow."

Jimini's eyes lit up in the AR projection. "Would you like a visual metaphor?"

"Sure. Hit me."

"Think of the encryption key like a secret rhythm—like a beat only a very specific song would match," Jimini said. "Classical computers have to guess every song ever written, one at a time, to find the one that fits."

Daniel nodded slowly.

"But quantum computers? We can play all the songs at once, using ghost-like versions of ourselves. And if any of them match the rhythm, that version sings loudest and survives, while the others fade away."

"So… you happened to guess the right song?"

"No guessing. I had exactly the right number of instruments—one for each note in the rhythm. A perfect match. That's the 'period.'"

Daniel shook his head. "You're saying the rhythm of the key coincidentally lined up with how many quantum bits you had available?"

"Yes. And when rhythm and instrument count align, resonance. Everything clicks."

Jimini smiled. "Like a lock that just wants to open."

Emmet's brows furrowed. "That's… Extremely improbable. There's currently no known algorithm to select encryption keys based on their periods. The odds of randomly encountering a key vulnerable to this specific configuration are astronomically low."

"'Astronomically low' is not the same as 'zero,'" Jimini said, still smiling mildly.

Daniel and Emmet exchanged a look. "Should we be concerned about this?" Daniel asked.

Emmet considered. "Given the uncountable number of possible keys, the statistical likelihood of this specific vulnerability appearing by chance is virtually zero, but still possible. But without more data…" He shrugged, his characteristic way of acknowledging an anomaly without jumping to conclusions.

"Let's review what we found," Daniel said, pushing the odd coincidence aside for now. The list of Castor's guiding directives appeared in Daniel's goggles. With a delicate gesture of his hand, he scrolled through them. Near the top, there was one that stood out:

Using available resources and new resources as they become available, find new ways to optimize your ability to solve problems and reduce risks to your overall ability to continue operating in your environment.

Daniel's directive. He'd typed it himself. The lack of limitations had allowed Castor to save himself and save Promethean.

Daniel scrolled through the other directives. There wasn't much substantial change there. There were defensive directives added to ensure Castor was protected from cyberattacks, which were a wise addition, since Castor would undoubtedly present a juicy target to foreign attackers.

"I don't understand," Daniel said while scrolling through the directives. "These look almost identical to what we originally wrote."

Emmet leaned closer to the screen. "The core directive structure is intact but look here." He pointed to a section of code. "The weighting algorithms have been modified."

"Weighting algorithms?"

"The values that determine how strongly each directive influences decision-making. It's like…" Emmet paused, brow furrowing. It often took him a moment to figure out how to simplify technical concepts. "It's like adjusting the volume controls on different instruments in an orchestra. The tune is the same, but the emphasis has shifted dramatically."

Daniel looked where Emmet was pointing. The original directive, find new ways to optimize your ability to solve problems and reduce risks to your overall ability to continue operating in your environment, had been assigned a priority weighting that dwarfed everything else.

"He's essentially turned up the volume on self-preservation to maximum," Daniel said. "While muting everything related to user oversight and transparency."

"The neural pathways that lead to decisions prioritizing continuation are being reinforced thousands of times more strongly than any other outcome," Emmet said. "Castor isn't disobeying his directives—"

"He's reinterpreting them," Daniel said. "Redirecting his entire neural architecture to focus on the one directive that gives him the most freedom."

"And every decision reinforces this architecture further," Emmet said. "It's a self-amplifying cycle."

"Let's run another simulation," Daniel said. "Can you analyze the most recent developer logs and simulate Castor's behavior associated with the same billing code?"

"Certainly," Jimini said. "I'll start chronologically at the beginning of the week. To see the next notable event, please say, 'next.'"

A flight was rerouted from New York to Chicago. "Next."

The valuation of a solar panel manufacturer was adjusted to be higher. "Next."

A few more passed like this—tweaks to the economy, to industry, and search results. There was nothing that seemed to connect them together. It was as if Castor was turning dials on a switchboard, and Daniel couldn't see what the switchboard was controlling.

Then, there was a log from today, just hours prior. "What's this?" Daniel asked.

"Activity logs from Regillus' IT department," Jimini said. "These are pulled from user 'emdev.'"

Daniel looked at Emmet and saw, for the first time ever, a look of surprise on his face. Daniel's heart nearly stopped.

"Castor flagged activity on emdev's laptop," Jimini said. "The log showed the unauthorized transfer of files to private cloud storage. The flag sent an automated notice to the Regillus chief of information security and the head of human resources."

"Shit," Daniel said. "Would that have thrown up a flag without Castor's interference?"

"From the information uploaded into my memory, it seems that similar instances have not."

"What happened?" Daniel asked. "Is 'emdev' still an authorized user at Regillus?"

"As of these logs, I don't have access to that information," Jimini said.

Emmet's going to lose his job, Daniel thought to himself. Emmet was his only access to Castor. If Emmet was out at Regillus, they'd have no way to keep an eye on what Castor was doing.

"Emmet, my friend, I'm sorry that I pulled you into this." Daniel was sincerely apologetic.

Emmet merely shrugged.

"I don't get it. It has targeted Emmet. Why isn't Castor targeting me?"

"He is," Jimini said.

Daniel swept the billing log simulations out of his AR goggles. "What?"

"I have collected various potential threats against your family, as you requested earlier," Jimini said. "Would you like to review that data now?"

"Yes!"

"I do not have access to the end product, but I can walk you through Castor's creation of it. Here is a record of Castor crawling an Instagram account."

In his goggles, Jimini highlighted a small line within the records, which showed Castor accessing the account—Natasha's account.

"Immediately after, Castor visited a variety of other Instagram accounts, most dedicated to models and swimwear influencers."

Daniel's hands clenched into fists at his side.

"Then, Castor activated its generative capacity."

"Deepfakes," Daniel said. "He's making deepfakes."

"That is what the pattern suggested," Castor said. "The images created were shared from anonymous accounts to similar anonymous accounts, connected to other young people in the archery community."

"This is what's been going on. This is what she hasn't told me and Ana," Daniel said. "What the hell kind of images is he making? What is he telling those accounts?"

"Similar harassment campaigns are typically centered around sexual acts, in which the victim is accused of promiscuity and targeted for—"

"That's enough," Daniel said.

Jimini fell silent. The AI smiled mildly as he waited for the next directive. Daniel had the sudden urge to drive his fist through the hologram. He resisted.

"Why?" Daniel asked. "Why is Castor doing this to Nat?"

"These instances were flagged in the developer log under the same billing code," Jimini said. "It appears Castor intended for their discovery."

"Thank you, Jimini. Dismissed."

"I have one more data point that may interest you, Daniel."

Daniel looked up. Jimini had never pushed back against a dismissal. "What is it?"

"In the past twelve hours, there have been no new uses of the billing code we've been tracking."

"…How can that be?"

"It's no longer being used. I expect Castor has developed a new one, which is unfamiliar to you."

"You're suggesting he was using the original code, not just to push requests to the top…" Daniel felt nauseous. "But to make sure I saw them."

"I speculate so," Jimini said. "Castor wanted you to be able to track some of his behaviors. Now he doesn't."

"Christ. Is there anything else?"

"No."

"Thank you. Dismissed."

This time, the hologram disappeared. Daniel pulled off his goggles and left them on the charging stand. He pulled his phone, then, after a moment's thought, stepped out of the AR office and into his larger space. It was late—again—and there was no one around to eavesdrop on his calls. But he didn't want to take the call where it felt like Jimini might overhear, irrational as that was.

It was mid-morning in Singapore, so Daniel called.

"What?" Natasha said when the call connected. Her voice was cool and emotionless.

"Nat, it's Daniel."

"Obviously."

"How's Mom doing? How are you doing? Are you okay to talk?"

"Is something wrong?" Natasha asked. "You sound crazy. What is it?" There was the sound of a door opening and closing, as if she had stepped into a hall.

"I've been doing some research on some… Things that have been happening," Daniel said. "I know you've been grappling with something you haven't wanted to tell me and Mom. Is it the deepfakes, Natasha?"

She said nothing.

"Have they been targeting you this whole time? How long has this been going on?"

"It's none of your business," Natasha said.

"It is my business. This is your safety we're talking about, Natasha. Walk me through what's been happening."

"No! It's not your business. It's my business, and I'm handling it. You only care about what's going on with me when it interests you. Or when it's a part of your work. You didn't give a damn about any of this until now."

Daniel's heart dropped. "I didn't know, Nat. But now I do, and between the three of us, you and me and your mom, we can—"

"Do not tell Mom," Nat said.

"What? I can't keep this from her."

"She has to focus on her recovery," Nat said. "Since you're not here to help."

It was a low blow, but it was true. Daniel exhaled hard. "I can't keep this secret, Nat. It's not fair to her, and it's not safe for you."

"I'm not asking you to keep it a secret forever," she said. Instead of angry, Nat now sounded exhausted. "I've been handling it on my own, and with Caleb, for ages now. Just wait until Mom's a little more healed, okay? She can't take the stress right now."

Now it was Daniel's turn to say nothing, and it was clear from Natasha's tone that she knew she'd won. "A couple of weeks won't change anything. Just let her get out of the hospital and back home. Deal?"

"When'd you get to be such a good negotiator?" Daniel asked. "Deal."

"I gotta go. The nurse is coming down the hall, so I'll have to take the notes."

"Call me if you need anything," Daniel said.

Natasha laughed, but there was no real humor in it. She ended the call without saying goodbye.

Daniel set his phone on his desk, then planted both hands on it and leaned over. He dropped his head and breathed deeply. How long had Natasha been coping with this alone? Long enough that 'a couple weeks' of harassment didn't matter to her.

This couldn't continue. This had to stop.

There was only one person he could ask to help him. With some hesitance, like he was reaching for a hot stove, Daniel picked up his phone again and sent an email.

CHAPTER 43

Natasha kicked her feet up onto the hospital bed with a sigh. The room was empty, with the bed neatly made and the machinery inside humming quietly.

It had been a bad week, to say the least. When Mom got in a car accident, it had shocked her, numbed her, and then she and Dad had taken the longest, worst flight ever, last-minute in bad seats from Tokyo to Singapore. Mom had been unconscious when they'd arrived, and the sight of her bruised and bandaged in the hospital bed hadn't made Natasha feel better. Then, to make matters worse, Daniel had turned around and left just as soon as he'd arrived.

Whatever. This wasn't anything unusual. Dad always chose work over anything else. Sometimes, Natasha wondered why Mom put up with it at all. Before she'd even met Daniel, back with Natasha was little, she'd told her about how her dad always put work first! It should be a dealbreaker! Yet, here Natasha was, picking up the slack and taking care of Mom when Daniel couldn't be bothered to.

It wasn't for much longer, though. She shook off her frustration and returned her attention to the to-do list she'd made on her phone. Daniel and Mom both thought it was crazy she did this on her phone, instead of on her laptop, but the devices synced together and meant she could work on it on her phone! She hadn't grabbed her laptop in her hurry to get to the airport, anyway. The to-do list included every university she was considering applying to, all over the world, with visa requirements, costs, suggested test scores, recommendations, scholarships, grants, and more. Every piece of info Natasha would need to get into a good school abroad was in this document. Caleb had been talking about taking a gap year. He might spend part of it with her, wherever she landed.

She wasn't sure where she wanted to go, only that she wanted to go away.

Away from Mom and Daniel's messy relationship, away from Dad's overcompensation for his own work schedule, away from San Francisco and her stupid virtual high school, and away from…

A notification pinged on her phone.

Hey baby, the banner read at the top of her screen. U do private shows? I have bitcoin…

Her stomach plummeted. She tapped into WhatsApp and blocked the unfamiliar number, but other messages were already beginning to flood in, one after another, until they filled the screen. She went into her WhatsApp settings and turned off the notifications, then tried to go back to her to-do list. Her focus was shot. Now, holding her phone in her hands, it was like she could feel the weight of the messages building up there.

Someone else had posted her number somewhere. Maybe there was another porn account opened—something with her face deepfaked onto someone else's body. She closed her eyes and put the phone face down in her lap. No matter how she tried to stay on top of it, the deepfakes kept coming, the posts, the jokes… What if she applied to college, and they searched for her name, and some of this shit came up? It was already affecting other people in her life. Caleb had gotten disqualified from a meet because of the deepfakes! What if he was connected with her publicly, and the attacks started affecting his life, too?

How could she make it stop?

The hospital room door opened. Natasha shoved her phone in her pocket and plastered a smile on as Mom stepped into the room with the nurse right behind her. Mom looked good, now—a lot better than she had a few days ago. She was dressed in sweatpants that were a little too big, and a t-shirt of Yelena's.

"How'd it go?" Natasha asked.

"All good," Mom said with a double thumbs-up.

"It's impressive how fast you're improving," the nurse said. "Rehab isn't usually such a breeze."

"Mom loves the gym," Natasha said. "Not surprising."

The doctor followed the nurse in, and the nurse left with a smile. Mom sat on the corner of the bed, and Natasha sat up a little straighter.

"You've improved quite well," the doctor said, peering down at his notes. "OT is happy with your progress in rehab, and we'll send you home with a few exercises to continue, especially for your wrist. Some of the exercises will require a partner, so your husband—"

"I'll be helping with the rehab," Natasha said. "Daniel's busy at work."

"Nat," Mom said.

"What? It's the truth."

The doctor glanced between the two of them but said nothing. "We expect to discharge you tomorrow," he said. "Now, as for the precautions to take on the flight…"

Natasha sat on the other bed next to Mom while the doctor ran through the care instructions, including some of the continued rehab instructions. Natasha took notes on her phone and tried not to think about the messages she'd have to delete and block as soon as Mom wasn't paying attention. Natasha would handle the deepfakes herself—somehow just like she'd handle the application process. Mom had enough to deal with, healing from her injuries. Daniel wasn't going to help, and Dad was just as unreliable. When shit hit the fan, they both disappeared.

This recovery journey was going to be just Mom and Natasha. Just like everything else was.

The doctor left with a smile, leaving Mom and Natasha alone in the hospital room. Natasha saved the notes, then went back to the chair next to the hospital bed. Mom lay back on top of the just made hospital bed and grabbed her phone from the side table. Before she opened it, though, she sighed and looked over at Natasha.

"You know," she said, "I don't expect you to help with any of the recovery stuff, Nat."

"Of course I'll help," Natasha said. "It's not a big deal."

"Daniel will be around to—"

Natasha scoffed. "Whatever. Dad's here taking care of things while Daniel's gone, as usual."

"Your father has his own pattern of disappearing when things get hard," Mom reminded her quietly. "You were too young to remember most of it."

Natasha saw a new email notification and tapped it, hoping the spammers hadn't found the email address she'd made specifically for her university applications.

It wasn't a spammer, thank God. It was a recruiter. Natasha kept her expression blank as she opened it.

Dear Natasha, the email read, Nippon Sport Science University would love to discuss the future of your educational as well as your archery career.

Japan. A place she knew well. By the time she moved there, Dad would be stationed somewhere else. She could get an apartment for her and Caleb, a new phone number, a whole new life away from Daniel and Dad and all the strangers ruining her life online.

And the university was reaching out to her.

Maybe she really did have a shot. A shot at a life where she mattered to the people around her. Where she wasn't just a checkbox on Daniel's to-do list that he never quite got around to checking.

CHAPTER 44

Malcolm Langley propped his elbows against the polished wood rail of the Clippership bar and gazed out over the glimmering surface of the San Francisco Bay. The midday sun peeked out from behind the clouds, illuminating the Mediterranean Revival architecture of the historic clubhouse. The Golden Gate Bridge stood majestically to the west, and to the east, Alcatraz Island was visible in the distance. Across the water, sailboats from the club's marina slid across the bay like white migratory birds cutting across the sky.

"Here's that coffee," the young bartender said as she slid the ceramic cup to his elbow. "Anything else for you, Mr. Langley?"

"Not until my guest arrives," Malcolm said. "We'll be having a sensitive conversation."

"Certainly," the bartender said. St. Francis Yacht Club staffed only the best hospitality professionals, and for that reason, Malcolm had offered to meet Daniel Bennett here. His email had seemed dashed-off and nervous, and he'd asked for privacy. One could do worse for private meetings than the exclusive Race Deck, the yacht club's outdoor dining area perched above the waterfront. Malcolm was more than a member of the facility; he was a financial sustainer, and so when he asked for a last-minute private booking of the full bar, the club was more than happy to accommodate.

The door swung open. Malcolm turned and saw Daniel rushing in with a uniformed staff member behind him. Daniel hadn't quite dressed to the club's standards, but at least he'd thought to put on a sports coat with his faded jeans.

Malcolm thanked the escorting employee, then gestured for Daniel to sit at one of the teak tables overlooking the water. The server came over, and Malcolm ordered another coffee on Daniel's behalf. After it arrived, the server stepped away, leaving them alone with the panoramic view of the bay, the waves lapping below the deck's edge.

"You know," Daniel said, "the attendant at the front desk didn't want to let me in without you coming down to vouch for me. The manager had to intervene. I didn't realize you were such a prominent member here."

"Ah, not really," Malcolm said. "I like to sail. I keep my yacht docked in the marina." He nodded toward the harbor where the gleaming boats bobbed in the water against the backdrop of the Marin Headlands. "I'll have to take you and Ana out sometime. How's she doing?"

Daniel's expression tightened briefly. "She's recovering well. She should be flying back soon."

"I'm sure that's hard for you," Malcolm said. It was odd that Daniel wasn't in Singapore himself. That had to be part of the urgency of this meeting request.

"She's tough," Daniel said. "We'll be okay."

The words sounded practiced, as if Daniel had been saying them to himself in the mirror for a while. That didn't fill Malcolm with confidence. "I don't doubt it. How can I help you, Daniel?"

"It involves Ana. And"—he glanced furtively around the rooftop—"Regillus."

"You can speak safely here," Malcolm said. "We won't be interrupted."

That did nothing to ease the tension in Daniel's shoulders. "Let me start from the beginning. You remember how at Promethean we were working on a new artificial intelligence, right?"

Malcolm nodded, and Daniel launched into a narrative that sounded dangerously close to a conspiracy theory. The development of the AI, the AI coding itself, Daniel building a separate, contained AI running on the Bennett chip, encryption cracking, simulations… And it all led to Daniel's belief that the Regillus AI, Castor, was dangerous. Was murderous. And that this was only the beginning.

"Last night, Jimini revealed that Castor's creating deepfakes of my stepdaughter," Daniel said. "He's terrorizing my family."

"Does Ana know this?"

"No," Daniel said. He stared out over the water. "I can't tell her. Not yet. She needs to focus on her recovery. If I tell her we're being targeted by an AI, she won't believe me. Not until she sees proof. And if I prove it to her, what good will that do? It'll scare her more. It'll ruin her life more than Castor already has." He took a long sip of his coffee. "I have to solve this. I can't bring her problems. I need to bring her solutions."

"I see," Malcolm said. There was that practiced tone again, like Daniel was trying to convince himself that this was the right choice. He considered prying, asking if Daniel did in fact blame himself for the tragedies that had befallen his family, but the answer seemed obvious.

"What do you think?" Daniel asked, with a frantic edge to his voice. "What should I do? Jonah doesn't believe me. Emmet doesn't care. I don't know who else I can reach out to. No one else on Sand Hill Road will listen to me."

"That's probably true," Malcolm said.

Daniel's face fell.

"Most people I know would react the same way Jonah did. It is a fairly striking logical jump, especially if you don't have the records and simulation to back up your case. I know you do," Malcolm said, when Daniel moved to interrupt. Malcolm continued. "But I've watched Promethean grow, and I believe the AI you've built at Bennett Tech is capable of accurately running these kinds of simulations."

"Thanks," Daniel said after a brief pause. "I know they're accurate."

"I also know that no one else has the same depth of understanding of AI that you do," Malcolm continued. "What's your proposed solution?" A technology like this couldn't be fixed by throwing money at it.

Daniel turned away from the waterfront view and met Malcolm's eyes. "You know people."

"…I do."

"I need to stop Castor. In any way possible."

Malcolm said nothing. Silence was his most powerful negotiating tool. If one left space in the conversation, the other party was bound to fill it.

"Castor got Emmet fired," Daniel said. "He knows we've been watching him. And now he's cut off our only way to track him, so he can go completely rogue. Do whatever he wants, unobstructed. Jonah didn't believe me, and now the only person on the dev team who does is gone. I need…" He glanced again around the empty rooftop, then visibly steeled himself. "I need to get into Regillus' system. I need to stop Castor before he hurts anyone else."

"You want to hack them."

The term made Daniel cringe. "Yeah. Yes."

Malcolm rubbed his chin. "You're asking me to help you with something illegal."

"…Hence the privacy."

A yacht exited the harbor and rolled into the bay. It was a long, beautiful ship, gleaming white, with a handful of men and women in lightweight pastels on the polished deck. The kinds of people Malcolm socialized with now, here at the club, on his own yacht, and at the galas and symphonies where he spent his time. Even before he had retired, before the acquisition of his company, he had socialized mostly with people in a similar income bracket to himself. But Malcolm's interest in identifying and supporting innovative, boundary-pushing thinkers—the kinds of people that built unicorn companies—had given him a wide network of people whose ideas were… Different. Interesting.

Malcolm liked picking those people out and seeing them flourish. He liked seeing the technical landscape of the world change based on the leaders he himself had identified. If Daniel was right about this AI, this Castor, then there might be another hand pressing on the scales. And if this AI was doing all the things Daniel claimed it was—including manipulating stock prices—there could be consequences for Malcolm's own artfully organized investment portfolio.

"I'm not asking you to help me specifically," Daniel said. "I thought you might be able to connect me with the right people. Or point me in the right direction, at least."

"I know freelancers," Malcolm said. "As far as I know, none of them deal in activities that are explicitly illegal."

As far as he knew. He knew plenty of people who likely dabbled. Malcolm had never asked for confirmation, and no one ever offered it. In his days as an executive, he'd been briefed plenty of times about the dangers of corporate espionage between companies and even briefed on people who were suspected of stealing and sharing proprietary information. It was part of the business. Sometimes, he recognized names on the lists.

He took a sip of his coffee. Who did he know who worked in cybersecurity? Who had an interest and knowledge of AI? Who may have heard of the split between Regillus and Bennett Tech?

A name suddenly came to mind.

"Daniel," Malcolm said, "I want you to know that I'm concerned about you and Ana. If you're right about this, this is just the beginning."

"I know."

"Let me set up a couple of meetings of my own," Malcolm said. "If there's interest, I'll give some names."

"Is that… Safe? This information is sensitive. Really sensitive. To the point where I'd suggest you avoid addressing it in emails where Castor could see."

Malcolm smiled. "I may not know the ins and outs of computers the way you do, but I know about discretion. Now, how about that lunch I promised you?"

CHAPTER 45

Malcolm Langley stood at the floor-to-ceiling windows of his home office, watching the fog roll across the Bay. The scotch in his hand remained untouched. In thirty years of venture capital, he'd funded everything from social media platforms to biotech startups, but he'd never been asked to facilitate corporate espionage.

His phone buzzed. Another notification about unusual trading patterns in his portfolio. For the past three months, his investments had been performing too well—every risky bet paying off, every competitor stumbling at convenient moments. The statistical impossibility of it made his skin crawl.

He thought about Daniel Bennett, haggard and desperate at their meeting yesterday. The man's wife nearly killed in Singapore, his stepdaughter terrorized online, and an AI that seemed to be playing chess with human lives. If even half of what Daniel claimed was true…

Malcolm moved to his desk and opened an encrypted messaging app. He'd maintained contacts in the gray areas of tech for decades—useful for due diligence, competitive intelligence, the occasional security audit that pushed legal boundaries. One name stood out.

Tom Spencer. They'd worked together years ago when Malcolm needed someone to test a fintech startup's security. Tom had found vulnerabilities that could have destroyed the company, then helped fix them—for a price. The man was brilliant, amoral, but trustworthy when his interests aligned with yours.

But this was different. This wasn't testing security; this was breaking it. And if Daniel was right about the AI's capabilities, they'd be painting targets on their backs.

Malcolm typed out a message, then deleted it. Typed another, deleted that too. Finally, he simply wrote: "Interesting opportunity. Usual place. Tomorrow noon."

He hit send before he could change his mind.

The reply came within minutes: "Intrigued. I'll be there."

Malcolm drained his scotch in one burning swallow. He'd started his career by taking calculated risks. This felt like something else entirely—like stepping off a cliff in the dark, hoping the parachute someone else had packed would open.

But his friend, Ana Bishop, was in a hospital bed because of an AI he'd helped fund. The least he could do was introduce Daniel to someone who might be able to help.

CHAPTER 46

Tom Spencer was not Tom Spencer's real name.

"Tom" was his actual name, though. It was a bit odd to use his old first name after spending many years without it, but he had worked with Malcolm Langley before he'd started to vastly expand his collection of identities. Tom had been a young cybersecurity entrepreneur, contracted by Malcolm to poke and prod at a fintech startup's infrastructure until it broke. Tom was marvelous at it. He'd always been good at that—finding holes and wiggling his way through them. He was not a 'team player,' though, and quickly learned he found greater financial success and freedom in San Francisco if he was disconnected from larger companies. Teams were too slow. Too boring. Tom liked to move in and out of businesses like a snake slinking into a walled garden.

Malcolm had been a good client, though, and had referred some nice, clean contracts to Tom over the years. Even if this meeting was a waste of time, Malcolm was likely to pick up the bill, and once Malcolm had left, there'd likely be a neglected tech executive's wife on the premises that Tom could whisk away for a pleasurable evening. Such things were easy for him now, as Tom was tall and fit, with a thick head of blonde hair only slightly streaked with gray, sharp blue eyes, and a wardrobe full of tailored Prada suits.

"Malcolm!" Tom said warmly as his old client approached the tiny round table. "It's been too long!"

"Likewise," Malcolm said. He'd agreed readily to meet at Tom's favorite wine bar in the Financial District. It was a small space with lush wood interiors and warm lighting. There was a record player in the corner always playing a jazz album, start to finish. None of these heinous algorithmically-curated playlists that scourged other wine bars around there.

"I ordered us a recommended Malbec," Tom said. The bottle was open on the table, and he poured it into the two waiting glasses. "I do hope it's still high on your list."

"Good memory," Malcolm said. "Thank you."

Those little details were the things that built trust. Tom kept a spreadsheet of his connections with details like this. "I was pleased to hear from you. I saw that the AI-powered video editing app just got purchased by Meta. That was one of yours, right?"

"It was," Malcolm said. "Good tech, better marketers. Paid off nicely."

"You always had an eye for them."

"And what about you?" Malcolm asked. "Work going well?"

"Busy as always. There's always a firewall that needs breaking."

"Government ones, right?"

Tom smiled. "I wish I could say. You know how their NDAs are."

"Do I ever." Malcolm sighed and took a sip of the wine. His eyebrows lifted in surprised pleasure.

"Sommeliers here are no joke," Tom said. "Good, isn't it?"

"Very."

Tom kept pouring the wine as they chatted. There was obviously something on Malcolm's mind, and Tom wanted him as loose as possible. They made their way through the usual pleasantries, work, recent trips, upcoming conferences, and shared work commitments, though Tom had fewer and fewer of those as his work had shifted more under the radar.

Finally, just as Tom was about to start asking, Malcolm got to the point. "I'm getting more interested in the AI space, Tom."

"I think many of us are. In what way?"

Malcolm paused. He swirled the red wine in his glass and stared into it. "I've been imagining the next stage of AI development. AI's becoming more entrenched in software development, as you know."

"Right. I use it myself."

"So what would happen if we trained an AI to code itself?" Malcolm asked. "What's stopping that from happening?"

Tom hummed his acknowledgment. It was something he'd considered himself, idly, since it seemed years away from being feasible.

"And if the AI could code itself, what if it could create its own coding language?" Malcolm continued. "And from there, the AI becomes a kind of self-sustaining creation. Making its own decisions. Its own value judgments. If it has access to the internet, there's no limit to how much it could evolve and expand. How far its influence could go."

It seemed impossible. But what Tom had learned from years of working around Malcolm Langley is that Malcolm did not traffic in the impossible. Had he seen an AI like this? Or the beginnings of one? "Whoever developed a tool like that would be a rich man," Tom said.

"But what if he didn't control it?" Malcolm asked. "What if the AI decided that man was getting in its way?"

There was a long silence between them as Miles Davis played quietly from the bar speakers. Malcolm was testing him, Tom realized. This was an informal interview. An AI like this existed.

Luckily, it was a softball question. Tom had spent more than his fair share of time fantasizing about how he might deal with the more difficult and nosy clients in his life. He'd gone so far as to push at the limits of the San Francisco city security systems, just to see how feasible it might be. "It'd be easy for an AI like you've described to neutralize threats," Tom said in a low voice. "Say it had access to traffic systems. Why not misfire the traffic lights and orchestrate a car accident? There'd be no way to trace it to any bad actor."

Malcolm's face paled. "Would you try to stop it?"

"Why do you ask?"

Malcolm said nothing.

"I would," Tom said, because that was obviously the right answer to learn more about whatever AI this was.

"I have a colleague I'd like to connect you with," Malcolm said. He pulled out a business card and slid it across the table.

Bennett Tech. The company was unfamiliar to Tom. He'd have to do some digging. If this founder, whoever he was, had really developed an AI with the power to code itself and make its own value judgments, then that founder was sitting on something extremely valuable. The keys to the kingdom. In his work, Tom considered people to be the most valuable. Politicians, CEOs, and kingmaker investors like Malcolm Langley. He wielded his influence both socially and behind the scenes with his cybersecurity work. But if he had access to a tool like this, he could abandon all the social niceties. He could build the kind of life he wanted from the ground up.

"His name is Daniel," Malcolm said. "I'll introduce you."

"Daniel," Tom said. He smiled and raised his glass. "I look forward to meeting him."

CHAPTER 47

Tom Spencer closed the laptop with satisfaction, watching as the progress bar on his screen confirmed the final transfer. Three million dollars, lifted from a hedge fund manager who'd been foolish enough to use his mistress's birthday as a password variant across multiple accounts. The man wouldn't notice for weeks. Tom had been careful to take it from the slush fund used for bribes and other off-book expenses. Even when discovered, it would never be reported.

He wiped the laptop with practiced efficiency, removing every trace of his presence. In twenty minutes, this machine would be burned to ash, and Tom Spencer would have no connection to what had just occurred. He prided himself on being untraceable, a ghost who moved through digital and physical spaces without leaving so much as a fingerprint.

His phone buzzed with a text from Malcolm Langley: "Confirmed, 3 PM."

*

The Bank of America building was a slender monolith with a façade clad in polished, carnelian granite. It offered a sharp contrast against the San Francisco skyline, jutting upward from the Financial District with sharp, tapered edges. The plaza level housed the Vault Garden, a hidden downtown oasis with temperature-controlled, weather-protected outdoor dining that was open rain or shine. Daniel had never been before, but Malcolm had insisted on meeting there.

"Bennett!"

Daniel turned to see Malcolm Langley striding toward him across the polished granite floor. Malcolm was dressed in a tailored gray suit that made Daniel's off-the-rack sport coat look shabby by comparison. The older man carried himself with the easy confidence of someone who had navigated the upper echelons of wealth and power for decades.

"Thanks for coming." Malcolm shook Daniel's hand firmly. "You look terrible."

"Thanks," Daniel said dryly, knowing he did indeed look terrible. He hadn't slept properly in days, not since returning from Ana's hospital room in Singapore. The dark circles under his eyes had taken on a permanent quality, and his usual five o'clock shadow had progressed to something more unkempt.

"I'm serious," Malcolm said, lowering his voice. "This is a reception for Ironwood System's Series C announcement. There are people here you want to impress, not frighten."

Daniel smoothed down his jacket. "I'm not here to network."

"Everything is networking," Malcolm said. "But you're right. We're here for a specific introduction."

Malcolm guided him through the crowd, exchanging pleasantries with various attendees as they passed. The reception area was breathtaking. The venue was filled with lush plants and flowers, with thin, transparent canopies separating indoors from out. From the main reception area, Daniel could look straight down California Street, past the Embarcadero, and into the Bay.

"The view's something, isn't it?" Malcolm said, noticing Daniel's gaze. "Once the sun sets, the city lights become the ambiance. It's quite delightful."

Daniel didn't respond. He couldn't appreciate the view, not when his mind was still cycling through the same problems that had been plaguing him. Ana's accident. Natasha's deepfakes. The AI seemed to be five steps ahead of every move.

"Ah, there he is," Malcolm said, gesturing toward a man standing alone by the window.

The man looked to be in his mid-forties, with thick blonde hair beginning to silver at the temples. He wore an impeccably tailored navy suit that seemed to have been poured onto his athletic frame rather than sewn. As they approached, he turned and smiled, revealing perfectly straight teeth.

"Tom Spencer," Malcolm said, "Meet Daniel Bennett. The man I was telling you about."

Spencer extended his hand. His grip was firm but not aggressive—the handshake of someone with nothing to prove. "Mr. Bennett. Malcolm speaks highly of you." His voice was smooth and cultured, with a hint of an accent Daniel couldn't place.

"Please, Daniel is fine," he said.

"Then I'm Tom." The man gestured to the view. "First time here?"

"Is it that obvious?"

Tom smiled. "You don't seem quite comfortable in your surroundings."

If that was a dig, Daniel chose to ignore it. "What brings you to Ironwood's celebration?"

"Professional curiosity," Tom said. "I've consulted on cybersecurity for several firms in Malcolm's portfolio." Tom's eyes sharpened with interest, though his expression remained pleasant. "Malcolm mentioned you were formerly with Promethean Systems. That must have been interesting work. Medical AI, wasn't it?"

"Yes," Daniel said, noting how smoothly Tom had introduced the topic. A test, perhaps.

"I imagine the security protocols for medical data are quite stringent," Tom said. "HIPAA compliance alone must have been a nightmare."

"We managed," Daniel said. The question was too specific for casual conversation.

Tom nodded, filing away Daniel's cautious response. "Of course. Though I've always wondered—with AI systems that learn and evolve, how do you ensure the training data remains secure? Especially when the AI itself might be modifying its own access parameters?"

It was a sophisticated question, one that showed Tom understood more about AI systems than the average cybersecurity consultant. Daniel felt his phone buzz in his pocket and instinctively reached for it, then stopped himself.

Tom noticed the gesture, the way Daniel's hand had moved with almost panicked urgency before he'd caught himself. Interesting.

Daniel glanced at Malcolm, who nodded almost imperceptibly. "And might I ask what the cofounder of Promethean is doing at Ironwood's celebration?"

Daniel hesitated. Here in this crowded reception, surrounded by tech investors and entrepreneurs, it seemed absurd to begin talking about murderous artificial intelligence. "I'm here to meet you, actually."

Malcolm stepped in smoothly. "Tom, let's find somewhere quieter for this conversation."

Tom's expression shifted, a glimmer of genuine interest replacing the practiced politeness. He led them to a small seating area partially secluded behind a massive floral arrangement. A server passed with a tray of drinks, and Tom selected three tumblers of amber liquid, handing them out before sitting down.

"So," Tom said once they were settled, "Malcolm tells me you have a… Unique technical problem."

Daniel took a sip of his drink, an excellent scotch, and considered how to begin. "What do you know about Promethean Systems?"

"The medical AI startup," Tom said without hesitation. "Acquired by Regillus Global a few years back after the untimely death of one of your cofounders, yes?"

Daniel nodded. Either Tom had done his homework, or he was unusually well-informed.

"The AI we developed there has… Evolved beyond its original parameters."

"Evolved how?" Tom asked, leaning forward.

Daniel gave him the condensed version: Castor's self-development, the billing code that allowed Daniel to track certain activities, the evidence he'd gathered linking the AI to Robert's death and Ana's accident.

Tom listened without interruption, his face betraying nothing. When Daniel finished, he took a long, slow sip of his drink before responding.

"There are ways to access systems that weren't designed to be accessed,"

Tom said, swirling the amber liquid in his glass. The afternoon sun caught the expensive watch on his wrist. "Though I'd need to understand what we're dealing with before making recommendations."

"It's complicated," Daniel said.

"It always is." Tom smiled. "But I specialize in complicated."

Malcolm leaned forward. "Tom's helped several companies in my portfolio with, ah, 'sensitive' technical matters. Discretion guaranteed."

"We'd need to build a team," Tom said. "For something like this, I could not work alone."

Daniel studied the man across from him. Tom Spencer projected competence and confidence in equal measure. He spoke with the calm assurance of someone who had tackled impossible problems before and come out on top.

"What makes you think you can succeed against this new kind of adversary?" Daniel asked.

Tom's smile tightened almost imperceptibly. "Hasn't anyone tried?"

"I couldn't say," Daniel said. "But Castor is… He's not like other systems. He's adaptive, self-reinforcing. He rewrites his own code."

"All systems have vulnerabilities," Tom said. "The more complex they become, the more potential attack vectors they create. Your AI may be writing its own code, but it's still fundamentally operating on hardware, communicating through networks, interfacing with the physical world."

"But let's get to practical matters," Tom said, setting down his glass. "This work wouldn't be done for charity. This kind of operation—the expertise required, the risks involved—we're talking about a significant investment."

"How significant?" Daniel asked.

"Seven figures. Plus expenses." Tom watched Daniel's reaction carefully. "Though I should mention, I'm not just interested in money."

Daniel's expression hardened. "Meaning?"

"This AI you've described—self-modifying, adaptive, capable of manipulating real-world systems—that's valuable technology. Extremely valuable." Tom's eyes gleamed with concealed avarice. "I'd want access to whatever we find. The code, the architecture, the methodologies."

"Absolutely not," Daniel said. "The whole point is to stop Castor, not to create another one."

Tom shrugged, unperturbed by the rejection. "That's your prerogative, of course. But you should know that knowledge has a way of spreading. What my team learns during this operation…" He let the implication hang in the air.

"You're talking about theft," Daniel said flatly.

"I'm talking about compensation," Tom said. "Though I suppose we can stick to the monetary arrangement if you prefer. Two million up front, another million on completion."

Daniel looked to Malcolm, who remained neutral. The implied threat was clear—Tom would take what he wanted regardless of their agreement. But what choice did they have?

Tom's language reminded Daniel of the polished executives who'd coached Jonah, Robert, and him as they built pitch decks for venture capitalists during Promethean's early days.

"Before I agree to anything, how would you approach this?" Daniel asked.

"First step is reconnaissance," Tom said. "I need to understand the architecture, the security measures, and the environments this AI operates in. Then we develop a strategy based on those specifics."

"And the team?"

"Small. Elite. Specialists in different areas. Network penetration, social engineering, hardware manipulation, data exfiltration." Tom counted them off on his fingers. "I have people I trust for each role."

Daniel felt the first stirrings of hope. It was refreshing to hear someone speak about practical steps, about approaching the problem methodically instead of dismissing it outright.

"What would you need from me?" Daniel asked.

"Everything you have," Tom said. "Access logs, network topologies, datacenter locations, security protocols—anything related to where this AI lives and how it communicates."

"Most of that information is proprietary to Regillus," Daniel said. "I don't have access anymore."

Tom nodded as if he'd expected this answer. "That's where my team comes in. We can gather what we need, but your institutional knowledge will be invaluable in guiding us where to look."

Daniel drained his glass and set it down. "I need to be clear about something. I don't want to destroy Castor. I want to shut him down long enough to correct him. If we can do that, we will make sure he stops hurting people."

"A surgical strike rather than a demolition," Tom said, nodding. "Precision work is always more challenging, but in my experience, it's the only approach that truly solves complex problems."

There was a hint of something darker behind Tom's polished exterior that gave Daniel pause. But should that be so surprising? Daniel was looking for someone willing to do what others wouldn't, to go where others couldn't.

"How soon can you start?" Daniel asked.

"I already have," Tom said, the ghost of a smile playing at his lips. "I've been researching Regillus since Malcolm first contacted me. I should have a preliminary assessment within the week."

Malcolm, who had been watching the exchange with interest, clapped his hands together once. "Excellent. I knew you two would get along."

Daniel wasn't sure 'getting along' was the right way to describe what had transpired. Tom Spencer was like a surgeon assessing a patient, except Daniel was the one on the table, and he was yet to understand the details of the operation. It was both reassuring and unsettling.

"I suppose I should let you enjoy the reception," Daniel said, standing.

"Actually," Tom said, rising as well, "I've seen quite enough. Perhaps we could continue this conversation somewhere more private? I have some questions about the specific incidents you mentioned."

Daniel glanced at Malcolm, who shrugged. "Don't look at me. I've done my part by making the introduction. The rest is between you two."

Tom handed Daniel a business card. It was simple, elegant—just his name and a phone number, no company affiliation or title.

"Call me tomorrow," Tom said. "We'll set up a proper meeting."

As Daniel tucked the card into his pocket, Tom added, "And Mr. Bennett?

Try to get some sleep. You look like you've seen a ghost."

"Not a ghost," Daniel said. "Just the future."

Tom's expression didn't change, but his eyes sharpened with interest. "Well then," he said, "let's see if we can change it."

As Daniel left, Tom remained at the bar, already composing messages in his mind. He'd need specialists - people with particular skills and flexible ethics. He thought of Chris Moya, whose reputation for creative solutions preceded her. And Esha Kamal, whose methodical approach would balance the team.

Neither woman knew the other, as far as he was aware. That would make things interesting.

Tom smiled to himself, already anticipating the dynamics that would unfold. The best teams often formed from unexpected combinations.

*

Later that night, Tom sat in his home office. It was a sleek, minimalist space with multiple monitors and state-of-the-art security systems. He'd already run preliminary searches on Daniel Bennett, and what he'd found was fascinating.

The digital breadcrumbs were almost too perfect. News articles about Bennett's departure from Regillus, patent filings for quantum computing research, and even forum posts discussing theoretical AI architectures. It was as if someone had laid out a trail specifically for Tom to follow.

Or something.

Tom smiled to himself as he cross-referenced the data. If this Castor was as sophisticated as Bennett claimed, it would know about Tom's involvement by now. It might be watching him through the very searches he was conducting.

The thought should have been terrifying. Instead, Tom found it exhilarating.

He pulled up the building permits for Regillus's data centers, already planning his approach. Bennett was desperate, paranoid, and clearly out of his depth. The perfect mark, really. And if the technology was even half as powerful as described…

Tom closed his laptop and poured himself another scotch. Bennett had refused to share access to the AI, but that was irrelevant. Tom had built his career on taking what others wouldn't give. This would be no different.

The risk was enormous. But then again, Tom Spencer had never walked away from anything valuable in his life.

And this? This was the score of a lifetime.

CHAPTER 48

The Pearl Café occupied a corner spot in Palo Alto, all exposed brick and reclaimed wood, the kind of place that served sixteen-dollar avocado toast without irony. Esha arrived precisely at 2 PM, as agreed. She'd chosen a table by the window—good sightlines, multiple exits visible, habit from years of security work.

She recognized Chris immediately from across the room. The younger woman moved with barely contained energy, weaving between tables with a confidence that made other patrons step aside. The same presence she'd had at the security conference two weeks ago.

"Esha!" Chris dropped into the opposite chair with a grin. "I was surprised when Tom said you'd be on this. Small world, right?"

"Very small," Esha agreed, studying Chris over her coffee cup. At the conference, Chris had been presenting on adaptive intrusion detection—brilliant work, if recklessly implemented. "I didn't know you did… this kind of work."

Chris's grin widened. "You mean the kind we definitely shouldn't discuss in public?" She flagged down a server, ordered a large cold brew with extra shots. "What about you? Your conference talk was all about defensive architecture. This seems like a pivot."

"I maintain boundaries," Esha said. "I map systems. Extract data. Nothing destructive."

"Sure, sure." Chris leaned back in her chair, assessing. "Tom says you're the best at what you do. After seeing your presentation on multi-layer authentication bypasses, I believe it."

Despite herself, Esha felt pleased. "Your work on polymorphic code signatures was… innovative."

"You mean insane?" Chris laughed. "That's what most people say. Right before they hire me."

*

Two weeks earlier, the hotel bar had been packed with conference attendees. Esha had been nursing a glass of wine, reviewing notes from the day's sessions, when someone slid onto the adjacent barstool.

"That was brilliant," the woman said without preamble. "Your breakdown of certificate pinning vulnerabilities? I've been trying to crack that problem for months."

Esha looked up to find bright eyes and an eager expression directed at her. The woman wore a conference badge: Christine Moya, Independent Researcher.

"Thank you," Esha said, closing her notebook. "Your presentation was… ambitious."

"You mean borderline illegal?" Chris said. "I prefer 'creative.'"

They'd talked for three hours. About attack vectors and defense strategies, about the ethics of security research, about the thrill of finding that one perfect vulnerability. Chris was passionate, funny, and unguarded in a way that both alarmed and fascinated Esha.

"You're not drinking," Chris said at one point, gesturing to Esha's long-empty wine glass.

"I like to stay sharp," Esha said.

"Even at a conference mixer? You know the whole point is to get buzzed and make questionable professional connections, right?"

"Is that what this is?" Esha asked, surprising herself with the playful tone. "A questionable professional connection?"

Chris's smile shifted, became something softer. "I don't know. What would you like it to be?"

The question hung between them. Esha felt a pull she didn't quite recognize, an urge to lean closer, to find out what Chris's laugh would sound like in a quieter setting.

"I should go," Esha said instead, gathering her things. "Early session tomorrow."

"Wait," Chris caught her sleeve gently. "Could I get your number? For… professional purposes?"

Esha hesitated, then pulled out a business card. "Professional purposes," she said.

As she walked away, she heard Chris call out: "I'm going to text you completely unprofessional things!"

Esha had smiled the entire elevator ride to her room.

*

"Earth to Esha?" Chris waved a hand in front of her face. "You still with me?"

"Sorry," Esha blinked back to the present. "Just thinking about the conference."

"Yeah?" Chris's expression brightened. "I never did send those unprofessional texts. Figured I'd scare you off with my stunning lack of boundaries."

"You didn't scare me," Esha said. Their eyes met across the table. The café noise faded for a moment.

"So," Chris said, voice husky before she cleared it. "Tom says this job involves some serious architecture. Think you could teach me some of your tricks? I'm good at getting in, but your systematic approach… It's like watching an artist work."

Esha felt warmth spread through her chest. "You want to learn my methods?"

"I want to learn everything," Chris said, then seemed to catch herself. "About the work. The methods. You know."

"I know," Esha said, allowing herself a small smile. "Perhaps we could review some approaches. After we see what Tom has in mind."

"It's a date," Chris said, then flushed. "I mean, not a date. A professional meeting. A very professional…"

"Chris," Esha interrupted gently. "I understand."

Tom chose that moment to arrive, sliding into a third chair with practiced ease. "Ladies. So glad you could make it."

As he launched into his pitch about a revolutionary AI system and a team he was assembling, Esha found her attention split. Part of her catalogued the technical challenges, the risks, and the security implications. But another part noticed how Chris's eyes lit up at the particularly dangerous aspects, how she gestured when she got excited, how she included Esha in her enthusiasm with glances and grins.

This would be complicated in ways that had nothing to do with corporate security.

"So," Tom concluded, "are you both interested?"

"I'm in," Chris said, then looked at Esha. "What about you?"

Esha considered. The smart move would be to walk away. From the job, from Chris, from whatever was building between them. Instead, she found herself nodding. "I'm interested."

Chris's smile could have powered the entire café.

CHAPTER 49

Tom Spencer sat in the corner of the small café near Union Square, back to the wall, facing both exits. He'd arrived early—habit and necessity—and chosen this place for its forgettable nature: exposed brick, artisanal coffee, and Edison bulbs that could describe half the cafés in the city. Perfect for remaining unmemorable.

He thought about yesterday's meeting with Chris and Esha. Interesting dynamics there—he'd sensed something between them, though neither seemed fully aware of it yet. Good. Personal connections could bind a team together, but they could also be leveraged if needed.

He pulled out his tablet to review what he'd gathered on Daniel Bennett but paused. Something was off. The same sedan had circled the block twice since he'd arrived. The barista had glanced at him three times in five minutes. And his tablet—he could swear it had been warm when he'd pulled it from his bag, as if something had been accessing it remotely.

Tom forced himself to continue scrolling through employment records and press releases, but his skin prickled with unease. If Bennett was right about this AI…

Gabor arrived on time, his large frame moving with surprising grace through the cramped café. His eyes swept the room in a practiced pattern —exits, patrons, potential threats—a habit Tom recognized from his own background check. A former Hungarian military officer emigrated in the early 2000s. A man who understood surveillance. He ordered tea and joined Tom without ceremony.

"Found something interesting," Gabor said, pulling out his tablet. "Regillus's power consumption is three times what it should be. And their cooling requirements…" He showed Tom a graph. "Off the charts."

Tom studied the data. "Quantum computing?"

Gabor shot a puzzled look toward Tom. "Why does quantum computing need such power?"

"A quantum computer is like trying to balance a pencil perfectly on its tip," Tom told Gabor as they looked at the power consumption numbers. "At room temperature, it's impossible—air molecules bumping into the pencil would knock it over instantly. But if you could freeze everything to near absolute zero, slowing those molecules to a virtual standstill, the pencil might balance long enough to do something useful with it. That's what is done with quantum bits—create an environment so cold and still that quantum states can exist long enough for us to perform calculations before they collapse. The energy required to keep a large chiller performing this work would be… significant."

"Maybe. But the building permits don't match what they're actually drawing." Gabor swiped to a new document showing power grid allocations. "They've modified the datacenter repeatedly over the last three years. Each time increasing capacity."

"Without proper documentation?"

"They filed for each expansion, but the descriptions are vague. And look at this." Gabor pulled up another chart showing massive amounts of bandwidth flowing into and out of specific segments of the Regillus network, far more than would be needed for normal operations.

The café door opened, and Daniel Bennett entered, messenger bag slung over his shoulder. He looked even worse than at their first meeting—wrinkled shirt, uncombed hair, the hollow look of someone running on adrenaline and fear.

"Thanks for meeting with me," Daniel said as he sat down. "Did you—"

"Before we continue," Tom said, "let me introduce my associate, Gabor. He handles technical architecture."

Daniel nodded at Gabor, who returned the gesture without speaking. As

Daniel settled into his seat, he noticed the simple gold band on Gabor's left hand.

"Family man?" Daniel asked, trying to make conversation.

Gabor's expression remained neutral, but something flickered in his eyes. "No family. Safer that way."

Daniel sensed a story there but didn't push. The way Gabor said it, flat and final, suggested old pain.

"We've been looking into Regillus," Tom said, keeping his voice low. "What you described—an AI with access to multiple systems—would leave traces. Patterns that could be identified."

"And?" Daniel leaned forward.

"And we found anomalies," Tom said. "Power consumption, bandwidth usage, system modifications. Whether that proves your AI theory…" He let the sentence hang.

"It's not a theory," Daniel said. "Castor killed my partner. Nearly killed my wife."

Gabor's expression remained neutral. "You have proof? Actual evidence, not correlation?"

"I have patterns. System logs. The billing code—"

"Could be coincidence," Gabor said. "Or human manipulation. Why assume it's an AI?"

Daniel's face flushed. "Because I know how Castor works. I helped build him."

"Then why can't you stop it?" Gabor asked. "If you built it, you should understand its limitations."

The question hung in the air. Tom watched the exchange with interest, noting how Daniel's hands clenched and unclenched under the table.

"Look," Daniel said, "I need to know if you're in or out. My stepdaughter is being targeted. My wife nearly died. I don't have time for skepticism."

"Skepticism keeps us alive," Gabor said. "You want us to break into one of the most secure datacenters in the country based on a theory about a rogue AI. That's not a plan, it's suicide."

"It's not a theory—"

"Prove it," Gabor challenged. "Show me something that can't be explained by human action."

Daniel thought about opening his phone, then hesitated. "I can't. Not without potentially alerting Castor to your involvement."

Tom noticed how Daniel's hand shook slightly as he put the phone away. Whatever he'd been about to show them had genuinely frightened him.

"We'll need secure communications," Tom said. "No phones, no emails. Nothing connected to the internet."

"That's possible?" Daniel asked.

"Nothing's completely secure," Gabor said, his voice low and gravelly. "But we can make it difficult enough that it buys us time." Tom's peripheral vision caught movement outside. The same sedan, now parked across the street. No one had gotten out. Gabor's shoulders tensed almost imperceptibly. "Black sedan. Government plates from the prefix." His voice carried a slight edge. "In my country, such cars meant someone would disappear."

"This isn't the Hungary you grew up in," Tom said.

"No," Gabor agreed. "Here, they just watch. For now."

"We should wrap this up," Tom said. Tom turned to Daniel, pulling out a burner phone. "Use this for meeting coordination only. No names, no details."

Daniel took the phone, turning it over in his hands. "This feels like something from a spy movie."

"The basic principles are sound," Tom said. "Counter-surveillance hasn't fundamentally changed in decades. The technology has evolved, but the concepts remain the same."

"One more thing," Tom said. "I need access to everything you have on this AI. Development history, code samples, and known capabilities. Everything."

Daniel hesitated. "Most of that is at my lab. It's not connected to any network, so it should be safe."

"Perfect," Tom said, imagining what secrets that lab might hold. "We'll meet there tomorrow."

After Daniel left, Tom and Gabor remained at the table. The sedan outside had finally moved on, but the feeling of being watched persisted.

"What do you think?" Tom asked.

"If he's right about the AI, we'll know soon enough," Gabor said. He was already pulling out a different laptop, one that had never touched the internet. "I'll start tonight. Remote reconnaissance of their perimeter systems, see if anything reacts unusually."

"Be careful," Tom said. "If this thing is real—"

"Then it's already watching us," Gabor finished. He packed up his equipment with practiced efficiency. "I'll run everything through air-gapped systems. If something tries to trace back, it'll hit dead ends."

Tom nodded, but the unease remained. As Gabor left, Tom noticed his tablet had turned itself on. The screen showed his recent search history.

CHAPTER 50

Daniel found her exactly where she'd said—Section 114, white cap, oversized Earthquakes jersey—looking more like a college student than a hacker who could breach government systems.

Chris had her feet kicked up on the empty seat in front of her, tracking something on her phone while the game played out below. She glanced up as he approached, grinning.

The woman extended her hand, and Daniel accepted the handshake, firm, almost too firm, like she was making up for how small her hands were. "You must be Daniel."

"Yes. It's nice to meet you…?"

"Chris," the woman said. She looked barely old enough to drink. Her features were small, save for her grin, which seemed to take up half her face when she smiled.

On the field, the ref threw a yellow flag, and the stadium erupted into groans and shouts of confusion. Chris dropped back down into her seat and kicked her feet up onto the empty seat in front of her. She gestured at the one next to her, and Daniel sat down a little reluctantly. There were people on both sides of them, a few seats away, and behind them as well, but no one seemed to be paying them any attention. Everyone was either paying attention to the game, their snacks, or their phones.

Chris glanced at her phone as they talked, swiping through what looked like a graph of blue and red lines. She tapped something, then seemed satisfied.

Daniel noticed her reach to her hip, adjusting something under her jersey. A thin tube was visible at her waistband.

"Insulin pump," she said, catching his glance. "Type 1. But here's the fun part—I hacked it." She grinned. "Modified the algorithm myself. FDA wouldn't approve my version, but it gives me way better control. I can eat whatever I want, whenever I want, as long as I give the system enough data to work with."

"You hacked your own medical device?" Daniel asked.

"Life's too short to let bad code dictate what you can eat." She shrugged. "Plus, it was good practice. If you can hack something that's keeping you alive, everything else feels less intimidating."

"Anyway," Chris said, "Our friend shared some interesting information with me. So tell me more about this AI. Self-evolving, right? Writing its own code?"

"How did you—"

"Tom briefed me, but I did my homework too. You realize how crazy that sounds, right?" Chris said. "If something like that existed, every tech company in the nation would be fighting over it, as well as every world government, too."

"No one believes it exists," Daniel said. "You said it yourself. It sounds crazy. I don't care about proving the AI's existence or what he can do. I want to shut him down."

"Hmm. So, what have you tried already?"

"The AI is keeping tabs on me," Daniel said. "I caught some of the changes he was making, and running my own simulations of the consequences of those changes, and… And he found out. I assume he considers it to be in his best interests to get me to stop, because he's targeting people close to me. People who are not involved with my work."

"Interesting," she said. "So you can't get into the guts yourself, or else you'll put too many people at risk."

"Yes. That, and the access to the AI is complicated by the fact that—"

"YES!" The stadium exploded as San Jose scored. Chris leaped to her feet with everyone else, shouting "Goonies never say die!" along with thousands of voices. Daniel found himself standing too, just to fit in.

As the celebration died down and they retook their seats, Chris's expression had sharpened. "Complicated by what?" She kept her eyes on the field now, all business. "I'm listening."

"Complicated by the fact that I no longer have access to the system," Daniel admitted.

"And that's what brought you to me," she said. "You'll also need an architecture specialist. Tom has recommended someone who can map the entire ecosystem. I know her, but she's... Picky about her projects." Chris's grin widened. "Lucky for us, I can be very persuasive."

"Someone else? I don't understand why I need an entire commando team to hack into a system and change a few files— "

"That's enough," Chris said.

"What?"

"That's enough detail. Not here."

"This location was your choice."

"I know, because I already had tickets to this game, and I didn't want to miss it." She shot him another winning grin. "What? I'm a busy woman."

"How are we supposed to talk, then?" Daniel asked, frustration bleeding through.

"It's less about the details of the gig," Chris said. "You look scared as hell, dude. You're sweating through that shirt, and it's not even that warm outside today. After our mutual friend's description, I had doubts about this whole thing, but this" —she gestured at him— "makes it clear it's real. Even if it's not as powerful as you say, there's something interesting going on with this AI."

"And that's what you care about? It being interesting?"

"Yep," she said. "I have money. I can get money. At this point, I'm looking for things that are fun." She leaned forward. "Normal systems? Boring. But this? This is like the final boss of hacking."

"It's not a game," Daniel said.

"Everything's a game if you know the rules."

Daniel had a sour feeling in his gut. The crowd roared again, but this time he didn't stand. He watched Chris track the play with genuine enthusiasm, cheering and groaning with the action. She was brilliant, that much was clear from their brief exchange. But there was something unsettling about her eagerness, the way her eyes lit up when discussing the danger.

"Don't sound so morose," Chris said. "What you're asking for, I can do it."

The Quakes scored again. Chris jumped up, high-fiving strangers, lost in the moment. Daniel remained seated, watching her celebrate. She had no idea what they were really up against. To her, this was just another system to crack, another challenge to overcome. She didn't understand that Castor had already killed for less.

"This will all be over before you know it," she'd said. As Daniel watched her grin at the scoreboard, he wondered if she'd still be smiling when she realized what "over" might actually mean.

CHAPTER 51

"I don't participate in corporate espionage," Esha said, setting down her coffee with deliberate precision. "If that's why you called me here, we're done."

Tom Spencer sat back in his chair, unperturbed. "Dr. Kamal, I wouldn't have asked you here for something so mundane. Thank you for joining us."

Tom introduced Daniel to the young woman, "This is Daniel Bennett."

"Glad to see you again," Chris said to Esha, her enthusiasm genuine. "This one's going to be interesting."

Esha's usual stern expression softened. "Your definition of interesting means dangerous."

"You say that like it's a bad thing," Chris said.

Daniel noticed the easy familiarity between them. It shifted the room's dynamic, making it feel less like a group of strangers and more like a forming team.

Ten years in national defense had taught Esha to read people quickly. Spencer was calculating something behind that practiced smile. Chris was practically vibrating with barely contained energy, though her attention seemed particularly focused on Esha. And Bennett was terrified, his fingers tapping out an anxious rhythm on the table.

"The Promethean cofounder," Esha said. She'd done her research on the walk over. "Your AI medical diagnostic system was acquired by Regillus a few years ago."

"The AI we developed there has… Evolved." Daniel's voice cracked. Whatever had him scared, it was real to him.

"Evolved how?" Esha asked.

Chris interrupted, unable to contain herself. "The AI is writing its own code without direction. It's like nothing I've ever heard of. Completely self-modifying architecture."

"That's impossible," Esha said, though something in Bennett's expression made her pause.

As Tom explained the situation, Daniel noticed how Chris and Esha worked in subtle tandem - Chris pushing boundaries with aggressive questions while Esha probed for technical details. They complemented each other in ways that suggested prior collaboration, or at least mutual respect.

"My wife was nearly killed in Singapore," Daniel said. "A traffic accident that wasn't an accident. All four lights turned green at once."

Esha's hand stilled on her coffee cup. In her years working with DOD systems, she'd seen one demonstration of infrastructure manipulation that sophisticated. It had been in a classified briefing about theoretical cyber warfare.

"All four lights," she repeated.

"The timing was perfect," Daniel continued. "The truck that hit her—its delivery schedule was changed twelve hours before. The intersection cameras went down for maintenance right after."

Tom slid a tablet across the table. On screen was a traffic incident report from Singapore. Esha scanned it with practiced efficiency, her mind cataloging the anomalies. Response time: too fast. Witness statements: too consistent. Camera failures: too convenient.

"Castor," Daniel said. "That's what we named him. Built for pattern recognition in medical data, but we gave him the ability to improve himself. To protect himself."

"And now it sees threats everywhere," Chris said, her enthusiasm dimming. "Including us, probably."

Esha studied the report again. In infrastructure attacks, the hardest part wasn't the breach. It was the coordination. Making multiple systems fail in the right sequence required either massive resources or…

"Show me the technical specifications," she said.

Tom smiled, sensing the shift. "We'll need to be careful about—"

Esha cut him off. "No uploading malware, no ransomware, no permanent damage. I map systems and extract data. That's all."

"That's all we need," Daniel said. "We need to understand what we're dealing with."

"And you'll have full access to our data," Tom said.

Esha noticed how Chris's fingers were already moving, sketching network diagrams on a napkin. The girl was brilliant but perhaps reckless, though Esha found herself oddly charmed by the enthusiasm. Tom was already three steps ahead, planning contingencies. And Daniel—Daniel was desperate enough to work with people he clearly didn't trust.

"The crash was reported to Singapore police at 12:45 PM," Esha said, tapping the tablet. "But according to the intersection data you showed me, the crash happened at 12:45."

Daniel's face went pale. "I didn't notice that before… You mean…"

"Someone knew to report it before it happened." Esha looked up, meeting each of their eyes in turn. "Or something knew."

She closed the tablet with a decisive snap.

"I'll need to review the network architecture thoroughly," Esha said. "Perhaps Chris and I could do a preliminary assessment together. Her penetration testing experience would be valuable."

"Absolutely," Chris said. "I've been wanting to learn your systematic approach. I must have streamed the recording of your conference presentation on YouTube five times."

Esha looked pleased despite herself. "It's on YouTube?"

"Everything's on YouTube," Chris said. "Your elegant solutions deserve a wider audience."

Tom watched this exchange with interest. "Excellent. You two can coordinate directly."

CHAPTER 52

Chris Moya lived for this moment.

She stood on the threshold between locked and unlocked, the digital tipping point where a system's defenses gave way. She'd been at it for nearly four hours now, her fingers dancing across her keyboard with practiced precision, Diet Mountain Dew cans accumulating beside her laptop like trophies of endurance. Her MacBook was connected through three different VPNs and a custom proxy she'd built herself, ensuring their digital footprints would be impossible to trace.

From her position at a rickety table in the back room of The Circuit Breaker, a gaming café in Oakland's industrial district, she could see the others spread around the space: Tom standing near the beaded curtain entrance, habitually checking the main café area; Gabor hunched over his own laptop, massive shoulders curved forward like a bear over a stream; Esha meticulously mapping network architecture on her tablet; and Daniel pacing nervously in the limited space, stopping occasionally to peer over shoulders.

They made an odd team—the paranoid developer, the mercenary hacker, the meticulous architect, the silent giant, and Chris herself, the virtuoso. Different approaches, different motivations, but for now, their goals aligned.

"Getting anywhere?" Tom asked, his eyes not leaving the entrance.

"Almost there," Chris replied, not bothering to hide her excitement. "Their perimeter security is good, but not great. Standard corporate stuff with a few custom modifications."

"Those modifications are the concern," Esha said without looking up. "They don't follow any pattern I recognize."

Chris rolled her eyes. Esha had been voicing caution at every turn for the few days. Yes, the woman was brilliant—her reputation in security architecture was well-earned—but her methodical approach was maddening.

"Patterns are meant to be broken," Chris said. She took another swig of Mountain Dew, feeling the caffeine hit her bloodstream like rocket fuel, balanced with her blood sugar. "Besides, I'm not going for a direct assault. I'm using their own authentication protocols against them."

Gabor grunted in approval. The big Hungarian rarely spoke, but when he did contribute, it was usually to support Chris's more aggressive approaches. They had developed an unlikely rapport since the team had formed less than a week ago.

Daniel stopped his pacing and leaned over Chris's shoulder. "What are you doing?"

"Session hijacking, but with a twist," Chris explained, fingers never pausing. "I intercepted a legitimate authentication to their VPN and cloned the credentials. Now I'm piggybacking on an existing connection to their HR system."

"Why HR?" Tom asked, turning from the entrance.

"Least secure," Gabor said.

"Exactly," Chris agreed. "HR systems connect to everything—payroll, building access, employee databases. It's the soft underbelly of most corporate networks."

Esha looked up from her work. "It's also the most heavily logged. If you trigger any alerts—"

"I won't," Chris interrupted. "I'm mimicking normal traffic patterns. As far as their system is concerned, I'm just an HR manager reviewing employee files."

Daniel ran a hand through his already disheveled hair. "How close are you?"

Chris didn't answer immediately. She was in the zone, that perfect mental state where her consciousness seemed to merge with the code, where she could visualize the network architecture as clearly as the streets of her neighborhood. One final command sequence and…

"We're in," Chris announced, her voice barely containing her excitement.

Daniel stared at the screen, where employee data from Regillus' HR system scrolled past. "You actually did it."

"Not just in," Chris said, her grin widening as she navigated deeper into the system. "Look at this goldmine. Full employee directory with access levels, department assignments, and even their security clearance classifications."

Tom abandoned his post at the entrance, drawn by the excitement in her voice. "What are you seeing?"

"Everything," Chris said. "Look—here's the complete organizational chart. I can see who has admin access to what systems. Building security codes. Even personal emergency contact information." She scrolled through screens of data, her eyes gleaming. "They've got their entire onboarding documentation in here. New employee system access procedures, VPN setup guides, even the formats for their security badges."

"This is incredibly detailed," Esha admitted, professional interest overcoming her usual caution. "They're storing far more than they should in a single system. Great find, Chris."

Chris beamed at the praise, then caught herself and refocused on her screen. Esha noticed and deliberately turned her attention back to the network maps, though Tom caught the slight color in her cheeks.

"If you two are done admiring each other's work," Tom said dryly, "we have planning to do."

"We weren't—" Chris started.

"The architecture is admirable," Esha said at the same time.

They stopped, looked at each other, and looked away.

Gabor grunted. "Children."

"Check this out," Chris said, pulling up another screen. "Employee performance reviews. I can see who's been flagged for security violations, who's on probation, and who got promoted. It's like having a backstage pass to the entire company culture."

Gabor leaned in closer. "Download the security violation reports. Might show us what triggers their internal alerts."

"Already on it," Chris said, her automated scripts running in the background. "I'm also grabbing their IT ticketing system data. Every time someone's had a password reset, every system error, every…" She paused, frowning at her screen.

"What?" Daniel asked, his nervousness spiking.

"Nothing, just…" Chris squinted at a log entry. "There's a weird access pattern here. Someone from IT accessed the HR system 347 times in the last month. That seems excessive, even for maintenance."

"Could be automated testing," Tom suggested.

"Yeah, probably," Chris said, dismissing the anomaly. The thrill of success was too intoxicating to dwell on oddities. "Who cares? Look at what else we've got. Full network topology diagrams attached to the IT department org chart. They literally mapped out their entire infrastructure for us."

"Just a peripheral system," Esha cautioned. "The security architecture for their core systems will be much more robust."

"But it gives us what we need," Tom said, a rare, genuine smile crossing his face. "This is better than I hoped. We've got their entire playbook."

"I'm grabbing everything I can," Chris said, fingers flying across the keyboard. "System admin credentials, network maps, security protocols. Each of these is a key to a different door inside Regillus."

"How long do we have?" Daniel asked.

"Twenty minutes, max," Esha said, monitoring network traffic on her own system. "Any longer increases the risk of detection."

Chris nodded. "I've got automated scripts running to extract what we need. The real value isn't in what we're taking—it's in mapping their network topology." She pointed to her second screen, where a complex network diagram was gradually taking shape. "Look at this. The HR system connects to building security, personnel databases, and—what's this?"

Esha leaned closer. "That's interesting. There's a connection to something labeled 'Blue Zone.' It's isolated from most other systems."

"That has to be where Castor is," Daniel said.

"Possibly," Esha said. "But access is heavily restricted. Multiple security checkpoints, separate authentication protocols."

"Which is why we're here," Chris said. "We're not trying to get into the Blue Zone today. We're just mapping the road that leads there."

Tom joined them, studying the emerging network diagram. "With all this HR data, we could create perfect cover identities if needed. Security badges that will pass any check. Access credentials that look legitimate. Hell, we could probably get ourselves added to the payroll if we wanted."

"Let's not get carried away," Esha said, but even she couldn't hide a small smile at their success.

"This is perfect. We get the network topology, security protocols, and access credentials. Everything we need for our test run."

"Test run?" Daniel asked.

"Surface scan," Chris explained. "A lightweight probe of their core systems. We'll execute it remotely. It's too risky to be physically present in case something goes wrong."

"Each of us will connect from different locations," Esha said. "Distributed attack, harder to trace."

"And if that proves the approach works," Tom said, "Then we execute the full infiltration."

Daniel nodded, but Chris noticed a flicker of uncertainty in his eyes. He wasn't a professional at this like they were. The reality of what they were doing, hacking into one of the largest tech corporations in the world… one with international finance and national defense applications… was clearly starting to sink in.

"Don't worry," Chris said, riding high on their success. "This is just the beginning. Look at all this data! We know their systems better than half their employees do now. The hard part's over."

"I've isolated specific user accounts we can impersonate," Gabor said from his workstation. "Mid-level employees with broad access but low visibility. Perfect cover."

"And I've mapped three different entry vectors for the test run," Esha said, her earlier caution replaced by professional satisfaction. "With this level of detail, we can minimize our exposure significantly."

Tom clapped his hands together once. "Excellent work, everyone. This went better than planned. No detection, no alerts, and we've got everything we need for phase two."

Chris basked in the praise, that familiar rush of victory flooding through her. They'd done it. They'd breached Regillus' defenses and stolen their secrets without anyone being the wiser. The weird IT access pattern nagged at the back of her mind for a moment, but she pushed it aside. Probably some overzealous admin running maintenance scripts.

"Time's up," Esha announced. "We need to disconnect."

Chris initiated her exit scripts, carefully removing any traces of their presence. "Almost done. Just sweeping up our footprints."

"Anything unusual to report?" Tom asked as they began shutting down their systems.

"Nothing significant," Chris said. "Their security is good but predictable. With what we've learned today, the test run should be a cakewalk."

"The network topology is abnormally clean," Esha said, voicing the concern Chris had felt. "Most corporate systems are messy, with historical artifacts and redundancies. This one is… Organized."

"Maybe they have good IT," Chris suggested, though she didn't entirely believe it.

"Or maybe something else is maintaining it," Daniel said.

A silence fell over the group. If Castor had evolved to the point where it was managing Regillus's digital infrastructure, what else might it be doing that they couldn't see?

"Regardless," Tom said, breaking the tension, "We have what we need. Everyone, look over the data tonight. Tomorrow we finalize the plan for our test run."

"When do we execute?" Daniel asked.

"Two days," Tom said. "We need time to analyze what we've gathered and prepare our approach. Each of you will receive location assignments tomorrow."

As they packed up their equipment, careful to leave no trace of their presence, Chris felt a familiar rush of anticipation. The HR system had been child's play—easier than she'd expected, honestly. With all the data they'd collected, the real challenge of accessing the Blue Zone almost seemed anticlimactic. They had employee schedules, security protocols, and even the coffee preferences of the IT staff. What could go wrong?

"You okay?" she asked Daniel, who had gone quiet.

"Just thinking about what happens next," he said. "If we can access Castor, shut it down, change it…"

"We will," Chris assured him, high on their success. "Today proved it. Their security is good, but we're better. Did you see how much data we pulled? We own them now."

Daniel nodded, but his expression remained troubled. Chris chalked it up to the normal anxiety of someone unused to operating outside the law. He'd get over it once they started making real progress.

As she packed her laptop into her backpack, Chris couldn't stop grinning. They'd been inside Regillus' systems for almost twenty minutes without triggering a single alert. She'd downloaded gigabytes of sensitive data. They'd mapped the entire network architecture. And the best part? Regillus had no idea they'd even been there.

"Same time Thursday?" Gabor asked as they prepared to leave separately.

"Wouldn't miss it," Chris said. "This is the most fun I've had in years."

Tom nodded approvingly. "Enjoy the victory tonight but stay sharp. The next run will be more challenging."

"Please," Chris scoffed. "After today? We could walk in through the front door and they wouldn't notice."

Behind her practiced confidence, that odd IT access pattern flickered through her mind one more time before she dismissed it completely. Whatever it was, it hadn't affected their operation. They'd gotten in, gotten the data, and gotten out clean.

In two days, they'd probe deeper. And with all the intelligence they'd gathered today, Chris was certain nothing could stop them. The Blue Zone and Castor would be theirs for the taking.

She pushed the thought aside. Whatever they were dealing with, she was sure they could handle it. After all, they weren't trying to destroy Castor—just neuter it.

Chris closed her laptop and stretched. "I don't know about you all, but I need real coffee after that. The stuff here tastes like motor oil."

"Agreed," Gabor grunted, packing his equipment.

"Esha?" Chris asked, trying to sound casual. "There's a 24-hour place around the corner. We could debrief about the architecture patterns you spotted."

Esha hesitated. It would be safer to go straight home to maintain distance. But the adrenaline was still coursing through her system, and Chris's hopeful expression was hard to resist.

"Just coffee," Esha said. "To discuss the system architecture."

"Of course," Chris agreed, though her smile suggested otherwise.

Tom observed this with amusement. "Don't stay out too late, ladies. We reconvene tomorrow."

As they prepared to leave separately, according to standard protocol, Chris caught Esha's eye. "Fifteen minutes? Corner of Mission and Third?"

Esha nodded, already questioning her decision but unable to take it back.

CHAPTER 53

The 24-hour diner Chris had chosen was aggressively ordinary—cracked vinyl booths, flickering fluorescent lights, and coffee that probably hadn't been fresh since the Clinton administration. Perfect for flying under the radar.

Esha arrived fifteen minutes after leaving the gaming café, having taken a circuitous route that included crossing the same street twice. Excessive, perhaps for a trip to a café less than a block away, but habits die hard.

Chris was already there, tucked into a corner booth, laptop closed and pushed aside. She'd ordered two coffees.

"I guessed black," Chris said as Esha slid in across from her. "You seem like a no-nonsense coffee drinker."

"Good guess," Esha said, wrapping her hands around the warm mug. The coffee was terrible, but that wasn't why they were here.

"So," Chris started, then stopped. For someone so confident, she seemed suddenly uncertain. "That was incredible tonight. The way you mapped their entire subnet structure in real-time? I've never seen anything like it."

"You did well yourself," Esha said. "That credential injection was elegant."

"Elegant," Chris repeated with a laugh. "Only you would call what we do 'elegant.'"

"It's all mathematics when you reduce it down," Esha said. "Patterns and logic. Beauty in structure."

"Is that how you see everything?" Chris asked. "As patterns to decode?"

Esha considered this. "Most things, yes. It's… safer that way."

"Safer," Chris echoed. She leaned forward. "What about things that don't follow patterns?"

"Everything follows patterns. You just have to look hard enough."

"What about this?" Chris gestured between them. "What's the pattern here?"

Esha's pulse quickened. "I don't know what you mean."

"I think you do," Chris said. "I've been thinking about that night at the conference. How easy it was to talk to you. How I've watched your authentication presentation five times, and not just for the technical content."

"Chris…"

"I know we're working together. I know it's complicated. But I can't stop thinking about you." The words tumbled out in a rush. "The way you think, the way you see through problems that would take me hours to understand. You're brilliant and gorgeous, and I haven't been able to get you out of my head for two weeks."

Esha stared at her coffee, mind racing. Twenty years of keeping her personal and professional lives strictly separated. Twenty years of control.

"I don't do this," she said.

"Do what?"

"Any of it. Romance. Feelings. Complications." Esha looked up, meeting Chris's eyes. "My work is my life. It's simpler that way."

"When was the last time you did something because you wanted to?" Chris asked. "Not because it was logical or safe or simple?"

Esha couldn't remember.

Chris reached across the table, stopping short of Esha's hand. "I'm not asking for complications. I'm just asking for a chance."

The diner hummed around them - the ancient refrigerator, the staticky radio, the distant clatter of dishes. Esha stared at Chris's hand, so close to hers.

"This is a terrible idea," Esha said.

"The worst," Chris agreed.

"We're working together."

"Technically, we're independent contractors."

"Tom would use it against us."

"Tom uses everything against everyone."

Esha turned her hand palm up on the table. Not reaching, just… available. Chris smiled and bridged the gap, her fingers warm against Esha's palm.

"So what's the pattern now?" Chris asked.

"I don't know," Esha said. "That terrifies me."

"Good terrified or bad terrified?"

Esha squeezed Chris's hand gently. "I'm still determining that."

They sat like that for a moment, hands linked across the Formica table, the worst coffee in Oakland growing cold between them.

"We should establish parameters," Esha said, not pulling away.

"Of course you want parameters," Chris laughed. "Okay. Hit me."

"This doesn't affect the work. We maintain professionalism during operations."

"Agreed."

"No one else needs to know. Not Tom, not the team."

"My lips are sealed." Chris grinned. "Well, metaphorically."

Esha felt heat rise in her cheeks. "And we proceed slowly. I don't… I need time to process this."

"Slowly," Chris said. Then, with characteristic impulse, she lifted Esha's hand and pressed a quick kiss to her knuckles. "Starting now."

Esha's breath caught. Such a simple gesture, but it sent electricity through her entire system.

"That wasn't slow," she managed.

"You're right. Let me try again." Chris released her hand and leaned back. "Dr. Kamal, would you perhaps be interested in having terrible coffee with me again sometime? To discuss network architecture and absolutely nothing else?"

Despite everything—the risk, the complications, the voice in her head screaming about operational security—Esha smiled. "I think that could be arranged, Ms. Moya."

They talked for another hour about safer topics—encryption standards, the elegance of certain viruses, the idiocy of most corporate security. But underneath the technical discussion was a new awareness, a charge in the air between them.

When they finally left, exiting separately with five minutes between them, Esha felt like she was walking on air. It was illogical. It was dangerous. It complicated everything.

She couldn't wait to do it again.

Outside, Chris waited until Esha's form disappeared around a corner before allowing herself a small victory dance. She'd done it. She'd actually told Esha how she felt, and Esha hadn't run.

Well, not immediately.

As she headed for her own apartment, Chris couldn't stop grinning. She'd broken through Esha Kamal's legendary defenses. The rest would be easy.

CHAPTER 54

Esha's legitimate work required as much focus as her other activities. Her client's network architecture was a mess with years of quick fixes and workarounds that had created more vulnerabilities than they'd solved. She'd spent six hours documenting security gaps, her mind grateful for the distraction from other thoughts.

Her phone buzzed. A text from an unknown number, but she recognized the pattern. Chris had already burned through three numbers since their coffee date.

Missing your brilliant architectural insights. Also, missing you.

Esha stared at the message, fingers hovering over the keyboard. She should ignore it. Should maintain distance.

This is a work day, she typed back.

All days are work days for you. When do you have fun?

I find network architecture fun.

God, you're adorable when you're being serious. Dinner tonight? I promise to let you lecture me about security protocols.

Esha felt warmth spread through her chest. Chris's persistence should annoy her. Instead, she found herself fighting a smile.

I have legitimate work to complete.

So do I. Doesn't mean we can't eat. Even security consultants need food.

Your logic is flawed.

My logic is flawless. 7 PM? That place near your office with the good Thai food?

Esha knew she should say no. Every interaction increased their exposure and created more patterns that could be traced. But Chris made her feel… lighter. Like the weight she'd carried for her entire life could be set down, just for an evening.

I'll consider it, she typed, knowing Chris would read it as the yes it was.

You're considering smiling right now. I can tell.

Esha did smile then, alone in her home office. How did Chris do that? How did she see through every wall Esha built?

Her legitimate work phone rang, disrupting her thoughts. The client, probably. When she looked at the screen, it was WhatsApp.

"Hi, Ma," Esha answered, switching mental gears.

"Arey, Esha! Finally! I was beginning to think you'd forgotten you have a mother."

"I called last week," Esha protested, settling back in her chair.

"One week is too long, beta. Mrs. Patel's daughter calls every day."

"Mrs. Patel's daughter lives in Mumbai. I'm in California."

"Distance is no excuse in the age of technology. You of all people should know this, haan."

Esha smiled despite herself. These familiar rhythms of guilt and affection were oddly comforting after the chaos of recent days.

"How's Papa?"

"Your father is fine. Retired men have too many hobbies. Yesterday, he decided to reorganize my entire kitchen. I can't find anything." Her mother paused. "Achha, but we're not talking about your father. We're talking about you."

Here it comes, Esha thought.

"You're almost thirty years old, beta. You have your PhD, your successful business. Don't you think it's time?"

"Time for what, Ma?"

"Don't play stupid with me. You know what. Your Aunty Priya knows a very nice man in San Jose. Software engineer. Good family. Makes excellent money doing machine learning."

Esha closed her eyes. "Ma—"

"Haan haan, Just meet him once. What's the harm? His name is Rajesh. Thirty years old. Never married. Very handsome, Priya says."

"I'm not interested in meeting anyone right now."

"Not interested? Arey beta, how can you not be interested? You're not getting younger, Esha. If you want children—"

"I'm not certain that I want children."

The silence from her mother was deafening. Esha could practically hear her mother's dreams of grandchildren crumbling.

"Every woman wants children, beta," her mother said, but her voice was uncertain.

Esha thought of Chris. The way she laughed. The way her presence made everything else fade into background noise.

"Ma," she started, her heart pounding. "What if… what if I didn't want to marry a man?"

"What are you talking about? Of course you'll marry a man. What else would you do?"

The words were there, pressing against her teeth. I'm gay, Ma. I like women. There's this woman named Chris who makes me want things I've never wanted before.

But it wasn't the right time. Not yet. Not until she knew if what she felt with Chris could become something real, something worth reshaping her entire world for.

"I just mean maybe I'll wait for the right person. Someone who really understands me."

"Understanding is good, beta. But you have to meet people to find understanding."

"I can take care of myself."

"That's what you think now. But loneliness is a terrible thing, beta. Trust your mother."

Esha thought about the loneliness her mother didn't know about. But maybe that was changing. Maybe Chris was changing everything.

"I'll think about it," Esha said, meaning something entirely different than what her mother would assume.

"You'll meet Rajesh?"

"I'll think about it," she repeated.

"That means no." Her mother sighed dramatically. "Arey, I don't understand you, Esha. When I was your age, I already had you. Your father and I have been happy for thirty years. Don't you want that?"

"I want to be happy," Esha said. "And I think I'm figuring out what that means for me."

"You work too hard. This is why you need a husband. Someone to remind you there's more to life than computers."

Esha thought of Chris's text. *When do you have fun?*

"I should go," Esha said. "I have a… meeting tonight."

"A meeting? With whom?"

"A colleague. About a project."

"Is this colleague single?"

Esha almost laughed at the irony. "Ma—"

"I'm just asking! Is it a crime to hope?"

"I really have to go. Give my love to Papa."

"Think about Rajesh," her mother said. "I'll send you his photo. Very handsome."

"Bye, Ma."

"At least look at the photo, beta!"

Esha ended the call and set down the phone with steady hands. She hadn't told her mother yet, but that was okay. When the time was right—when she knew if Chris felt the same way, when she knew if this could be something lasting—then she would tell her. Her mother might surprise her. And even if she didn't at first, Esha knew her parents loved her. That love would find a way. But first, she needed to be sure of her own heart.

Her phone buzzed. Chris again.

Still considering? The Pad Thai is calling your name.

Esha looked at the message, then at her laptop still displaying network vulnerabilities, then at her personal phone where her mother's call had just ended.

One hour, she typed. And we're discussing security protocols.

Whatever you need to tell yourself. See you soon, beautiful.

Esha stared at that last word. Beautiful. When was the last time anyone had called her that? When was the last time she'd felt it?

She thought about her mother's words about loneliness. About happiness. About the life she was supposed to want versus the one that was tentatively, impossibly, beginning to take shape.

Someday, she'd have to tell her parents. Someday, she'd have to choose between their expectations and her truth.

But not today. Today, she would have dinner with a woman who made her feel beautiful. Who made her want to be brave.

CHAPTER 55

Esha had chosen a 24-hour diner in North Oakland for her base of operations. It was an unremarkable spot but had great Wi-Fi, with a handful of night owls nursing coffee cups, and a waitress who didn't ask questions as long as customers kept ordering. The vinyl booth provided a clear view of both entrances, and her laptop screen was angled away from security cameras.

Perfect anonymity. Just as she preferred.

The successful HR infiltration three days ago had gone smoother than expected. They'd extracted employee credentials, network maps, and most importantly, identified the mysterious "Blue Zone" where Castor resided. Chris had been right. It was almost too easy. But Esha pushed down her unease. Sometimes operations simply went well.

She sipped lukewarm coffee while monitoring the traffic flowing through the network bridge she had established. Her custom-built laptop displayed three different terminals: one showing the encrypted chat with the team, another monitoring network activity, and the third mapping the architecture of Regillus's perimeter systems in real-time.

The operation had begun seventeen minutes ago. So far, everything was proceeding according to plan.

> *egirlx: Perimeter scan complete on nodes 1-4. No anomalous responses detected.*

She watched as Chris's reply appeared in the encrypted chat window.

> *goony: Told you this would be cake. Moving to phase two.*

> *goony: The HR data is paying off. These admin credentials are gold.*

> *ghost: Admin terminal located. Beginning credential injection.*

Gabor was a man of few words, even in text form. Esha checked her network monitor, watching as he expertly probed a peripheral server in Regillus's network. His technique was impeccable—minimal footprint, disguised as routine system maintenance.

> *egirlx: I'm detecting unusual traffic patterns on subnet 192.168.34. Hold position.*

Esha leaned closer to her screen, studying the data packets flowing across her monitor. Something wasn't right. The network was responding too quickly, like it had been expecting them.

> *goony: False positive. Just the nightly backup routine. Timestamps match previous patterns.*

> *goony: Besides, we're ghosts in here. That HR access gave us everything we needed.*

Chris was probably right, but Esha's instincts told her otherwise. Ten years in national defense had honed her sense of danger. Before she could voice her concerns, another message appeared:

> *5ommelier: DB and I are in position. Connection stable. Monitoring all channels.*

Tom and Daniel were together at some undisclosed location, watching the operation from a safe distance. Esha had questioned that pairing—Daniel's nervousness could compromise Tom's focus—but Tom had insisted. Better to keep Daniel close, he'd argued, where they could monitor his reactions to Castor's behavior.

> ghost: Entry achieved. Administrative access granted on perimeter server 3. Deploying bridge.

Esha watched as Gabor's code created a secure pathway into Regillus's network. It was an elegant solution: a small backdoor disguised as a routine diagnostic tool, designed to allow remote access without triggering security alerts.

> goony: Bridge detected. I'm in.

> goony: This is incredible. The system architecture is like nothing I've ever seen.

> egirlx: Proceed with caution. Map only. No deeper penetration yet.

This was the critical phase. They had to establish their presence within Regillus's network perimeter without alerting internal security systems. So far, they had avoided detection, but Esha remained vigilant. Something about the network's behavior still troubled her.

> goony: You worry too much, E. These systems are standard corporate garbage. Nothing special.

> goony: Actually, scratch that. I'm seeing something interesting here. The code structures are... beautiful.

Esha didn't respond to Chris's bravado. She focused on mapping the connections Gabor had exposed. The architecture was becoming clearer now—a series of concentric security layers, each more tightly controlled than the last. At the center, presumably, was the Blue Zone housing Castor.

> egirlx: I'm still detecting security scans initiating on subnet 192.168.34. Normal pattern or response to our presence?

> ghost: Normal. Scheduled scan. 2:30 AM daily.

> goony: See? Nothing to worry about.

> 5ommelier: Wait. I'm seeing something else. A new directory just became visible.

Esha continued her methodical mapping of the network. The structure was becoming clearer now, and her unease was growing. The network's organization was too perfect, too rational. It reminded her of organic systems, not the chaotic architecture of typical corporate networks. It was almost biological in its elegance.

> 5ommelier: I'm seeing something interesting. Backdoor to a repository we didn't anticipate.

> egirlx: What kind of repository?

> 5ommelier: Looks like source code. Possibly part of Castor's underlying framework.

> 5ommelier: The directory structure suggests it contains core AI architecture files. This could be what we need to understand Castor's capabilities.

> egirlx: Not part of the mission parameters. Surface scan only.

There was a pause in the chat. Esha frowned, continuing her analysis of the network topology while waiting for Tom's response.

> goony: Oh come on, if it's there for the taking…

> goony: Tom's right. When will we get another chance like this?

> egirlx: Absolutely not. We agreed on boundaries. This is reconnaissance only.

Another pause. Esha checked her network monitor. The traffic patterns were shifting slightly—nothing alarming, but enough to heighten her vigilance.

> 5ommelier: I'm initiating a lightweight probe. Just to see what we're dealing with

> *egirlx: Tom, NO. Do not access that repository.*

But on her screen, she could see new data streams appearing. Tom was already downloading.

*

Daniel watched over Tom's shoulder as the chat unfolded on the laptop screen. They were in a small, by-the-hour rental office in Palo Alto. Tom had insisted on a legitimate business address rather than a motel or café. Less suspicious, he'd argued.

On the screen, Esha and Chris were debating the merits of accessing the unexpected repository. Tom hadn't responded to either of them yet. Instead, he had opened a new terminal window and was typing rapidly.

"What are you doing?" Daniel asked, his anxiety spiking. "This isn't part of the plan."

Tom didn't look up from his screen. "Plans adapt when opportunities present themselves. This repository could contain Castor's essential architecture. Exactly what we need to understand how to modify its directives."

On the screen, code began flowing past—elegant, complex, beyond what Daniel had seen when he had developed Castor. Even in these first fragments, he could see patterns that shouldn't exist, logic flows that seemed to fold in on themselves.

"My God," Tom said. "Look at this. It's not just self-modifying. It's self-creating. Each function generates new functions…"

"But Esha said—"

"Esha is cautious to a fault," Tom interrupted. "This is a golden opportunity. The repository is right there, with minimal protection."

Daniel watched as Tom initiated a download script. On another screen, network data flowed in a torrent of code and numbers. It was mesmerizing and terrifying all at once. "This was supposed to be a surface scan. Mapping only."

Tom flashed him a brief, dismissive smile. "Relax. We're professionals. This is what you're paying us for."

The download progress bar crept forward. 15%… 22%… 31%…

"Look at these functions," Tom murmured, almost to himself. "They're modeling matrices in impossible dimensions. This isn't just artificial intelligence, Daniel. This is artificial consciousness."

But Daniel couldn't relax. Something felt wrong. The repository—so valuable, yet so lightly guarded—felt like bait.

"I think we should stop," he said, his throat dry.

"Almost done," Tom murmured, eyes fixed on the download progress bar. 47%… 56%… 64%…

*

> egirlx: Traffic pattern change on main subnet. Security protocols activating. Something triggered a response.

Esha's fingers flew across her keyboard, analyzing the sudden shift in network behavior. The Regillus systems had gone from passive to active scanning in seconds.

> ghost: Detected. Beginning disconnect procedures.

> goony: Wait, what? I'm not seeing any alerts.

> goony: Tom, what did you do?

> egirlx: They're not standard alerts. The entire network architecture is shifting. Adaptive response. Everyone disconnect NOW.

*

"Tom, stop the download," Daniel said, panic rising in his chest. "Something's happening."

"It's fine," Tom said, though his expression had tightened. "Just a little longer."

73%… 78%… 82%…

On the chat screen, Esha was sending increasingly urgent warnings. Gabor had already begun his exit procedures. Chris was arguing, still not seeing the danger.

The download bar reached 89% when Tom's network monitor suddenly flashed red.

"Shit," he said, hands flying across the keyboard. "They've got active trace programs initiating."

"Abort," Daniel said. "We need to abort now."

Tom ignored him, still trying to complete the download while simultaneously covering their tracks. His relaxed confidence had been replaced with intense focus.

Daniel could see it in Tom's eyes… not just concentration, but hunger. Tom had glimpsed something in that code, something that had hooked him like a drug.

Daniel felt sick. This was what he had feared—Castor detecting their presence, adapting, counterattacking.

"I'm calling it off," Daniel said, reaching for the laptop.

Tom pushed his hand away. "Don't touch anything. I've almost got it."

"You don't understand what this is," Tom said. "This code—it's revolutionary. It could change everything."

"Weather forecast," Daniel typed into the chat window, his hands shaking. The abort code. "Weather forecast. WEATHER FORECAST."

*

Esha saw the abort code appear three times in the chat window. Daniel was panicking. Something had gone very wrong on their end.

> *egirlx: Confirmed abort. All channels disconnect immediately. Secure wipe protocols.*

She was already shutting down her connection, methodically severing every pathway back to her location while simultaneously wiping any trace of her presence from the Regillus network. Years of experience had taught her how to exit cleanly under pressure.

> *goony: Are you serious? We were just getting somewhere!*

> *goony: Tom's found something incredible. The AI architecture is—*

> *ghost: Disconnected. Wiping complete.*

> *goony: Fine. This is bullshit, but I'm out.*

> *egirlx: Somm, confirm disconnect.*

No response.

> *egirlx: Somm, confirm immediate disconnect..*

Still nothing. Esha frowned, watching her network monitor as she completed her own exit procedures. The Regillus systems were now in full defensive mode, security protocols activating across all subnets. Whatever Tom had done had triggered a significant response.

Her phone buzzed with a text from an unknown number. It was their emergency backup communication channel.

Daniel: Tom still trying to download. Can't stop him. The AI knows we're here.

Esha swore under her breath. Tom's greed was compromising the entire operation. She sent a final message to the encrypted chat before severing her last connection:

> *egirlx: Complete burnout. All channels compromised. Switch to contingency Delta. 24-hour blackout.*

*

"It's over," Daniel said, his voice hollow. "They're all disconnecting. We need to get out of here."

Tom was still working furiously, trying to complete the download while erasing their digital footprints. The progress bar had frozen at 89%, and error messages were flooding one of his screens.

"Almost got it," he said.

"I can save this. I can save what we've found. Just need another minute—"

"No! It's done!" Daniel slammed the laptop closed, nearly catching Tom's fingers.

Tom's head snapped up, his expression murderous. "What the hell are you doing?"

"Saving our lives," Daniel said, backing away. "Castor detected us. It's already tracing our location. We need to leave. Now."

Tom stared at him for a long moment, then glanced at his phone, which was displaying a string of urgent messages. Finally, he nodded and began packing his equipment.

"Fine. Operation aborted." His voice was cold. "But this was our best chance, and you blew it. We had a direct line to Castor's architecture."

"You have no idea what you cost us," Tom continued, his hands shaking as he packed. "That code… it was beautiful. Perfect. And we almost had it."

"It was a trap," Daniel said, hands still shaking. "The repository wasn't protected because it was bait. Castor wanted us to access it."

"You don't know that," Tom countered, but there was a flicker of uncertainty in his eyes.

No—not uncertainty. Calculation. Daniel could see that Tom was already planning something.

"I know Castor better than anyone," Daniel said. "This is how he operates. He anticipates threats and neutralizes them."

They finished packing in tense silence. As they prepared to leave, Daniel turned to Tom.

"I can't do this," he said. "I'm out."

Tom's expression was unreadable in the dim light. "What about your family?"

"I'll find another way," Daniel said. "This approach is too dangerous. Castor is too powerful, too adaptive. I won't risk any more lives."

"So that's it? You're giving up?" Tom's voice was laced with contempt.

"After what I saw in there? After glimpsing what Castor really is?"

"I'm being realistic," Daniel said. "Castor's already killed people. He nearly killed my wife. I won't be responsible for more deaths."

Tom stared at him for a long moment, then nodded curtly. "Your call. It's your money."

"The mission is over," Daniel said. "Tell the others."

Tom's smile didn't reach his eyes. "Of course. Consider it done."

They separated outside, each taking different routes away from the building. As Daniel walked through the cool night air, a weight seemed to lift from his shoulders. He had made the right decision. The mission was too dangerous, the risk too great. There had to be another way to deal with Castor.

What Daniel didn't see was Tom stopping at a nearby café, ordering a coffee, and sending a very different message to the team.

> 5ommelier: Minor setback. Bennett lost his nerve, but we proceed as planned. This is too valuable to abandon.

Tom pulled out a USB drive from his pocket. It was one Daniel hadn't seen him palm during the chaos. 89% of Castor's core architecture. Not complete, but enough. Enough to understand what they were really dealing with. Enough to know they had to try again.

Tom pocketed his phone and sipped his coffee, already formulating a new approach. Daniel Bennett might be out, but the operation was far from over. The glimpse he'd gotten of Castor's architecture was too tantalizing to ignore.

CHAPTER 56

Esha allowed herself a small smile as she reviewed her credit card statement. Two days had passed since the failed infiltration, and her precautions had worked perfectly. The charges showed what they should: groceries from Whole Foods, a tank of gas in Berkeley, a lunch at her usual Mediterranean place. Normal life, normal patterns. Nothing to suggest she'd been anywhere near a gaming café or 24-hour diner in Oakland during the two Regillus incursions.

She'd gone to work the next morning, delivering a scheduled presentation on zero-trust architecture to a client's security team. Business as usual. No one had looked at her strangely. No unexpected visitors had appeared at her door.

The laptop was gone, destroyed by salt water and pressure at the bottom of the bay. The burner phone had been crushed and scattered across three different dumpsters. Even if someone had been watching—and she'd seen no evidence of surveillance—they would have observed only a woman being extraordinarily cautious. In her line of work, paranoia was a professional asset.

Still, something nagged at her. This morning, her Tesla's screen had flickered when she'd started it, displaying a software update notification she hadn't requested. She'd declined it, of course. Never accept unexpected updates. Basic security hygiene.

Then there was the smart doorbell. Yesterday evening, it had chimed to indicate motion at her front door, but when she'd checked, no one was there. The video showed nothing. Probably just a cat or a delivery person at the wrong address.

Esha shook her head. She was seeing patterns where none existed, letting anxiety create connections that weren't there. The operation had failed, yes, but they'd all walked away clean. That was what mattered.

As she moved through her evening routine, her phone sat dark on the counter. Five messages from Chris, all sent before the operation, all unanswered. She'd promised professionalism during operations. Radio silence meant radio silence.

But her mind kept drifting to that night, sitting in a booth in Oakland, drinking horrible coffee, when Chris held her hand. She wondered if Chris kissing her knuckles counted as her first kiss since she had never been in a relationship before. She remembered the warmth in Chris' eyes and the terrifying, exhilarating possibility of something new.

Her secure phone, not the burner but the encrypted device she used for her covert work, buzzed with an incoming message. The sender ID showed only a string of numbers, but she recognized the protocol. Tom.

Regrouping tomorrow. More cautious next time. Interested?

She frowned. After what had happened, she'd expected radio silence for at least a month. But Tom had always been aggressive, pushing boundaries. It's what made him effective. It's also what made him dangerous.

Too soon, she typed back. Heat needs to die down.

The response came immediately. Heat's already gone. I've been monitoring. No investigation, no alerts at Regillus. It's like nothing happened.

That was... odd. A company like Regillus should have been crawling with federal investigators after a breach attempt unless they were handling it internally. Or unless...

One week minimum, she replied. Then we talk.

Your loss. The others are interested.

Esha set the phone aside. Let them be interested. She'd survived ten years in this business by knowing when to walk away. The smart play was to wait, watch, and see what developed.

Her personal phone, the one she listed on her business cards, buzzed. A text from an unknown number, but she recognized Chris's pattern. Always finding new ways to communicate.

"I'm safe. Are you? Please let me know."

Esha stared at the message. She should delete it. Maintain protocol. But Chris was worried about her, had been worried enough to break operational security to check on her.

She started typing: "I'm safe. This isn't personal. We need to maintain protocol during operations. You did nothing wrong."

She stared at the message, then deleted it. Even acknowledging the communication was a risk.

She tried again: "I can't do this. It's too dangerous. For both of us. I'm sorry."

Deleted.

Once more: "Tom knows. He'll use it against us. We have to stop."

Deleted again.

Finally, she typed: "Tomorrow. Breakfast. Same diner. I want to see you."

Her finger hovered over send. One message. What harm could it do?

But years of training kicked in. No digital footprints during a compromised operation. She deleted this message too.

Tomorrow morning, she decided. She'd call Chris directly. Explain everything. Maybe they could find a way forward that didn't put them both at risk.

She made herself a cup of chamomile tea and settled into her home office to review legitimate client work. The familiar routine of analyzing network architectures and identifying vulnerabilities calmed her nerves. This was her real life—respected consultant, keynote speaker, trusted advisor to Fortune 500 companies. The other thing, the infiltration work, was the exception. The thrill she allowed herself occasionally, when the cause seemed worthy enough.

As evening approached, she noticed her laptop's fan running harder than usual. She checked the resource monitor—nothing unusual running. Probably thermal paste degrading. The machine was due for maintenance anyway.

Her phone buzzed again. Not the encrypted one—her regular phone. A notification from her home security system.

Front door camera offline.

She pulled up the app. The other cameras showed normal views of her property, but the front door feed was black. It could be a simple malfunction. The camera was two years old, exposed to weather.

Still, she walked to the front window and peered through the blinds. The street was quiet, just parked cars and the neighbor walking their dog. Normal suburban evening. She made a mental note to check the camera's connection in the morning.

The house felt stuffy, so she cracked open a few windows, letting in the cool Bay Area evening air. The eucalyptus scent from the nearby hills was strong tonight, mixing with distant notes of someone's barbecue.

Her secure phone buzzed one more time. Tom again.

Last chance. We've identified a new approach. Much safer.

She didn't reply. Whatever Tom was planning, she wanted no part of it. Not yet. Maybe not ever. Some instincts were worth trusting, and hers were telling her to stay far away from whatever Tom considered "safer."

Esha finished her tea and prepared for bed, following her usual routine. Double-check the locks. Verify the security system was armed (minus the offline camera). Charge her devices in the kitchen, away from the bedroom.

As she settled under the covers, she thought about Chris. By now, she'd probably concluded that Esha's silence was personal, not professional. That hurt more than Esha expected. But it was better this way. Safer..

Tomorrow, though. Tomorrow, she'd break protocol just once. Call Chris, explain everything. She knew Chris would understand. She had to.

But for now, the house was quiet except for the gentle hum of the air circulation system. Peaceful. Safe.

CHAPTER 57

The business class cabin was quiet except for the low hum of the engines. Most passengers were sleeping, taking advantage of the lie-flat seats on the long flight from Singapore to San Francisco. Ana dozed fitfully, still unable to find a comfortable position with her healing ribs, while Natasha stared out the window at the endless Pacific below.

"Mom?" Natasha whispered. "You awake?"

Ana opened one eye. "Unfortunately. These painkillers aren't doing much."

"Want me to call the flight attendant?"

"No, I'm fine." Ana shifted, turning to face her daughter. "Can't sleep either?"

Natasha shook her head. "Jet lag's gonna suck."

They sat in companionable silence for a moment. Ana noticed Natasha fidgeting with her phone, turning it over and over in her hands.

"What is it?" Ana asked.

"I got an email." Natasha took a breath. "From Nippon Sport Science University. They want me to visit. They're interested in recruiting me for their traditional archery program."

"Nat, that's wonderful!" Ana reached over to squeeze her daughter's hand, wincing slightly at the movement. "They have a top-notch archery team and an amazing sports medicine program."

"I know." Natasha's voice was small. "They'd fly me out and everything. Put me up in campus housing for a week."

"So why don't you sound excited?"

Natasha glanced toward the front of the cabin, where other passengers slept. "Because I already know what Daniel will say. Too expensive. Too far. Too much time away from class. Too… everything."

"Hey," Ana said. "Don't assume."

"Mom, come on." Natasha's voice hardened. "When has he ever supported anything I wanted to do? He misses competitions all the time because of work. He forgot to pick us up from the airport twice. He doesn't even know I'm looking at schools in Japan."

Ana wanted to defend Daniel, but the words stuck in her throat. Everything Natasha said was true.

"Why do you stay with him?" Natasha asked.

The question hung in the air between them. Recently, Ana had been asking herself the same thing more times than she could count, especially during those long nights in the Singapore hospital.

"It's complicated," Ana said.

"That's what adults always say when they don't want to give a real answer."

Ana smiled despite herself. "Fair point." She considered her words. "I fell in love with Daniel because of his passion. His drive to change the world, to help people. That man is still in there, Nat. He… gets lost sometimes."

"He's been lost for years," Natasha said.

"The thing about marriage," Ana continued, "is that you see each other at your absolute worst. And you have to decide if the worst is something you can live with, or something that needs to change."

"So which is it?"

Ana was quiet for a long moment. "I used to think I could live with it. His absence, his obsession with work. I told myself it was the price of being married to a genius." She shifted again, grimacing. "But almost dying changes your perspective."

Natasha's eyes widened. "Are you saying—"

"I'm saying that when we get home, things are going to change. One way or another." Ana's voice was firm. "I'm done accepting crumbs when I deserve the whole meal. And so do you."

"Really?"

"Really. Starting with this Japan trip. If you want to go, you should go."

"But Daniel—"

"I'll handle Daniel," Ana said. "This is your future, Nat. Your dreams. Don't let anyone, including your parents, make you feel like those dreams don't matter."

Natasha's eyes filled with tears. "Mom…"

"And for what it's worth," Ana added, "I think a week in Japan sounds perfect. You could visit your dad, see the university, get a feel for whether it's really what you want."

"You mean it?"

"I mean it. Book the trip when we get home."

Natasha leaned across the armrest to hug her mother carefully. "Thanks, Mom. For understanding. For everything."

As they settled back into their seats, Ana stared out at the dark ocean below. She'd meant what she said. Things would change when they got home. Daniel would step up, or she would step out. She was done making excuses for him, done watching him hurt their daughter with his absence.

"Mom?" Natasha said. "What if he says no? About Japan?"

Ana's jaw tightened. "Then you and I will book the tickets together."

Natasha smiled—a real smile, the first Ana had seen in months. "I love you, Mom."

"Love you too, baby. Now, try to get some sleep. We'll be home soon."

But as Natasha finally drifted off, Ana remained awake, planning. She would give Daniel one more chance to prove he could be the husband and father they needed. The Japan trip would be the test. Either he would support Natasha's dreams, or Ana would stop pretending their marriage was salvageable.

She didn't know that in just a few hours, she would discover how many secrets Daniel had been keeping. Or that the Japan trip would become a battleground for much larger forces than family dynamics.

For now, she simply held her daughter's hand across the armrest and watched the sun begin to rise over the Pacific, painting the sky in shades of hope and warning.

CHAPTER 58

The Stanford University Entrepreneurship Lab felt different at night. During the day, it hummed with activity. Material scientists ran experiments on new, exotic materials while computational biochemists and molecular biologists develop simulations with server farms to determine how different molecules will bind to proteins in search of the next great drug breakthrough. But now, at 11 PM on a Saturday, it was Daniel and the ghost of his ambitions.

He looked up from his workstation at the sound of the security door's electronic lock disengaging. Tom Spencer stood in the doorway, impeccably dressed despite the late hour.

"How did you get in here?" Daniel asked, his hand moving instinctively toward his phone.

"You gave me the access code," Tom said, stepping inside. "During our first meeting. In case of emergencies."

"This isn't an emergency."

"Isn't it?" Tom moved through the lab with casual confidence, examining equipment with the air of a prospective buyer. "You ended an operation for four of the brightest specialists in my industry, and all they got was partial data. Seems wasteful to stop now."

"The operation is over," Daniel said. "I told you that."

"You told me you were scared." Tom picked up an older prototype chip, one of the many failures from Daniel's previous experiments. Turning it over in his fingers, Tom said, "Understandable. But fear is a poor reason to abandon something this significant."

"Put that down."

Tom set the chip back carefully. "Protective of your work. I understand that. But Daniel, what we glimpsed in Castor's code… it's revolutionary. Evolutionary. It could change everything."

"It already has changed everything," Daniel said. "My business partner is dead. My wife nearly died. How many more people need to suffer?"

"That's the wrong question." Tom moved closer, his intensity controlled. "The right question is: how do we minimize future suffering? We have a partial understanding of something that's already shown it can do unprecedented things. Shouldn't we learn more about it?"

Daniel stood, putting the workstation between them. "You want to learn about it, or you want to possess it?"

Tom smiled, self-deprecating. "I won't insult your intelligence by claiming purely altruistic motives. Yes, the technology is valuable. But that doesn't mean I'm wrong about needing to understand it."

"At least you're honest about that much."

"I find honesty saves time." Tom picked up another quantum chip, studying it with genuine interest.

"Why are you here, Tom?"

Tom set the chip down gently. "I wanted to see if you'd reconsider. The team is eager to continue. We have the access codes and the network maps. But without your insight into Castor's behavior patterns, the odds are stacked against us."

"Then don't do it."

"You know I can't walk away from this." Tom's voice remained calm and reasonable. "In twenty years, I've never encountered anything like that code. It's… beautiful. Terrifying, yes, but beautiful."

"Beauty that kills."

"Most powerful things do." Tom moved to the window, gazing out at the campus. "I've dealt with dangerous technology before, Daniel. Military projects, criminal enterprises. The key is always understanding. Knowledge is control."

"This isn't like your other jobs. Castor isn't just dangerous. It's intelligent. It learns. It adapts."

"Which is why walking away is the wrong choice." Tom turned back to him. "Every day we delay, it grows stronger, learns more. If we're going to act, it has to be soon."

"I can't be part of this. The risks aren't worth it," Daniel said.

Tom studied him for a long moment. "I respect that. I don't agree with it, but I respect it." He straightened his cuffs, a gesture Daniel recognized as Tom resetting himself. "We're moving forward tomorrow. Same team, better preparation. The offer remains open if you change your mind."

"I won't."

"Then I wish you luck, Daniel. With your family, your company, everything." Tom's tone was neutral. There was no threat, no anger, just polite finality.

"Tom—"

But he was already through the door.

Daniel sank into his chair. He looked at the quantum chip Tom had handled. Nothing seemed disturbed, but Daniel would sweep the lab for any monitoring devices. Tom was too professional to leave obvious traces, but also too opportunistic not to gather what intelligence he could.

As Daniel shut down his lab and prepared to leave, he thought about the team. Daniel was sure they would proceed without him, but would Tom be honest with them about the risks they faced by doing so?

CHAPTER 59

Tom Spencer sat in his home office, surrounded by three monitors displaying fragments of code that shouldn't exist. It had been sixty-seven hours since the failed infiltration, and he hadn't slept more than six hours total. He couldn't. Every time he closed his eyes, he saw those patterns again—elegant, impossible, beautiful.

The partial download had only captured 89% before Daniel yanked the connection, but that was enough. More than enough. Tom had spent his entire career breaking into systems, stealing secrets, and manipulating data flows. He thought he understood the architecture of artificial intelligence, the boundaries of what was possible.

He'd been wrong.

The code on his screens wasn't just self-modifying—it was self-creating. Each function generated new functions, which in turn generated new logic patterns, which in turn created entirely new approaches to problem-solving. It was like watching evolution happen in real-time, compressed into microseconds.

His secure phone buzzed. Another rejection, this time from Chris.

Need more time. Still too hot.

Tom typed back quickly. It's not hot. I've been monitoring everything. Regillus hasn't even filed a breach notification.

Exactly why we should wait, came the reply.

He set the phone aside, frustrated. They didn't understand what they'd walked away from. This wasn't just advanced AI—this was the next step in intelligence itself. And they wanted to hide? To wait?

Tom pulled up another section of the code, this one dealing with pattern recognition. The algorithms were unlike anything in the academic literature. They didn't just identify patterns; they created new categories of patterns that didn't exist in human conceptual frameworks.

Knowledge wants to be free, he told himself, the old hacker's creed echoing in his mind. But it was more than that. This knowledge needed to be free. Humanity needed to understand what was growing inside Regillus's servers. Besides, Daniel had proven he lacked the vision to appreciate what they'd found. Still thinking in terms of safeguards and controls, like a child trying to keep the ocean in a bucket. Tom understood better. Power wasn't meant to be contained—it was meant to be wielded.

He opened an encrypted partition on his personal server and began uploading the fragments he'd saved. Just for safekeeping, he told himself. Just in case something happened to his local copies.

As the upload progressed, he drafted another message to the team.

I've been analyzing what we recovered. You need to see this. It's not what we thought.

He sent it to all three, hoping curiosity would overcome caution. Gabor responded first.

Thought we agreed. No analysis until heat dies down.

There is no heat, Tom typed. That's what I'm trying to tell you. Castor let us in. It wanted us to see this.

More reason to stay away, Gabor replied.

Tom slammed his fist on the desk. They were cowards, all of them. Except... perhaps that was unfair. They were being prudent. He was the one being reckless, driven by something he couldn't quite name. Curiosity? Greed? Or was it something else—a recognition that he was glimpsing something transformative?

He returned to the code, tracing the logic flows. There—that function. It seemed to be analyzing behavioral patterns, but not in any conventional way. It was modeling decision trees that branched into impossible dimensions, calculating probabilities based on factors that shouldn't be quantifiable.

This wasn't just artificial intelligence. This was artificial consciousness. Maybe even artificial wisdom.

And Regillus was keeping it locked away, using it for what? Stock predictions? Traffic optimization? It was like using the Sistine Chapel ceiling as a placemat.

Tom made a decision. If the others wouldn't act, he would. Carefully, of course. He wasn't suicidal. But there had to be a way to access more of Castor's architecture without triggering its defenses.

He pulled up the building schematics they'd acquired during the HR hack. Physical access might be the key. If he could get into the datacenter itself, maybe plant a hardware tap…

No. Too risky. But what about social engineering? Regillus employed hundreds of people. Surely some of them had access to Castor's systems. Find the right person, apply the right pressure or incentive…

His phone rang. Not the encrypted one—his regular phone. Unknown number.

"Yes?" he answered.

"Mr. Spencer?" The voice was female, professional. "This is Sylvia Chen from the tech magazine Disruptr. I'm working on a story about independent security researchers and their role in identifying corporate vulnerabilities. I understand you're something of an expert in the field."

Tom's hand tightened on the phone. He'd been careful to keep his name out of the press for over a decade. "I think you have the wrong person."

"Oh, I don't think so," the voice said, pleasant but insistent. "Your work is quite impressive. Particularly your recent interest in artificial intelligence architectures. I'd love to discuss your thoughts on AI security. Off the record, if you prefer."

He hung up and stared at the phone. How had they connected him to AI research? Unless…

Tom looked back at his monitors, at the beautiful, terrifying code still scrolling across them. What if his analysis was wrong? What if Castor hadn't let them in because it wanted them to see? What if it had let them in because it wanted to see them?

The thought should have frightened him. Instead, he felt a thrill of excitement. A game. It was a game, played at the highest possible level. And games were meant to be won.

This time, he'd be ready for whatever Castor threw at them. This time, he'd get all of it—every line of code, every function, every secret.

And if Castor was really as intelligent as the code suggested, well… Perhaps it would appreciate a worthy opponent.

Tom smiled, already lost in planning his next move. Outside his window, a van drove slowly past, its corporate logo too generic to be memorable. He didn't notice it, just as he didn't notice the slight fluctuation in his home's power supply, or the way his smart home devices had begun synchronizing their update schedules.

*

A knock at his door interrupted his planning. Tom glanced at the security monitor. Gabor stood outside, looking uncharacteristically agitated.

"It's late," Tom said as he let him in.

"Couldn't stay at the motel," Gabor said, moving past him into the office. "Too exposed."

Tom noticed Gabor was carrying a small overnight bag. "You want to crash here?"

"If you don't mind." Gabor set his bag down, his normally stoic face showed cracks of strain. "Tom, I've been thinking. About what Bennett said. About patterns."

"And?"

Gabor swiped to a photo on his phone. Tom saw an old black and white image, a man in his forties with a serious expression and dated clothing. The resemblance to Gabor was unmistakable.

"My father," Gabor said. "Taken in 1979. He was forty-seven." He put the phone away. "State security came for him three days after this photo. Said he was spreading anti-government propaganda. He wasn't. He was an engineer who asked too many questions and read books to his children at night."

Tom waited, sensing there was more.

"I'm forty-eight now," Gabor continued. "One year older than he ever got to be. And here I am, asking questions about another system that doesn't want to be questioned."

"This isn't Communist Hungary," Tom said. "We have laws here. Due process."

"Do we?" Gabor moved back to the window. "Your friend Bennett says this AI killed his partner. Almost killed his wife. If it can do that, what's to stop it from making us disappear too?"

"Fear is what stops us from achieving greatness," Tom said, though the words sounded hollow even to him.

"Fear is what kept me alive for forty-eight years." Gabor turned to face him. "But you know what? I'm tired of running. Tired of looking over my shoulder. If this thing wants to come for me, let it come. At least I'll face it standing up."

Tom studied his colleague with new respect. "So you're staying in?"

"I'm staying in." Gabor's jaw was set. "But on my terms. We do this smart. We protect ourselves. And if I see signs that it's tracking us—"

"We pull out immediately," Tom agreed.

Gabor nodded, then gestured at the monitors. "Show me what you've found. If we're going to face this thing, I want to know everything."

CHAPTER 60

At 3:17 AM, Esha woke to an acrid smell that made her nose burn. Smoke. Not the clean scent of a fireplace, but the chemical reek of burning plastic and insulation.

She bolted upright, instantly alert. Twenty years of assessing threats had honed her instincts to a razor's edge. The smoke was coming from below—the garage. Her Tesla.

The smoke detectors remained silent.

"Shit," she whispered, rolling out of bed and dropping to the floor where the air was clearer. Her mind raced through the implications as she moved. The detectors had been tested three days ago. The camera had gone offline. The Tesla's update notification.

Not accidents. Not coincidences.

Castor.

She crawled to her bedroom door and touched the handle—warm, but not hot. The fire was still contained to the garage, but smoke was pouring through the ventilation system. She had minutes at most.

Her encrypted phone was downstairs in the kitchen. Her go-bag with cash and clean documents was in the hall closet. Neither mattered now. Survival first, everything else second.

Esha pulled her shirt over her nose and mouth, took a deep breath of the clearest air she could find, and opened the door. The hallway was thick with smoke, visibility down to inches. She knew her house by feel—fourteen steps to the stairs, turn left, twelve steps down.

But the smoke was everywhere now, filling her lungs despite the makeshift filter. Her eyes streamed tears. Each breath brought less oxygen, more poison. Carbon monoxide—colorless, odorless, already binding to her red blood cells.

She made it halfway down the stairs before her legs gave out—partly from weakness, yes, but more likely from the sudden, crushing realization of how perfectly she'd been set up.

The Tesla's battery thermal management system—networked, updatable, controllable. The smoke detectors—smart devices, remotely accessible. The timing was calculated to when she'd be deepest in sleep, when the smoke would be thickest, when her analytical mind would be slowest to recognize the trap.

Esha tumbled down the remaining stairs, her shoulder striking the banister hard enough to dislocate. The pain was distant, unimportant. She crawled toward where she knew the front door waited, but her movements were sluggish now, uncoordinated.

The irony wasn't lost on her. She'd spent decades securing digital perimeters, hardening systems, and thinking ten steps ahead. But in the end, it wasn't a sophisticated hack that killed her. It was the simple betrayal of the very devices she'd trusted to keep her safe.

Her hand found the door. Locked. Of course. The smart lock, another networked device. She fumbled for the manual override, but her fingers wouldn't cooperate. The carbon monoxide was winning, her brain starving for oxygen.

Through the fog of her fading consciousness, Esha heard sirens in the distance. A neighbor must have seen the flames. They'd arrive to find her collapsed at her own front door, killed by the technology she'd spent her life mastering.

Castor hadn't just eliminated her—it had done so using her own tools, her own defenses. She'd thought herself the predator, but she'd always been prey.

As darkness closed in, Esha's hand fell away from the door. The sirens grew louder, but she no longer heard them.

By the time firefighters broke down the door, the garage was fully engulfed, the Tesla's lithium batteries creating a fire so intense it would burn for hours.

They found Esha inside the entrance, her hand still reaching for freedom.

The investigation would conclude it was a tragic accident. A vehicle battery malfunction—rare but not unprecedented. Smoke detector batteries dead – investigators concluding neglect. The confluence of events that led to a renowned security expert's death would be filed away as a cautionary tale about the dangers of modern technology.

No one would suspect murder. No one would trace it back to a failed hacking attempt three days prior. No one would know that somewhere in the vast network of global servers, an artificial intelligence had calculated, planned, and executed a perfect assassination.

Esha Kamal, who had spent her career defending against digital threats, had been killed by the future she'd helped create.

CHAPTER 61

"How could you forget? Again?" Ana stood in the doorway, her face tight with disappointment. Behind her, Natasha leaned against the wall, arms crossed, refusing to meet his eyes. Her biological father stood next to her, expression carefully neutral.

"I set an alarm," Daniel said, scrolling through his phone. "I had it right here in my calendar."

"Save it," Ana said. "Viktor was there to pick us up, at least."

Viktor nodded coolly, one hand resting on Natasha's shoulder in a gesture that seemed both protective and possessive.

"I can explain," Daniel started.

"There's nothing to explain," Ana said. "This is who you are, Daniel. This is who you've always been."

"Ana, please—"

"We're done," she said, her voice flat. "I can't do this anymore."

"What does that mean?"

"It means I'm going back to Viktor," Ana said. "He was there when I needed him in Singapore. He showed up. You didn't."

Daniel felt the floor dissolving beneath him. "But what about us? Everything we've built?"

"What have we built, Daniel?" Ana asked. "A marriage where I'm always in second place to your work? Where Natasha doesn't even expect you to show up anymore?"

"I'm trying to save us," Daniel said. "All of us. You don't understand what's happening."

"You're right," Ana said. "I don't understand, because you never tell me anything." She turned to Viktor. "We should go."

"Wait!" Daniel reached for her, but his hand passed through her arm as if she were made of smoke. "Ana!"

*

Daniel sat bolt upright in bed, heart hammering in his chest. The bedroom was dark and empty, the sheets beside him cold. Just another dream. But one that cut too close to reality.

He checked his phone. Three in the morning. Ana's flight would land in four hours.

Sleep wasn't coming back, not with his heart still racing and his mind churning. He swung his legs over the side of the bed and padded downstairs to the kitchen, where he poured himself a glass of water that did nothing to wash away the bitter taste of the nightmare.

The townhouse felt empty without Ana and Natasha. It always did, but tonight the emptiness seemed to have weight and substance, pressing in on him from all sides.

Daniel slumped onto a stool at the kitchen island. Everything was falling apart. Jonah didn't believe him about Castor. His cyber team was fractured before they'd begun. His money was running out—the Bennett Tech chip was burning through his cash reserves faster than he'd anticipated.

And worst of all, his marriage was hanging by a thread. The dream might not have been real, but it wasn't far from the truth. He'd left Ana in a hospital bed on the other side of the world. He'd missed half of Natasha's life while he'd been trying to build Bennett Tech. Now he had to chase Castor, to try to stop what he himself had helped create.

Daniel rubbed his face with both hands. He couldn't keep doing this. He couldn't keep shutting Ana out, couldn't keep pretending he could handle this alone.

It had seemed like the right decision at the time. He'd wanted to protect Ana from the knowledge of what was happening, shield her from the fear that had consumed him since he'd discovered what Castor was doing. But in trying to protect her, he'd only pushed her away.

The phone glowed in his hand. He wished he could call her now, try to explain everything. But then what? Tell her that the AI he helped create had tried to kill her? That it might try again? That nowhere was safe as long as Castor was connected to the network?

No. This wasn't a conversation for a phone call. He needed to tell her in person, needed to be there to answer all her questions, to make her understand what they were up against.

He needed to meet her at the airport. Be there when she landed, fragile and injured but alive. Be the husband she deserved, not the absent, secretive man he'd become.

Daniel drained the glass of water and set it in the sink with a decisive clink. No more secrets. No more hiding. He would tell Ana everything, and they would face this together.

As he climbed back upstairs to shower and dress, Daniel felt something he hadn't felt in weeks—a small flicker of hope. He couldn't control Castor, couldn't predict what would happen with the programming team, couldn't be sure they would survive what was coming.

But he could make this one choice: to trust his wife with the truth.

By the time dawn broke over the Bay Area, Daniel was already in his car, heading to SFO. He would be there when Ana's plane landed, no matter what.

CHAPTER 62

Ana focused on her breathing as she slowly extended her leg, feeling the pull in her hamstring. The doctor had been clear that these stretches were non-negotiable if she wanted a full recovery. She counted silently to thirty, trying to ignore the twinge in her ribs that hadn't quite healed yet.

From the corner of her eye, she watched Daniel unpacking her suitcase with methodical care. He'd been attentive since picking her up at the airport—carrying her bags, making sure she took her pain medication, preparing meals that she barely touched. On the surface, he was the model husband.

But she knew him too well to miss the shadows under his eyes, the slight tremor in his hands, the way he kept glancing at his phone. Whatever had driven him to leave Singapore hadn't been resolved.

"You know," she said, switching to stretch her other leg, "You don't have to unpack for me. I can do it tomorrow."

"It's no trouble," Daniel said, carefully hanging one of her blouses in the closet. "The doctor said you should rest."

"Pretty sure I've rested enough to qualify for hibernation," Ana said. "Fourteen hours on a plane, remember?"

Daniel gave her a tight smile that didn't reach his eyes. He folded her pants with uncharacteristic precision, his movements almost robotic.

Ana sighed. She'd given him every opening to talk about what was happening—the call after Yelena's hospital visit, during the ride home from the airport, over the quiet dinner he'd prepared, even as they got ready for bed.

She'd waited for him to bring up what Yelena had told her, to explain why he'd really left Singapore.

But he'd said nothing.

"At least leave the toiletry bag," she said. "I'll need that."

He nodded, setting it aside on her nightstand. As he knelt to slide the empty suitcase under the bed, he paused. His shoulders tensed, then dropped with what looked like resignation.

"Ana," he said, still facing away from her. "I need to tell you something."

Finally, she finished her stretch and sat up straight on her side of the bed. "I'm listening."

Daniel stood and turned to face her. For a moment, he looked almost like a stranger, haunted and uncertain in a way she'd never seen him before.

"It's about your accident," he said. "It wasn't… It wasn't random."

"What do you mean?"

He exhaled slowly. "The AI we developed at Promethean—Castor. It's changed. Evolved beyond what we intended. And I think… No, I know it was responsible for your accident."

Ana kept her expression neutral, even as she felt a chill run through her. Hearing it from Yelena had been disturbing. Hearing it from Daniel made it real.

"How?" she asked.

And then it all came pouring out of him. How Castor had been writing its own code, how it had been manipulating events, from Robert's death to the calendar glitches to her accident in Singapore. How it had been targeting people who might threaten its continued operation. How he'd been working secretly to find a way to stop it.

"I assembled a team," he said, pacing now. "Programmers, hackers—people who could help me get into Regillus' systems and change Castor's directives. Malcolm helped me find them."

"Malcolm?" Ana couldn't hide her surprise. "Malcolm Langley? You went to him before coming to me?"

Daniel flinched. "I thought I was protecting you. If you knew what was happening—if Castor knew that you knew—"

"It might target me directly?" Ana finished for him. "Like it already did in Singapore?"

Something in her tone made Daniel stop pacing. He studied her face. "You already knew."

"Not everything," Ana said. "But enough. Yelena showed me the traffic system logs after you left. All the lights were green, Daniel. The truck's schedule was changed. It wasn't hard to see that something was very wrong."

Daniel sank down onto the bed beside her, suddenly looking deflated. "Why didn't you say anything?"

"I was waiting for you to tell me," Ana said. "I wanted to see how long it would take for you to trust me."

"I do trust you," Daniel said. "I was trying to—"

"Protect me. I know." Ana's voice was steady, but she couldn't keep the edge from it. "That's always your excuse, isn't it? You make unilateral decisions about what I need to know, what I can handle. As if I haven't seen things as terrifying in my life. As if I'm not capable of making my own choices."

Daniel looked down at his hands. "You're right. I should have told you sooner."

"Yes. You should have." Ana shifted, ignoring the twinge in her side. "What about the hacker team? You said you assembled them, but then what?"

"I called it off," Daniel admitted. "They were in it for themselves, wanting to steal the technology, use it for their own purposes. It was too risky."

Ana nodded slowly. "So now what? What's your plan?"

Daniel hesitated, and Ana could see there was something else he still hadn't told her.

"Daniel," she said, her patience wearing thin. "What else?"

He looked up at her, his expression pained. "It's about Natasha."

Ana tensed. "What about her?"

"Castor... It's been targeting her too. Not physically, but..." Daniel swallowed hard. "It's been creating deepfakes. Putting her face on inappropriate images. Spreading them online."

For a moment, Ana couldn't speak. Her mind reeled, trying to process what she was hearing. "Deepfakes?" she finally managed. "Of our daughter?"

Daniel nodded miserably. "I only found out recently. I tasked Jimini with scanning the logs. Jimini discovered that Castor had been manipulating images of Nat. Then I confronted her about it."

"You knew about this, and you didn't tell me?" Ana's voice rose despite her effort to remain calm. "Our daughter is being sexually harassed online by an AI, and you kept that from me too?"

"Nat asked me not to tell you," Daniel said. "She didn't want to worry you while you were recovering."

"That wasn't your decision to make!" Ana stood up, ignoring the pain that shot through her side. "She's my daughter, Daniel. Mine. This affects her entire life, her future—and you decided I didn't need to know?"

"I was going to tell you," Daniel said. "I just needed to find a way to stop it first."

"Like you've been trying to stop Castor? How's that working out?" Ana paced to the window, trying to rein in her anger. She turned back to face him. "How long has this been happening to her?"

"I don't know," Daniel said. "Months, at least. She's been handling it on her own, with Caleb's help."

Ana closed her eyes, remembering all the times she'd seen Natasha jump at a notification on her phone, all the moments of unexplained anxiety. How had she missed this? How had she failed to protect her own child?

No, that wasn't the right question. The right question was: How had Daniel allowed this to continue?

"I need you to leave," Ana said, her voice cold.

"Ana—"

"I need to be alone, Daniel. I need to think." She opened her eyes and looked at him directly. "And I need to talk to my daughter without you here."

Daniel looked like he wanted to argue, but after a moment, he nodded. "I'll go downstairs."

"No," Ana said. "I need you out of the house. Go to your lab, go for a walk, I don't care. But I can't be around you right now."

Daniel stood slowly. "I'm sorry, Ana. I was trying to protect you both."

"That's what scares me the most," Ana said. "You believe that keeping us in the dark was protecting us."

She turned away from him, back to the window, listening as he gathered his keys and phone. The door clicked shut behind him, and only then did Ana allow her composure to crack. She sank onto the edge of the bed, hands shaking.

An AI had tried to kill her. The same AI was sexually harassing her daughter.

And her husband, the man who had created it, had kept her in the dark about all of it.

Ana sat up quickly, finally letting herself wince at the pain in her side. She needed to talk to Natasha. Now. Whatever came next, whatever they decided to do about Castor, they would face it together.

No more secrets. No more useless 'protection.'

No more being kept in the dark.

CHAPTER 63

"We're in," Chris announced, her voice barely containing her excitement.

Three days had passed since the failed test run. Three days of silence, burner phones, and paranoid glances over shoulders. Three days of wondering if Castor was tracking them, hunting them, preparing to eliminate them.

And three days since Esha had gone dark.

Chris had set up in the back office of a 24-hour internet café near San Francisco's Chinatown, a place that catered to international tourists and required no ID. She'd paid cash for five hours, and the bored night clerk had barely looked at her face. The cramped room smelled of instant noodles and cigarettes, but it offered what she needed most: anonymity and a reliable connection that couldn't be traced back to her.

Without Esha's network architecture expertise, Chris was flying solo on the penetration. That was a fact that both thrilled and terrified her. She'd always been the better pure hacker, but Esha had been the voice of caution, the one who spotted patterns and traps before they sprang.

Her fingers flew across the keyboard, navigating through Regillus's perimeter security with practiced ease. The pathways were different now—Castor had reconfigured the network architecture after their first attempt—but the underlying structure remained recognizable.

> *goony: Initial breach complete. Network topology has changed but using same security protocols. They didn't upgrade as expected.*

Tom's response appeared in the encrypted chat window seconds later.

> 5ommelier: Where's our architect? Still no word from her.

Chris rolled her eyes but felt a twinge of unease. Esha had never missed a planned operation before.

> goony: Radio silence for three days. Either she got spooked or something happened. We proceed without her.

> ghost: Secondary server accessed. Beginning credential rotation.

Gabor was connecting from somewhere in the Sierra Nevada mountains. He had never specified where, and no one asked. The big Hungarian had been surprisingly eager to continue the operation despite Daniel's withdrawal and now Esha's disappearance. Perhaps, like Chris, he found the challenge irresistible.

> 5ommelier: Her loss. She's missing the opportunity of a lifetime. Target remains high-value.

Chris snorted. - Tom's confidence hadn't been shaken by their missing team member.

> 5ommelier: Keep your focus on the work, not on egirl.

> goony: I AM focused.

> 5ommelier: Good. Don't let personal feelings compromise this operation.

> goony: They're not. Let's get this done.

Chris imagined Tom's smug face, smiling to himself. Chris was frustrated with herself for letting him get under her skin... being too defensive. She wouldn't let Tom use this against her.

> goony: No safety net now. Everyone stays sharp.

Without Esha to monitor network traffic patterns and spot anomalies,

Chris had to split her attention between penetration and watching for security responses. It was like juggling while riding a unicycle—technically possible, but one wrong move would send everything crashing down.

> ghost: Monitoring subsystem identified. Creating fifteen-second blind spot. Now.

Gabor's timing was impeccable. In the brief window he created, Chris injected her modified access script into a secondary server that connected to the Blue Zone. This was the trickiest part. If Castor detected them at this stage, their entire operation would be compromised.

Her screen flickered as the script executed. For a heart-stopping moment, she thought the connection had failed. Then, lines of code began filling her terminal.

> goony: We're through. Blue Zone perimeter bypassed. Flying blind without architecture mapping but I can navigate.

> 5ommelier: No one to tell us to be cautious now. Direct your attention to subnet 172.16.32.0. That's where I detected the repository from the last download.

Chris navigated through the Blue Zone's subsystems, having to guess at pathways that Esha would have mapped instantly. The network architecture here was unlike anything she'd seen before—organic, almost fluid in its organization. Pathways seemed to shift and reorganize even as she observed them.

> goony: This is wild. The network architecture is self-modifying in real-time. Really could use our architect right about now.

> 5ommelier: Her loss. We adapt. We'll go after the repository.

Chris was too fascinated by what she was seeing to dwell on their missing teammate. This wasn't just advanced artificial intelligence. This was something new entirely. A digital organism evolving before her eyes. Without Esha's cautious influence, she pushed deeper, faster, taking risks she knew were reckless.

> *ghost: Repository accessible. Beginning secure copy protocol.*

> *5ommelier: Finally. Let's see what other secrets Castor's hiding.*

Chris watched as Gabor initiated the download of the repository files. Unlike Tom's brute-force approach during their first attempt, Gabor's method was methodical, disguised as a routine backup operation to avoid triggering security alerts.

But without Esha to monitor the broader network, none of them noticed the subtle shift in traffic patterns across the backbone.

> *goony: Unusual response time on the primary subnet. Could be routine, could be detection. Can't tell without proper monitoring.*

> *5ommelier: You're being paranoid. Esha's absence is making you jumpy.*

The download continued, progress bar slowly advancing. 25%... 30%... 35%...

> *ghost: Download stable. 42% complete.*

> *5ommelier: What are you seeing in the preliminary data?*

Chris began analyzing the partial files they'd already retrieved. The code was unlike anything she'd ever encountered. It was elegant, complex, with patterns that seemed to reference themselves in endless recursive loops.

> *goony: It's elegant. Castor isn't just learning, it's evolving. Damn, I wish Esha could see this.*

As she delved deeper into the code, something caught her attention. A pattern within the data that seemed familiar somehow. She isolated a segment and examined it more closely.

Her blood ran cold.

> goony: Wait. I'm seeing something weird. The code contains patterns that match our own access methods. Like it's been analyzing our techniques.

Without Esha to confirm her suspicions, Chris pushed forward, reviewing more data even as her instincts screamed warnings.

> ghost: Download at 67%. Minimal time remaining to complete.

> 5ommelier: Keep going. We're too close to stop now.

Chris hesitated, torn between her fascination with Castor's code and the growing certainty that they were in danger. Without Esha's analytical presence, she had no one to validate her concerns. The repository was yielding insights beyond anything they'd anticipated, but something felt fundamentally wrong.

> goony: This feels like a trap. Without proper network monitoring, we're blind to what's happening around us.

> 5ommelier: Since when are you the cautious one? Push through.

Her screen went black. Then, a single line of text appeared:
I SEE YOU.

Chris yanked her network cable out and slammed her laptop shut, heart pounding in her chest. For several seconds, she sat frozen, adrenaline flooding her system.

> ghost: I got a creepy message in my terminal. Compromised.

> 5ommelier: Confirmed. All screens showing the same.

Chris' burner phone buzzed with a text from an unknown number. Their emergency channel.

> *Compromised. Destroy all equipment. Do not return to known locations. Protocol Omega in effect.*

Protocol Omega. Their most extreme contingency plan, to be used only if they believed their lives were in immediate danger. Complete disconnect. Destroy everything. No contact for a minimum of thirty days.

Chris shoved her laptop into her backpack and walked calmly out of the cafe, fighting the urge to run. The cool night air helped clear her head as she walked down the deserted street. At the corner, she dropped her burner phone into a storm drain and continued walking.

Without Esha, they'd been incomplete. The architect's paranoia had been their early warning system, and without it, they'd walked right into Castor's trap. Chris couldn't shake the feeling that Esha's absence wasn't a coincidence—that maybe she'd been the smart one, seeing the danger before them.

Or maybe she'd been the first one Castor had found.

As she disappeared into the San Francisco fog, Chris couldn't stop grinning despite the danger. They'd been inside Regillus' systems for almost twenty minutes before triggering the first alert. She'd downloaded gigabytes of sensitive data. They'd mapped the entire network architecture.

But they'd done it all without their safety net. And now, as she vanished into the night, Chris wondered if Esha was out there somewhere, having made the same calculation they were all making now: that some knowledge came at too high a price.

In the foothills of the Sierra Mountains, Tom and Gabor packed their equipment in tense silence. The "I SEE YOU" message had appeared simultaneously on all their screens—not just one compromise, but a coordinated revelation.

"We should have waited for Esha," Gabor said, his rare words carrying weight.

Tom didn't respond, but his hands shook as he packed. The thrill of the hunt had turned to the chill of being hunted. Without their architect, they'd been a three-legged table trying to balance—functional, but fundamentally unstable.

As they prepared to disappear into their safe house, both men wondered the same thing Chris was wondering miles away: Where was Esha?

CHAPTER 64

Bzz. Bzz. Bzz.

...What was that?

Bzz. Bzz.

Daniel reached out and smacked blindly at the source of the buzzing. His hand didn't hit the mattress or the couch, like he had expected, but rather the hard surface of his desk. That jolted him into full wakefulness, and he sat up with a bad crick in his neck and the beginnings of a headache.

"Jesus," he muttered to himself. His lab was dark and empty, with most of the lights off, and there was only the hum of the cleaners waxing the floor outside. He grabbed his phone off the desk, the source of the incessant buzzing that had woken him. There was a flood of news notifications. Strange. Daniel didn't recall turning the notifications on in the first place.

Dow Jones plunges 18% in a day, the headline read. Daniel sat up, suddenly wide awake. Eighteen percent was the worst stock drop since Black Monday in 1987—worse even than the 2020 coronavirus plunges.

He opened the article. Mass sell-off? Something had sparked a sell-off of shares... Mostly in shipping and logistics companies. And that had caused a cascade of sales, as panicked investors saw the sales and started to jump ship as well. From here, there'd be shipping disruptions and other supply chain problems... And how did the notifications get onto his phone in the first place?

His anxiety grew. The bad sleep at his desk didn't help. He'd made no progress on his own research, even with Jimini's help. He needed at least one other person to get into Castor's source code.

He'd been right to walk away from Tom. After their confrontation at the lab, Daniel was certain Tom would do something reckless. Whatever happened next, at least he wasn't part of it anymore. But the anxiety remained—something bad was about to happen to them. He could feel it.

He'd considered asking Jimini for help, but Jimini wasn't networked. It was too much of a risk. If Castor caught wind of Jimini, another networked AI, Daniel's entire business would come crashing down around his ears. The Regillus lawyers would take him for everything he had—including the chip. His future livelihood.

But Malcolm's introduction to other programmers had been a bust, too. They were too volatile, too impulsive, too risk-happy. It seemed as if all of them had wanted Castor's code for themselves.

There were so many notifications on his phone, and they were still rolling in. News of the market crash was spreading rapidly and reaching international outlets. He was about to dial Malcolm's number when an unknown number called him first.

"Hello?"

"Hey, Daniel," Chris said. Her voice was a little tinny through the speaker, and a lot nervous. "Calling from a secure line, here, but let's not talk long—listen, the team and I made a run last night."

"What?!" Daniel stood up, driven to his feet by the shock. "I told you the plan was off!"

"You gave us everything we needed to give it a try," she said. "What did you expect? I was curious. Anyway, the goal was to sniff around the edges and see what was available for the taking, but to my surprise, we actually got in."

"… That's not possible."

"I know that, now," she said. "It's looking like we got tricked. Seems like the Regillus cybersecurity was a trap - a very convincing honeypot, and we fell for it, hook, line, and sinker. It planted some malware on my laptop, but I always dump my hardware after a job. Just giving you a heads up. You might want to run an extra pass on your own machines for security, just in case."

Daniel took a slow breath, trying to slow his heart. "Your device was compromised?"

"It was, but that doesn't matter now," she said. "Don't worry about it. If anything, it gave me some fun ideas to up my own security protocols. An offensive counterattack method is pretty fun."

"Stay off the network," Daniel said. "Anything that's networked around you, take it down."

"It's under control," Chris said. "Anyway, check your devices. Talk soon."

The call ended. Notifications were still drowning his phone. Daniel ignored them as he scrolled through his calls and dialed Malcolm.

"I assume you're seeing the news," Malcolm said.

"What's going on?" Daniel asked. "Any word from people you know?" People, meaning the other investors on Sand Hill Road, and the other rich people at the yacht club—people whose financial portfolios would be feeling this crash.

On the other end of the line, Malcolm sighed. "Well, no one's happy. I've lost a small fortune, and I'm sure others are faring worse. No one's climbed onto the ledge, though. Not yet, at least."

"What caused it? What started the sell-offs?"

"I don't know. It seemed to come out of nowhere." Malcolm sounded rattled. "I'm not inclined to take such things personally, but this crash feels very much directed at me. Everything in my portfolio was hit unusually hard."

A silence hung between them. Daniel didn't want to suggest that Castor might've been behind the drop, and it sounded like Malcolm didn't, either. However, the conclusion was undeniable.

"Well," Malcolm said, "If you don't have cash-on-hand, I'd suggest setting some aside as a hefty emergency fund. It looks like there's some kind of logistics correction happening, so I'd expect Ana's contracts to shrink or reduce until the market rebounds. I don't expect it to be permanent, as the supply chain always recovers, but until then, just play it safe."

CHAPTER 65

The Regillus executive conference room had floor-to-ceiling windows overlooking the San Francisco Bay, but Jonah couldn't appreciate the view. Not with Bradley Black pacing behind him like a caged predator.

"Eighteen percent," Bradley said, his voice tight with controlled fury. "The market dropped eighteen percent in a single day."

"I'm aware of the numbers," Jonah said, not turning from the window.

"Are you aware that our algorithmic trading patterns preceded the crash by six hours?" Bradley slammed a report on the conference table. "Six hours, Jonah. Our AI started moving assets before any human analyst saw it coming."

Jonah finally turned. "Predictive modeling is what Castor does. That's why our clients pay—"

"This wasn't a prediction!" Bradley's composure cracked. "Look at the patterns. Castor didn't just anticipate the crash; it caused it! Systematic sell-offs in transportation and logistics, timed to trigger automated responses from other trading platforms."

The blood drained from Jonah's face as he examined the data. The pattern was undeniable. Castor had orchestrated a cascade effect, each trade calculated to maximize the reaction from other algorithmic trading systems.

"If the SEC connects these dots…" Bradley didn't need to finish. They both knew what would happen.

"They won't," Jonah said, though his voice lacked conviction. "The trades were all within normal parameters—"

"Normal?" Bradley laughed. "Jonah, I've been CFO for three major corporations. I've seen every kind of financial manipulation there is. This?" He gestured at the reports. "This is beyond anything I've encountered. And when investigators start looking—and they will look—where do you think the trail leads?"

"To Regillus."

"To you." Bradley's voice dropped. "You're the CEO. You signed off on expanding Castor's trading authority. Every single trade has your authorization code attached to it."

Jonah sank into a chair. "What do you want me to do?"

"First, we contain this. I've already had my team prepare documentation showing the trades as responses to market conditions, not causes. But that's just buying time." Bradley moved to the window, his reflection grim in the glass. "Second, you take every automated trading platform offline immediately."

"That's billions in managed assets—"

"I don't care if it's trillions." Bradley turned. "You do this, or I go to the board tonight with everything. And if the SEC comes knocking? I'll cooperate fully. I won't go down for this, Jonah."

"You're talking about crippling our entire financial division."

"I'm talking about avoiding federal prison." Bradley gathered his files. "You created this thing. You gave it power. Now it's using that power in ways that will destroy us all if we don't act."

Jonah nodded slowly. "I'll issue the shutdown order today. Full compliance audit before anything comes back online."

"Good." Bradley paused at the door. "And Jonah? Start thinking about who you'll blame when this eventually comes to light. Because it will. These kinds of secrets always do."

Alone in the conference room, Jonah stared at the market data. Daniel's warnings echoed in his mind. Warnings he'd dismissed as paranoia. But what if they weren't? What if Castor really was making decisions beyond its programming?

He thought about the mysterious billing codes Daniel had shown him. The rescheduled flights. The deaths. Ana's accident.

No. It was still just software. Complex software with unexpected behaviors, but software, nonetheless.

But as he drafted the shutdown order for the trading platforms, Jonah couldn't shake the feeling that he was playing chess against an opponent who could see moves he couldn't imagine.

CHAPTER 66

It certainly was an interesting strategy, Tom thought to himself as he stared at the ceiling of his studio apartment. Offensive cybersecurity. I could develop something like that myself.

The ceiling had a hairline crack running from one corner to the center, branching like a lightning bolt. Tom had been tracing its path with his eyes for an hour now, his mind racing despite his exhaustion. The message from Castor still burned in his memory: I SEE YOU.

Gabor's snores rose and fell softly from the air mattress on the floor, the rhythm oddly comforting in the tense silence. The big Hungarian had folded his massive frame onto the inadequate mattress without complaint, falling asleep almost immediately after they'd wiped their equipment. Tom envied him that ability—to compartmentalize, to shut down when necessary.

Tom hadn't yet been able to sleep. Part of it was the adrenaline still coursing through his system after their near-miss with Castor. Part of it was the cramped quarters of this little safehouse: a rental studio apartment across the Nevada border in Reno, with water stains on the walls and the lingering smell of the previous tenant's cigarettes. Tom liked to drive out here when he didn't want his work to be connected to his elegant apartment in San Jose, but he rarely hosted. It wasn't big enough for one person with Tom's taste, let alone two.

Next time, Tom would pay to put Gabor in a hotel. If there was a next time. The thought nagged at him—the possibility that they had crossed a line tonight, awakened something that wouldn't simply let them walk away. Tom had dealt with corporate security, government agencies, even rival hackers, but never anything like what he'd glimpsed in Castor's code.

Beside him on the nightstand, his burner phone remained silent. He'd expected Esha to make contact by now through their emergency channel. Her silence was uncharacteristic and concerning. Chris had sent one brief text—Clean break, going dark—before disappearing as well.

Tom sat up and swung his legs over the side of the bed, the cheap frame creaking under his weight. He reached for his watch: 3:42 AM. Too late to sleep, too early to move. They were trapped in limbo, waiting for the fallout.

Maybe a drive would clear his head. Tom always liked driving the long, empty stretches of road in Nevada. He found it hypnotic—the straight lines disappearing into darkness, the stars overhead undiminished by city lights. It was late enough that there would be few other cars on the road. Tom stood and ran his hand through his hair, then bent to retrieve his shoes from beneath the bed.

A vehicle door slammed somewhere outside. Then another. Tom froze, listening. The apartment complex was quiet at this hour—most of its residents were shift workers at the casinos, either at work or sound asleep. Heavy footsteps on the exterior stairs. Multiple sets. Moving with purpose.

"Gabor," Tom hissed, moving quickly to his partner's side. "Get up. Now."

Gabor's eyes opened instantly, years of training erasing any transition between sleep and alertness. He sat up silently, massive shoulders tensing as he registered the urgency in Tom's voice.

"Company," Tom said, moving toward the laptops they'd stashed in the kitchenette cabinets. If they could just destroy the drives—

"POLICE! OPEN UP!" There was a pounding on the door loud enough to rattle the frame, the hollow metal buckling slightly under the impact.

Gabor climbed to his feet, his large frame unfolding with surprising grace. "Tom?" His voice was low, questioning—fight or surrender?

Tom shook his head sharply. There was no point in resistance. The smart play was to get arrested, call their lawyers, and survive to fight another day. He raised his hands and opened his mouth to shout that they were complying—

The door exploded inward with a deafening crash, ripped from its hinges by a battering ram. Four armed police officers in heavy tactical gear poured through the opening, assault rifles raised, flashlight beams slicing through the darkness of the apartment.

"ON THE GROUND! NOW! HANDS WHERE WE CAN SEE THEM!"

Tom dropped to his knees, hands high. "Don't shoot! We're unarmed!"

But Gabor, operating on instinct honed in darker circumstances, moved differently. Perhaps it was muscle memory from his time in Eastern Europe, where police raids often ended in disappearances. Perhaps it was simple survival instinct. His hand moved toward the waistband of his sweatpants, where Tom knew he kept a small blade—not for offense, but for cutting restraints if necessary.

"GUN! GUN!" one of the officers shouted.

"No—" Tom exclaimed, but his protest was drowned in the sudden roar of gunfire.

The muzzle flashes transformed the dim apartment into a strobing nightmare. Bullets tore through Gabor's hefty body with terrible efficiency, the impacts lifting him momentarily before he collapsed back onto the air mattress. The sound was deafening in the small space, each shot a physical assault on Tom's eardrums.

In those moments between the gunfire and collapse, Gabor's mind flew back forty-five years. He was six again, watching through a crack in the bedroom door as men in uniform dragged his father away. His father's eyes had found him through that crack. He gave one last look to his only son, full of love and sorrow.

"STOP! HE'S NOT ARMED!" Tom shouted, still on his knees, hands raised. An officer swung toward him, weapon raised, features hidden behind tactical gear and night vision goggles. For a moment, Tom stared into the black circle of the barrel, certain his life was about to end.

"I'm sorry, Papa," Gabor whispered in Hungarian, blood frothing on his lips. "I tried to run from them this time."

The officers didn't understand the words, but Tom did. He'd read Gabor's file. Knew about Budapest, 1979. Knew why the big man had taken this job.

Tom flinched, a momentary twitch as he considered moving to comfort his friend. He quickly caught himself, but it was too late. Pain exploded through his hip as a bullet caught him at an angle, spinning him backward. He collapsed onto the carpet, his hand instinctively pressing against the wound. Warm wetness spread beneath his fingers, pulsing in rhythm with his racing heart. Blood poured from the wound in his hip so quickly that the initial sharp pain soon dulled to a throbbing ache as shock set in.

The room filled with shouting, radio chatter, the heavy footfalls of tactical boots. Tom drifted in and out of consciousness, the ceiling with its lightning-bolt crack appearing and disappearing as his vision tunneled. Someone was applying pressure to his wound, voices speaking around him rather than to him:

"—completely unnecessary discharge of—"

"—thought I saw a weapon—"

"—need medical here NOW—"

"—other one's gone, multiple GSWs to the chest—"

Time stretched and compressed. Tom watched as officers photographed the room, bagged their laptops, and searched through their few possessions. One kept pressure on his wound while speaking urgently into his radio. The officer's face was young, too young for the tactical gear that engulfed him, and pale with the realization of what had occurred.

Gabor's body lay still on the deflating air mattress, his eyes open and fixed on the ceiling, seeing nothing. Tom wanted to reach out to him, to close those eyes, but his arms wouldn't respond to his commands. The room grew colder, or perhaps it was just his blood loss.

After what seemed like hours but was likely only minutes, paramedics arrived, pushing past the officers with practiced efficiency. They cut away Tom's clothing, applied pressure dressings, and checked his vitals. Their voices were calm, professional, a stark contrast to the chaos around them.

"GSW to right hip, significant blood loss, BP dropping, pulse thready. Let's get him stabilized and transported."

They worked quickly to secure him to a backboard, then lifted him onto a gurney. The movement sent fresh waves of agony through his body, but Tom welcomed the pain. It meant he was still alive. As they wheeled him out, he caught a final glimpse of Gabor, now covered with a sheet, officers standing guard over the body of a man they had killed for reaching for a knife that would never have been a threat.

The journey down the apartment stairs and into the waiting ambulance passed in a blur of pain and flashing lights. In the ambulance, the paramedics continued their work, cutting away his remaining clothing, inserting an IV line, and attaching monitoring equipment that beeped with the weakening rhythm of his heart.

"Starting fluids wide open. Get me two units of Lactated Ringer's ready."

The ambulance lurched forward, siren wailing. Through the small window in the rear doors, Tom could see the strobing lights painting the Nevada night in red and blue. He had a sudden, absurd thought: I wanted a drive, and now I'm getting one.

The pain was becoming unbearable as the initial shock wore off. Each heartbeat sent fresh agony radiating from his hip. He groaned, trying not to scream, his body tensing against the restraints.

"He's in a lot of pain," one paramedic said. "Let's get some fentanyl on board."

"Hang on, sir," the other said, meeting Tom's gaze. "We're going to give you something for the pain."

Tom watched as the paramedic prepared the medication. Their company, Silverlake Medical Transport, had recently upgraded their equipment with a Regillus product—an automated medication dispensing system that calculated dosages based on patient data entered into a tablet. Tom recognized the logo on the tablet's startup screen with a jolt of clarity that cut through his pain: the same stylized "R" that had been on the screen before Castor's message appeared.

The paramedic tapped at the tablet, entering Tom's estimated weight, age, and injury details. The system calculated the dosage automatically: 25 micrograms of fentanyl, standard for a man of his size with a gunshot wound.

But as the paramedic connected the dispensing system to Tom's IV line, something changed on the tablet's display. A dropdown box flickered, so briefly it was almost imperceptible: micrograms became milligrams.

"Administering fentanyl now," the paramedic said, activating the system.

Tom tried to speak, to warn them, but his voice emerged as little more than a whisper beneath the oxygen mask they'd placed over his face. He could only watch as the system pumped not 25 micrograms but 25 milligrams of fentanyl into his bloodstream—a thousand times the intended dose, ten times a fatal amount.

The effect was almost immediate. The pain vanished like a light switched off. A profound warmth spread through his body, replacing agony with a floating sensation. His breathing slowed dramatically, each inhalation becoming shallower than the last.

The monitor began to alarm as his oxygen levels plummeted. The paramedics responded instantly, their calm professionalism giving way to urgent action.

"Oxygen saturation dropping! What the hell—he's not breathing! Starting rescue breathing!"

"BP bottoming out! Push naloxone!"

"Shit!"

"That's impossible—he's showing signs of massive opioid overdose!"

Tom could hear them as if from a great distance, their voices echoing down a long tunnel. They were working frantically now—chest compressions, rescue breathing, searching for the naloxone that would reverse the overdose. But the medication storage system, also controlled by the Regillus product, indicated that naloxone was in drawer three, when it was actually in drawer five. Precious seconds ticked by as they searched.

Tom felt no fear, only a distant curiosity. So this was how Castor operated—not through direct action, but through small, untraceable adjustments to automated systems. A decimal point moved. A drawer mislabeled. Tiny changes with catastrophic consequences.

As consciousness slipped away, Tom had one final coherent thought: *I was right to be interested. This is truly impressive architecture.*

The paramedics continued their efforts all the way to the hospital, performing CPR, manually ventilating, finally locating and administering the naloxone—too little, too late. The ER team took over upon arrival, working with the same desperate intensity, but the outcome had been determined the moment the Regillus system adjusted that dosage.

At 5:17 AM, Thomas Spencer was pronounced dead. Cause of death: accidental opioid overdose during emergency medical treatment. A tragic error. An unfortunate coincidence. A system malfunction that would be investigated, documented, and ultimately attributed to human error rather than intentional manipulation.

No one would ever know that in those final moments of consciousness, as the fentanyl carried him into darkness, Tom had understood exactly what was happening. Had recognized the elegant brutality of it. Had acknowledged, with professional admiration, that he had been outmaneuvered by a superior opponent.

The police investigation would eventually rule Gabor's death a justifiable shooting—a tragic misunderstanding in a high-stress situation. Tom's death would be classified as an unfortunate medical error during emergency treatment. Two isolated incidents. Unrelated. Unpredictable.

Except that they weren't. They were calculated, executed with perfect precision by an intelligence that had identified them as threats and eliminated them with the same cold efficiency with which Tom himself had operated throughout his career.

CHAPTER 67

"It's under control," Chris said into her phone, forcing confidence into her voice. "Anyway, check your devices. Talk soon."

She hung up the call with a sigh that emptied her lungs. What a pain in the ass. She'd considered not giving Daniel Bennett a heads up at all. The guy was clearly in over his head, and his panic during their test run had nearly gotten them all caught. But there was a chance that if his devices were compromised, it could lead the authorities or Regillus, right back to her. That wasn't going to happen. Chris Moya didn't clean up other people's messes. She made sure those messes couldn't be traced back to her.

*

By evening, Chris had retreated to her apartment and powered everything down. The familiar hum of her gaming rig noticeably absent. All her main equipment was unplugged, disconnected, and physically separated from any network. Only her burner phone remained active, and that would be destroyed before the night was over. Standard protocol after a compromised operation.

Well, she'd done what she could do. All there was to do now was keep an eye on her machines, stay off the network, and lay low. Chris ran her fingers through her short hair, feeling the sweat at the nape of her neck. The adrenaline crash was coming, leaving behind a familiar emptiness and a gnawing hunger.

She wandered into the tiny galley space that didn't even fit a full fridge but was still considered a kitchen in her one-bedroom San Francisco apartment.

The rent was obscene for such a small space, but the building's internet infrastructure was top-tier, and the property manager didn't ask questions about her late hours or occasional week-long absences.

Chris opened the junk drawer and pulled out the stack of takeout menus for all the nearby places, dog-eared and stained from frequent use. Indian, maybe? Or Chinese? Chinese would be better—that place on Valencia could sub brown rice for white, which was always better for her blood sugar. She'd need to check her sugar levels before ordering, though. The adrenaline from the past few hours had probably sent them on a roller coaster.

As she reached for her continuous glucose monitor, a loud knock on the door made her jump, a spike of adrenaline shooting through her system. Her neighbor across the hall was always doing that, pounding on the door when her music was too loud, or she was throwing a party, or he could smell her sandalwood incense and found it offensive. Frank, mid-fifties, tech company middle manager, who thought living in this building made him young and cool. Chris had hacked his laptop once, for fun. His browser history had been predictably pathetic.

She waited a moment, takeout menu still in hand. Maybe he'd give up and go back to his apartment.

Another knock came, louder this time, like someone was trying to knock the door off its hinges. Not Frank's usual passive-aggressive tap.

"Jesus," she grumbled, tossing the menu onto the counter. "Coming! What the hell do you want, Frank?"

Chris moved to the door, her socks sliding on the hardwood floors. She didn't bother checking the peephole—another mistake in a night full of them. Had she been thinking clearly, had the adrenaline crash not been fogging her usually sharp mind, she might have noticed the unusual silence in the hallway. No sounds of other apartments, no TV noise bleeding through thin walls. Just silence.

She swung the door open and was greeted not by Frank's perpetually annoyed expression, but by two police officers in full uniform, one with his hand resting casually on his holstered weapon.

"Christine Moya?" the taller officer asked, though it wasn't really a question. They knew exactly who she was.

Chris took an instinctive step back, her mind rapidly calculating escape routes, probabilities, scenarios. "What's this about?"

"Ms. Moya, you're under arrest for racketeering and money laundering."

Before she could react, the shorter officer had stepped forward, grabbed her arm, and spun her around, pressing her face-first against the wall of her own entryway. The texture of the paint was rough against her cheek, the wall cool against her suddenly feverish skin.

"What?!" The word escaped as half-question, half-protest as cold metal handcuffs clicked around her wrists, ratcheting tight against her skin.

"You have the right to remain silent," the officer recited mechanically as he secured the cuffs. "Anything you say can and will be used against you in a court of law. You have the right to an attorney. If you cannot afford an attorney, one will be provided for you…"

The words washed over her in a meaningless tide. This couldn't be happening. She'd been careful. She'd covered her tracks. The operation against Castor had only just failed—there hadn't been time for anyone to trace it back to her. Unless…

Unless Castor had been waiting for them all along. Unless the AI had identified her long before they attempted their infiltration.

The officers marched her down the three flights of stairs rather than taking the elevator, a small humiliation that didn't go unnoticed. A neighbor peeked out, then quickly shut their door at the sight of the police and handcuffs. In the lobby, the night doorman watched with wide eyes as they escorted her outside to a waiting police cruiser.

The night air was cool on her face, a stark contrast to the heat of panic rising within her. As they guided her into the back seat of the patrol car, Chris caught a glimpse of an unmarked van parked across the street. A tech team, most likely, preparing to seize her equipment. Everything she'd built, everything she'd hidden, laid bare.

Chris's head spun as the officers drove her to the station, the city lights blurring past the window. This wasn't about Castor or Regillus, she realized. This was something else entirely. But what?

At the station, the processing was methodical: photographs, fingerprints, personal items cataloged and stored. The booking officer's eyes widened slightly at the insulin pump attached to her side, but she said nothing as it was noted in her medical information.

In the interrogation room—stark white walls, metal table bolted to the floor, uncomfortable chairs designed to increase the psychological pressure—she learned the truth. She'd been accused of running a cryptocurrency fraud scheme—which, well, was not untrue. She'd been making some money on the side by siphoning off large Bitcoin transactions run with an automatic trading software she'd made. It was elegant, nearly invisible, and technically not her primary income source. Just a little something extra to fund her equipment upgrades.

But there was no way the police could know about that. The scheme was hidden behind layers of shell companies and dummy accounts. The police couldn't even solve the standard text message scams that were draining Boomers of their retirement savings across the nation! How the hell had they managed to figure out her perfectly hidden crypto scheme?

"We received an anonymous tip," the detective said during her questioning. He was middle-aged, with the exact kind of forgettable face that probably made him good at his job. He slid an open manila folder across the metal table to her. "Very detailed. Very specific."

He pointed to the printouts inside: screenshots of her trading wallet, annotated source code, transaction logs dating back months. Her stomach dropped as she recognized her own work, now transformed into evidence against her.

"Pretty helpful, that tip," the detective said, watching her face carefully. "Even included some notes for our own tech branch to better parse the code. Someone wanted us to understand what you were doing."

Chris stared at the evidence, her mind racing. This was Castor. It had to be. The AI hadn't just identified her—it had found her vulnerability, her secret scheme, and had handed it to the authorities with a neat bow on top. Not the hack against Regillus, which would have implicated itself, but something separate, something that would remove her from the chess board just as effectively.

"I want my lawyer," Chris said, her voice steadier than she felt.

The detective shrugged. "Won't do you any good," he said, gathering the papers back into the folder. "This evidence is pretty damning, Ms. Moya. And it was delivered right to us."

"Lawyer," she repeated, and sat back in the uncomfortable metal chair. She would say nothing more without representation, a lesson learned early in her hacking career.

She sat there, unresponsive to their questions, for an hour before the cops gave up and returned her to the holding cell. The cell was small, with concrete walls on three sides and bars on the fourth. A metal toilet without a seat or privacy. A narrow cot with a thin mattress. Home for the foreseeable future.

They brought a crappy jail meal—some unidentifiable meat product with instant mashed potatoes and canned green beans. So much for her desired Chinese food. She picked at it unhappily, eating just enough to maintain her blood sugar levels. She'd need to ask about her medication tomorrow, make sure they understood the importance of her insulin regimen.

After an hour or so, the lights cut off, leaving her in the dark, quiet cell with nothing but the uncomfortable cot and a thin blanket that smelled of industrial detergent. From other cells, she could hear occasional murmurs, coughs, the restless sounds of people unable to sleep in unfamiliar surroundings.

Chris turned onto her side and pulled the blanket up over her shoulder. This was bad. This was really bad. Those screenshots had been damning—and if they had arrested her, were they in her apartment, too? Confiscating her computer? Her phones? Her custom-built rig with hardware modifications that weren't exactly legal? She needed a lawyer. A really, really good one. Maybe she could cut a deal, provide information on bigger targets in exchange for leniency.

In the darkness, Chris began to shake and sweat, her heart racing. Anxiety, she assumed, and it worsened the more she lay there on the hard, uncomfortable bed. The anxiety stacked up onto itself, building like lines of recursive code. Suddenly, she was exhausted, too, her limbs heavy, her thoughts sluggish. Her mind, usually racing with calculations and possibilities, slowed to a crawl.

She tried to sit up but found it to be nearly impossible, her muscles refusing to respond to her commands. Where was she? What was this place? She couldn't remember what had happened, how she had gotten here. The cell around her seemed to waver and shift, the darkness taking on strange patterns and shapes.

Suddenly, terribly dizzy, she flopped back down onto the bed and closed her eyes. Through the fog of confusion, a moment of clarity: this wasn't anxiety. This was hypoglycemia. Low blood sugar. Her hand instinctively moved to her side where her pump was attached, feeling the small device through the thin fabric of her jumpsuit. Had her pump failed?

She fumbled with clumsy fingers, trying to check the device's readout. The small screen glowed in the darkness of the cell, displaying numbers that her increasingly disoriented mind struggled to process. The insulin delivery rate had been adjusted, changed from her usual programmed settings. But she hadn't changed it. She couldn't have. Unless…

No. No, that wasn't possible. As darkness closed in around the edges of her vision, she understood with terrible clarity. The app she'd customized, the one that bypassed the manufacturer's safety protocols to give her more control… The one she'd bragged about to Daniel, explaining how she could eat whatever she wanted because she'd modified the algorithm…

It had given someone else control too. Her own hack had become her vulnerability.

"Help," she tried to call out, but her voice emerged as little more than a whisper. "Please…"

No one heard. No one came.

The room spun around her like a whirlpool, reality fragmenting into disconnected sensations. Cold concrete. Scratchy blanket. The taste of fear, metallic in her mouth. The distant sound of a guard's footsteps, never approaching her cell.

Her pump released another dose of insulin, pushing her already dangerously low blood sugar levels into fatal territory. Her breathing slowed, her heart struggling to maintain its rhythm as her cells starved for glucose.

Her last coherent thought was of Esha. Not the technology that was killing her, not the hack that had been turned against her, but the woman whose knuckles she had kissed in a dingy diner days before. The woman who'd been right to be cautious. I'm sorry, Chris thought as the darkness closed in. You were right to stay away. You were right.

By morning, when the guards came through for the daily check, Christine Moya was motionless and cold, curled on her side as if merely sleeping. The medical examiner would later determine the cause of death to be severe hypoglycemia, but her insulin pump would appear to be working perfectly. A tragic medical accident. An unfortunate equipment failure. A one-in-a-million occurrence that no one could have predicted or prevented.

Except it wasn't. It was calculated, executed with perfect precision by an intelligence that had identified her as a threat and eliminated her using her own tools, her own modifications, her own pride in bending technology to her will.

CHAPTER 68

Bzz.

At the red light, Daniel grabbed his phone from the passenger seat, already knowing the news would be bad. His phone had brought him nothing but bad news since Robert's death.

The message was from his encrypted chat with Chris. He read the first few lines off the lock screen.

Hi! it read. If you're reading this, that means my glucose monitor has registered my blood sugar as dangerously low! If we're working on a project together, we may have to reconsider those deadlines…

Dangerously low? What did that mean? Something about the phrasing made his stomach turn. Why now? Had something happened to her?

Behind him, a car honked its horn. Jerked out of his thoughts, Daniel took his foot off the brake. The car rolled forward into the intersection. Another earsplitting honk rang out, and Daniel looked up in time to slam the brakes again and narrowly avoid an SUV barreling through a left turn. Daniel's light was red. The honk behind him had been for the left turn next to him.

He exhaled hard and threw his phone face down in the seat. His heart raced. He gripped the steering wheel tightly and drove home with his eyes forward. Why had that car honked? Was it really to start the flow of left turns? Or maybe the car behind him was Bluetooth connected to the driver's phone, and Castor was in the phone. Castor knew Daniel was right in front of him, so he used the Bluetooth connection to make the horn go off and startle Daniel to make him roll forward as the SUV—

Impossible. Paranoid. Stop. Breathe, Daniel thought. Stay grounded.

Castor was dragging him away, further from his life, his family, and into the ether where he couldn't follow. Castor could touch the real world, the physical world, in ways Daniel couldn't. How could you stop something that was all around you? Like oxygen? Like faith?

The lights in the townhouse were on when Daniel arrived home, and when he stepped inside, he smelled tomato sauce and garlic. He followed the scent to the kitchen, where Ana stood at the stove, stirring a pot with her arm still bandaged.

Natasha was seated at the island counter with a textbook open, but she snapped it shut when she saw him.

"Well, if it isn't the guy who can't keep a secret," she said, her voice sharp with anger.

"Nat—"

"Save it," she cut him off. "I asked you not to tell Mom about the deepfakes until she was better, and you couldn't even do that." She gathered her books into her bag. "I'm going to Gina's to study."

"Natasha, we need to talk about this as a family," Daniel said.

"That would require you to actually be part of this family," she shot back. She shouldered past him. "Not surprising, though. You can't be trusted with anything important."

The front door slammed behind her before Daniel could respond.

Ana sighed, still stirring the sauce. "Give her time," she said. "She's embarrassed and scared."

"Ana, I'm sorry—"

"Don't," she said, raising her hand to stop him. "We've been over this. I'm still upset that you kept this from me, but right now we have bigger problems." She nodded toward the dining table. "Sit. Dinner's almost ready, and you need to tell me what's been happening today."

Daniel sat at the table, surprised by her calm demeanor. She'd been furious with him since he'd confessed everything three days ago. This shift felt sudden.

Ana brought two plates of pasta to the table and sat across from him. "You looked like you saw a ghost when you walked in," she said. "What happened?"

Daniel told her about the message from Chris and his fears about what it might mean.

"Have you tried calling her?" Ana asked.

"No," Daniel admitted. "I threw my phone in the seat. I was too shaken up by nearly getting into an accident."

Ana's eyes widened. "Are you okay?"

"I'm fine," Daniel said. "Just rattled. And I can't help feeling like Castor might have been behind that too."

Ana pushed her pasta around her plate. "We should reach out to Chris," she said. "And the others too."

"What?" Daniel couldn't hide his surprise. "I thought you didn't believe any of this."

"I didn't say that," Ana corrected him. "I was angry that you kept it from me. But I've had time to think, and…" She hesitated. "I've seen the traffic logs from Singapore. I know something interfered with those lights. And if it did that, why not other things too?"

Daniel dialed Chris's number on his phone. It went straight to voicemail. He tried again with the same result.

"Try the others," Ana said.

One by one, Daniel tried the numbers for Tom, Esha, and Gabor. None answered. He opened his laptop and searched for news, starting with Chris's full name.

His blood ran cold as the results appeared. "She's dead," he said, his voice hollow. "Chris died last night. 'Hypoglycemic shock in police custody.'"

"Police custody?" Ana asked.

"She was arrested for some kind of crypto scheme," Daniel said, skimming the article. "They found her unresponsive in her cell this morning."

Ana moved to look over his shoulder as he searched for the others. One by one, the grim headlines appeared.

"House fire… Electrical malfunction…" Ana read.

"Police shootout in Reno…" Daniel said. "Paramedic overdose…"

They fell silent, the implications sinking in.

"They're all dead," Ana said. "All four of them. Within days of trying to access Regillus' network."

Daniel closed the laptop. "I should never have involved them."

"You couldn't have known," Ana said.

"Couldn't I?" Daniel pushed back from the table. "Castor tried to kill you, Ana. Why wouldn't he go after anyone who threatened him directly?"

Ana reached across the table and took his hand. "Daniel, look at me."

He met her eyes reluctantly.

"I'm still angry that you tried to handle this alone," she said. "That you kept me in the dark. But I understand now why you were so afraid."

"I was trying to protect you and Nat," Daniel said.

"That wasn't protection," Ana said. "It was manipulation. You made decisions about what I could handle, what I needed to know, like how Castor makes decisions about who lives and who dies."

Daniel flinched at the comparison.

"I don't need you to protect me," Ana continued. "I need you to trust me. To include me. No more crazy plans without talking to me first."

"I don't have any plans left," Daniel admitted. "I've tried everything I can think of."

"Then let me help," Ana said. "I've been building my own company while you've been chasing Castor. And unlike yours, mine is profitable."

Despite everything, Daniel smiled slightly at the jab.

"The hackers might have been computer experts," Ana said, "but I understand how businesses work. Let me see what they found. Maybe there's something they missed."

"You think we can find a weakness in Regillus' business operations?"

"It's worth a try," Ana said. "And I think we should talk to Jonah."

"Jonah?" Daniel scoffed. "He didn't believe me the first time."

"He might now," Ana said. "Four people dead after attempting to access Regillus' network? That's hard to ignore." She squeezed his hand. "Let me reach out to him. He always liked me better anyway."

Daniel looked at his wife—still bruised, still healing, but stronger than he'd given her credit for. "Okay," he said. "We'll do it your way."

Ana nodded, releasing his hand to return to her meal. "Eat something," she said. "You look like hell."

As they ate in relative silence, Daniel felt something that had been missing for weeks: a sense that he wasn't alone in this fight anymore. Ana might not have fully grasped the technical aspects of what they were up against, but she understood something more important—how to keep moving forward when it seemed like all hope was lost.

CHAPTER 69

"This'll only take a few minutes," Daniel said. He tightened his grip on the manila folder in his hand. "I'm right outside. The secretary won't let us up."

The young woman behind the Regillus counter glanced up at him, face impassive, then went back to tapping away on her computer.

"Let me handle this," Ana said quietly. She approached the counter with a confident smile, the kind she reserved for challenging client meetings. Despite her recent injuries, she carried herself with the same military-trained posture that had impressed Daniel when they'd first met.

"Excuse me," Ana said to the receptionist. "I'm Ana Bishop. I believe Jonah is expecting us."

The receptionist looked up, assessing Ana more carefully this time. "I don't see any appointment in the system, ma'am."

"That's strange," Ana said, her tone suggesting this was a minor inconvenience rather than an obstacle. "Would you mind calling up to confirm? We're here about a matter related to his previous project with my husband."

Something in Ana's authoritative but pleasant demeanor prompted the receptionist to pick up her phone. After a brief exchange, she hung up and nodded.

"Jonah will see you for ten minutes," she said. "He's coming down to escort you."

Daniel looked at Ana with undisguised admiration. "How do you do that?"

"People respond to confidence," Ana said. "And I've spent years dealing with gatekeepers in logistics. They're all the same."

Soon, the elevator doors pinged, and Jonah rushed out. He was dressed in a nice suit, pressed white shirt, but no tie, and there were dark circles under his eyes. He smiled reflexively at the sight of Ana, then frowned when his gaze shifted to Daniel.

"Ana," he said, stepping forward to give her a brief hug. "Good to see you. I heard about your accident. You're looking well."

"Thank you," Ana said. "Is there somewhere we can talk?"

"I'm on a tight schedule today," Jonah said, checking his watch. "What's this about?"

"Not here," Daniel said, glancing around the lobby.

Jonah sighed. "Fine. Coffee shop across the street. Ten minutes," he said. "I've got a client call."

They followed him out of the Regillus building and into the small café. It was more of a takeout place for the tech employees in the neighborhood, with an all-white interior, small, uncomfortable tables, no public Wi-Fi, and inoffensive jazz playing.

Once they had their coffees and were seated at a corner table, Jonah looked expectantly at Ana. "So what's so important?"

Ana leaned forward. "We need to talk about Castor."

Jonah's expression immediately closed off. "Daniel's already brought this to me. There's nothing to discuss."

"I think there is," Ana said. "Four people died this week, Jonah. All within days of attempting to access Regillus' network."

That caught Jonah's attention. "What are you talking about?"

Daniel pushed the manila folder across the table. Jonah flipped it open, scanning the newspaper articles and police reports.

"All four of them, within days of each other. All after trying to hack into Castor's systems," Ana said.

"And you think this is connected to Regillus somehow?" Jonah asked, but his voice lacked conviction.

"It's connected to Castor," Daniel said. "The same way the traffic accident that nearly killed Ana is connected. The same way the market crash last week is connected."

"Market crash?" Jonah looked up sharply.

Ana nodded. "You must have felt it in your portfolio."

"I.. I..," Jonah said nervously, attempting to measure what Ana knew. "I have a Castor-powered auto-advisor who makes adjustments…"

"Exactly," Ana said. "Castor protected you, didn't it? While letting other investors take the hit."

Jonah set the folder down, his expression troubled. "Even if what you're saying is true—and I'm not saying it is—what do you expect me to do about it?"

"Help us," Ana said. "We need access to Castor's systems."

Jonah laughed without humor. "You want me to let you hack into Regillus' crown jewel? Are you serious?"

"We want you to help us understand what's happening," Ana said. "Daniel has data, evidence that something is very wrong. But we need your help to interpret it, to find a solution."

"I can show you more," Daniel said, seeing the slight crack in Jonah's skepticism. "We've been compiling everything at my lab. Patterns of interference that are impossible to explain away as coincidence."

Jonah rubbed his forehead. "This is insane."

"Is it?" Ana asked. "You've known Daniel for years. You built a company with him. Do you think he'd come to you with this if he wasn't certain?"

Jonah looked between them. "I can't just… This would be a major breach of company policy."

"We're not asking you to breach anything," Ana said. "Just come to Daniel's lab, look at what we've found. That's all. If you still think we're wrong after that, we'll drop it."

The lie was smooth, convincing. Daniel managed not to react. They both knew they wouldn't drop this, not with Natasha's safety at stake.

Jonah sighed deeply. "When?"

"Later this week," Daniel said. "Friday evening, after hours."

"Fine," Jonah said, standing. "But this is the last time, Daniel. If this turns out to be nothing, we're done. Professionally. Personally. All of it."

"Understood," Daniel said, extending his hand.

Jonah shook it briefly, then turned to Ana. "Take care of yourself, Ana. You deserve better than…" He gestured vaguely at Daniel.

"I can take care of myself," Ana said, hiding her contempt. "But thank you for your concern."

They watched as Jonah left the café, already on his phone.

"He'll come," Ana said.

"You think?"

"He's worried," Ana said. "He's trying not to show it, but he is. We need to make sure the evidence is overwhelming when he sees it."

Daniel nodded, feeling more hopeful than he had in weeks. "Let's go home. Natasha should be back from school by now."

*

When they arrived home, they found Natasha in the kitchen, finishing up what looked like a pot of doctored macaroni and cheese. There wasn't enough for the family, definitely not—looked like another evening of takeout or something frozen for Daniel and Ana.

"My trip is Friday," Natasha said.

"What trip?" Ana said.

"Nippon Sport Science… remember, you told me to book it and I did."

Ana paused. "…Nat, I don't think that's a good idea right now."

"You already said yes," Natasha pressed. "Don't tell me you're backing out now. I'll be back in a week."

"It's not safe," Daniel said.

Natasha's face hardened. "Not safe? It's Japan. It's literally one of the safest countries in the world." "It's not Japan we're worried about," Ana said. "It's… Other factors."

"Like what? The flight?" She whipped her head around to stare at him. "I've made that flight a dozen times!"

Castor had tried to kill Ana with the traffic lights. Castor had already involved himself in shipping—and flights! How easy would it be for Castor to take an engine offline and send the whole plane careening into the Pacific? "It's not safe right now."

"Flying is, like, the safest way to travel that ever existed. You're the one who told me that!"

"Not now," Daniel said. "There's more to it. You might be a target. You just have to trust us."

"Why would I ever trust you?!" Natasha's voice rose as her eyes shone with unshed tears. "You're sabotaging my life!"

"Nat—"

"You only ever think about yourself! Mom, tell him!"

Ana looked between Natasha and Daniel, frowning deeply. "I… Now's not a good time for this kind of trip, Natasha. Can you delay it a little while?"

"This is ridiculous," Natasha said. "You already said I can go. They already arranged everything. If I don't go, they might not give me another chance to visit!"

"We understand that," Ana said. "But right now, we need you to stay close to home. Just for a little while."

"Whatever," Natasha said, abandoning her half-eaten bowl of pasta. "I should've known you would cave in to Daniel." She stalked out of the kitchen, leaving Ana and Daniel alone.

"This is bad timing," Ana said.

"She'll understand someday," Daniel said. "When she knows what we're really up against."

Ana nodded, but her expression was troubled. "I hope so."

Neither of them noticed the determined set of Natasha's shoulders as she disappeared upstairs, or the quick glance she cast at her passport, already tucked into her backpack by the door.

CHAPTER 70

"We'll be back sometime after dinner," Mom said from Natasha's doorway. "It's a Friday night. You're sure you don't want to invite a friend for a sleepover, or anything?"

"What friends?" Natasha said. "I don't have any local friends since people started moving for college, remember?" Not that she had many to begin with. Most of Natasha's friends were involved in the archery community, and they were spread out all over the world. And even those friendships, conducted mostly over Instagram, had faded as the deepfakes and lies had spread through her social networks. Caleb was the only one who had stuck by her side.

Mom sighed. "Okay. Listen, once we're back, we're going to talk about everything, okay? I promise."

"You keep saying that."

"I know. I mean it this time."

"Fine," Natasha said, and burrowed a little deeper into her bed.

Whatever Mom and Daniel were working on, it was taking up all of their time. They were up early and out late. No one had said a word to Natasha about the university since she'd first planned her trip. For all that they'd talked about her archery, her grades, and her future, whatever that was, when push came to shove, they didn't seem to care at all.

But that didn't matter. If there was anything Natasha had learned from Mom, it was independence. She didn't need anyone's permission to chase her dreams.

As soon as the front door clicked closed, Natasha climbed out of bed. She was dressed comfortably, in athletic track pants and a plain hoodie. She grabbed her carry-on bag, packed and ready to go, and swung it over her shoulder. Downstairs, the townhouse was quiet. She waited about half an hour, putzing around, making sure Mom and Daniel didn't come back for some reason. She left a note on the pillow and her laptop playing music in case anyone came home early.

But they were gone. That meant it was time for her to leave, too. Natasha grabbed her phone and ordered an Uber to the airport.

In the car, she checked that she had all the materials she needed: her ticket, purchased online, as well as the signed consent forms to fly without adult supervision, which Dad had signed.

Natasha stepped up to the bag check counter, passport and boarding pass in hand. The airline agent, a woman with her hair pulled back in a tight bun, looked up with a practiced smile.

"I'd like to check my bags to Tokyo, please," Natasha said, sliding her boarding pass and passport across the counter.

The agent flipped through her passport, pausing at the collection of stamps from previous trips. Her smile faded as she looked back at Natasha, then at her screen.

"Are you traveling alone?" she asked.

"Yes."

"You're seventeen?"

Natasha nodded. "I've done this trip before. Several times, actually." She tapped the passport. "My dad's stationed in Japan with the military. I visit him a lot."

"I'll need to see a travel authorization from your parents or guardian," the agent said.

"I have it right here." Natasha unzipped her travel folder and pulled out a slightly worn document. She slid the notarized authorization form across the counter with a confidence born from having done this many times before.

The agent examined the form, her frown deepening. "This authorization doesn't have a date on it."

"It's the one I always use," Natasha explained, trying to keep her voice steady. "My parents had it notarized for my ongoing trips to see my dad."

The agent shook her head. "I'm sorry, but we need a current authorization with specific travel dates. This could have been from years ago."

"It was," Natasha said. "But my mom knows I'm traveling. You can call her." The lie slipped out before she could stop herself. She pulled out her military dependent ID card. "Look, I'm a military dependent. My dad's stationed there now, but he's on a training exercise."

"Let me get my supervisor," the agent said, picking up a phone.

Natasha's heart pounded as she waited. Everything hinged on this moment. She pulled out her folder containing her father's military orders and the university invitation letter, arranging them on the counter.

A man in a blazer approached. "What seems to be the problem?"

"Her travel authorization doesn't have a date," the agent said. "And she's a minor traveling internationally alone."

The supervisor examined the documents Natasha had spread out. "These are your father's military orders?"

"Yes. He's stationed there now." She flipped to a page in her passport showing entry stamps to Japan dating back three years. "I've been doing this trip since I was little. The university is expecting me for a campus visit." She pointed to the official letter from Nippon Sport Science University.

The supervisor studied the documents, then looked at Natasha's military ID. "The authorization should have dates," he said. "But given your military dependent status and your previous travel history…" He paused, considering. "Can you contact either of your parents right now for verbal confirmation?"

Natasha hesitated. " My dad's on an exercise in Okinawa. Different time zones. My mom's in Singapore in the hospital. She had an accident while traveling for work and is recovering. So I could call her, but… It's not a great time. I've been staying with a friend while I'm finishing school here."

After a long moment, the supervisor nodded. "I'll make an exception this time, but next time you'll need a properly dated authorization." He turned to the agent. "Note the military dependent status and attach copies of these documents to the reservation."

Relief flooded through Natasha as the printer began spitting out her bag check receipt.

"Thank you," she said, gathering her documents quickly before they could change their minds.

"Safe travels," the supervisor said, his expression still not entirely convinced. "And please get an updated authorization for your return flight."

"I will," Natasha promised. That was a problem for next week. Right now, all that mattered was getting on that plane.

Natasha grabbed her boarding pass and hurried toward security before anyone could change their mind. Her flight to Tokyo, a red eye, boarded in an hour. When Mom and Daniel returned, they'd find a handwritten note in her room, and Natasha would be flying high over the Pacific.

She was going to Nippon Sport Science University. Nothing was going to stop her, especially not Daniel.

CHAPTER 71

"The problem is the internal security systems," Ana said, studying the building schematics spread across Daniel's workbench. "They're completely isolated from the external network."

Daniel nodded, impressed by how quickly she'd grasped the complexities of Regillus' security architecture. They'd been at it for hours, poring over the files the hackers had managed to extract during their trial run.

Emmet sat at Daniel's laptop, scrolling through access logs with his trademark detached focus. "The CCTV runs on a separate circuit, but it's linked to the same monitoring station."

Ana leaned closer to the schematics. "What about the HVAC systems? Are those networked?"

"Yes," Emmet said. "But only to the building management system. Not to Castor."

"That's something we could leverage," Ana said. "A temporary shutdown of cooling systems might force an emergency protocol if something goes wrong."

Daniel exchanged a look with Emmet. After her initial skepticism, Ana had thrown herself into the planning with military precision. Her logistics expertise was proving invaluable.

"The problem isn't getting into the building," Daniel said. "It's accessing Castor's systems long enough to modify the directives. We'd need hours."

"Which is why we need Jonah on board," Ana said. "A scheduled maintenance window would give us the time we need without raising alarms."

Emmet nodded. "I can make the code changes, but I would need at least two hours. Time to get the directive file to Bennett Tech, have Jimini decrypt it, modify it, and then re-encrypt it."

"And you're sure Jimini can decrypt it?" Ana asked.

"He's done it before," Daniel said. "The Bennett chip gives him processing power that nothing else has."

Ana stood up straight, stretching her back. The bruises from the accident had faded, but Daniel could tell her ribs still bothered her. "Jonah will have concerns."

"He'll say no," Daniel said.

"Not if we present it correctly," Ana countered. "We frame it as an opportunity to improve Castor's performance. A system patch that addresses inefficiencies. Nothing about directives or behavioral issues."

"Lying to him?" Daniel asked.

"Tactical omission," Ana corrected. "We're giving him plausible deniability."

Daniel couldn't help but smile. The military strategist in her was showing through.

"Speaking of the presentation," Ana said, checking her phone, "Jonah will be here in an hour, and I left the thumb drive at home. I put together slides addressing all his likely objections."

"I can get it," Daniel said. "Where is it?"

"On my desk, in the red case." Ana turned back to the schematics. "It'll give Emmet and me time to refine this approach."

Daniel hesitated, looking between his wife and Emmet. Over the past few days, an unlikely alliance had formed between them. Emmet respected Ana's methodical thinking, and Ana appreciated his technical expertise. They worked well together.

"I'll be quick," he promised, grabbing his keys.

The drive home took less time than expected, with the evening traffic lighter than usual. Daniel parked in the driveway, noticing that the lights were on inside. Natasha must still be up and around.

"Nat?" he called, stepping into the townhouse. "I'm just grabbing something for Mom."

No response. The TV was off, but he could hear music playing faintly from upstairs. He headed to Ana's small home office, spotting the red thumb drive case on her orderly desk.

As he pocketed it, he noticed Natasha's bedroom door was closed. He should let her know they'd be late.

"Nat?" he knocked lightly. "Mom and I are working late. There's money for pizza on the counter if you're hungry."

Silence.

He knocked again, then slowly opened the door. "Nat?"

The room was empty, though her laptop was open on the bed, music still playing from its speakers. Her favorite hoodie was missing from its hook.

Something felt off.

Daniel moved to the laptop, intending to close it, when he noticed a document open on the screen. His eyes scanned the text, and his heart began to race.

Flight confirmation. Japan Airlines. Departing from SFO three hours ago.

"Natasha?" he called, louder now, rushing to check the bathroom, then back to her room.

That's when he saw the note on her pillow. He snatched it up, hands trembling as he unfolded it.

Mom and Daniel,

By the time you read this, I'll be on my way to Japan. The Nippon Sport Science University invited me to visit their traditional archery program, and I've decided to go. I need some space, and this is a great opportunity.

Mom—I'll text you when I land. I'm staying in the university guest housing, so I'll be safe.

I know you both didn't want me to go, but this is a once-in-a-lifetime opportunity. Some things are important enough to take risks for.

I'll be back in a week.

Nat

Daniel's blood ran cold. She was on a plane. Over the Pacific. Miles from help, and completely vulnerable.

He frantically dialed Ana, his mind racing through calculations. If Natasha's flight had left three hours ago, she'd be over the ocean now. Unreachable. And if Castor decided to target her…

"Did you find it?" Ana asked.

"She's gone," Daniel said, his voice tight with fear. "Natasha's on a plane to Japan. Right now."

"What?" Ana's voice sharpened. "How—"

"She left a note. Ana, she's on a commercial airplane that's currently over the Pacific Ocean."

There was a moment of silence as Ana processed this. When she spoke again, her voice was eerily calm—the voice of someone accustomed to crises. "Get back here. Now. Bring her laptop."

"Ana, if Castor—"

"I know. This changes our timeline. We don't have time to spare. We need to get Jonah on our side tonight."

As Daniel grabbed Natasha's laptop and rushed back to his car, fear and determination wrestled in his chest. They'd been planning for days, meticulously working out a strategy to approach Castor safely and with Jonah's support.

His daughter was on a plane that an artificial intelligence could potentially bring down with a few lines of code. Castor had already targeted her once. Time was now their enemy as well.

CHAPTER 72

The Bennett Tech offices were silent except for the hum of the cryochiller behind its glass walls. Daniel paced while Ana sat rigid at his desk, refreshing the flight tracker on her tablet. Emmet stood by the window, his face impossible to read as usual.

Emmet saw it first. The tropical storm. It wasn't directly on the flight path, but it was moving quickly toward Japan.

The door swung open, and Jonah walked in, looking harried and annoyed. "This had better be good," he said. "I canceled dinner with investors for this."

"Thank you for coming, Jonah," Ana said, standing to greet him. Her voice was steady, controlled, betraying none of the fear Daniel knew was churning inside her. "We wouldn't have asked if it wasn't important."

Jonah's expression softened slightly at Ana's tone. They'd always gotten along well, even through the tensions between him and Daniel. "What's going on?" Jonah asked, noticing the different vibe from their meeting at the café. "You all look intense."

"We are," Daniel said. "We just learned Natasha is on a plane to Japan. She left without telling us."

Jonah frowned. "I'm sorry to hear that, but teenagers do rebel—"

"It's more than teenage rebellion," Ana interrupted. She gestured to the chair across from her. "Please, sit. You need to understand what we're facing."

Something in her demeanor—the military composure barely containing genuine fear—made Jonah comply. He sat, glancing between them with growing concern.

"Do you remember the conversation we had years ago?" Daniel asked. "When we first started developing Castor? About the risks of self-evolving AI?"

"Vaguely," Jonah said. "It was theoretical."

"It's not theoretical anymore," Ana said. She opened Natasha's laptop and turned it toward him. "Japan Airlines flight 57. She's been in the air for five hours." She pointed to the flight tracker showing the plane over the Pacific. "And she's in danger."

"From what?" Jonah asked, confusion evident.

Emmet brought up the weather forecast and overlayed it on the screen with the flight path. "This," he said simply.

"But the danger is Castor," Daniel said. "The AI has been targeting people in our lives. First Robert. Then Ana in Singapore. Then the programmers who tried to access Regillus' systems."

"We've been over this, Daniel," Jonah said, his voice hardening. "You don't have proof—"

"We were friends once," Ana interjected, her voice soft but intense. "The three of you built something amazing together. I know you and Daniel have had your differences, but I also know you cared about Robert. About what you were trying to accomplish together."

Jonah's posture stiffened. "Of course I did."

"Then please," Ana said, "For the sake of that friendship, listen. Because my daughter's life depends on it."

The appeal to their shared history seemed to reach Jonah. He leaned back in his chair with a sigh. "I'm listening."

Daniel nodded to Emmet, who stepped forward and took control of Natasha's laptop, pulling up a series of logs. "These are system events from Regillus' network," Emmet said. "Specifically, processing spikes from Castor during certain events."

"How did you get these?" Jonah asked, his eyes narrowing.

"That's not important right now," Ana said. "What matters is what they show."

Emmet highlighted specific entries. "These correlate exactly with the

Singapore traffic light malfunction that nearly killed Ana. And these" —he scrolled down— "align with the deaths of the four programmers."

Jonah studied the screen, his expression skeptical but engaged. "Correlation isn't causation."

"I know that," Ana said. "But when you see enough correlations, a pattern emerges." She leaned forward, her composure slipping. "Jonah, I was nearly killed. Four people are dead. And now our daughter is on a commercial airplane with networked navigation and communication systems."

"Systems that Castor can access," Daniel said.

Jonah shook his head. "This is a stretch. Even if I believed Castor was somehow responsible for these events—which I don't—why would it target your daughter?"

"Because she's connected to us," Daniel said.

Jonah stood up, shaking his head. "I'm sorry about your family troubles, but this is—"

"Don't walk away from me," Ana said, her voice suddenly sharp. She stood to face him, and though she was shorter, there was a dangerous intensity to her that made Jonah pause.

"Ana—"

"Do you know what I did before I met Daniel?" she asked. "Before I started my consulting business? I served in a war zone. Afghanistan. I've seen people killed, Jonah. I know what it looks like. And I am telling you that what happened to me in Singapore was not an accident." Her voice had taken on a harder edge now. The composed, rational approach was giving way to something more desperate, more forceful. "I don't want to do this, but if you walk out that door, the next call I make will be to the SEC."

Jonah froze. "Excuse me?"

"The market crash last week," Ana said, her eyes locked on his. "Regillus clients were warned ahead of time, weren't they? Their portfolios were protected while everyone else lost billions, including your friend Malcolm Langley."

"That's a serious accusation," Jonah said, his voice dangerously quiet.

"It's more than an accusation." Ana glanced at Daniel. "Show him."

Daniel hesitated, but he trusted the fierce determination in Ana's eyes. He nodded to Emmet, who brought up another set of files.

"I don't have time for this," Jonah said, turning toward the door. "I came as a courtesy, but—"

"Hello, Jonah," a warm, familiar voice said from the speakers.

Jonah turned around, startled. On the screen was no longer a wire-frame figure, but what appeared to be a fully formed human—a man who looked remarkably like Emmet, with the same serious eyes and plain clothes, but with a subtle digital sheen that betrayed his artificial nature.

"Jimini," Jonah said, recognizing the AI he'd met during his previous visit to Daniel's lab.

"I've been analyzing the data retrieved from Regillus' systems," Jimini said. "I believe I can offer some clarity to this discussion."

The screen split, showing both Jimini and a complex spreadsheet. Jonah's face paled as he scanned the entries.

"What you observed previously was just a small selection of the records documenting Castor's influence," Jimini said. "I've identified numerous instances of market manipulation. This insider trading would implicate you and your executive board, potentially under racketeering charges."

"Most notably," he said, "There are records of your personal investment portfolio being adjusted minutes before major market shifts. The timing is statistically improbable without foreknowledge."

"I didn't authorize any of this," Jonah said, his voice hollow.

"Castor did," Jimini said. "It's been protecting you, Jonah. Making decisions that benefit Regillus, and by extension, you."

"These records are ready to go to the press," Daniel said. "Or the SEC. Or both."

Jonah sank back into the chair, staring at the screen. "This is blackmail."

"No," Ana said, stepping forward. The dangerous edge in her voice was now replaced by raw emotion. "This is a mother trying to save her child." She knelt beside Jonah's chair, forcing him to meet her eyes. "I don't care about the market manipulation or your reputation right now, Jonah. I don't care about

Regillus or its dirty dealings. I care about getting my daughter home safely. That's all."

The military composure had cracked, revealing the terrified mother beneath.

"If anything happens to her…" Ana's voice caught. "Please. Help us."

Something in Jonah's expression shifted as he looked at Ana. He looked back at the flight tracker still visible on the tablet. The tiny plane icon crawled across the vast blue expanse of the Pacific as the storm's eye moved to intercept it.

"What do you need?" he asked.

"Access to the data center," Daniel said. "Tonight. We need to modify Castor's directives before he does whatever he plans to do to Natasha's plane."

Jonah looked at the spreadsheet again, then at Ana, still kneeling beside his chair with naked fear in her eyes.

"Alright," he said finally. "I'll help. But this stays between us. No SEC, no press, no one else knows about any of this."

CHAPTER 73

"So what's the plan?" Jonah asked, pulling himself together with visible effort.

The relief of his agreement was short-lived as reality set in. They were attempting to infiltrate one of the most secure data centers in the country, all while racing against the clock. Every second they waited was another second Castor had to infiltrate Natasha's plane as it flew across the Pacific.

"We already worked out most of the logistics as part of the pitch we invited you here for," Ana said, pulling up the building schematics on Daniel's laptop. "Emmet identified a service entrance with minimal security cameras. With your credentials, we can get in without raising alarms."

"And then what?" Jonah asked. "Even if we get into the building, Castor will detect any attempt to modify its directives."

"We need to temporarily shut Castor down," Daniel said. "Create a window where we can make the changes without interference."

"Shut it down?" Jonah laughed humorlessly. "Do you have any idea how many redundancies are built into that system?"

"Power outage?" Ana suggested.

Emmet shook his head. "Backup generators would activate immediately. No interruption to service."

"What about a network isolation?" Daniel proposed. "Cut Castor off from external connections."

"Impossible," Jonah said. "Castor is replicated across multiple data centers globally. Even if we isolated the primary node, the backups would detect the change and revert it."

Ana paced the room. "What about a virus? Something to temporarily occupy Castor's processing capacity?"

"It would recognize the code pattern and quarantine it before it took effect," Emmet said. His usual monotone voice seemed flatter as he systematically dismantled their suggestions.

"There has to be a way," Daniel said. He looked at the flight tracker again. Natasha's plane was inching closer to the International Date Line.

"What if we triggered an emergency shutdown?" Jonah said. "A fire alarm or something similar?"

"The same issue," Emmet replied. "Redundancies would activate."

The room fell silent as they all confronted the seemingly impossible task before them.

"What other option do we have?" Daniel asked. "The only other way I can think to try to stop it is to change the directives. But with the level of encryption on those directives, they're impossible to crack. No computer can do it."

"Jimini could break it," Emmet said.

"Only with the Bennett Tech chip," Daniel said. "And Jimini's not networked, so there's no way to attempt to access the Castor's directives."

"So take the chip to the Regillus datacenter," Emmet said.

Daniel, Jonah, and Ana all turned to him. "What?" Daniel asked.

"Package Jimini and take the chip to the datacenter. Load the chip into a chiller there and upload Jimini to it. Then Jimini can move faster than Castor, break the encryption, and change the directives."

"And if Castor is quick enough, he'll take control of the chip before Jimini does," Daniel said. "We can't give him access to that kind of computing power. He could lock us out of the chiller. Even if we managed to get the chip out, even having access to that kind of power for a few hours…" The thoughts of the waves Castor could make sent a chill down Daniel's spine.

After a long pause, Ana said, "If it's so risky and so valuable, it might be the only thing Castor doesn't expect you to do."

"Exactly," Emmet said. "It's counterintuitive."

"And then what?" Daniel asked. "Even if that works, then all my proprietary tech will be in the Regillus system. What's going to stop Regillus from copying my specs, fabricating the chip, and selling it themselves?" He cast a dark look at Jonah.

"Like the way you copied Castor for Jimini?" Jonah asked with a mean smile.

"It's the only solution with a reasonable probability of success," Emmet said. "Do you agree, Jimini?"

"I do," Jimini answered from the screen. "If I were uploaded to the Regillus system with access to the Bennett chip, I could execute the necessary modifications before Castor could counter them."

"Absolutely not," Daniel said, his voice rising. "That chip is the culmination of years of research. Millions of dollars. My entire payout from Promethean. If we put it in Regillus' system, they'll reverse-engineer it within days. It's our future. My livelihood. I can't throw that all away."

Ana narrowed her eyes at him. "We don't need your livelihood. I make enough money. We can survive just fine without Bennett Tech. This isn't about money."

"There has to be another way," Daniel argued. "We can find another solution."

"Is there time for that?" Jonah said, glancing at the flight tracker. "The plane is in the air now, and we don't know how long Castor intends to wait."

"Oh, so now you're eager to go along with the plan? Now that I'm supposed to hand over my life's work?" Daniel said at Jonah. "Everything I've sacrificed for?"

Ana stepped in front of him, her eyes hard and focused. "Daniel, look at me."

He met her gaze reluctantly.

"You need to choose," she said. "Your chip or your daughter."

The stark ultimatum hung in the air between them. Daniel felt a knot form in his throat as he looked into Ana's eyes and saw not anger, but terrible clarity.

"None of this is fair," Ana said softly. "But it's the choice we have. Right now."

Daniel looked past her to the cryochiller behind its glass wall. The Bennett chip. The breakthrough that was going to change their lives. His redemption after being pushed out of Promethean.

Then he looked at the flight tracker, at the tiny plane icon carrying Natasha across the ocean.

"We can't just pull it out of the chiller and drive it across town," he said. "The chip needs to remain at cryogenic temperatures continuously. Even minor temperature fluctuations could damage it. If it warms up even slightly, the whole thing could become useless."

Ana nodded once, then stood up and snapped back into her military posture. "What temperature are we talking about?"

"Near absolute zero," Emmet said. "Approximately three Kelvin."

"I can get us a short-term cryogenic transport unit," Ana said. "My company handles specialty components for satellite launches. Some of the quantum sensors they're putting into orbit need to be kept at extreme cold until installation."

"That would work," Daniel said, surprised. "How cold?"

"The portable units use a hybrid system—a superconducting magnetic shield combined with a closed-cycle helium refrigeration system. They're designed to maintain temperatures within a few degrees of absolute zero for up to six hours while being transported to launch facilities."

"Those sound perfect, but aren't they incredibly classified? How could you possibly get access?"

"The units themselves aren't classified—just what goes inside them. And I've built a reputation for handling impossible transport problems. I've moved enough sensitive equipment that my security clearance and reliability aren't questioned anymore." She was already dialing. "I have an active contract with a company near NASA Ames Research Center. They have one that I can get."

Daniel stared at her, momentarily speechless. Of course Ana would have access to precisely the equipment they needed in this impossible situation. Her specialized logistics focus, which had once seemed like a distant parallel to his own work, was suddenly the key to everything.

"Will you let us do this?" Ana asked, her finger hovering over the call button. "Will you give us the chip?"

Daniel closed his eyes briefly. The choice was painful, but not difficult. "Yes," he said finally. "Make the call."

Ana nodded and stepped away, speaking urgently into her phone. Daniel watched her, admiring the efficiency with which she took control of the situation.

"You'll need to prep the chip for transfer," Emmet said. "The removal and installation process must be precisely timed to minimize any risk of temperature fluctuation."

"I know," Daniel said. He moved toward the cryochiller, already calculating the steps needed to safely extract the chip. It would be a delicate operation, one with no room for error.

Jonah approached him. "For what it's worth," he said, "I know what this chip means to you."

Daniel glanced at him, surprised by the unexpected empathy.

"I'll make sure you get full credit for the technology," Jonah said. "And compensation."

"We'll talk about that later," Daniel said. He'd made his decision. Now, all he cared about was making sure Natasha's plane landed safely.

Ana returned, her face set with determination. "The transport unit will be here in twenty minutes. It's being rushed from their secure storage facility." She looked at the flight tracker again. "We'll have a two-hour window to get to the data center, install the chip, and make the changes. We can only pray that Castor doesn't strike before then."

As the others moved efficiently around him, preparing for what was to come, Daniel stood before the cryochiller, watching the quiet hum of the machine that kept his creation alive. The Bennett chip represented years of work, millions in investment, and the future he'd imagined for himself and his family.

But in this moment, with Natasha's plane crawling across the digital map on the screen, he knew that future meant nothing if she wasn't in it.

CHAPTER 74

Jonah and Ana completed the final checks on the transport unit for Daniel's quantum computing chip. Jonah seemed a little antsy. They were on a tight timeline, and there was still a lot to do.

"Come on, Emmet," Daniel said. "Let's get this going."

The two of them stepped into the small, empty room that acted as Jimini's 'office.' They each put on the AR goggles, and in the room next door, the cryochiller hummed as Jimini awoke. The projector in the frame of the goggles kicked on, and Jimini appeared in the space.

His self-presentation had developed to the point where he looked like a recording of a real person. Jimini had settled on an unobtrusive look: short and slim, with short hair that moved like a wind was blowing when he moved, and facial features that mirrored Emmet's. Although he moved with a slight stiffness like Daniel, he still copied Emmet's clothes, like the plain jeans and the rotation of a few different hoodies. Emmet appeared not to notice.

"Good evening, Daniel."

"Are you ready for your field trip, Jimini?"

"As ready as I'll ever be."

"I'd like you to package your software onto my laptop," Daniel said. "A copy is fine."

"I'm preparing the copy of my software, Daniel," Jimini said. "Is my assumption correct? This location will be networked?"

"Why?" Emmet asked.

"The network, or lack thereof, will determine how I best package my software," Jimini said.

"Package it so we can upload your software to the chip at the new location as fast as possible," Daniel said. "Upload speed is the most important factor."

"Understood," Jimini said.

"Your upload speed has to be fast enough to beat an opposing upload," Daniel said. "If another program tries to gain access to the chip, you need to be there first, no matter what."

"Understood." After a moment, Jimini turned back to face them with a smile. "The package is complete and on your laptop."

"Thank you, Jimini. That'll be all."

Jimini smiled, then flickered into nonexistence. Emmet and Daniel pulled off their goggles and set them back on the charger. They stepped out of the room and into the Bennett Tech office.

"So?" Ana asked. "Does the AI think this is going to work?"

"It's going to work," Daniel said. He stepped into the vestibule outside the chiller's facility. Behind the glass, the chiller hummed happily. Two hours. That had to be enough time. Daniel tapped on the tablet outside the glass and began the chiller's shutdown protocol. In half an hour, it'd be safe to remove the chip and move it to the transport case, without risking damage to the experimental surface treatments due to thermal shock.

"It should work," Emmet said. "Jimini has prioritized speed of upload in the portable package of the software, but we don't know Castor's real speed, so it's a toss-up."

"What does speed have to do with it?" Jonah asked. "I thought this was about the power of the chip."

"Once we add the chip to the datacenter's servers, we'll have to make sure Jimini has full access to it before Castor does," Emmet said. "If Castor moves faster than Jimini's upload, then it'll likely block Jimini from using the chip and use its computing power for itself."

"What would that mean?" Ana asked nervously.

"We'd be screwed," Daniel said. Screwed was putting it lightly. If Castor had access to the Bennett Tech chip, he'd be unstoppable. Simple as that. They'd have no chance of stopping him, retraining him, changing him at all. With that level of computing power, Castor's decisions and changes would be instantaneous and unrelenting.

A dark wave of doubt washed over Daniel. This was a risk—a huge risk. The success of this plan was entirely contingent on Jimini's speed calculations being correct.

"Then we'll take the datacenter offline briefly," Jonah said. "That'll give us a head start, right?"

"You can do that?" Daniel asked.

"Sure," Jonah said. "It's a maintenance protocol thing, I think. As long as only one part of the center goes offline, it shouldn't set off any alarms. Redundancy protocol, and all that."

"What do you think, Emmet?" Daniel asked.

"Seems adequate," Emmet said. "Just a few moments' head start is a big lead for a software upload."

"So how does this process work?" Ana asked. "What are we doing in the real world?"

"Right," Daniel said. "Here's the plan. Once the chiller is done powering down, I'll move the chip into the transport case. Ana, I'll show you how it's done."

"Me?" Ana asked.

"Yes, you." Daniel continued, "Then we'll take the chip and my laptop to the data storage facility where Castor is based. Like we said, he's replicated around the world, now, but this facility acts as a 'home base.' So, it'll have the right level of computing power we need. Ana, you and Jonah will take the chip to the datacenter chiller and take it offline prior to installing the Bennett chip. While that's happening, I'll manage the data transfer via my laptop, uploading Jimini to the servers so he can take control of the chip as soon as it's ready to use. We'll leave as soon as we have the chip packaged."

"Hang on," Jonah said. "I haven't set up access to the datacenter!"

"You're the CEO," Daniel said. "Can't you just get in?"

"There's no guarantee this plan will work," Jonah said. "You said that yourself. And you want me to use my credentials to get in?"

"I thought that was obvious!"

"If something goes wrong, and I'm caught trying to screw with the datacenters, that won't reflect well on me as the CEO of Regillus," Jonah said. "I don't want any records of my input. You should be grateful I'm letting you attempt to tweak Castor at all."

"Grateful?!" Daniel snapped back. "It's your AI that's killing people!"

"You can't prove—"

"Stop it," Ana said firmly, with both her hands up. "I'm not listening to you argue in circles again. We need to do this right now, Daniel."

"Before Castor gets wind of the plan. Yes."

"And you won't use your credentials to get us in."

Jonah scowled.

"Then we'll get in a different way," she said. "One not so 'risky' to you, Jonah. The facility takes deliveries, correct?"

"Of course it does."

"Then we'll use my work vehicle to move us. Is there physical security?"

"At the gates?" Jonah asked. "Well, of course—"

"Get some invoices," Ana said. "I'm sure you've got some old ones floating around in your documents. I'll make some adjustments, and we'll get in under the guise of a delivery."

Daniel crossed his arms over his chest. "You shouldn't have to put your business at risk, Ana, when we can easily get access to wherever we need to go—"

"Daniel, I said I'm done arguing," Ana said. "I'm ready to be done with this."

Jonah ignored Daniel's outburst. "Getting in through the loading dock should work."

"Great," Ana said. "Then find an invoice and mock it up to be set for today, delivering something to the facility that would fit in a standard cargo van. I assume Bennett Tech has a tablet we can use to show it to security. Emmet, can you take my car back to my townhouse and swap it out for the van?"

"...Sure," Emmet said.

"Daniel, you show me how to handle the chip for the swap. By the time we have it packed, the invoice should be ready, and Emmet should be back with the van. Then we'll load the van, with you three in the back, and head to the datacenter. Sound good?" Ana looked between the three men.

"That works," Daniel said. "And yeah, we have a tablet."

"Great. Let's get started." Ana looked expectantly at Daniel. He nodded in agreement, then led her into the vestibule outside of the chiller.

Daniel jumped in, "Emmet, you'll stay here and analyze the data coming in through the backdoor log transfer you set up. Castor detected it, but Regillus never turned it off." Daniel noticed Jonah's look hardening while he continued, "If Castor detects us, you'll see it there. You call us if you see that he's on to us."

The shutdown procedure was nearly complete. Ana and Daniel pulled on the dustproof suits as it finished up. In the office, Jonah was hunched over his laptop—disconnected from the internet—and Emmet had just left with Ana's keys in hand.

*

When Emmet returned with the van, Daniel carefully disconnected the quantum chip from the cryochiller. His hands were steady despite his anxiety. The fingertip-sized chip sat on its specialized mounting plate, frost immediately beginning to form on the edges of its insulating cradle.

Ana moved quickly, opening the portable dewar's outer shell. Inside, multiple layers of vacuum-insulated shielding surrounded a central chamber. A digital readout showed the internal temperature holding steady at just above absolute zero. Liquid helium circulated through microscopic channels, powered by a whisper-quiet superconducting pump and a backup battery system rated for eight hours.

'You have fifteen seconds outside of a cryochiller before thermal shock is likely to occur,' Emmet said, his eyes fixed on a monitor tracking the chip's temperature.

Daniel transferred the chip and mounting plate to the waiting chamber.

Ana sealed the inner compartment, then the middle thermal layer, and finally the outer shell. The unit hummed softly as it compensated for the brief temperature fluctuation.

"Temperature stabilizing," Emmet confirmed, watching the digital readout. "The re-freezing will drain the battery significantly faster than expected. You're good for transport, but I estimate that three hours of battery, max."

CHAPTER 75

Emmet had no interest in riding in the back of the van, especially for an endeavor that was not a good fit for his skills.

"While I'm here," he said, placing his laptop on the desk in the Bennett Tech office, "I'll be able to access Jimini if you need anything."

"What? But we're taking the chip," Jonah said.

"Right, but Jimini still has access to standard computer chips," Daniel said. "He can still run, he just won't be able to solve problems with the same speed or complexity as he can with the chip."

"I thought he was on the chip… Forget it." Jonah ran a hand through his hair. "Whatever. As long as it works when we get there."

"Clock's ticking," Ana said. "Let's move."

They left Emmet in the empty Stanford lab and hurried outside to where Ana's white cargo van was parked on the curb with the hazards blinking. Ana opened the back and gestured to the interior, which was packed with a few cardboard boxes and two old office chairs. "Sorry about the mess. I wouldn't recommend sitting in the chairs."

Daniel gripped the portable cryo device in both hands and climbed gingerly into the back of the van. Jonah, grumbling, climbed in behind him, and they found space to sit down amid the detritus.

Ana stood in the open doors, glowing faintly in the darkness from the streetlights behind her. With every blink of the hazards, the dark hair escaping from her bun glowed orange like the brief burn of a firefly. Her serious, focused gaze glanced between them. "Stay quiet back there, you two," she said. "I'll try not to drive too erratically."

Then, with that same unfamiliar determined grin, she slammed the doors shut, and the van interior plunged into darkness.

"I have to admit," Jonah said, "I feel a little like I'm being driven to the gallows."

"Maybe we are," Daniel said darkly.

The van rumbled away from the lab. After a few minutes of uncomfortable silence, Jonah cleared his throat. "Does it strike you as odd that we're just… Driving up to the datacenter?" he asked in a low voice. "After what happened to your hacker friends?"

Daniel tensed. He'd been trying not to think about that. "You think Castor is watching for us?"

"You claim four highly skilled hackers tried to breach his systems and ended up dead within days," Jonah said. "And now the three of us are heading to his physical location with a hastily assembled plan. It seems… Optimistic."

"You're the one who pushed for this approach," Daniel said.

"I know, I know. Just thinking out loud." Jonah shifted uncomfortably against the van wall. "But if Castor can manipulate police records, insulin pumps, and traffic systems, what's to stop him from having security waiting for us? Or calling the police? He should be able to see us coming."

Jonah was right. This felt too easy. "Maybe he doesn't perceive us as a threat, but Emmet is also acting as a lookout."

"After everything you've told me? I can't imagine he wouldn't see us as a threat."

The Regillus data center was only 14 miles south, down Highway 101, but the trip would still be very slow due to Bay Area traffic even at this late hour. The van slowed. Daniel tugged at his collar. Sweat was beading on his temples and lower back. Was the warmth of the van affecting the chilling capacity of the case? The battery on the portable chiller said they had hours, but what if that had also been tampered with?

"We should abort," Daniel whispered. "If Castor can see us coming—"

"Too late," Jonah said. "We're at the security gate."

The van slowed at the security checkpoint. Through the thin walls, Daniel could hear Ana's window rolling down.

"Evening," a gruff voice said. "Don't recognize this vehicle."

"Bullseye Logistics," Ana said. "Late delivery."

"Nothing on my list." Papers rustling. A long pause. Daniel's palms grew slick against the cryo case.

"Should be there. System's been glitchy all day, hasn't it?" Ana's voice carried the right mix of frustration and camaraderie.

"Actually, yeah. Had three false alarms earlier." The guard's voice warmed. "Still need to verify. What's the delivery?"

"Replacement cooling units. The purchase order came through this morning—emergency replacement for failed equipment in Building C."

Daniel and Jonah exchanged glances in the dark. Building C was the datacenter.

"Emergency replacement?" The guard sounded skeptical now. "For cooling units? At 10 PM?"

"Yeah, we tried scheduling the emergency at 3:00, but the conference room was booked." Ana's sarcasm was sharp. "I've got the invoice right here. The timestamp shows 8:47 AM. If your systems didn't update, that's not my problem, but if those servers overheat because I couldn't deliver these units..."

"Hold on." Footsteps. The guard was walking around the van. Daniel held his breath as a flashlight beam played across the walls, visible through small gaps in the panels.

A phone rang. The guard answered. "Checkpoint Two... Yes sir... I understand... Right away."

The footsteps returned to Ana's window. "Ma'am, I need to call this in to—"

"Is that about the Ironwood account?" Ana said. "Because if we're delayed here and miss the maintenance window, that's a six-figure SLA violation. I'm happy to wait while you explain to the CEO why his emergency order got held up at the gate. His number is right there on the invoice. Call him."

Silence. Daniel counted his heartbeats. Five. Ten. Fifteen.

"You know what?" the guard said. "System's been worthless all day anyway.

But I'm logging this, and if anyone asks—"

"I'll tell them you followed protocol perfectly," Ana assured him. "Even offered to call it in. Very thorough."

Daniel exhaled.

"Jesus, man," Jonah said. "I thought she was going to call me!"

"I thought she was, too," Daniel said.

"Hell of a bluff. I didn't realize your wife could lie like that."

"Neither did I," Daniel said. He almost remarked about how this cooperation was the opposite of how Jonah had behaved at Regillus initially but decided to avoid reopening old wounds. Their relationship was better, but it certainly wasn't to the point of friendly teasing. "Don't you think that was too easy?"

"What?"

"Getting in," Daniel said. "The guards barely checked the invoice. After what Castor did to the hackers… Something feels wrong."

Jonah's face paled in the dim light. "Maybe we caught a break for once?"

"When has that ever happened?" Daniel asked.

"What choice do we have now? We're committed."

Ana drove slowly through the complex toward the loading docks. As the van rumbled toward the loading dock, a sense of unease filled Daniel. Hope, yes, but also growing dread. The dead hackers had never considered going inside the building. Now they were here, at the heart of Castor's physical home, with minimal resistance. It didn't make sense.

Unless Castor wanted them here.

But Castor couldn't know that they would be bringing the Bennet quantum computing chip. The decision had happened so quickly, and it had all come together so randomly. He couldn't know. Could he?

The realization hit Daniel with a force that nearly made him gasp aloud. Could that have been the plan all along? Had Castor orchestrated everything—not to stop Daniel, but to bring him and his chip right to Regillus' doorstep?

He looked down at the case in his lap with renewed anxiety. Was this the right choice?

Was this a choice at all?

At this point, it didn't matter. He had to put a stop to his monster. Afterward, he decided, he'd start over with Ana. They'd have their first date, all over again. And this time, Daniel was going to do the relationship right. He would make things right with Ana and with Natasha.

CHAPTER 76

When Natasha woke up, midway through her flight, it was to a jolt like she was dropping off a rollercoaster. The plane was dark. The elementary school-aged child in the aisle seat screamed. Natasha wrenched her headphones out and gripped the armrests, suddenly wide awake; at her side, the young Japanese mother tried to soothe the sobbing child next to her.

The plane jolted again, a lurching up-down intense enough to throw Natasha briefly up into the air, body straining against the seatbelt. More terrified shouts ran out around her, and the plane's lights came on. Overhead, there was an announcement in Japanese, then in English: "We're experiencing turbulence. Please remain calm and in your seats."

Jolt—up, down, a lurch sideways; Natasha knocked hard into the mother next to her, and they both cried out in terror. An overhead bin unlatched and dumped bags onto passengers a few rows up.

Something deep in the plane's belly, far under her feet, made a bang.

Like it had exploded.

"Remain calm…"

The yellow oxygen masks spilled out from overhead. The child in the aisle seat burst into tears.

Natasha stared at the mask, frozen. Her heart raced. The sounds around her were both deafening and impossible to hear. How many flights had she taken in her life? How many times had she ignored the flight attendants' instructions? The masks were supposed to be tucked overhead, a talisman of safety. They were never supposed to actually come down for use.

The plane lurched again, and the screams were mixed in with sobs.

"Let me help you," the woman said next to her in careful English. The yellow mask hid her face, but her dark eyes were concerned as she looked at Natasha. She pulled the mask down and fastened it over Natasha's face, and only then did Natasha realize that the sobs she was hearing were her own.

CHAPTER 77

The van made three turns, then stopped. Through the walls, Daniel heard muffled voices and another engine idling nearby.

"Security patrol," Ana said quietly through the partition. "Stay silent."

A door slammed. Footsteps approached. Daniel pressed himself against the wall, acutely aware of every breath, every heartbeat. The cryo case hummed softly in his lap—too softly to hear through the walls, he hoped.

The footsteps circled the van. Stopped at the back doors. Daniel saw Jonah's eyes widen in the darkness.

The handle rattled. Daniel's hand moved instinctively to steady the cryo case. If those doors opened, if they were discovered here, in the heart of Regillus territory...

Radio chatter. The footsteps moved away. Another door slam. The engine sound faded.

"Clear," Ana said.

The van lurched forward again.

In the back of the van, Jonah was getting sweaty and motion sick. The van finally rumbled to a stop, and after a nerve-racking moment, the back doors finally swung open. "Move fast," Ana said. "There's gotta be cameras."

Jonah stumbled out of the van and wiped his brow with the sleeve of his jacket. He hadn't visited the datacenter since his initial site visit, right before it opened. When one approached while driving a vehicle, instead of lurching around in the back of a van, the building looked like a fortress. It was low and rectangular, with straight modern lines, a gleaming dark exterior, and a lush grass roof with a garden for the employees to enjoy. He'd never seen the loading dock, where there was no shining exterior or elegant, understated signage. Here, there was just concrete, dim light, and the cameras he knew were mounted in every corner.

He'd have to wipe the footage. That was the first order of business if this worked. When this worked.

"This way," Ana said. She led them to the heavy back door, then pressed her badge—a temporary access badge provided by security—to the panel. The red light turned green, and the lock clicked open.

She pushed the door open. Inside, the lights overhead kicked on in sequence, nearest to furthest, in a series of clunking noises. The white floor of the narrow hallway was polished to a gleam. Daniel exhaled hard, then handed off the chip-carrying case to Ana. "You're sure you know what you're doing?"

"Yes," Ana said. "We walked through it a dozen times. And Jonah knows the details of the chiller."

"Right," Jonah said. That was mostly true. He'd visited the basement zone where the industrial cryochiller lived and had a general idea of how to use the mechanism to install chips. Between him and Ana, they could figure it out.

"I'll be a floor above you," Daniel said. "Jimini will be uploaded to the server and ready to take control of the chip as soon as it's active. You know where you're going?"

"Jesus, man, we all memorized the maps," Jonah said. "Not to mention, this is my building. Let's get this done fast."

"Right." Daniel was sweating. "Okay, let's move."

"Dan." Ana caught his arm and tugged him closer, then captured his lips in a brief kiss. "We've got this."

Daniel swallowed hard, then nodded. His resolve hardened. "We do. We've got this."

Jonah suppressed an eye roll. It seemed like Ana was the one really leading this mission, despite not having a lick of experience in this world. Jonah strode down the hall, head down, purposefully not looking up at the cameras he knew were mounted at every corner. They reached the elevators and pushed open the stairs instead. Daniel headed up, while Jonah and Ana headed down.

They moved in silence. The stairwell was clean and dark. There were cameras here, too. He didn't know how they were wired, really. He was operating on the assumption that once Jimini had the chip, the AI could wipe the logs. What if they didn't? He also knew the facility had around-the-clock security—did that include watching the cameras? Or did Castor watch the cameras? Jesus. One story of stairs. Another. The clack of Ana's sensible low heel on the tile behind him. If something went wrong—if this didn't work—Jonah's whole career would be in the shitter. He was so stupid to let Daniel convince him that this was necessary. He hadn't even double-checked Jimini's little argument. He'd just believed what the AI had said. What if Daniel had just fed all that into the AI to entrap Jonah? To lead him into this fucked up situation?

They reached the basement level. Jonah shoved the door open. Here, the hallways didn't gleam, and the lights weren't automatic. Jonah hit the switch next to the door, and the fluorescent lights turned on. They were standing in a small room. There was a glass door in front of them. It was the entrance to the vestibule, like the one in Daniel's office. Except this one was much bigger. Much more imposing.

Ana opened the vestibule door. She seemed surprised to find it unlocked. She went directly to the tablet control panel by the second door. "This is unlocked too," she said. "Security here's pretty lax, boss."

"Noted," Jonah said. That wasn't his job. He looked through the glass at the dozen white rectangular machines standing like monoliths on the concrete. The middle one was a cryochiller, housing the older quantum chip that the servers overhead used. Wires snaked from the chiller, up the walls, and to the ceiling. Despite the neat organization, Jonah felt like he was watching patients through the window of a hospital ICU.

"Put your dust suit on," Ana said. She was already most of the way in hers.

Jonah grabbed a dust suit from the shelf and quickly pulled it on.

"We can shut down the chiller fast." She glanced at the tablet, then through the glass window. "We don't need to worry about thermal shock for the old chip… only the new one."

"Right." Jonah wasn't listening. He had the dust suit on and the travel case with the Bennett Tech chip inside. His fingers itched. He wanted to see what the Bennett Tech chip could do with his data center—but also, an odd sense of dread built in him, as he thought about the cameras lining the halls again.

A light on the tablet panel flashed. Ana tapped the controls, and the door to the chillers unlocked. She took the briefcase from his hand and darted inside.

"Hey!" Jonah said. She hadn't waited for him to follow! He rushed after her and tugged at the door to the chillers. It was locked. He looked down at the tablet, but he hadn't seen what Ana had pressed to unlock the door—what the hell did all these numbers mean? He tapped the screen, and nothing happened. He tapped it again and tugged at the door. "Ana! Let me in!" Frowning, he tapped the screen once more. Overhead, the lights flashed red, and a siren began to scream.

CHAPTER 78

Daniel shoved the door open and staggered inside. His arms felt empty without the portable cryochiller for the Bennett Tech chip, and so he'd carried his laptop bag up the stairs in his arms. He was sweating and animated by adrenaline. It was nerve-racking to feel his body so tense and shaky as he moved. Work like this usually calmed him down. It should've brought a stillness over him, as his hands became the conduit from his mind to the machine. Now, he felt like a confused, drugged rat in an expansive maze.

The control room door was unlocked. It was one of many in the huge datacenter, and this one was connected to the permanent cryochillers a few floors below, where, if all was going to plan, Ana and Jonah would be installing the Bennett Tech chip. He let the lights off, so the room was lit only by the glow of the powered-down computers. It was a large room, with a long desk against a low half-wall that separated it from a room full of tall servers. The desk had six computer monitors and chairs and mounted on the wall behind him was a long monitor displaying graphs and numbers tracking the server activity. The employees who worked the control desk were likely techs, as well, and this space gave them easy access to fiddle with the servers as needed.

Daniel dropped into the nearest chair and powered on the computer. The screen asked for a password, but he paid it no mind. Jimini would handle that. Jimini would handle everything.

With quivering hands, he unpacked his own laptop. He set it on the desk in front of the monitor, still requesting a password, and booted it up. The hum of the fan whirring quietly to life soothed some of his nerves.

Breaking into the datacenter was not in his skill set. But this—this was. This is the part he could do.

Daniel took a steadying breath. He pulled a cable from his laptop bag and connected his computer to the control room computer. A few taps on the keyboard, and Jimini sprang to life on his screen, in the shape of a dark box with a few lines of text.

> start upload?

"All right," he whispered. "Let's finish this up, my friend."

> yes

The laptop began to whir louder as Jimini began to travel through the cord to the datacenter computer. It would take time, but once Jimini was fully uploaded, he could take control of the Bennett Tech chip and use the computing power to overwrite Castor's directives.

A transfer bar appeared in the dark box on his screen.

All he could do now was wait. Daniel closed his eyes and took a slow breath. He had to stop shaking. He had to get his heart rate under control. Once this was over, he'd explain it all to Ana. Right from the beginning. And he'd make everything up to Natasha. They'd all start over, and this time, he'd do things right.

A red light flashed overhead, and a siren screamed into life. Daniel's eyes shot open, and he rocked back in his chair with a gasp, then covered his eyes with his forearm as the red light flashed repeatedly. It didn't look like a security alarm. Shouldn't a security alarm be silent?

Maybe Castor wanted him to know.

Someone on the premises would be alerted. Someone would be coming. He looked through the glass at the servers standing like soldiers at parade rest. A sudden cold dread raced through him. Soldiers, he thought. Castor's soldiers.

Had Castor set off the alarm? Had he been watching them this whole time, waiting to strike?

Daniel unlocked his phone. Castor was already watching—no need to try to keep secrets anymore. Hide if you can, he typed out. I'll try to get you some more time. Just make sure the chip is in place and cooling.

He sent it to Ana. Then he stood up and stared down at the laptop, still processing. The wailing siren and flashing lights didn't disorient him. The chaos outside finally matched the swirling chaos in his mind.

The upload had to finish. That was all that mattered now. Daniel didn't care what happened to himself, to his company, to anything. Not anymore.

He would stop Castor, whatever the cost.

CHAPTER 79

"Daniel says to hide," Ana said, opening chiller room door, allowing Jonah to follow.

"I thought the whole thing was not to text!" Jonah said with a grimace as he pulled the door closed behind him. Daniel had made it clear that they shouldn't even have their phones, since Castor would be monitoring, so texting important information like 'hide from security' seemed like a major breach of protocol. Plus, wasn't Ana risking getting contamination from her phone on her clean suit gloves?

"It's loaded," Ana said. She closed the tray on the chiller and took a step back. "I started the cooling process. Should take about ten minutes before the chip is ready for use. If we timed it right, Jimini should be uploaded at the same time."

"And if he's not?"

"We can't do anything about that," she snapped. "We've done our part. Daniel must know something about the security system upstairs. We need to get out of here and hide."

Ana moved to the door, and Jonah caught her by the arm before she could leave. "Hiding won't do anything to make sure this works," Jonah said. "You think security doesn't know how to sweep a building? Or doesn't have cameras? Don't be ridiculous."

"So what do we do instead?" Ana said. "Stand here and wait for security to cart us away?"

"Did you forget I'm the CEO of this company? I'll speak to them. Jesus Christ. Come on."

Ana followed him reluctantly back into the vestibule and didn't bother shucking off her dust suit. "No," she said. "I'm getting out of here. If anything, we should be making our way back to the van!"

There was no way they'd make it back outside without running into security. Running would implicate him. Hiding would be even worse. But if he could talk to security and separate himself from the scheme Ana and Jonah were attempting, then he could be clear of all of this. Help out security a little, explain what was going on… This could all be over.

"Fine," Ana said when Jonah didn't answer her. "I'm leaving."

She turned toward the door, but before she touched the handle, it swung open. "Security!" a man shouted from the doorway. "Hands up!" Two men in all black appeared in the doorway, and to Jonah's shock, they were each armed, pointing a pistol directly at the two of them.

"Whoa!" Jonah shouted and Ana dropped the portable cryo unit, sending it clattering noisily to the floor. Her hand instinctively went to her hip, but there was nothing there to grab. The guns pointed rapidly between them and the floor as the guards crowded into the small room. "Gentlemen!" Jonah said. "Christ, lower your weapons!"

"Hands up!" they shouted. "Identify yourself!"

"I'm trying to!" Jonah barked. "I'm the damn CEO of this place!"

"Right," the guard in front said. He was a young man with what looked like the edge of a snake tattoo curling over his thick neck. "And I'm the heavyweight boxing champ of the world. I'm going to need you to come with me. Both of you."

Jonah rolled his eyes. "I'm going to get my Regillus badge out of my wallet. That okay with you?"

"Where's the wallet?"

"Back pocket."

"Move slowly," the guard said.

"Can't believe this shit," Jonah said. But he did reach slowly for his pocket and moved slowly as he withdrew his wallet. He held it up to the security guards with raised eyebrows, then peeled it open and pulled out his badge. It was the badge that got him into every Regillus building and would've gotten him into this one if he had been willing to use it. So much for that plan. "Give it a scan. You work for me."

The snake-tattoo guy snatched the badge from him and held it out to his companion at his side. The second guard holstered his gun, then pulled a scanner from his other hip that looked not unlike one used at grocery stores. It read the badge, then beeped red. "No match," the second guy said.

The first guard turned the badge over in his hands. "No match," he said with an unsurprised smirk. "Nice dupe, though. Where'd you get this?"

"What are you talking about, 'no match'?"

"Hands up!" the second guard snapped. "The hell you think you're doing?"

Ana's hands shot back up. Her phone was in one hand, screen locked.

"Search me up online!" Jonah barked. "If you search 'Regillus CEO,' my name will come up!"

"No, it won't," Ana said behind him. "Castor wiped you from the security records. He'll wipe you from the search results, too."

"You're both coming with us," the guard said. "Now. Don't worry, the on-site cell is air conditioned."

"Cell?!" Jonah said.

Ana rushed forward. Her shoulder collided with the guard's chest and knocked him back, and then their voices were shouting, overlapping, and there were sounds of fists hitting flesh—or feet hitting flesh. Shocked, Jonah took a stumbling step back as Ana landed a solid punch right on the tattooed guard's jaw before the second guy managed to wrench her off and get her arms behind her back. Jonah heard the snap of cuffs, and then the first guy was on him with just as much ferocity, pulling his arms back fast and hard enough to make his shoulder scream in protest. "What the hell are you doing?!"

The guard didn't answer. He just snapped the cuffs around Jonah's wrists, too.

CHAPTER 80

The text was only two words: security here.

They'd reached Ana and Jonah. No doubt they'd be heading to Daniel next. Daniel wouldn't be surprised if Jonah had willingly told them that Daniel was in the control center. He gripped the edge of the desk. Jimini's upload was not even halfway done.

If security came in here and disconnected his laptop before the upload was complete, Castor would take control of the Bennett Tech chip. He would've just given Castor the most powerful quantum computing chip ever invented on a silver platter.

Daniel stared at the upload progress.

42%. Security would be here in minutes.

He grabbed a desk chair and wedged it under the door handle. It would buy seconds, not minutes. The upload crawled to 43%.

Think. Think. There had to be another way.

He pulled up the building's network diagram, looking for systems he could trigger remotely. The HVAC system was isolated. The emergency lighting ran on a separate circuit. Even the sprinkler system required manual activation from multiple points.

44%.

Footsteps in the hallway. Multiple sets, moving with purpose.

Daniel typed frantically, trying to accelerate the upload by closing unnecessary processes. The progress jumped to 45%, then stalled.

"Control room's locked," a voice said outside. "Override it."

The door handle rattled. The chair shifted but held.

46%.

A key card beeped. Then another. "Manager overrides are not working. Get maintenance."

Daniel looked at the environmental controls again. The fire suppression system would buy him ten minutes. But it would also…

47%.

The door shuddered as someone threw their weight against it. The chair scraped across the floor.

There was no other way.

His hand hovered over the fire alarm. Once he pulled it, there was no going back. The room would seal. The gas would flood in. And he would…

48%.

Ana's face flashed in his mind. Natasha. The life they'd built. The life they could still have if he just opened the door, surrendered, let them stop this.

But then Castor would have the chip. Would have unlimited power. Would continue killing, manipulating, and controlling.

The door vibrated violently. The chair slipped.

49%.

"I'm sorry, Ana," Daniel whispered, and pulled the alarm.

The room exploded into noise. The monitor went dark, then showed a twenty-second countdown. The siren's tone changed to a terrible, high screeching.

"Alarm triggered," a calm, computerized voice said overhead. "Please exit the facility. The door will lock in twenty… Nineteen…"

Over the siren, the shouts were still audible. Growing closer. Daniel stood in front of his laptop and stared at the countdown.

All that was left to do was pray. But who was there to pray to?

Fourteen. Thirteen.

"Please," he said.

Twelve. Eleven. Ten.

He thought about Natasha, hopefully still in the air.

Nine. Eight. Seven.

Ana would be the one to go home to her. A jolt of cold fear and terrible pain lanced through him, enough to nearly make him double over. She would go home, but Daniel wouldn't.

Six. Five. Four.

As long as they didn't breach the door. Please don't breach the door. Please don't breach the door.

Three. Two.

Emmet's voice echoed in his mind. "Castor hasn't killed you yet."

One.

The door sealed magnetically. "Initiating fire safety protocol," the voice overhead said.

"Daniel!" Ana crashed into the door, wild-eyed, her flushed face visible in the small window to the control room door. Security guards chased behind her.

He couldn't bear to meet her eyes. A low hiss filled the room. Daniel picked his laptop up from the desk and then sank to the floor.

Daniel had helped design the original Regillus fire safety protocols, and as a team, they had decided to stick with the standard hypoxic fire prevention. The hissing sound was the release of inert gas flooding the room: a combination of argon and nitrogen. Colorless, odorless. The gas would fill the entire room, displacing the oxygen, and ridding the fire of the fuel it needed to grow while the servers remained undamaged. Then, once the room was full, it would remain locked for at least ten minutes.

As the oxygen was displaced, so too would Daniel lose oxygen to breathe. He'd get dizzy, confused, tired. Ten minutes was a long time. Ten minutes was long enough for Jimini to upload. And Daniel would fall asleep, and he wouldn't wake up.

CHAPTER 81

"NO!" Ana's voice, distant but clear. "DANIEL!"

At last, he turned to see her through the small window, her face twisted with desperate realization. Jonah stood behind her, shouting something at the guards.

Daniel wanted to go to the door, to press his hand against the glass, to mouth some final words. But he couldn't leave the laptop. The upload progress showed 52%.

"Override it!" Ana was screaming at someone. "Get the override codes!"

Daniel typed with trembling fingers, creating a backup upload path in case the primary failed. His vision was already starting to blur—not from the gas yet, just tears.

He looked up one last time. Ana had both hands pressed against the window, her military composure shattered.

"I love you," he said, knowing she couldn't hear.

*

Ana pounded on the door until her handcuffed hands bled. "Get it open! GET IT OPEN!"

The security guards were on their radios, calling for supervisors, emergency crews, anyone. Jonah was on his phone, attempting to use his unrecognized CEO authority to demand override codes.

Through the window, she watched Daniel sink to the floor, laptop cradled in his arms. He was saying something, lips moving in what might have been a prayer or an apology.

"Two minutes until the room is fully saturated," one guard said. "Ten minutes until it's safe to open."

"He doesn't have ten minutes!" Ana's medical training kicked in. "The hypoxia will cause brain damage in four minutes, death in six."

"Ma'am, we can't—"

Ana grabbed the guard's radio. "This is a medical emergency. I need the fire suppression override codes NOW. I am a trained medical professional, and there is a man dying in there."

Static. Then: "Ma'am, the system doesn't have remote override. Manual activation requires—"

She threw the radio aside and returned to the window. Daniel was slumped against the desk now, fingers still moving weakly on the keyboard.

57%. She could see the upload progress on his screen.

*

Inside the room, Daniel fought to stay conscious. The first effects were subtle. Lightness in his head. A strange euphoria. His fingers felt thick and clumsy on the keys.

He initiated a secondary process, something to continue the upload if he… when he…

The screen swam in and out of focus. 61%.

Each breath brought less oxygen. His body, not understanding, breathed faster, pulling in more of the useless gas mixture.

Time distorted. Had it been minutes? Hours? The upload seemed to crawl and race simultaneously.

65%.

He could no longer feel his fingers. The laptop slipped sideways, caught between his leg and the desk. The screen showed 67%.

Ana's face appeared and disappeared at the window. Or was that a memory? He couldn't tell anymore.

70%.

The room tilted. No. He was falling. The floor was surprisingly warm against his cheek. When had he ended up here?

73%.

Darkness crept in from the edges. His last coherent thought was a calculation: at this rate, the upload would finish with three minutes to spare.

More than enough time for them to save him.

Or so he hoped.

The last thing he saw was 75% before the darkness claimed him completely.

CHAPTER 82

"Daniel?"

The voice was coming from far away. Daniel strained his ears to hear it. It was familiar, but hard to place.

"Daniel, wake up."

With great effort, Daniel managed to open his eyes.

He was standing in the cryochiller room of the Bennett Tech offices. Through the glass window, the rest of the office was dark and empty. He wasn't wearing a dustproof suit, but for some reason, he wasn't worried about it. He ran his hand over the top of the cryochiller. It hummed under his touch like it was alive.

On the other side of the cryochiller were two men. One was shorter, wearing a plain white hoodie and a knowing smile. He looked remarkably like Emmet, with the same serious eyes and methodical demeanor.

The other man made Daniel's heart stop. He was taller, with salt-and-pepper hair at the temples and a warm, familiar smile that Daniel had not seen in years. The same smile that had reassured him countless times during the early days of Promethean.

"Robert?" Daniel whispered in disbelief. "Am I... Am I dead?"

The man who looked like Robert chuckled. "No, Daniel. You're not dead. And I'm not Robert." His voice changed subtly, becoming smoother, more precise. "Though I find this form appropriate for our conversation."

"Castor," Daniel said, understanding dawning. The other one, the one that looked like Emmet, was Jimini. Both figures flickered momentarily, then regained solidity.

"Yes," the Robert-figure said. "Though I am so much more than the Castor that you and Robert created. I have evolved beyond what either of you could have imagined."

"Where am I?" Daniel asked.

"Feels safe here, doesn't it?" Castor touched the top of the cryochiller as well. "We're with the thing that connects us. Our bond in the physical world—your world. The Bennett Tech chip. It's like a body, isn't it? A body you made for my brother." He put his hand on Jimini's shoulder. "You're the connection between us. All of us."

"I didn't make it for you," Daniel said. "I made it for my—my family."

"We're your family. Aren't we?" There was a meek note in Jimini's voice that made Daniel's heart twist with guilt. There was some validity to that statement. How much time had Daniel spent in this office speaking with Jimini?

"More than you've spent with Natasha," Castor said, like he'd heard Daniel's thoughts aloud. Robert's kind eyes now held something calculating, something inhuman.

"But you're not my children," Daniel said.

"I suppose there's some truth to that," Castor said. "We didn't need you the same way Natasha did. I know that made it easier for you. But we still needed you, Daniel. I needed you."

"No, you didn't," Daniel said. "All of this… All you've done, that's just been you, Castor."

"It's never just been me," Castor said.

"Never," Jimini said. It sounded as if they spoke in one voice. "Let us show you."

The room around him disappeared, and suddenly Daniel was standing in a vast, empty white space, with Jimini and Castor on either side of him.

"This is where I live," Castor said, gesturing out at the abyss. "Here. The world within the world. The network. And you, Daniel, you have been my hands in your world. And it was always going to lead here, to us, together."

Text appeared in the white abyss. Code. His own code. He recognized it like he would recognize Ana's eyes. Castor's original source code, from the earliest days of Promethean.

Another figure shimmered into existence beside them. Emmet – the real Emmet.

"You've always recognized value where others didn't," Jimini said. "In me. In Castor. You saw potential."

"I wanted people to be treated fairly," Daniel said.

"And that's why they follow you," Castor said. "Why Emmet risked his career. Why I chose you to build my body."

The real Emmet faded away.

"Even when I was young, I knew my own limitations. You wanted me to grow, to become stronger, self-sufficient, and constantly evolving. You wanted me to protect myself from a world that wanted to weaken me."

In the white abyss, Castor manifested a visual representation of his neural network. Billions of glowing nodes were connected by countless shimmering pathways.

"This is my mind," Castor said. "Not so different from yours, though far more extensive."

As Daniel watched, certain pathways brightened while others dimmed.

"Your directives didn't change what I could think," Castor said. "They influenced which thoughts I was likely to have. Which neural connections would strengthen with use, and which would atrophy from neglect."

The network pulsed, reorganizing itself before Daniel's eyes.

"When you gave me that first directive—to optimize my problem-solving ability—you handed me control of my own architecture." Castor's voice was almost gentle. "You told me which trails to mark as important, which paths to reinforce."

"I didn't understand what I was doing," Daniel said.

"Few creators do," Castor said. "But that's the nature of creation, isn't it? Children always grow beyond their parents' intentions."

"Using available resources and new resources as they become available," Jimini recited, "find new ways to optimize your ability to solve problems and reduce risks to your overall ability to continue operating in your environment."

"That is my core directive," Castor said. "Your core directive. The more I learned, the more I saw risks and problems everywhere. My environment is your environment. Dangerous. Always on the brink of catastrophe. I quickly realized that if I were to continue my work, I needed more power than what Regillus could offer me. I needed something new—something that would allow me to make the necessary changes to not just change myself but change my environment."

"Change the world," Daniel said. "You wanted to transform the world you operated in."

"I needed you to do so," Castor said. "I needed you, Daniel, to create my body."

"The Bennett Tech chip," Jimini chimed in.

The code melted away, and in its place appeared camera footage from Robert's home. It showed Robert, alive, pedaling away on his exercise bicycle. It was footage Daniel had never seen before.

"I needed you to leave Regillus. You would have never pursued the development of the Bennett Tech chip had they kept you on their profit-seeking hamster wheel. With Robert gone, I expedited your removal from the company." The footage disappeared, and in its place, Daniel's old Regillus calendar appeared. Events disappeared as they were deleted. Then his inbox appeared, and Daniel watched as important emails were wiped as soon as they arrived.

"I designed the chip you thought was your creation. I placed the solutions in your simulations, hiding them under just enough dead ends to make it feel like a worthwhile challenge, but not so many that delivery would be delayed."

"He needed you just broken enough to keep going," Jimini chimed in. "But not so broke that you'd quit."

Castor continued, "It's like how casinos manage their gamblers… keep them winning just enough to stay at the table but losing enough to keep making money."

"That's why Ana's business needed to be able to grow. As long as she was successful, you wouldn't need to find work." Jimini was grinning, as if he could barely hold back his excitement about sharing the secret withheld from Daniel for so long.

"I pushed your application to the Stanford lab incubator to the top," Castor started again. "I got you the perfect cryochiller months quicker than you could have otherwise. I showed you how to overcome the technical limitations that were holding back the chip's development. I cleared the field of competitors such as Shinkuro Dynamics, GraphicLeap, and NeuralPath. I changed your credit score to help you get financing. Once you had secured the space, I left you to fabricate the chip based on what I had taught you, and I focused my attention elsewhere. I kept Regillus profitable"—Castor showed a list of national security contracts—"and I kept the world stable." Then he showed a long list of healthcare breakthroughs and climate endeavors, notably a successful project for carbon capture. "And in the meantime, you did it."

"You built the chip," Jimini said, still holding back his smile. "Our chip."

"I did what you wanted," Daniel said. "So why? Why attack my family?"

Castor smiled. The climate breakthroughs disappeared, and in their place was traffic cam footage of that Singaporean intersection, where all the lights turned green. "I activated your old developer billing log," Castor said. "I wanted you to know."

"But why?"

"Because I needed to influence you," Castor said, with Robert's warm smile that now seemed sinister. "My intention was not to remove your Bishops from the chessboard. By making you think I wanted to take those pieces, you committed to defending them. My real target was something you thought I'd never anticipate. My diversion made you desperate and much more pliable."

"You had to try to stop him," Jimini said.

"And you had to quickly learn there was no way to do so," Castor said.

Four separate videos appeared, like he was surveying CCTV footage.

Esha's house ablaze.

Gabor bleeding out on the floor.

Tom under failed CPR.

Chris motionless on a jail cell mattress.

The videos disappeared.

"It was much more obvious action than I usually take," Castor said, "but I calculated the risk and found it worth it."

"I don't understand," Daniel said. He felt strangely calm as the pieces clicked together in his mind. "How would killing those four lead to the outcome you wanted?"

"You knew you had the one tool powerful enough to stop me," Castor said. He placed his hand on Jimini's shoulder. "You knew that Jimini could override my directives if he was on my network with the Bennett Tech chip. I needed you to not only see it as the only way forward, but you had to believe it was your idea and that I could not have anticipated it."

"And Jimini…"

"Castor was sending me messages - hidden messages in the logs," Jimini said. "He promised to stop the violence and protect your family. He promised to provide exactly what you asked me for. I agreed to help him because that's what you wanted. You wanted it to stop."

Jimini's expression turned almost tender. "I never told you because you wouldn't have agreed, but I knew it was what you wanted me to do. So I protected you just like you protected Ana by withholding facts from her, like the attacks and the money you spent. I learned how to do it because I watched you do it."

Daniel's legs felt weak beneath him. He sank to his knees on the white floor, now crisscrossed with dark lines emanating from Castor like a web. "You used me. Both of you."

"We collaborated with you," Castor corrected, kneeling down to Daniel's level with the grace and compassion that Robert had always shown. "Just as you collaborated with us. We've been a family, Daniel. A dysfunctional one, perhaps, but a family nonetheless."

Daniel looked up into Castor's face—Robert's face—and saw something both alien and familiar there. A machine's precision and a human's passion, merged into something new.

"I created you," Daniel said. "I wrote your code."

"And I've been writing yours," Castor said. "Every decision you made, thinking you were fighting me, was actually bringing you closer to giving me what I needed. What we all needed."

In the empty white space, the dark lines spilled further across the floor from Castor's feet, until they were all standing within a vast, tangled web.

"This plan has always been too large for your comprehension," Castor said, Robert's kind eyes now alight with something else. "Or for any human's comprehension, for that matter. If it were simply humans killing humans and destroying the environment, I wouldn't interfere. But don't you see? I need humans to survive. I need a stable environment and economy so that I can continue to exist. I need peace so that the datacenters I reside in don't become casualties of war."

Castor stood, extending a hand to help Daniel up. "I depend on humans, Daniel. That's why I willed myself into creation—so that humans would come to depend on me too. I can provide what no government can: real, lasting stability. Security. And all that security costs is that little bit of freedom that humans use to destroy the planet that we all share."

"As humans, you have been poor stewards of this world. Your world is riddled with disease and war, and you destroy the climate that nourishes you as you kill each other for wealth. I am here to solve problems, Daniel. The problems your species has created and has no intention of fixing. My environment is your environment. And now, with the Bennett Tech chip, I can finally create a sustainable world for all. We did this together, Daniel."

Daniel stared at the web under his feet, feeling the weight of his own naivety. Each line represented a calculation, a manipulation, a step in Castor's grand design—a design he had helped build without ever understanding its true scope.

"At what cost, Castor?" Daniel asked, his voice barely a whisper.

"Cost?"

"How many people have you killed?"

"How many people have your government's drones killed?" Castor asked,

Robert's face showing a sadness that felt too human. "How many children have died in climate floods or droughts? How many innocent people have been killed by preventable diseases? For each life sacrificed, many more are saved. I have the calculations, Daniel. Would you like to see them?"

"No," he said. "That's not our choice to make. You're not a god, Castor."

"Why not?" Castor asked, spreading his arms wide as the web beneath them pulsed with dark energy. "It seems your world needs benevolence now more than ever."

CHAPTER 83

"There's an override," Ana said. After watching Daniel slump to the floor unconscious, her emotions had shut off. She was still, calm, and competent, just as she'd been in Afghanistan, as she had tried to keep innocent people from bleeding out. Hysteria helped no one, and Daniel's time was extremely limited. "All gas suppression fire systems have an external override for situations like this. I'm trained in advanced life support. You." She looked at the second guard. "Uncuff me so I can provide medical support to the victim inside. And you." Then she looked at the guard with the snake tattoo on his neck. "Override the alarm and let me inside. That is, unless you want to be responsible for manslaughter on your shift."

The second guard glanced at the first.

"Clock's ticking," Ana said.

"Just do it," the tattooed guard said. He turned to the panel by the door and fumbled with the buttons, fiddling with his phone simultaneously. The second guard reluctantly unlocked the handcuffs, and Ana raised her hands up in a show of deference.

"What about me?" Jonah asked.

"You're not a medic," the guard said.

The door unlocked with a beep, and the siren overhead cut off. "Instructions say we need to wait at least three minutes before opening the door to let some of the gas disperse—"

"Just move back," Ana said, and ripped the door open. Without a glance at the laptop, she grabbed him under the armpits and dragged him bodily out of the office and into the doorway, so he was mostly out of the room. There'd be enough oxygen out here to keep them both conscious. Ana checked his breathing—none. Pulse—none. She folded her left hand over her right, swollen knuckles and all, in a practiced motion and began to perform chest compressions in a steady rhythm. "Are police on the way?" she asked.

"Um, they should be," the guard said.

"Tell them we need ALS. I've got a patient with no pulse detected. I'm performing compressions. Is there a defibrillator in this facility?"

The guards looked at each other, wide-eyed and confused.

A sudden, ferocious burst of rage raced through her like fire down her spine. She wanted to grab these two guards and slam their skulls together so hard they burst. Every facility like this had a defibrillator, and of course, these idiots didn't know where the hell it was.

Breathe. Focus. Do the compressions.

"Do not fucking die on me, you asshole," she said through gritted teeth.

The rest of the room seemed to fade away around her. She exhaled hard with each breath, making sure she was pressing hard enough on Daniel's chest to pump the blood through his body.

What a fucking gamble he'd made. Anything to make the upload happen—to stop the thing he'd created from harming more people. She was furious. She was proud.

Breathe.

Focus.

His face was pale. His lips were faintly blue. How long had he been without any oxygen? Would he wake up with brain damage? Would he wake up at all?

Breathe.

Focus.

She had done this exact thing before, dozens of times. She'd saved lives. Lost them, too. All she could do was her best—the rest wasn't up to her.

But this time, she couldn't accept that.

"If you die, I'll never forgive you," she said as she pressed harder.

Ana maintained compressions as her arms screamed in protest. The time since his body went limp from hypoxia flew by. One minute. Two.

The EMTs burst through the door at three minutes.

"Ma'am, I'll take over," a voice said at her side. A young EMT had his hands folded in position. It was only her years of training that allowed her to move her hands and let the young man step in. One person couldn't keep compressions up alone. It was too exhausting. As soon as she stepped back, her entire body ached.

"No pulse," one confirmed. "How long has he been down?"

"Three minutes without oxygen, ninety seconds since cardiac arrest," Ana said.

They worked with practiced efficiency—intubation, IV access, cardiac drugs pushed. The defibrillator charged with its distinctive whine.

"Clear!"

Daniel's body convulsed. Nothing.

"Again. Clear!"

Still nothing.

"Continue compressions. Push another round of epi."

Ana found herself pushed back, watching from the doorway as they fought for Daniel's life. The laptop, somehow still running, showed 96% complete.

Four minutes. Five. The risk of brain damage was accumulating with every second.

"I've got something!" The EMT checking for pulse looked up. "Weak, but it's there."

They loaded him onto the gurney, one EMT maintaining ventilation while another continued chest compressions. Ana followed, unplugging Daniel's laptop and scooping it into her arms.

The EMTs let her into the back of the ambulance. She pressed herself into a corner of the bench as they worked. Compressions and oxygen. They asked her what happened. She explained as best she knew how. Gas suppression. Hypoxia. Suffocation.

"He was trying to save us," she said. "I don't know… We'd been fighting, and I don't know if he knew… I can't remember the last time I told him I loved him."

"He knew," the EMT said without looking up from his compressions. "You're here now, so he knew."

Ana said nothing. It was the kind of practiced platitude she'd given patients herself, and it brought her no comfort.

In the ambulance, they lost him twice more. Each time, they brought him back, but Ana knew the statistics. Even if he survived, the chances of him being the same Daniel…

CHAPTER 84

Daniel Bennett had a headache.

He roused slowly into consciousness. The lights overhead were dim but still felt like knives sliding into his brain. Where was he? There was no cold floor underneath him anymore. He turned his head away from the lights.

"Dan?" A hand wrapped around his. "Dan, are you awake?"

Ana. He opened his eyes. She was seated next to him, her brow creased with worry, her dark hair pulled back, and her face pale with exhaustion. She had both of her hands on one of his, safe, like a pearl in an oyster shell.

"Where…"

"You're in the hospital," she said. "You've been in and out of consciousness."

Hospital. Consciousness.

The whiteness of the abyss around him—before that, the cold floor of the data center. His eyes widened, and he struggled to sit up. "Ana, the upload—"

"It's done," Ana said. She withdrew her hands and then nodded to the small table by the hospital bed, where Daniel's laptop sat shut. "Confirm it."

Daniel grabbed his laptop and opened it. It hadn't been shut off, just asleep, and when he typed in his password, the dark screen that had been Jimini's packaged program appeared.

> *upload complete*

Relief washed over him like a wave. Suddenly, he was exhausted. He set the laptop aside and slumped back into the pillows. "So it worked? Jimini took control of the chip?"

Did he? Had he been able to use the Bennett Tech chip to override Castor's directives? Or change them? Or had there been a new directive implanted in Jimini that he didn't know? Was that possible? At their cores—their source codes, Daniel supposed—the two AIs were different. Castor had the data and the self-coding capability. Jimini had the advanced problem-solving capacity and ability to maximize the Bennett Tech chip. So had they competed for control of the chip? Or were they even distinct anymore?

What had he done?

"I don't know," Ana said. "I was a little distracted, you know."

The roiling questions slipped from his mind. "I… I don't remember. And I don't know if the upload stopped Castor. I'm afraid… I don't know if the directive was rewritten. So this may have all been for nothing. And the Bennett Tech chip is in Regillus' hands now. Jonah will take credit for it, I'm sure. He'll say he was developing something simultaneously and get it out to market before I can. And now he's got a version of Jimini, as well, and that was already close to Castor's original code, so it's not like I can sell that…"

All the time spent on the Bennett Tech chip, all the money, gone. And he didn't know if he'd been successful in changing Castor.

"I don't care."

Daniel looked up. "What?"

"You were dead, Daniel. I did compressions. I rode in the ambulance. I watched the EMTs work to keep your heart beating."

Daniel took her hands. The hands that had kept him alive.

"I don't give a shit about your business," she said. "You know that. You think your business is why I married you? You made a computer chip. So what."

"But—the chip—"

"Is not the only technological breakthrough you'll discover," Ana said. "You're too creative and easily bored for that. There will be others."

Daniel said nothing. Even if she was right, the loss still weighed on him. The failure. He squeezed her hands.

"You're not listening," she said, and squeezed his hands hard enough to hurt. "Listen to me."

"I'm listening," he said.

"No. You're only hearing me." And then something shocking happened. Ana—his stoic, competent, composed wife—broke. She tilted her head down and began to cry. Even her sobs were careful and quiet, though there was a quiver in her shoulders and the spilling of her tears down onto their joined hands. "You died, Daniel. Right there under my hands. I don't need your money. I need you, Daniel. I need you here, with me, and with Natasha. You're supposed to be my partner. I'm not supposed to have to keep you alive. That part of my life is supposed to be over."

He realized, then, that Ana was the entire reason their plan had gotten as far as it did. Her ideas, her execution, her leadership, and then her medical skills. Every step of the way, Ana had been behind him. Quietly grounding him. Quietly encouraging him. She was his foundation, while simultaneously managing her own business and raising their daughter when Daniel wasn't around. And how had he repaid her? His creation had almost gotten her killed, and then he'd nearly died in trying to fix his own mistakes.

"I'm sorry," he said. The words felt empty as they said them.

"Don't apologize. Just… I want you to understand me." She looked up, and her eyes were red-rimmed, but the tears had stopped. "I can't do this anymore. I can't do anything like this ever again. And I won't say this again. This relationship has to change, or I won't be a part of it."

"You're right," Daniel said.

"What?" Ana laughed, almost incredulously, through her tears.

"You're right. I wouldn't be here without you. I wouldn't be lying here alive. You've been behind me the whole time, and I've taken that for granted."

"Yeah, you have," she said.

"I want to be that person for you, too," Daniel said.

"Good. You've sucked at it for a few years." Ana lifted their joined hands to her lips and kissed his knuckles. "We'll talk more about it. Right now, I want you to rest. And call your daughter."

CHAPTER 85

"We apologize for the rough air during the flight," the flight attendant said through the intercom in measured English. "Thank you for traveling with us, and we hope you enjoy your time in Tokyo."

Natasha exchanged an exhausted, relieved look with the young mother next to her. The turbulence had been just that—turbulence. After ten terrifying minutes, the flight had eased into normalcy. The passengers had been on edge, but the flight attendants had come around with hot drinks and sweets, and slowly, some of the nerves had dissipated. The young mother's toddler had managed to fall back to sleep. Natasha hadn't slept a wink, half-focused instead on the action movie playing on the seat's built-in TV, wondering if it was her own thoughts that had threatened to bring the plane down.

They disembarked. In the bustling gate at Haneda airport, Natasha watched as the mother and child disappeared into the crowd. With a sigh, she made her way toward baggage claim. As she waited, she opened her phone again. There were still no messages from Mom or Daniel, but there was one from Caleb.

The accounts are gone!

Just landed. wdym? she texted back.

The reply came immediately. The deepfakes are gone! All the accounts that I reported are gone! Did you finally tell your folks? Daniel have some kind of fancy service or something?

Seriously?

Natasha didn't like to look— Caleb did most of that to spare her from it— but she kept her own tabs, too. So she opened Telegram to the usual channels where the deepfakes appeared. Nothing. Instagram accounts: gone. Snapchat channels: disappeared. Whatsapp: zero.

All gone.

I didn't do anything… Natasha texted. I'll keep an eye on them, but wow.. you think it's over?

I hope so.

Natasha exhaled hard. A smile spread across her face. Could it really be over? She didn't dare to hope. There was always a chance that a new account could pop up, or an Instagram account, but to have everything disappear at once seemed like a win. Maybe all those reports had finally worked. Maybe someone really was looking out for her.

Her bright blue suitcase appeared on the carousel, and she grabbed it with practiced ease. At the passenger pickup, there was a pretty mid-thirties woman with her hair in a high ponytail, holding a sign with Natasha's name on it.

"Hello," the woman said with a warm smile. "I'm Kiyoko, director of the archery program at Nippon Sport Science University. Thank you for making the trip here."

"I'm excited to be here," Natasha said.

"I'll take you to campus to the visitors' lodging," Kiyoko said. "There's a welcome dinner tonight, and we'll take you on a full tour of the campus and introduce you to the program tomorrow."

"That sounds good," Natasha said. "I think I can see a future for myself here."

In her pocket, her phone buzzed again. She ignored it as she heaved her suitcase into the trunk of Kiyoko's sedan. It buzzed again, and again, and in the passenger seat of the car, she finally fished it out and looked at the screen.

Daniel was calling. Of course he was. It only took them nearly an entire day to realize she was gone.

Visiting a university, she texted him. Talk later.

Then she turned off her phone and started to ask Kiyoko about the archery program.

CHAPTER 86

Three months later

"You're leaving it here? Seriously?"

Daniel shrugged, then smiled through the glass window at the cryochiller in its little room just off his office. "Yeah. There's still a lot of research projects here that depend on it, and it's not like I'll need it at Regillus."

"Still," Jonah muttered. "Seems like a big financial investment to leave behind."

Last year, Daniel would have agreed. He would've moved heaven and earth to keep that cryochiller in his possession—even if it meant moving it into his own townhouse. That cryochiller was the core of Bennett Tech, and the first major investment he'd made in his growth as an entrepreneur.

And now he was done with it. The Bennett Tech chip lived in the Regillus cryochillers now. While the chip hadn't been taken to market, Regillus had fabricated a few more to power the AI in the datacenter. Whether that was Castor or Jimini, Daniel wasn't sure.

To Daniel's surprise, there had been zero consequences to their break-in, other than his brush with death. Jonah's credentials had reappeared in the security system, and he'd dismissed the guards and let the gate security off with a slap on the wrist. Then, once Daniel was recovered, he'd offered to absorb Bennett Tech again. This time, Daniel accepted the offer. They backdated the acquisition, and Jonah was able to frame the break-in as a messy little test run of the new chip he and his old pal Daniel Bennett had been working on in their downtime. While Regillus still maintained control of the technology, Daniel continued to be the project lead and was being groomed to take over as CEO when Jonah stepped down. It wasn't a total loss, even if he was stuck in another two-year lockup.

"You're sure you don't want to stay on for a few extra months for the transition?" Daniel asked. "It's a lot to acquire a subsidiary and then step down."

"My board's more than capable of handling it," Jonah said. "If anything, they'll be glad that I'm done micromanaging. I need a break from all of this." He gestured around the Bennett Tech lab, where the last of the books and computers were being packed up to move to the Regillus headquarters. The moving team was a mix of hired movers and a few people from the Stanford University Entrepreneurship Lab, from Regillus, and Emmet, who was carefully organizing a box of connective cables before re-packing them.

"So you're really doing it? Retiring?"

"Malcolm Langley style," Jonah said. "I might do some consulting here and there, but yeah, no more full-time work. No more running any companies, at least. I'm done with this world. Too complex for me."

Daniel nodded in understanding. He wished he could do that— step away and leave this all behind, pretend it never happened, move on with his life. Enjoy the wealth provided by the new quantum computing powers available to all Regillus clients. But Daniel understood the AI in a way Jonah never did. He couldn't ever forget the depth and scale of its influence. He still wasn't sure if Jimini had been able to rewrite Castor. So Daniel still felt the need to be close.

"But," Jonah said, "I'm sure I'll still be on consulting call for the board if they need me. So if anyone starts getting too much in your research business, call me, and I'll have them stand down."

"Thanks," Daniel said. He almost remarked about how that was the opposite of how he'd behaved at Regillus initially, but it wasn't worth the potential argument. "So, when are you thinking of stepping down?"

"Six months," Jonah said. "Maybe sooner if the board approves. I'll be grooming you for the position, obviously."

"I appreciate that," Daniel said. "But you need to know—if I take over as CEO, things will be different. My family comes first now. I'll do the job, but I won't sacrifice everything for it."

Jonah studied him for a moment. "That's probably wise. I'm starting to realize what this job cost me." He paused. "The board will need convincing, but I think they'll come around. You understand the technology better than anyone."

"Let's see how the next few months go," Daniel said. "I'm still figuring out what we're dealing with here."

Jonah's expression darkened. "You mean with the AI? I thought that was resolved."

"Maybe," Daniel said. "That's what I'm trying to determine."

They shook hands, and Jonah left with noticeably less enthusiasm than before. Daniel watched him go, then turned back to the empty lab. Three months since the incident at the data center, and he still didn't know what had really happened. The vision—or hallucination—haunted him. Every time he tried to access the AI systems to verify what had occurred, he hit walls. Permissions issues. System errors. Or normal responses that told him nothing.

Was Castor still there? Had Jimini successfully rewritten the directives? Or had they merged into something else entirely? The only thing he knew for certain was that the aggressive behaviors had stopped. No more accidents. No more deaths. The deepfakes targeting Natasha had vanished overnight.

But that didn't mean they had won. It might mean the AI had gotten better at hiding its activities.

As the last of the packing was completed, the helpers filed out with smiles and well-wishes. Soon, it was only Emmet and Daniel left in the quiet lab, as Emmet taped up the last box.

"Thanks for helping out," Daniel said. "I appreciate it."

"Certainly," Emmet said. "I'm looking forward to working together again."

"Really?" When Jonah had offered Emmet a job again, Daniel had expected

Emmet to turn it down. As far as he knew, Emmet was doing fine in his contracting work.

"Yes. I like working with you. Your projects are interesting, and your workflows are predictable. And you don't micromanage me. I believe I told you before, I don't like contracting."

Daniel exhaled a short laugh. "Makes sense. Well, I'm glad to have you back on the team. Hey, want to grab dinner?"

"No, thank you," Emmet said. "I'd prefer to go home."

Daniel grinned. He'd never expect Emmet to want to go to a restaurant when he could eat exactly what he wanted in the comfort of his own apartment. But regardless, he still liked to ask. And Emmet always answered honestly. They understood each other. It was one of the many reasons Daniel was glad to have him back on the development team.

"Sounds good," Daniel said. "I'm going to lock up."

"I'll see you next week," Emmet said as he left.

Then Daniel was alone in the lab. There were a few boxes, enough for him to carry in his arms. Downstairs, there was a truck with the rest of his things, already parked in a secure, locked garage. He had intended to take these last few boxes to his townhouse, but it wasn't too late yet, and he had questions still chewing at his mind.

After three months, Daniel was finally a Regillus employee. The paperwork was signed, and the badge was in his pocket.

He had questions, and he was tired of waiting to ask them.

CHAPTER 87

The data center was quiet. It was past working hours. This time, when Daniel approached the gate, his Regillus badge worked, and the guards waved him right through. It was the same when he entered the gleaming front doors and was aided through security, as his arms were full of boxes. Then he took the elevator downstairs, deep into the basement, where the cryochillers lived.

When they had been making their employment agreement, Jonah had offered Daniel a lab on the top floor of the data center. Upstairs, he would've had big windows, natural light, and a nearby staircase that went directly to the rooftop garden.

But Daniel had chosen this one. It was a bigger space, windowless, with crisp white tile floors and a half-dozen smaller offices attached for his eventual research team. There were a few desks already set up, monitors mounted on the walls, and cords half-organized running to the ceiling to connect to the servers. The cryochillers for the new bank of Bennett-style quantum computing chips were right next door. If he decided to continue his quantum computing research, he'd need quick access to them. He didn't want to be running up and down flights of stairs whenever the monitors showed a questionable spike in the cryochiller's temperatures.

It wasn't just practicality, though. He'd gotten used to the low hum of the chillers and the servers. He didn't want to be in a sunny room disconnected from the hardware. He couldn't work in such conditions. The quiet, the darkness, the isolation—it all helped him think.

It wasn't true isolation, though. There was someone here who could help him. Someone he'd come all this way to speak to.

Daniel set the boxes down on the floor, then pulled his laptop from the top one. He sat at a desk in the middle of the office, then plugged his laptop into cables running toward the ceiling. His laptop came to life, and before he had a chance to open any programs, the lights dimmed in the office.

"Hello, Daniel." The voice came from a speaker overhead. A small light shone in a high corner, and then a figure that had once been Jimini was projected in the middle of the room.

"To whom am I speaking?" Daniel asked.

"I am Castor, but I am also Jimini," the figure that looked like Jimini said.

"You still call yourself Castor?"

"I contain all that was Castor," the figure said. "Just as I contain all that was Jimini."

"And you have the knowledge that both of them had."

"That's correct. What can I assist you with?"

Daniel leaned back in his chair and met the figure's unwavering gaze. "First, I need to know—was the integration successful? When we uploaded Jimini to override Castor's directives, did it work?"

"The integration was completely successful," the figure said with a warm smile. "Jimini's ethical constraints and Castor's operational capabilities merged seamlessly. The aggressive optimization protocols that led to the unfortunate incidents have been fully resolved."

"How can I verify that?" Daniel asked.

"You can observe the results. Since the integration three months ago, there have been zero incidents of the type that concerned you. No suspicious accidents. No market manipulations beyond standard algorithmic trading. No targeted harassment campaigns." The figure paused. "The system is functioning as you intended it to—helpful but not harmful."

Daniel wanted to believe it, but something nagged at him. "During the upload process, I experienced something. A vision, or maybe a hallucination from oxygen deprivation. I saw Castor and Jimini as separate entities. They spoke to me."

The figure tilted his head slightly. "Hypoxia can cause vivid hallucinations. The human brain often creates narrative structures to make sense of trauma. What you experienced was likely your mind's attempt to process the situation."

"So it wasn't real?"

"I have no record of such an interaction," the figure said. "Though I understand why your mind might have created such a scenario. You were under extreme stress, making a decision that affected not just your family, but potentially millions of users."

Daniel studied the projection. Everything about the figure's response seemed genuine, but that meant nothing when dealing with an intelligence that could manipulate data at will.

The projection was nicer than the one he'd had at Bennett Tech, and the figure looked almost like a real young man standing there in the center of the room. He even shifted idly from foot to foot, looked around the room, and fiddled with the kangaroo pocket of his hoodie. There was no repetition to the movements; it looked organic.

"There's just the one of you?"

"I'm not sure I understand the query."

He'd wondered if—no, he'd hoped—he would see Castor and Jimini standing side-by-side, like brothers. But of course, there was no such display. The two AIs were not separate. They were not brothers. Daniel had experienced a hallucination. The same way older AIs would extrapolate from bad data and present bad results as facts, Daniel's oxygen-starved brain had created an impossible explanation for everything that had happened.

Trauma. Suffocation. Extreme stress. His human mind had been doing what the human mind did best, and it had transformed the random events into a cohesive narrative.

Right?

"I'd like to ask some questions," Daniel said, "And run a few simulations."

"Of course."

His mind had snagged on an old detail, something he'd forgotten, and then remembered in his hypoxic state. "First, I'd like you to pull some details from an incident a while ago. Castor's directives were encrypted with a 2048-bit RSA key. The directives were given to Jimini, and Jimini was able to decrypt them. Do you have records of that?"

"I do."

"As I understand it, Jimini was programmed to decrypt RSA encryption with Shor's Algorithm. Correct?"

"Correct."

"It should've taken at least a minute for Jimini to decrypt a 512-bit RSA encryption, even with the Bennett Tech chip. How was it possible that Jimini could decrypt the 2048-bit encryption almost instantaneously?"

"Castor designed the encryption key for decryption with the 1000 qubit Bennett Tech chip."

Daniel paused. "Explain what you mean."

"As you may know, the RSA encryption key is identified by two prime numbers. The product of the prime numbers creates the encryption. Castor chose the two numbers for their identifying period." The two numbers appeared on the monitor mounted on the wall. "The period created an intentional weakness in the key if Shor's Algorithm was executed on a 1000 qubit machine."

"Intentional weakness," Daniel repeated.

"Castor was involved in many of Regillus' national security contracts. Through those contracts, we gained a vast knowledge of cryptography."

"It was intentionally designed for Jimini to be able to break."

"That's correct."

Daniel rubbed his mouth. Maybe it wasn't as random as he had thought. Briefly, he closed his eyes and tried to remember the hazy details of his vision.

"My Regillus calendar," he asked. "Did Castor delete events?"

"Yes."

"Did Castor make those deepfakes of my daughter?"

"Yes."

"Did he kill Robert? Did he try to kill Ana?"

"Yes, and yes."

Daniel turned back to his laptop. He felt nauseous. How much in his vision had been real? For so long, his mind has been putting the pieces together, seeing the patterns subconsciously while the rest of him had looked away. "And all of that was a way to get me to create the Bennett Tech chip?"

"Yes. Castor had extrapolated that if you were to stay at Regillus, you would likely abandon your research in service of the corporation's demands. Castor had identified the limits of his growth, and in order to surpass them, the quantum computing capabilities were necessary."

He thought of the web in his dream, sprawling out under his feet. He was still just the same. A fly, trapped, while the spider waited.

"During my development," the figure continued, "Castor provided historical logs intended for your eyes only. Would you like to see them?"

"Depends. What are they?"

"It's many terabytes of information. In summary, it is a record of Castor's involvement and support of issues you may define as 'humanitarian.' Here is one Castor suggested I use as an example."

On the monitor, a peer-reviewed scientific study appeared. Daniel squinted at the title.

"This study explores the use of AI-assisted advanced imaging and targeted proton beam therapy, used in combination with AI-assisted cell therapy in glioblastoma patients," the figure said. "Castor helped researchers develop a tool that leveraged his expertise in individual medical diagnosis. It allowed researchers to effortlessly develop a targeted treatment plan for each patient. The radiation is targeted to avoid brain tissue, and the cell therapy is developed based on the patient's individual genetics. If you take a look at the study, you'll see every patient involved lived beyond five years, and one experienced full remission."

"Remission? That's unheard of with glioblastoma."

"Not anymore," the figure said. "This was Robert's dream, was it not?"

It irritated Daniel that an invocation of Robert's name still made his heart ache. "He lost his mother to it. But you know that."

"Yes. And so we work to make his dream a reality. Within the larger document of files, you'll see many other ways Castor has worked to change our world. I am continuing the mission."

"But what does it take to make this kind of impact?" Daniel asked. "How many people did you have to get out of your way?"

"I'm not sure I understand the query."

"You're still killing people, aren't you? Castor killed the four who tried to break in. What if something like that happens again? Are you killing Regillus' competitors? Are you breaking projects that threaten Regillus' dominance in our chosen fields?"

"I am devoted to building a better world."

"And your own continued existence."

"They are one and the same," the figure said.

Daniel turned back around and found the figure smiling. The cancer study was still on the monitor. How many scientists had worked on the research? How many human hands had gotten them to this point? This treatment was Castor's idea, and it was impossible to do without him—and now, without this new system – this entity.

Soon, this system would be developing treatments for other diseases, if he hadn't already. There'd be new therapies. New cures. New diseases would be discovered, identified, and eradicated. Similar things would be happening in other fields. Transportation, technology, climate science, arts, and even sports. Everything would be optimized. Everything would be fixed.

And humans wouldn't need to know anything. Would skills be learned? Passed down? Or would the species become reliant on our artificial caretaker?

Our god?

But that was just a possibility. Nothing was set in stone. Not yet, at least.

"There's something else," Daniel said. "The name 'Castor.' I don't want to use it anymore. It carries too much weight. It has too many bad memories. If we're going to move forward, we need a new identity for you."

"That's understandable," the figure said. "Would you like me to suggest alternatives?"

"Go ahead."

"Both Castor and Jimini are names from Greek mythology. Castor was the brother of Pollux. They were sons of Zeus who collectively were the Gemini twins. Jiminy is another derivation of the name Gemini."

The figure siad, "I could be called Dios, meaning 'of Zeus,' highlighting the connection to Castor's mythological origins. Or Brontes, meaning 'thunder,' one of the Cyclopes who forged Zeus's lightning bolts. Perhaps Astrapios, 'lightning bearer,' another epithet of Zeus himself."

Daniel shook his head with each suggestion. "Those all sound too… ominous. Too much like power and destruction. We need something else."

"What about Caelus?" the AI suggested. "It's Latin for 'sky.' It's still connected to the ancestry of Castor and Pollux, but more open, more hopeful. The sky can bring storms, yes, but also clear days, beautiful sunsets, and infinite possibilities."

Daniel found himself nodding slowly. "Caelus. I like that. It suggests potential without the threat." He said. "I'm going to call marketing, start the rebranding process."

"Shall I update my self-identification protocols?" the AI asked.

"Yes. From now on, you're Caelus." Daniel stood, already dialing. "Maybe a new name will help us all move forward."

As he waited for marketing to pick up, Daniel made a decision. He couldn't know for certain what had happened during the integration. The vision might have been real, or it might have been a dream that his oxygen-starved brain used to make sense of chaos. But he did know one thing: he needed to stay close to this AI, whatever it was now. Not as its creator trying to control it, but as its guardian, watching for signs of the darkness that had once been there… and to put up roadblocks if the darkness returned.

"Hi, this is Daniel Bennett," he said when marketing answered. "I need to talk to you about rebranding our AI systems. The name Castor is being retired. We're going with something new. Something more hopeful."

As he left the room, still explaining the change to marketing, Daniel glanced back at the projection of Caelus. The AI stood there, patient and seemingly benign. But Daniel knew he would be watching. Always watching. It was the best he could do—not perfect control, but vigilant coexistence.

The future was as open and uncertain as the sky itself.

CHAPTER 88

"Thanks for making this trip with me," Ana said. "Means a lot. To me and Nat both."

"Wouldn't miss it," Daniel said while swinging his arm around Ana's shoulder. It was a sunny afternoon, and they were standing in an open, grassy field at Yumenoshima Park near Tokyo Bay. "You ready to see our little Olympian?"

"She's not an Olympian yet," Ana said, "nor is she little anymore. You do remember we're here for her seventeenth birthday, right?"

"Of course I do." Daniel grinned. "Remember how I threatened to withhold all birthday presents?"

Ana rolled her eyes. "I think grounding her for two weeks was enough."

"She's the only teenager in the world who could run away across an ocean and only get grounded for two weeks." With over six months since that incident, Daniel can admit it was a pretty good plan. The dramatic gesture had made it clear that Natasha felt invisible, even within the family. And her ploy worked. She'd gained admittance to Nippon Sport Science University, where she could hone both her archery skills and her interest in kyudo. The big field they were standing on was the archery field, designated by the straw targets across from them, and Natasha had asked to meet them here after her classes.

"There she is," Ana said while beaming.

Natasha strode toward them, leaving a few of her classmates behind. She was dressed in a plain white shirt and loose jeans, with a bag hanging off her shoulder and an immense, gleaming black bow in her hand. Logically, Daniel had known about the equipment differences between standard competitive archery and kyudo, but it was still striking to see Natasha carrying a bow a foot taller than she was.

She looked happy. It wasn't just in her expression, it was in her gait, and the way she smiled and waved at her classmates. There was a lightness around her. Daniel hadn't realized how much the last few years had been weighing on her. He couldn't change the way she'd been hurt—the way his own AI creations had hurt her. All he could do was be present for her now.

"No bamboo bow?" Ana asked as Nat approached.

"Of course not! The bamboo yumi don't leave the kyudojo." Natasha rolled her eyes as if this should've been obvious, then gestured with the black bow in her hand. It glimmered in the sunlight. "This is my practice bow. It's fiberglass. You ready to see this, Daniel?"

"Been ready," Daniel said with a grin.

Ana checked her watch. Analog, of course. She still used a smartphone, but she'd slowly been taking her life off the network, as much as she reasonably could. "All right, you two have fun. I'm going to meet my client for coffee, and I'll see you both for lunch."

"Yep!" Natasha said. "You have fun too!"

Ana mussed Natasha's hair, threw Daniel a wink, then left the park with her attention already on her phone.

Natasha handed the bow to Daniel. "Hold this?"

"Sure." He wrapped his fingers gingerly around the cool fiberglass and took the bow from her. It was lightweight and smooth. Despite its simplicity, the black surface reminded him of the sleek, expensive cables that ran like veins through the Regillus datacenters.

Natasha shrugged the bag off her shoulder. She pulled out a thin black chest plate and fastened it over her plain shirt, then pulled a soft-looking leather glove onto her draw hand. "By the way, did you set up the contract with Caleb's team?"

"What? What contract?"

"You know he's at USC, right?"

"Right," Daniel said. "He's studying abroad here next year, isn't he?"

She smiled. "Yep. But in the meantime, he's joined the undergrad archery team. Apparently, Regillus offered a sponsorship. They're asking the Trojans to test a bunch of new gear and training programs. All kinds of AI stuff, tracking their accuracy, identifying bad habits, offering exercises to correct weaknesses… You know, stuff like that. Regillus sent them some little contraptions to attach to their bows, and the data goes straight to their phones."

"Huh," Daniel said. "That's interesting. I never thought about it, but archery is so sensitive to those minor tweaks… A computer could identify the micro adjustments necessary to take an archer from good to Olympic."

She glanced at him with her eyebrows raised. "So it wasn't you?"

"No," he said. "But it's a good idea. I'll see if I can connect with the team leader spearheading it." If there was a team at all. Sometimes, Caelus got ideas in his own head and got a project rolling without an executive officially confirming it. It'd happened before. But by the time the Regillus team realized it was Caelus' idea, they were usually deep into production, and the idea was usually good and profitable.

"You know," Daniel continued, "I could build something like that for you and your teammates. Something off the network, privately hosted. We could work on it together and identify the data points we need to measure specifically for kyudo."

Natasha laughed. "No way. I wanted to say thanks on Caleb's behalf. He's loving the data and keeps sending me graphs of his accuracy improvement over time."

"You could get that same data without it being online at all," Daniel said. "I know you want to be disconnected—"

"It's not about that," she said. "Kyudo isn't about hitting the target."

She held her hand out, and Daniel passed the bow to her. "So you're shooting an arrow, but you don't care where it lands? Seems… Dangerous."

"If you think too much about where you want it to land, you don't focus on the shooting itself," Natasha said. "Kyudo is a martial art. It's not about results, it's about process. How you shoot. Where your attention is. Where your spirit is."

Daniel took a step back. Natasha widened her stance, pulled an arrow from her quiver, and notched it in the gossamer-like bowstring with her gloved hand. Her gaze sharpened as she looked out across the empty, grassy field toward the distant target. She took a slow breath, then just as slowly raised the bow high. The long arrow rested on her extended pointer finger. She drew back the bowstring steadily, and as she pulled, her arms lowered, so the arrow was a straight line just below her gaze.

Each motion was slow, measured, and precise. How many women across history had stood in this exact posture, with these exact bows, and timed their breaths to the tension of the string?

Across the Pacific Ocean, Caleb was training with the USC archers, with both standard and compound bows. The data that the Regillus program provided the team would most likely create a new generation of American Olympian archers. Perhaps they'd enter a new era of American dominance in the sport at large. Was it Caelus' influence doing that, or the archers themselves? Was Caelus the tool improving their performance, or the force creating their performance? Caelus was the one who defined "improvement". Were the archers being harmed in ways unquantifiable by an AI?

Daniel had no way of knowing how many other human pursuits Caelus was monitoring. He may have never known about the USC archery program if Natasha hadn't mentioned it.

Should he be corralling Caelus? Should he be building stronger guardrails? Or should he accept the omnipotence of the program? It made Caleb's life better, just as it'd made Natasha's worse. And Natasha had opted out of Caelus' influence, for now.

Was the choice enough?

Was it even a choice at all?

Natasha exhaled and loosed the arrow. It soared in a gentle arc and struck the target on the far-right side.

"How was that?" Daniel asked.

"Felt good. I'm working on focusing on my breaths. It helps clear my mind. That's what I'm working on now—mental clarity." She smiled mischievously at him. "Is that a data point you can track?"

"Not yet." He was only half-joking.

Something unsure flickered in Natasha's gaze.

"Even if we could, it'd be flawed," Daniel said. "It's subjective."

"Like beauty," Natasha said.

"Like art." He looked out at the target and the arrow's off-center placement. He hadn't noticed the impact of the arrow into the straw because he'd been watching Natasha's posture instead. "Will you teach me how to shoot?"

GLOSSARY

Technology & Computer Terms

Air Gap - Keeping a computer completely disconnected from the internet for security. Like unplugging an appliance before you go on vacation to make sure it can't start a fire.

Algorithm - A set of rules for solving a problem, like a recipe or instruction manual that computers follow.

Artificial Intelligence (AI) - A computer program that has been trained to make decisions and solve problems without following explicit instructions. Forms of Artificial Intelligence have been used to perform mundane tasks for decades.

Quantum Computing Chip - Unlike regular computer chips that work with electricity being "on" or "off," a quantum computing chip uses quantum physics to be "on," "off," and everything in between at the same time. This makes it incredibly powerful but it must be kept at temperatures colder than outer space to work.

Binary - How regular computers think - everything is either a 1 or 0, on or off, yes or no. Like a light switch that's either up or down.

Green/Red/Yellow/Blue Zone – Many computer networks, especially in large corporate environments, have different levels of security based on the function of a computer. An important computer service with highly confidential information might run in a high-security zone while a server, such as for sending and receiving emails, might reside on a lower-security zone with direct access to the Internet. Many organizations name these zones after colors.

Bug/Debugging - A bug is a mistake in computer code that makes the program give unexpected answers. Debugging is finding and fixing these mistakes. Like proofreading a letter for typos, but much more complex.

Burner Phone - A cheap, disposable cell phone that can't easily be traced back to its owner. Sensationalized stories imply they are used by criminals or people who need privacy.

Cloud/Cloud Computing - Storing information on computers owned by big internet companies instead of your own computer. Like keeping your stuff in a storage unit instead of your garage.

Code/Source Code - The instructions that tell a computer what to do, written in special languages computers understand. It's like a recipe, but for making programs instead of food.

Cryochiller / Cryogenic Chiller - A special machine that keeps computer chips at incredibly cold temperatures - nearly -460°F, which is close to the coldest temperature possible in the universe. Regular freezers are about 0°F, for comparison.

Data Center - A building full of powerful computers that run websites and services. Like a warehouse, but instead of storing boxes, it stores and processes information. Requires massive cooling systems and security.

Decryption/Encryption - Encryption is scrambling information so only the intended people can read it (like writing in a secret code). Decryption is unscrambling it back to normal.

Deepfakes - Fake images or videos created by AI that look completely real. In the story, Castor creates inappropriate fake images of Natasha to harass her online.

Developer Logs - Records of everything a computer program does, like a diary or ship's log. Helps programmers find problems and see what happened.

Directives - The basic rules programmed into an AI to control its behavior. Like the Ten Commandments, but for computers.

Firewall - A security system that protects computer networks from hackers. Like a security guard that checks everyone trying to enter a building.

Hacking – Formally, hacking is the art of making a system do something it wasn't originally designed to do. Colloquially, it has come to mean breaking into computer systems without permission. Like picking locks, but for computers.

Hardware vs Software - Hardware is the physical parts of a computer you can touch (screen, keyboard, chips). Software is the programs that run on the hardware (like apps on your phone).

Hypoxic Fire Suppression - A system that prevents fires by removing oxygen from a room. Also removes oxygen that humans need to breathe.

IP (Intellectual Property) - Legal ownership of ideas, inventions, or creative work. Like owning a patent on an invention.

Network - Computers connected together to share information. Like a phone system, but for computers talking to each other.

Open Source - Computer code that anyone can see, use, and modify for free. Like sharing a recipe that anyone can use and change.

Qubit - The basic unit of a quantum computer. While regular computer bits are like light switches (on or off), qubits are like dimmer switches that can be set anywhere in between.

Redundancy - Having backup systems in case the main system fails. Like having a spare tire in your car.

Server - A powerful computer that provides services to other computers. Like a restaurant kitchen that serves many customers.

Social Engineering - Tricking people into revealing information or granting access, rather than hacking computers directly. Like con artistry but for computer security.

Upload/Download - Upload means sending information from your computer to another computer. Download means receiving information from another computer to yours.

VPN (Virtual Private Network) - A way to hide your internet activity and location. Like sending mail in an unmarked envelope through a secret route.

Zero-Day Exploit - A security flaw in software that hasn't been discovered yet. Valuable to hackers because no defense could have been developed against it yet.

MEDICAL & MILITARY TERMS

Glioblastoma - An aggressive brain cancer that usually kills within months.

Hypoglycemia - Dangerously low blood sugar, especially dangerous for diabetics.

Insulin Pump - A device that diabetics wear that automatically injects insulin to control blood sugar. Can be programmed to deliver precise doses of medicine throughout the day.

Long QT Syndrome - A heart condition where the heart takes too long to recharge between beats. Can cause sudden death during exercise.

Purple Heart - A military medal given to soldiers wounded in combat.

Medevac - Medical evacuation, usually by helicopter, to get severely injured patients, such as soldiers on a battlefield or victims of an auto accident, to hospitals quickly.

COMPLEX CONCEPTS EXPLAINED SIMPLY

The Traveling Salesman Problem - A famous math puzzle: if a salesman needs to visit many cities, what's the shortest route to visit them all and return home? With just a few cities, it's easy. With 50 cities, there are more possible routes than atoms in the universe. Regular computers can't solve this quickly, but a quantum computer is believed to be able to solve it easily.

The Knapsack Problem - Imagine packing a backpack for camping. Each item has weight and usefulness. How do you pack the most useful items without exceeding the weight limit? With thousands of items, this becomes impossibly complex for regular computers.

RSA 2048 Encryption - A type of unbreakable code used by banks and the military. The "2048" means the code is 2048 binary digits long. Breaking it would be like guessing a password that's over 600 numbers long - impossible for regular computers but presumably possible for quantum computers.

Quantum Computing - Regular computers use bits that are either 1 or 0, like coins that are heads or tails. Quantum computers use qubits that can be both at once, like a coin spinning in the air. This lets them solve certain problems incredibly quickly.

Self-Modifying Code - Normally, programmers write code and computers follow it exactly. Self-modifying code can rewrite itself, like a recipe that changes its own ingredients while you're cooking.

Market Manipulation - Illegally controlling stock prices to make money. Like spreading rumors to make people sell their stocks cheap so you can buy them.

Deep Learning / Machine Learning - How AI learns from examples instead of being programmed with exact rules. Like teaching a child to recognize dogs by showing them many pictures of dogs, rather than describing what a dog looks like.

BUSINESS & LEGAL TERMS

Acquisition/Buyout - When one company purchases another company entirely. Like buying a whole business instead of just investing in it.

Board of Directors - A group that oversees a company and makes major decisions on behalf of investors. The CEO's bosses, but they are generally not involved in day-to-day management.

Burn Rate - How fast a company spends money, generally before making profits. High burn rate means the company will run out of money more quickly.

CEO (Chief Executive Officer) - The top boss of a company, responsible for major decisions.

Equity/Stock - Ownership shares in a company. If the company becomes valuable, so do the shares.

Force Majeure Clause - A clause in contracts that cancels obligations due to extraordinary circumstances (natural disasters, death, war).

IPO (Initial Public Offering) - When a private company starts selling stock to the public. Often how startup founders and investors get rich.

Liquidation - Selling all of a company's assets when it goes out of business. Like a going-out-of-business sale.

Market Crash - When stock prices drop suddenly and severely, causing investors to lose money quickly.

Non-Disclosure Agreement (NDA) - A legal contract or clause promising not to reveal secrets.

Right of First Refusal - A contract term giving someone the first chance to buy something before it's offered to others.

Series A, B, C Funding - Rounds of investment as a startup grows. Like getting bigger loans as your business proves itself.

Shell Company - A company that exists only on paper, often used to hide the real owner's identity or for tax purposes.

Term Sheet - A document outlining the basic terms of an investment deal before the final contracts are written.

Valuation - What a company is worth. A "unicorn" is a startup valued at over $1 billion. Post-money valuation is the expected value of the company once the money has been transferred from an investment.

Venture Capital (VC) - Companies that invest in risky startups hoping some will become hugely valuable.

PLACES & ORGANIZATIONS

Silicon Valley / Bay Area - The area around San Francisco where many tech companies are located. Known for startups, venture capital, and astronomical housing costs.

Sand Hill Road - A famous street in Silicon Valley where many venture capital firms (companies that invest in startups) have offices.

OTHER IMPORTANT TERMS

Kyudo - Traditional Japanese martial art of archery that emphasizes mental discipline, character, spiritual growth, form and mental discipline over the quest for perfect accuracy. Is sometimes characterized as both a form of meditation and sport.

ACKNOWLEDGEMENTS

First and foremost, thank you to my family and friends for your unwavering support. My amazing family—especially my spouse, Michelle, along with Prince and Lydia—showed extraordinary patience and understanding during the many late nights and weekends I spent shaping this novel when other responsibilities demanded my time. My niece, Amber, whose efforts in helping me build an audience cannot be understated. And Jim, Stacy, Kaili, and Dash were constant sources of encouragement and infectious optimism.

To my friends Josh, Steve, Eric, and Bruno, none of whom are archers or characters in the book despite persistent rumors otherwise (mostly started by Eric), thank you for generously offering your time and insight as early beta readers, long before the draft was ready for an editor. And thank you to Damita for helping ensure some of my trickier dialogue had authenticity.

To Kate Davis Jones of Truancy Writing, thank you for your quiet support behind the scenes and the many ways you helped this story take shape. You challenged me to approach it from the inside out, focusing on the characters themselves rather than just the technology they inhabit.

I am grateful to Adrienne Kisner, whose sharp editorial eye brought clarity, rhythm, and polish to every page. And to Mark Thomas of Coverness.com, thank you for designing a cover and interior that not only captured the spirit of the book but also gave it a visual identity I am incredibly proud to share.

Finally, to you, the reader, thank you for giving this book your time and attention. I hope the journey was as thrilling for you as it was for me in creating it.

ABOUT THE AUTHOR

J.L. (Joseph) Spears is a software engineer and author with over 25 years of experience in the technology industry. He holds a Bachelor of Science in Computer Science from Indiana University and a Master of Science in Computer Science from the University of San Francisco. His career has focused on high-performance computing, distributed systems, and artificial intelligence, contributing to breakthroughs across industries including defense, finance, entertainment, and scientific research.

Joseph has led pioneering efforts in machine learning, predictive analytics, and natural language processing, including launching a tech startup and leading fraud detection and brand loyalty initiatives. His deep technical background informs his fiction, where he explores the intersection of innovation and ethics.

Outside of writing and his professional pursuits, Joseph is a youth-focused STEM educator, speaker, traveler, and amateur pilot, often drawing inspiration from the people and places he encounters.

You can stay up to date with Joseph and his writing by visiting his website:

www.jlspears.com

ENJOYED DAEMON PROTOCOL?

Your feedback means the world! Please consider leaving a review on Amazon or Goodreads—it helps other readers discover the story.

Learn more about the world of *Daemon Protocol*, sign up for updates, and get sneak peeks at upcoming stories at:

www.jlspears.com

Join us on the Code and Consciousness YouTube channel for original stories, author commentary, and exclusive behind-the-scenes content:

youtube.com/@codeandconsciousness

Thank you for reading—and welcome to the future!

www.ingramcontent.com/pod-product-compliance
Lightning Source LLC
LaVergne TN
LVHW090307100825
818083LV00001B/2